For my great-niece and goddaughter, Amber Walden, whose voice is as golden as her name. Keep your eyes always on the horizon. A dream waits for you there.

For my great-nephew, Dustin Christean, who, as the eldest, must blaze the trail for those who follow. Do great things! I know you can.

For my great-niece, Wendy Walden, who sometimes makes me feel that I'm looking in a mirror.

For my great-niece, Nichole Bowyer, who is living, breathing proof that dynamite comes in small packages.

And last, but definitely not least, for my great-niece, Halcy Atwater, a tiny little angel sent by God in answer to our prayers.

Harper
Monogram

Comanche Magic

 CATHERINE ANDERSON

HarperPaperbacks
A Division of HarperCollinsPublishers

This is a work of fiction. The characters, incidents, and dialogues are products of the author's imagination and are not to be construed as real. Any resemblance to actual events or persons, living or dead, is entirely coincidental.

HarperPaperbacks *A Division of* HarperCollins*Publishers*
10 East 53rd Street, New York, N.Y. 10022

Cover illustration by Pino Daeni

First printing: October 1994

Printed in the United States of America

HarperPaperbacks, HarperMonogram, and colophon are trademarks of HarperCollins*Publishers*

❖ 10 9 8 7 6 5 4 3 2 1

1

July heat hung over the yard like a blanket.
A cluster of bees hummed nearby, feeding on drips of
whey that seeped through the butter muslin hanging
from the fence. In the barnyard adjacent to the house,
the cow lowed every once in a while, harmonizing with
the shrill and sporadic grunting of the pigs. Not to be
outdone, the hens in the squat log chicken coop clucked
and flapped every time the breeze lifted, which wasn't
nearly often enough, given the temperature.

After unbuttoning his blue chambray shirt to mid-
chest, Chase Wolf repositioned his shoulder against
the pine tree and closed his eyes to absorb the smells.
He smiled at the images they brought to mind of his
boyhood and other July days when he had run wild
along the creek that bordered his parents' property.

This summer he didn't reckon he'd be doing much

running. The smile on his mouth thinned to a grim line. He considered rolling himself a smoke, then decided against it for fear it might make him cough. Coughing, like all other activities that called for muscle movement, was a luxury he couldn't afford, not with three cracked ribs. This would teach him not to let any moss grow under his feet the next time two logs tried to make a sandwich out of him.

If he didn't move, the pain wasn't too bad. Moving, though—that posed a problem. Until recently, Chase had never realized how active he was. Maybe it was the Comanche blood in his veins, but unlike some folks, he didn't cotton much to idleness. Like now, for instance. How long had it been since he'd sat in his ma's backyard under this old tree, listening to the bees hum? A long spell. Twenty-five last March, he had been working the timber since age eighteen. There hadn't been much time for lollygagging since. Now he had nothing but time on his hands, and he was a mite bored.

Placing a hand over his ribs, Chase shifted his hips on the mattress of pine needles and bent a denim-clad leg. A hank of mahogany hair fell into his eyes. He stared through the strands for a bit to get a new perspective on things. Then he spent some time counting the scars on the heel of his boot, came up with a tally of twenty-two, and passed some time pondering how they'd gotten there. Probably when he was logrolling, he decided, which led him down a path of pleasant memories that occupied him for a few more minutes.

When he resurfaced to the present, he rolled himself a smoke, ribs or no, struck a lucifer, and inhaled. His tobacco tasted like dry cow dung. He needed fresh.

Maybe later on this afternoon he would mosey over to the general store, mosey being the key word. It hurt like hell to walk.

With a disgusted grimace, he pinched the fire off his cigarette with calloused fingertips, pocketed the unsmoked portion, and closed his eyes, determined to take a nap, since he had nothing better to do. A bit later, he awoke to the sound of feminine giggles coming from down along the creek. He listened for a second and identified one of the giggles as belonging to his sister, Indigo. Twenty-four to his twenty-five, she had a husband and two children now. He grinned. Leave it to her to beat the heat by playing in the creek. The other wives in town, including his ma, were at home doing household tasks, a fair number baking bread if the smells on the morning air were an indication.

Chase pushed to his feet, drawn toward the creek by the sound of laughter. He might not be up to romping in the water, but sitting on the sidelines to watch was bound to be more entertaining than sitting all alone in Ma's backyard.

With one hand pressed over his side, he moved slowly through the sun-dappled woods. Dogwood and myrtle branches networked above him. The polished green leaves of Oregon grape and poison oak bushes formed a dense undergrowth at the base of the trees, the creamy white of dogwood and the deep pink of wild rhododendron blossoms lending splashes of vivid color. Wild strawberries encroached on the path, their vines contrasting with the red clay. The sight of them made his mouth water. As kids he and Indigo had gotten the stomach complaint at least once a year from gorging themselves on the sweet fruit. He cast a fond glance around, saddened because those days were forever lost to him. In his mind lingered the echoes of long-ago voices and laughter. There truly was no place quite like home, he guessed.

Amber warmth shafted through the oak and pine limbs above him, bringing a sheen of sweat to his brow and making the chambray of his shirt stick to his shoulders. He swiped a strand of hair from his eyes and winced at the resultant pain that knifed across his midriff. Taking care where he placed his booted feet, he finally reached the river rock that bordered Shallows Creek. Enjoying the mist that cooled the air, he paused in the shade of two intertwined oaks. More the fool he for not coming down here straight off. The banks of Shallows Creek always had provided a respite from the summer heat.

Heading toward the voices, Chase rounded a bend in the stream. Expecting to see his tawny-haired sister, he was surprised to see a petite blond instead. If she was from Wolf's Landing, Chase had never met her. She was as pretty as a picture, not the kind a man with eyes was likely to forget. He leaned a shoulder against an oak, happy to stay hidden so he could enjoy the view.

Indigo's pet wolf Sonny, napping in a spot of shade near the water, lifted his silver head and sniffed the air. An instant later, he spotted Chase. Recognition flickered in his golden eyes, and after a moment, he lowered his head back to his paws to resume his snooze. The instant of eye contact with the animal left Chase feeling oddly empty. There had been a time when he'd had the same gift for visual communication with animals and people that Indigo had. Not so anymore, compliments of these last seven years he'd been working away from home. Somewhere along the line, he'd lost touch with that part of himself.

Chase shoved away the thought and returned his attention to the young woman in the stream. Stripped down to her camisole and bloomers, she was cavorting in the water with Chase's four-year-old nephew, Hunter. The drenched muslin of her undergarments was nearly transparent with wetness and clung to her body like the skin on an onion. The rosy nipples of her small breasts were taut with cold and thrust against the cloth in impertinent little peaks. Some men might say she had been shorted in the bust, but Chase maintained that anything more than a mouthful was a waste, anyway. Besides, with her tiny waist and coltish limbs, small, pink-tipped breasts were just the thing to set off her figure to perfection.

Content to stay right where he was, Chase lowered himself carefully to the ground and draped his arms over his bent knees. On a hot day like today, it'd be downright unchivalrous to show himself and spoil her swim. He was nothing if not thoughtful.

Apparently she was in competition with his nephew to catch salamanders, commonly known in these parts as water dogs. Over the last few years, the women in Chase's acquaintance had been preoccupied with more carnal pursuits, the exhibitions of their charms well-practiced and usually executed to the rhythm of bawdy saloon music. A grin settled on his mouth and he got himself situated a little more comfortably. This beat the hell out of watching Ma's whey drip.

Whoever she was, she looked like an angel. A shaft of sunlight ignited her golden hair, turning it to a halo around the crown of her head. She had petal-white skin, as flawless as ivory in contrast to his Indian darkness. Her facial features were delicate and cameo-perfect except for her small nose, which was so turned up at the end, she'd drown in a heavy rainstorm. He decided he liked that. It gave her an impish, little-girl appeal.

His gaze dropped to her waist and lower as she slogged through the shallows and pounced to catch a water dog. With little-boy enthusiasm, Hunter dived to reach their quarry before she did and sent up a spray. She shrieked and staggered, laughing as she rubbed the water from her eyes.

"Dibs!" Hunter cried.

"My foot! I saw it first!"

Hunter shot triumphantly to his feet, his small brown hands curled into tight fists around his slippery catch. "I'm up to—" He broke off and frowned. "How many do I got?"

"Three," she said with an impish giggle.

"No, sir! You're cheatin'!"

"Pay attention to your ma during lessons so you learn to count, and I won't be able to cheat."

Holding the water dog threateningly aloft, Hunter lunged at her. With another shriek, she sloshed through the water to get away from him, her laughter chiming like crystal. "Don't you dare, you little rascal! You stick that thing in my drawers, and I'll drown you!"

"Hunter Chase Rand!" Indigo called from somewhere out of Chase's sight. "You drop that water dog down her bloomers, and I'll tell your pa. You mind your manners."

Unintimidated, Hunter made a grab. The blond clutched the waist of her underwear and fled a bit farther to get safely beyond his reach. She had a perfect little ass with plump cheeks that jiggled just enough to kindle a man's imagination and make him wonder how soft she'd feel pressed against him. When she turned toward him again, he could see the golden triangle between her slender thighs. He lifted his gaze to her breasts, and his mouth drew up as though he were sucking a lemon.

Too late, Chase began to wonder if sitting here was such a champion idea. It had been a spell since he'd had a woman, and suddenly his jeans felt about a half-size too small at the inseam. As frustrating as it had been watching Ma's whey drip, at least he hadn't ached for a taste. He hated cottage cheese with a passion. Too bad he couldn't say the same for tight little nipples that begged to be kissed.

With the short attention span typical of a four-year-old, Hunter spotted another water dog and went chasing upstream after it. The angel with the turned-up nose went unnaturally still. Chase dragged his gaze upward from her breasts and found himself staring into the biggest, most startled-looking green eyes he'd ever seen. Now that he came to think of it, they were the only true green eyes he'd ever seen, not greenish blue or gray, but the color of new spring leaves.

She gasped and cupped her hands over her breasts. The next instant, she knelt in the water to hide her nether regions. Chase stared, unable to think of anything to say. Howdy, maybe, but that didn't seem appropriate. Hello, there? That didn't do it, either.

He settled for, "It sure is a hot one, isn't it?"

She jerked at the sound of his voice, and her small face flushed. Chase could have sworn every drop of blood in her body surged to her cheeks, but upon further study, he noted she was pink all over. Dark as he was, that was a phenomenon worthy of speculation. On the few occasions in his life when he had grown flushed, no one but he had known. This girl lit up like a whore's lantern.

When she remained in the same frozen position for several seconds, Chase started to feel ashamed of himself. The sensation started with a tight feeling in his chest that rose to the region of his throat. He reckoned she wasn't too happy to find out she had male company when she was dressed only in her camisole and bloomers, both sopped and see-through. Not that he could blame her.

"Chase Kelly? Is that you?"

Indigo stepped out from behind a stand of brush, her sleeping daughter, Amelia Rose, cradled in her arms. Indigo was dressed in only her camisole and drawers as well, but given the fact it was her brother come calling, she didn't blush straight off. That came a few seconds later when it began to dawn on her what he'd been up to. Her big blue eyes flashed with silver fire.

"Chase Kelly Wolf, for shame! What're you doing, hiding up there? Spying on us? Didn't Ma ever teach you any manners?"

If Ma had, Chase guessed he had forgotten. He was starting to feel like a low-down skunk. Acutely aware of those startled green eyes still riveted on him, he forgot his sore ribs and shrugged. The movement made him wince. He considered thinking up a quick lie, but even with seven years' practice, lying still didn't come slick to him. "I was bored," he admitted. "When I heard y'all down here, I didn't figure you'd mind if I joined you."

"Which we wouldn't. If you had joined us." Indigo came striding up the bank, her graceful legs flexing under her bloomers. She handed Chase his sleeping niece. "Make yourself useful while I find Franny's clothes." As she scampered back down the bank, she cried, "For shame, for shame. I beg his pardon, Franny. To say he's an ape-brain would be a compliment."

Chase Kelly? She made him sound like a ten-year-old. And an ape-brain? Leave it to a sister to keep a man humble. It had been a while since anyone had dared to call Chase names.

He smoothed Amelia Rose's curly hair and tried to get comfortable holding her. At eighteen months, she was a sweet armful, baby-plump and pink all over. She had her daddy's raven hair and eyelashes, with her ma's delicate features. Her lacy undershirt was damp from playing in the creek. Chase curled a hand over her bare bottom and smiled. Now he knew where the saying "soft as a baby's behind" had originated. Her skin felt like velvet.

"Hi, Uncle Chase!" Hunter came slogging from the water, his skinny little body glistening like wet bronze in the sunshine. His grandfather's namesake, the boy looked more Comanche than white, his hair pitch black and as straight as a bullet on a windless day. "You wanna catch water dogs?"

Chase looked over the child's bobbing head to see Franny, the green-eyed angel, trying to wade from the creek without showing off any of her charms. Since he had already seen all there was to see, he could have saved her the trouble, but he figured Indigo might hang him if he said as much. "I'm too stoved up with these ribs for water dog chasing, Hunter. Maybe another time."

"Ah, please. Playin' with girls ain't no fun."

Chase figured that depended on how the girls were dressed and who was doing the playing. Hunter was obviously too young to appreciate the female form, which explained why his ma and her friend Franny felt free to flit around in front of him in nothing but their small clothes.

Keeping his gaze politely averted from the women, Chase watched Hunter return to the creek. Within seconds, the boy recovered from his disappointment and dove for another water dog. When Chase chanced another look in the women's direction, Franny stood on the bank wearing a white choker-collared, long-sleeved blouse and a blue flared skirt, both of which clung to her wet body. Still rosy-cheeked, she pushed ineffectually at her mussed hair, repinning the twist at her crown.

"Franny, I'd like you to meet my brother, Chase Kelly Wolf," Indigo said sharply. "As I'm sure you recall, I told you the other day that he was home recuperating from a logging accident."

Indigo's tone made Chase feel like a case of influenza. He dragged his gaze from the back of the blond's clinging skirt and said, "Pleased to meet you, Franny." He thought "Fanny" would suit her better. "I apologize for interrupting your swim."

Her face flooded with color again. "That's quite all right," she said in so low a voice he had difficulty catching the words. She swatted at her skirt and avoided his gaze. "Well, Indigo, I think I'll be getting along."

With that, she nodded in Chase's direction, still not looking at him. Then she jerked on a bonnet with wide ruching that concealed her face. After tying the chin ribbon, she grabbed her shoes and wadded stockings, then started up the footpath. Since Chase was sitting in the middle of it, holding a sleeping child, she came to a halt after taking several steps and lifted her wide green eyes to his. Chase knew damned well she wouldn't dare strike off through the brush, not unless she wanted a bad case of poison oak. In these hills, the stuff grew as thick as hair on a dog's back, and most people were allergic to it. Especially fair-skinned individuals.

Even shadowed by the bonnet ruching, those eyes of hers packed a wallop. Chase gave her a lazy smile, oddly pleased that he was sitting in her way. Suddenly, the thought of staying most of the summer in Wolf's Landing with nothing better to do than twiddle his thumbs didn't seem such a cross to bear. "No need to hurry off, Franny."

The tip of her turned-up nose pulsed scarlet. "I really must. I believe I can get around you. Please don't disturb yourself."

Chase had no intention of twitching so much as a muscle. As she stepped around him, he turned an eye to her bare feet and the fetching glimpse of ankle her uplifted skirt provided. She had slender little toes with delicate nails that put him in mind of translucent flower petals. A fanned network of fragile, delineated bones graced the top of each foot. He raised his gaze to her face.

Her eyes met his, and for an instant, Chase felt as if he had once again been sandwiched between two logs. Talk about pretty, this young woman gave a whole new definition to the word. It wasn't so much that her face was perfect. What struck Chase was how sweet and innocent she looked, the kind who made a man want to fight mountain lions for her and win. He forgot all about his ribs.

Not wishing to startle her, he tempered his voice and said, "I hope you'll come again, Franny. Maybe next time you'll stop by the house afterward and have some of Ma's lemonade. It's the best in Wolf's Landing."

For a moment, she froze there and stared at him, for all the world as if she couldn't credit her ears. Then her face flushed crimson again. Without a word, she swept on by and disappeared into the trees, never looking back.

"That wasn't very nice," Indigo said in a quavery voice. "How could you, Chase? I didn't think you had it in you to be so mean."

Chase's bemused smile disappeared and he turned to regard his sister, who stood near the water, hands on her hips, her tawny head tipped angrily to one side. Chase didn't mind being accused of orneriness when he had it coming, which he admitted was most of the time, but he felt this reprimand was uncalled for.

"It was mean to invite her for lemonade?"

"You know very well she'd never impose on Ma. Not to say Ma wouldn't welcome her, and our father, too. But Franny's too sweet to put them on the spot that way. You know how all the holier-than-thou people in this town are. Tongues'd buzz for a week if a woman of Franny's occupation was to call on anybody."

Chase digested that. "Did I miss something?" He glanced around to make sure Hunter was still preoccupied with catching water dogs. "The way you talk, you'd think she was the local whore."

Indigo's eyes went wide. "Surely you can think of a politer word than that, and it isn't funny, you acting as if you don't know. I swear, working with those rough-talking loggers has ruined you for respectable company."

A vision of Franny's sweet face swept through Chase's head. With those gigantic, innocent eyes of hers, she couldn't be a— No, it was impossible. Chase didn't claim to be a connoisseur of women, but after living in logging camps for so many years, he sure as hell recognized a fancy skirt when he saw one.

"Indigo, are you trying to tell me Franny's a whore?"

She made a frustrated sound. "Don't call her that, I said. What she is is my best friend, and I won't have you saying mean things about her. If you've got to call her something, call her an unfortunate."

Chase didn't give a shit what Indigo called it; a whore was a whore. An image flashed in his head of the flamboyant, curly-headed blond with the garishly painted face who worked over at the saloon. Out of respect for his parents, Chase had never frequented the upstairs rooms of the Lucky Nugget during his brief visits home, so he hadn't paid close attention to the soiled dove who worked there, but now that he thought on it, he recollected that the woman harkened to the name of Franny. He narrowed an eye. "That girl is the prosti—" He broke off and swallowed. "That's the unfortunate who works over at the Lucky Nugget?"

"Sort of."

"Sort of?" Chase stared at his sister. This was one of her jokes. Leave it to Indigo to try pulling his leg. "What d'ya mean, sort of?"

She wrinkled her nose, clearly impatient with his limited male intelligence. "She isn't exactly there when customers come calling." She shrugged a slender shoulder. "It's difficult to explain. Just don't be ornery to her. Promise me, Chase?"

A sort of whore who wasn't exactly there when her customers came calling? Chase could see that this made perfect sense to Indigo, but damn it to hell if he understood what she was talking about.

"It isn't her fault she's in this pickle," Indigo went on. "There but for the grace of God goes every other woman in this town. You men haven't given us females a lot of options when it comes to earning our bread. Franny truly is an unfortunate."

Chase could see that Indigo was dead serious. He shot a glance up the bank at the spot where Franny, the angel, had disappeared. Then he looked back at his sister, still unable to believe what he was hearing.

Franny, the blushing, green-eyed angel, was a prostitute?

2

Three hours later, Chase rocked back on one of his sister's kitchen chairs, a mug of coffee held to his lips. Across from him, Jake Rand, his brother-in-law, sat with Amelia Rose on his knee, feeding her a horrible-looking mess of meat, gravy, and mashed spuds, all mixed together. Amelia Rose kept rolling out her tongue and gagging, her huge brown eyes swimming with tears.

"Honey, you've got to eat," Jake informed his daughter in a cajoling tone. "One more bite for your pa?"

Amelia Rose skimmed the gook off her tongue with her teeth and let it plop in her lap. She blinked and shuddered. Jake sighed and tried to wipe the mess off her pretty little dress.

"That's the sorriest looking excuse for a supper I've ever seen," Chase commented. "No wonder she won't eat it."

Jake arched a black eyebrow, his brown eyes alight with laughter. "The voice of experience?"

"I don't have to be a papa to have common sense. Why muck her dinner all together like that? It makes me gag just looking at it."

Indigo turned from the sink. With a mischievous glint in her eye, she scooped her daughter off of Jake's lap and handed her to Chase. "Show us how it's done, Uncle Chase. If you get her to eat, I'll bake you an apple pie every day for a week."

His manner challenging, Jake shoved the baby's bowl across the table. Chase surveyed the unappetizing mixture, then studied his niece. He loved apple pie too much to pass. Biting back a grin, he grabbed the honey jar from off the table and dribbled a generous stream over the top of Amelia Rose's food. The little girl's brown eyes lit up with interest.

"That's cheating," Indigo cried, her cheeks flushing a pretty pink. "I swear, Chase Kelly, you're impossible. Now you've ruined her supper, and I'll have to grind more venison."

Chase gave Amelia Rose a large bite. The child chewed, blinked, swallowed and opened her mouth for another spoonful. Chase flashed his sister a sultry look. "Tell me I don't know how to work my way around females. Make the offer sweet enough, and they go for it every time."

Indigo rolled her large blue eyes. "You're rotten clear through."

Jake chuckled. "Whatever works. If she doesn't eat, she'll be as skinny as her ma." As Indigo walked past, he gave her well-rounded bottom a pinch through the seat of her buckskin pants. "Not that I'm complaining."

His tawny-haired wife flashed him a warning glance and returned to washing dishes. Chase continued to shovel honey-laced gook into his niece's mouth. "Roll out the pie dough, half-pint. I've won this bet."

Indigo shook her head. "She's got a sweet tooth, and no mistake. Trust you to encourage her. And don't call me half-pint. You know how I hate it. Hunter repeats everything he hears."

"Since Hunter's already back outside playing, I reckon I can call you whatever I want." At Indigo's indignant glare, Chase laughed, winced when the movement pained his ribs, and then resumed the chore of shoveling spoonfuls of Amelia Rose's dinner into her mouth. After a moment, he sobered and glanced up. "Speaking of name-calling, that reminds me. What did you mean earlier today when you said Fanny was only sort of a prosti— sort of an unfortunate?"

Indigo turned from the dish board. "Franny, not Fanny, and I can't make it much plainer. She just sort of is, but not really."

Chase slid a questioning glance to Jake, who shrugged and shot a look toward the ceiling—a look that said, plainer than words, that there was no figuring Indigo sometimes. Chase agreed. His sister was odd-turned. Of course, folks had once said the same of him. He reckoned it'd be a trick for either of them not to be a little different, raised as they were by a Comanche father and a staunch Catholic mother.

Jake pushed up from the table. "Reckon I'll go split tomorrow's cookstove wood. Want to come, Chase?"

"I'll be right along." Chase scraped Amelia Rose's

bowl clean and put the last spoonful in her mouth. The baby dimpled a cheek at him. Taking care to protect his ribs, he leaned over to put her down. "I'll be expecting my pie tomorrow evening, half-pint," he said to his sister as he stood.

Indigo raised a delicately drawn eyebrow. "You aren't going to hold me to that, are you? Not when you cheated."

Chase winked. "You didn't say I couldn't use honey."

Chase followed Jake outside and leaned against the woodpile to watch while his brother-in-law deftly wielded the ax. He wished his ribs were healed enough for him to help, but that would take a couple of more weeks. Frustrated at feeling useless, he searched for something to talk about. Since it was a subject he couldn't seem to let rest, he decided to resurrect the conversation they'd begun in the kitchen.

"Doesn't it worry you, Jake, having your kids subjected to a whore's influence?"

"I'm surprised at you, Chase. I thought your father taught you better than to judge others by the world's measuring stick."

Chase scuffed the sole of his boot in the dirt. Over the last few years, his father's teachings had become a sore point with him. Trying to walk in Hunter Wolf's footsteps was a surefire way for a man to get his teeth kicked down his throat. "I'm not judging her."

"Sure sounds that way to me."

"Call me cautious. I've never met a whore yet who didn't have her eye out for an easy dollar. It's no secret in Wolf's Landing that you come from a wealthy family, Jake, and Indigo wears her heart on her sleeve, always has and always will."

"It's not such a bad way for Indigo to be," Jake replied on the tail of a grunt. "I kind of like her that way."

"How are you going to feel when there's no bacon on the table because she gave all your money to the local whore? I'm telling you, watch out. What else could attract a gal like Fanny to someone like my sister? Indigo's sweet, but exciting, she definitely isn't."

Jake chuckled. "I find her exciting. Guess it's all in the eye of the beholder, hm? And that *gal's* name is Franny, not Fanny. Tells me where your mind's at."

"Where else? For the right price, that cute little fanny of hers is any man's playground."

Jake's jaw flexed, and he hesitated in his swing, putting more weight behind the ax when he finally cleaved the wood. "Keep your voice down. Hunter's playing just over yonder."

Chase glanced that way and lowered his pitch. "I just don't think you understand how serious a situation this could become. Indigo would give her last pair of moccasins away to anyone with a sad story to tell. Trust me to know."

"Because you're so much alike? Or should I say used to be?"

"People change."

Jake paused to study Chase for a moment then shook his head. "You've changed so much, though. I'm not sure I even know you any more."

"Of course you know me. I've just grown up, that's all. Happens to the best of us."

"Let me stay a kid at heart forever then."

That stung. Chase folded his arms and smiled, pretending he didn't care. But the truth was, he was getting pretty damned tired of everybody in his family finding fault with him. "My line of work gives a man a few rough edges. That doesn't mean I'm not the same person underneath."

Upending a length of log, Jake took a moment to balance it. "It's not your rough edges I'm concerned about, Chase, but how you look at things nowadays. Talk about people with sad stories, something tells me you've got one of your own to tell. Care to share it with me?"

Chase laughed at that and threw up his hands. "Jesus, Jake, would you listen to yourself? I'm not exactly alone in my opinion of prostitutes."

"Nope. You're definitely not alone, more's the pity. I just wonder what happened to make you take such a harsh stand. Sounds like bitterness talking to me. You been trying to rescue whores, Chase?"

"Not since I learned better."

"Got burned, did you?"

"You might say that."

"Well, don't let one worm ruin your taste for apples. Indigo claims Franny's a sweet gal, and I have to take her word on that. You know as well as I do that she has a way of seeing straight to the heart of a person."

"Whores aren't sweet, Jake. They have to be hard as nails to survive."

"Not Franny. According to Indigo, she escapes into dream images while she works. In the morning, she wakes up the same shy Franny, unaffected by what passed the night before."

"That must be some trick," Chase said with a snort.

"It's the only thing that makes sense." His brother-in-law raised an eyebrow. "You've met Franny. If you have another explanation for her being so shy and reserved, I'm all ears."

"She's a damned fine actress, that's what. No woman in her line of work could be that shy. I'm warning you, be leery. The girl's after something. She just hasn't laid her cards on the table yet."

"She and Indigo have been friends for years. Kind of slow on the take, isn't she?"

"Famous last words, and mark mine. You'll live to regret not heeding what I say."

"It'll be my regret. At risk of making you mad, Chase, who Indigo and my kids associate with is my concern, not yours."

"She's my sister. I guess I have a right to be concerned."

"I guess I have to give you that. She is your sister, and I know you love her." Balancing the ax on his shoulder, Jake met Chase's gaze. "I'm too fond of you to risk our friendship by forbidding you to interfere," he said softly. "But before you say or do anything you might regret, do me one favor and think twice. If for no other reason than you'll be leaving soon. You can't expect to drop in on us once or twice a year for a couple of days and make major changes in the way we go about things or the way we think. Franny is important to Indigo. If you say or do anything to damage their friendship, it'll break her heart."

"I don't want to see her hurt. That's the whole point." Chase sighed and shook his head. "I'll try to stay out of it, okay?" he finally relented. "But I won't make any promises. Just the thought of my sister chumming around with a prostitute makes my hackles raise. I feel just that strongly about it."

"I can see that you do," Jake mused softly.

Later that evening, stars as brilliant as diamonds peppered the indigo sky. At the north end of town, Chase sat on the front porch of his parents' house and tried to concentrate on the milk-faced glow of the moon rather than the two upper story windows of the Lucky Nugget, Wolf's Landing's only saloon. One of the windows was faintly illuminated by the glow of a lantern, the other as dark as death. Chase figured the lightless glass probably looked out from May Belle's quarters. Rumor had it that she was retired now and lived on her savings and a percentage of Franny's income. The older woman was most likely asleep by now while Franny worked in the adjacent room with the lighted window.

Franny. He couldn't get those startled green eyes of hers out of his mind. They had haunted him all afternoon and evening. Now here it was bedtime, and what was he doing? Staring at her window, wondering what in hell she was doing right now.

As if he didn't know. Though he took care not to flaunt his living habits in front of his parents and sister, seven years of living in logging camps had seen him in more than one house of ill repute. Redheads, blonds, brunettes, all garishly painted. After a time, they became blurred in a man's mind. An unmarried logger led a harsh, lonely existence, and poker, whiskey, and women offered the only respites.

There had been a time when Chase couldn't have imagined thinking the way he did now. But no one stayed innocent and idealistic forever. Except, maybe, for his father. Hunter Wolf was different than most men, though, purer of heart and noble to his bones. He had set an example that Chase had found impossible to emulate once he left Wolf's Landing.

"Do it unto others before they get a chance to do it to you," was the golden rule he lived by now. The real world beyond these mountains demanded that of a man if he meant to survive.

Chase doubted he could ever make his father understand that, or, for that matter, his mother. To them, there was right and wrong with no gray in between. Chase knew they were disappointed in him.

Hell, if he was brutally honest, he guessed he was even a little disappointed himself. An inexplicable sadness washed through him. Foolishness. A man had to grow up and walk his own way. It was being home again, he supposed, not for a quick visit as had been his habit these last few years, but for days on end. It had left him with too much time to think, too much time to remember how things used to be.

Things had seemed so clearly defined during his boyhood. Back then, he had believed his father had all the answers. Chase gazed at the illuminated upstairs window of the Lucky Nugget and was transported back through the years to the first time he had visited a whorehouse over in Jacksonville. Ten minutes for five dollars. He couldn't remember much about the woman, only that her name had been Clare, and that she was fat and stank. No small wonder, the latter.

He'd gone calling at the brothel with five friends and had been fourth in line.

To this day, Chase could remember how expectant he had felt standing in that dingy, dirty hallway, awaiting his turn. At that age—sixteen, if he remembered right—he had been all crotch and no brains, with one driving force in his life, to do it. All his friends had come out grinning and whooping, saying manly things like "what a honeypot that was," which led him to believe he was about to have the most exhilarating experience of his life. When he had finally gained the chamber of delight, the only thing that saved his fragile male pride was that he had been so worked up before entering that he hadn't lost his prowess quite as quickly as he had his enthusiasm.

As if the night's deeds had been wired back to Wolf's Landing, his father and the fathers of his friends somehow knew what their sons had been up to in Jacksonville. Each boy had received a lecture, Chase included. Only Chase's father, unlike the others, didn't talk about disease and discretion and such. Chase's lecture had consisted of one unforgettable sentence:

"He who preys upon the helpless and offers coin to salve his conscience will one day see the underside of a man's boots and find no solace in a dollar."

As with many of his father's sayings, that one had left Chase pondering its meaning for nigh onto a year afterward. He didn't see how it had anything at all to do with his diddling a fat whore. Helpless? By his calculations, Clare had more money in her coffer than a collection basket on Sunday.

Then one unforgettable night when he accompanied

his father to Jacksonville to attend a miners' meeting, Chase learned what his father meant. After that meeting, all the men had come back to Wolf's Landing and congregated at the saloon. Several of them, married or not, had gone upstairs with a sad-eyed May Belle whose bright smile seemed pasted to her mouth. Chase was scandalized, for most of those who availed themselves of her services were men who attended church regularly and wouldn't have nodded to the poor woman on the street. It was blatantly obvious to Chase that they didn't care a rap about May Belle's feelings, if indeed they believed she had any. Because she was growing older and less attractive, they didn't even pay her the going rate of ten dollars.

When the aging whore worked her way down the counter to Chase and his father, Hunter Wolf placed four ten-dollar gold pieces in her hand, enough for eight visits, according to Chase's calculations. For a horrible moment, he thought that his father, whom he had always believed to be perfect, planned to betray his mother and go upstairs. But then Hunter Wolf had said something Chase would never forget.

"My woman says her door is still open. You will find friends within our walls if your footsteps lead you there."

Now, nine years later, Chase stared at the upper story windows of the Lucky Nugget and realized that the circle was never-ending. May Belle's day as a marketable commodity was finished, and an angelic-looking young woman with startled green eyes had taken her place. *"There but for the grace of God goes every woman in this town. You men haven't given us a lot of options."*

Chase leaned his head back against the porch post and closed his eyes, remembering the young whore who had fleeced him a few years back. The same old bitterness welled within him, but here in Wolf's Landing with the lessons of his childhood whispering to him at every turn, its effect on him was different. Instead of feeling justified, he felt guilty for thinking the way he did. Even so, he doubted he would ever change. Some of life's experiences left marks that ran so deep, one never escaped them.

Franny with the green eyes had made her bed, and by God, she could sleep in it.

Shadows . . . Franny felt them around her, shifting, whispering, touching. But they weren't real. Sometimes, their whispers sounded like questions, and if the questions fit into the dialogue of her dreams, she replied. Otherwise, she didn't bother. Nobody paid her for talking, anyhow.

She closed her eyes and lost herself in sunshine. She was in the buckboard on the way to church. The morning breeze was sweet with the smell of wildflowers, and Ma was singing hymns. Franny pressed her little brother Jason's head to her breast and hugged him close, directing his unfocused gaze toward the field of daisies they were passing. His lax mouth spread in a silly grin. She borrowed Ma's handkerchief to wipe the drool from his bottom lip.

"Say you love me. I wanna hear you say it."

Franny's chest swelled with happiness at hearing Jason speak. "Oh, yes, I love you." She smoothed

Jason's hair, wondering if he knew how very much she loved him, and how sorry she was for what had she had done to him. Ma's affliction was one thing. At least Franny could make her mother's burdens lighter and care for her. But Jason's life had been finished before it began; now he lived in a dim world from which he could never escape. And it was all her fault. "I love you . . . I truly do. I love you with all my heart."

The shadow moved away, and Franny heard coins chink. She pressed her cheek against the chenille and smiled again. They were in church now, and the ushers were walking the aisles to pass the collection baskets for Pastor Elias. Franny leaned across her sister Alaina to press money into her ma's hand. Then she guided Ma's arm so she could drop their tithe into the basket. Though Franny earned whatever coin her family had, it seemed more fitting that her ma should be the one to make their donation, she being a widow and the head of their household.

Another shadow moved over Franny. She heard a voice say, "We're gonna have a fine time, honey." She gave a dreamy smile and said, "Oh, yes, a fine time."

She was in the parlor at home. It was Ellen's birthday, and Franny had a grand surprise for her hidden behind the horsehair settee, a brand-new pair of special ordered high-heeled slippers from Montgomery Ward and Company, her very first ladylike shoes. Before opening presents, of course, they'd play games and have cake. Ma was nearly finished cranking the ice cream machine. That was something her ma could do without help once Franny got her started, and she seemed to enjoy it. Probably because she felt necessary.

Too often, Ma sat on the sidelines wishing she could participate, her head tipped to hear better, her big gray eyes fixed straight ahead. Franny knew it wasn't easy on her, being trapped in darkness.

But enough of sad thoughts. This was a time to celebrate. Ellen's fourteenth birthday! Franny could scarcely believe her little sister had grown up so fast. Oh, what a fine day. The nine of them were going to have a grand time. Jason loved ice cream.

"Talk to me, sweetheart. Tell me how good it feels."

Franny lifted her skirt and twirled around the parlor in her brother Frankie's embrace. She was teaching him to dance at the expense of her toes. At seventeen, he stood a head taller than she, and he had gigantic feet that went every direction but the way he wanted. He was quick to learn, though, and Franny was ever so proud of him. He looked so much like their pa.

"Oh, that's perfect," she cried. "I feel like I'm floating on air."

Frankie blushed and said that having her in his arms felt like heaven. Franny giggled. He said the silliest things sometimes.

At last, the shadow moved away from Franny, and she heard the coins land on her dresser. Waiting to hear the door close, she kept her eyes squeezed tightly shut so she wouldn't glimpse the man's face in the brief spill of light that came into her room from the upstairs landing. To do otherwise would mean she'd have to face reality, and unless it was absolutely forced upon her, Franny avoiding doing that.

The men who visited didn't seem to mind the unorthodox manner in which she provided her services. A female who could be rented, that was all any of them truly wanted, and in a place as small as Wolf's Landing, she had no competition to worry about and was allowed her idiosyncrasies. She was available from nightfall until one in the morning, no exceptions. Always in the dark, a time limit of thirty minutes, absolutely no extras. Most of her customers were regulars who accepted those stipulations without question, took a third of the time allotted, and could be trusted to leave her fee lying on the dresser. Sometimes, if a man was a little short, he'd leave extra after his next visit to cover the difference. On the rare occasion when strangers came into town and wanted female companionship, Gus, the saloon owner, explained the rules and collected her money for her downstairs. The arrangement saved Franny from having to deal with any business transactions.

To distance herself still more, Franny conjured a picture of Shallows Creek, and with the ease of long practice, she slipped quickly into it. Sunshine. Indigo and her children. As the image came into sharper focus, she smiled slightly, watching herself in her mind's eye as she slogged through the water, laughing with little Hunter as they raced to catch the same water dog.

Then her dream picture took on a chill. Someone was watching her. Franny glanced up at the tree-shaded bank. A dark-haired man sat with one muscular shoulder pressed against an oak, his strong arms resting on a bent knee. The breeze ruffled his hair and draped it in unruly waves across his high forehead. His searing blue eyes held her transfixed. She couldn't move, couldn't breathe.

The way he looked at her made her feel naked. And pretty. She guessed who he was, Indigo's brother, Chase. But from the admiration she saw glowing in his eyes, she knew she had him at a disadvantage. Without her face paint and wildly curled hair, he didn't recognize her.

For a crazy instant, Franny wished he never would. He was incredibly handsome, dark and burnished, with an aura of leashed power emanating from his relaxed body. His mischievous grin flashed straight, white teeth and lent his blue eyes an irresistible twinkle. She had known lots of men, but none had made her feel like this, as if she had been waiting all her life to set eyes on him.

No sooner than the feeling registered, Franny shoved it away. As handsome as he was, Chase Wolf wasn't for her. She didn't know why she even entertained such foolishness. The last thing she needed or wanted in her life was a man.

With a weary sigh, she pulled herself from the picture inside her head and forced her eyes open to search the shadows. She was alone, and by her inner clock, she guessed her shift was over. From downstairs came the sound of laughter and piano music. Tightening the sash of her wrapper, she slipped from the bed. After opening the door to flip the sign over to read *Occupied*, she closed it and ran the dead bolt home. Then she moved across the room to the washbasin. As was her habit, she washed away all trace of her professional encounters before lighting her lamp. It made it all seem less real that way.

When the room was once again illuminated by the

lantern, she pushed aside the privacy screen that concealed her hobby table. A smile touched her mouth as she lowered herself onto her sewing chair and lifted the dress she was making for Alaina, who was about to turn sixteen. Pink, her favorite color. Franny plucked a pin from the cushion and resumed the task of fastening the ruffle to the hem.

Within seconds, the sounds coming from downstairs faded into the background, and she became aware of only those familiar things around her that constituted her reality. Her gaze shifted to the arrangement of pressed flowers under glass at her elbow—a gift she was making for Indigo. On the table by her rocker was her open Bible, the passage where she had stopped reading marked with a ribbon. Lying by her new sewing machine was the clown-face pillow she was embroidering for Jason.

Franny searched with her foot for the sewing machine treadle. Her day's toil was done, and now she could work on her sister's new school dress without further interruption. This was what was real, she assured herself. And all that truly mattered. Her vague recollections of what had passed earlier were consigned to that dark, secret corner of her mind where only nightmares lurked.

3

Sunlight slanted under the eave of the over-

Sunlight slanted under the eave of the overhang and dappled the planks of the boardwalk. Drawing
the ruching of her sunbonnet forward, Franny kept her
head bent as she hurried past the stores. On the morning
breeze, the delicious smells of maple, cinnamon, and
yeast drifted from the bakery. From the barbershop
came the mingled scents of bay rum, razor strop paste,
bergamot, and men's bath salts.

As she passed the dress shop, she glimpsed a new
display in the show window and slowed her footsteps
to admire a lady's spring cape made of perforated
black kersey and trimmed with black silk embroidery.
It was just the sort of thing Franny had been thinking
about making for her mother, fine enough for attending church, but not so dressy it would be out of place
around town. The high-standing collar was edged with

delicate black lace, and a matching Venice hat was pinned to one shoulder.

As much as she yearned to linger and study the wrap's pattern, she didn't dare. Perhaps when she visited home next weekend, the dress shop in Grants Pass would have spring capes of a similar design in stock.

As she hurried on her way, she heard voices coming through the open doorway of the general store. Sam and Elmira Jones had one-hundred pound sacks of spuds on special, and despite the early hour some of the local ladies were already out and about to do their daily shopping, probably in hopes of getting best pick of the potato shipment. Franny couldn't help but envy those women their casual friendships with one another. How nice it would be not to fear recognition, to be able to hold one's head high and greet passersby with a smile.

Don't think about it. Casting glances right and left to make sure the way was clear, she stepped off the boardwalk and into the street. As she ran across the packed dirt thoroughfare, she heard a low whistle and a man's voice. She didn't falter or look up. The man recognized her only because Franny, the whore, was known to dart furtively about town wearing a sunbonnet that concealed her face. If she were to doff the hat and turn to confront him, she would bear little similarity to the wildly coiffed and gaudily painted Franny from the Lucky Nugget, the woman he believed her to be.

That Franny didn't exist, not really.

As she neared Indigo's house, Franny slowed her footsteps. There were no other residences at the south end of town, only the schoolhouse, and it was empty now because of summer. There was little chance of bumping into someone unexpectedly here.

Today she and Indigo planned to make saltwater taffy. An insane idea in this heat, Franny knew, but she still couldn't wait to get started. Hunter would have a grand time when it came time to butter their hands and begin the pulling. With a grin, Franny remembered the last time she'd pulled taffy. Her younger brother Frankie had lost his grip on the candy and landed flat on his backside.

Taking a deep breath, she tugged off her bonnet and lifted her face to the sunshine. The odors from town didn't reach this far, and the air smelled of pine and oak, a wonderfully earthy scent that beckoned to her as nothing else could. Until dusk when she would have to creep back to the Lucky Nugget and assume her other identity, this was her reality, Indigo and her children and the sunlit morning.

It was enough for Franny because she knew it had to be. She would be forever grateful for Indigo's friendship. Without that distraction, Franny felt sure she would go stark raving mad. Finances made it impossible for her to visit home more than one weekend a month. The twenty-eight days that stretched like an eternity in between would be unbearable if she were never able to escape the tawdry trappings of the saloon. She had an incurable case of insomnia that allowed her to sleep only a few hours a night, and her sewing and crafts took up only so much of her waking hours.

Voices drifted to Franny through the open windows of Indigo's small house. She recognized Jake Rand's velvety tenor and deduced that he was late leaving for work. Wishing to avoid him, Franny crept around the corner of the house to wait until he left for the mine.

Shade from a tall pine fell across her, and she pressed her back to the shake siding of the house. Withered lilac carpeted the ground, the parched and faded petals rustling under her shoes. Closing her eyes, she inhaled their faint perfume and listened to the Rand family laughing together. Amelia Rose squealed with delight, and Franny pictured her father tossing her into the air before kissing her good-bye. Hunter's husky giggles drifted to her.

Once, so very long ago, Franny had had a loving father like Jake Rand. She could still remember how wonderful it had felt when he hugged her. Francie, he had called her, his little Francie girl. Though Frank Graham had been dead for nearly ten years, her memories of him were so precious that she would carry them with her always.

"Eavesdropping?"

The question, uttered in a deep, teasing voice, made Franny jump. She turned to see Indigo's brother, Chase Wolf, walking toward her, gilded with morning sunlight one moment, bathed in shadows from the tree above him the next. He held a blue ceramic mug in one hand, a sturdy finger crooked through the handle, his calloused knuckles pressed against its base. She saw steam waft upward and guessed the mug held freshly brewed coffee.

For a man with cracked ribs, he moved with unnerving agility, long legs measuring off the distance between them, his broad shoulders shifting with the loose-hipped swing of his stride. Mahogany hair lay across his bronzed forehead in rebellious waves. His eyes were a startling dark blue in contrast to his Indian darkness, but even so it was all too easy to imagine him on the Texas plains, raiding and pillaging, perhaps even kidnapping white women.

Today he wore blue jeans and a collarless white shirt, the latter homemade and simply patterned, the cuffless sleeves turned back over his broad forearms, the front placket unbuttoned and hanging open to reveal the burnished planes of his chest and the strips of stark white muslin that bandaged his ribs. The shirt, soft from many washings, skimmed the muscular lines of his torso like a caress, the tails blousy at his lean waist and tucked loosely into his trousers. Franny dropped her gaze to his boots, heavy and thick-soled lumberman pacs with spiked soles, the type most loggers wore. Yet he stepped with an eerie soundlessness, the inbred grace and wildness of his Comanche ancestors evident in every movement.

Because he had already seen her face yesterday, there was little point in putting her bonnet back on. He studied her as though he meant to sketch her, and an awful sense of foreboding washed over her. She averted her gaze, afraid of him without knowing for certain why.

Ridiculous. He was nothing to her, just Indigo's brother, home to recuperate from an injury. He wouldn't stay in Wolf's Landing long enough to be a threat to her. And by chance that he did, why would he wish her harm?

Franny forced herself to look up at him again and

then wished she hadn't. He didn't speak, but there wasn't a need. His eyes held hers in a relentless grip. She had the unsettling feeling that he could read far more from her gaze than she wished. Down at the creek yesterday, she hadn't sensed that about him, but now she realized he might be as intuitive about the feelings of others as his sister. Indigo's uncanny ability to strip away a person's layers didn't bother Franny because they were such good friends, and she trusted her.

Chase Wolf was a horse of a different color.

The teasing glint in his eyes was different from the one she had noticed yesterday. Harder, somehow, and laced with carnality. He had learned the truth about her; it was written all over his face.

Franny had an insane urge to run. But she couldn't. His gaze held her fast. As if he knew he had her helplessly ensnared, he smiled slowly, his mouth quirking slightly at the corners in a way that made her heart skitter.

"It sure is a beautiful morning, isn't it?" His tone was low and silken, not at all threatening or jarring, yet her nerves twanged with every inflection of his voice.

As he stepped closer, his nearness made her feel dwarfed. She guessed him to be well over six feet tall, an extraordinary height, no doubt inherited from his father who stood head and shoulders above most of the men in the community. To amplify his stature, he had the powerful musculature of someone who constantly pitted himself against the elements. His scent, sharpened by the humidity of morning, moved around her. Her nostrils picked up traces of bergamot and soap, which she recognized as the ingredients in shaving compound, and bay rum mixed with glycerin, used in homemade liquid shampoo. On another man, the combination of smells might have seemed commonplace, perhaps even mundane, but on Chase Wolf, it seemed potently masculine.

Not wishing to let him know his size intimidated her, Franny flattened herself against the house. As though he sensed her discomfiture and found it amusing, his smile deepened as he perused her. Those eyes. They were so intense and incredibly dark a blue, lined with thick, silken lashes the same shade as his hair. When she looked into them, she found it difficult to think clearly, let alone make intelligent responses.

"You *are* a puzzle," he murmured. "And I never have been able to resist a puzzle."

Franny tried to swallow but her throat refused to work. No matter, for her mouth had gone as dry as dust. "I . . . I have to go."

"Don't run off."

His expression still mischievous yet martially arrogant, he reached toward her. She flinched as his leathery fingers grazed her ear. As he drew his hand back, she saw that he held a gleaming gold coin. With practiced fingers he rolled it in a shimmering path over his palm, gave it a flip, and caught it within the circle of his thumb and forefinger.

Flashing the money at her, he said in a silken voice, "Ten dollars. Fancy that, me plucking it out of thin air." His gaze trailed lazily to her bodice. "And there's more where that came from." His white teeth flashed as he spoke, and his eyes heated with blatant invitation. "How many ten-dollar gold pieces would I have to find behind that pretty little ear of yours to talk you into spending the morning with me?"

Franny felt so humiliated she wanted to burrow into the dirt and disappear. "The morning?"

"The morning," he repeated. Squinting, he glanced up through the pine boughs at the cloudless sky. "It's a perfect day to find a private place along the creek somewhere and while away the hours with a very pretty and accommodating young lady."

She blinked, not at all certain how to handle this. Men sometimes tried to stop her on the street, but she had always managed to evade them. Chase Wolf stood so close she felt like a slab of meat sandwiched between two slices of bread, the house at her back, his chest blocking her escape.

"I . . . um . . . " She searched frantically for something to say. "I don't see gentlemen outside the saloon."

"I'm no gentleman." He twisted the coin before her nose. "How much, Franny? How does fifteen strike you? If you prove to be talented at your trade, I'll kick in another five and make it an even twenty. I'd venture a guess that's twice what you usually make."

"No, I—"

With a flick of his broad wrist, he emptied the contents of his coffee mug onto the grass. Bracing an arm against the house, he leaned in close and caressed her bottom lip with the coin. The teasing lights disappeared from his eyes to be replaced by a piercing glint.

"What's your game?"

"I beg your pardon?"

He laughed, the sound breathy and mocking. "Oh,

you are good. Do you practice that thing you do with your eyes in front of a mirror, or does it come naturally?"

Franny had no inkling of what he meant. "What thing? You're not making any sense, Mr. Wolf."

"Let me put it a little plainer then. Why would a female of your persuasions want to spend so much time with a sweet young woman like my sister? What's in it for you? And please don't tell me you enjoy playing nursemaid to two children."

A female of her persuasions? Franny had heard herself described in far baser terms, but even so it hurt. "Indigo is my friend. I enjoy being with her, that's all."

"Bullshit," he shot back. "I know your kind, don't think I don't, and you always have an ulterior motive. What is it, money? You hope to play on her sympathy and get into her pockets?"

"No," Franny denied weakly. "I'd never—"

He silenced her by pressing the coin firmly against her mouth. "Listen up, and listen good. You may fool some of the people some of the time, namely Indigo and Jake, but you can't fool all of the people all of the time, namely me. Stay away from my sister and her kids. The last thing she needs is a tarnished little whore playing on her sympathy and messing up her life."

Outrage lent Franny a flash of courage. Freeing her mouth, she said, "I believe you're stepping beyond your bounds, Mr. Wolf. If and when Indigo asks me to stay away from her, I shall happily comply, but the likes of you certainly won't dictate to me."

"Won't I? Let me list a couple of facts for you, sweet cheeks. Prostitution is on the real shady side of respectability. A word dropped here and there, and it wouldn't take much to get all the fine, highfalutin ladies in this town to heat up a caldron of tar and start plucking their chickens. Do you get my drift?"

Franny certainly didn't need him to paint her a picture. More than one woman in her profession had been run out of a town on the rails. "What have I ever done to—"

"Nothing," he said, cutting her off. "It's not personal, honey. Just looking out for my own. The members of my family, from my father on down, are too naive to be a match for your sort. The same isn't true of me. Save yourself a lot of heartache, hm? Stay away from my sister, and you and I will get along just fine."

Rather than meet his gaze, Franny looked down her nose at the coin. She realized now that he hadn't been serious about his proposition. He had only used it as an opening to warn her off. She didn't want any trouble, especially not from a man of Chase Wolf's ilk. Indigo's brother or no, he had a dangerous edge, and if he got it in for someone, she had a feeling he'd go for blood. She couldn't afford a scandal. Grants Pass was only forty miles away, enough of a distance to ensure none of her customers were likely to be men from her hometown, but not so far that news from Wolf's Landing never reached there.

"Do we understand each other?" he asked softly.

"Yes," she whispered, unable to say anything else. As bleak as the summer might be without Indigo's friendship, Franny figured she had best steer clear of her—at least until Chase went back to the logging camps.

"I thought you looked like a smart girl."

As he straightened and allowed her a little more

room, Franny closed her eyes on a wave of nausea. She prayed she wouldn't embarrass herself by emptying her stomach all over his boots. When she felt a little more in control, she lifted her lashes to find him regarding her with an uncertain expression clouding his gaze. In that instant, she knew that under the sharp-edged steel Chase Wolf wore as armor, he had a compassionate side—a side that regretted being so cruel.

Feeling suffocated by his nearness and masculine scent, Franny stepped around him. After all, he had said what he had come to say. He must have watched for her to leave the saloon this morning and followed her here, which explained their chance encounter. An ambush, more like.

To her surprise and dismay, before she managed to get completely beyond his reach, he grasped her arm and drew her to a halt. The grip of his fingers burned through the cloth of her sleeve. Gooseflesh rose on her skin, and she strove not to shiver. Throwing him a startled and questioning look, she waited for him to draw more blood with that razor tongue of his. Instead, he slipped the gold piece into her hand and folded her fingers around it. The minute he relaxed his grip, Franny did likewise and let the money fall soundlessly to the grass. She didn't mean to let him salve his conscience so easily.

She met his gaze, hoping her contempt for him shone in her eyes. It was so easy for him condemn her. If he went looking for a job in Wolf's Landing, he could probably have his pick of a half dozen before noon, all offering a decent wage. Did he think she wouldn't happily work alongside him in the timber if someone would hire her? Did he actually believe she liked the way she earned a living? God forgive him, if only he knew what it was like for her, he wouldn't be so self-righteous.

The instant he released her arm, Franny gathered her skirts and stepped across the dewy grass, resisting the urge to run. She wouldn't give him that satisfaction.

Chase stared after Franny's diminishing form, his throat tight with an emotion he couldn't name. That look in her eyes. He didn't think he'd ever be able to wipe it from his mind. Not just contempt, but a hurt that ran too deep for tears. Watching her, he couldn't help but draw a comparison between her and all the other prostitutes he had ever known. There was no similarity. Franny whatever-her-last-name-was had the mark of a lady. Even the way she moved was prim and proper.

A brilliant flash caught Chase's eye, and he glanced down to see the gold piece lying in the grass at his feet where she had let it fall. So she scorned his money, did she? He toed the coin then flipped it across the ground, loath to pick it up. For all he cared, it could lay there and grow moss.

"What did you say to her?"

Indigo's accusing voice lashed through the morning air to bring Chase's head around. He stared at her, as reluctant to admit what he had said as he was to retrieve his money. "Nothing that didn't need saying."

Her blue eyes stricken and giving him no quarter, Indigo hugged her waist and came toward him. "What do you mean? What needed saying, Chase?"

It had been a spell since Chase had felt like a boy

called onto the carpet. Angry that he should be made to feel guilty when his only crime had been to watch after his sister, he swallowed to moisten his throat. "A whore has no business being as thick as thieves with a decent young woman. You're too sweet for your own good, honey. What about your reputation? And if you don't give a flip about that, what about your kids? When they reach school age, do you want them humiliated because the other children whisper about their mother and the company she keeps?"

Indigo's eyes widened and her naturally burnished complexion went deathly pale. She glanced down, saw the gold piece lying at his feet, and moaned. "Oh, Chase, what have you done?"

"What had to be done," he replied gently. "I know you care about her, Indigo. But you can't take the woes of the world on your shoulders. Franny has chosen her path. Don't walk it with her. You have your family to think about."

Tears filled Indigo's eyes, and her mouth started to quiver.

"Indigo," he started.

"Don't," she said shakily. "Please don't say anything more. I think you've already said quite enough."

Chase couldn't believe her reaction. True, he had expected her to be upset. But this? He had done what any concerned brother would do. Couldn't she see that?

"I know you're angry at me right now," he put in gently, "but in time you'll see I only acted in your best interests."

"And what of Franny's best interests? I'm the only friend she has, Chase."

He gave a derisive snort. "Since when do whores expect to have friends? Jesus, Indigo, surely you can't be that naive."

"Naive? Or compassionate. And while we're on the subject of not being able to believe, I can't believe how hard you've become."

"Indigo . . . " he tried again.

"Don't you Indigo me. I want you to go directly to the Lucky Nugget and apologize to Franny. I mean it, Chase Kelly. She won't come back to visit me anymore until you do."

"Good."

"Good? Chase, you're going to apologize to her, so help me."

"Apologize?" he echoed. "For what?"

Indigo averted her face. "Until you figure that out for yourself, maybe it would be better if you didn't come around here."

"Excuse me?"

She turned that accusing gaze on him again. "You heard me. If I'm going to shield my children from all the ugliness in this world, maybe I should start with you."

"Are you serious?"

"Dead serious."

Chase could see that she was. Forgetting his ribs, he bent to pick up his mug and had difficulty straightening. Indigo reached out to grasp his arm. He jerked away. "Don't touch me. My ugliness might rub off."

"Oh, Chase," she said shakily. "I don't even know you anymore. Where has my brother gone?"

"To hell and back," he bit out. "You live here in

your sheltered little world and think you know it all. The truth is, Indigo, you don't know anything about women like Franny. None of you do. I was only trying to help. But, hey. If this is the thanks I'm going to get, why bother? Learn your lesson like I did, the hard way. Just don't come whining to me when her true colors start to show."

With that, he strode away, so furious he shook with it. To hell with her. For someone so dead set against being judgmental, she sure didn't hesitate to judge him.

4

Crickets serenaded in the darkness, and mosquitoes buzzed around Chase's head. After taking another swig from the jug of bourbon he had purchased over at the saloon, he wiped his mouth and rested his back more heavily against the pine tree, his gaze fixed on the boughs silhouetted against the cobalt sky above him.

One arm draped over his upraised knee, he held the whiskey jug dangling by its handle from the crook of a finger. With his other hand, he patted his shirt pocket for the half-smoked cigarette he had rolled earlier. Striking a lucifer on the seam of his jeans, he squinted against the bright flare of the match and took a deep drag. As he exhaled smoke, he laughed, softly and bitterly, while shaking his head.

As his uncle Swift was so fond of saying, if this

wasn't a hell of a note, he didn't know what was. Here he was, a grown man hiding from his parents in the backyard. All evening, his mother had been walking around looking as though she were sucking alum. His father had little if anything to say to him. Chase could scarcely stand to be in the same house with the two of them.

All in the world he had done was proposition a prostitute. If that was a criminal offense, add his name to a long list. Sex was the girl's business, for Christ's sake. It wasn't as if he had insulted a lady or something. Every time Chase thought about it, he did a slow burn.

Though his folks hadn't said anything, he knew Indigo had told them about his talk with Franny. He supposed the whole lot of them expected him to go to the saloon, hat in hand, to apologize. To a whore, of all the crazy things, and for doing nothing more than offering her money for what she peddled every blooming night of the week. He had done what needed doing—what Jake or his father should have done—and he didn't feel the least bit remorseful.

Taking another belt of whiskey, Chase tried to estimate how much longer he might have to stay in Wolf's Landing. Too long, that was a certainty. The instant his ribs healed, he was making tracks. And if his family thought he'd be back to visit them again any time soon, they all had another think coming. He'd had enough of this bullshit.

"Good whiskey?"

The sudden sound of his father's voice startled Chase, which bore testimony to just how intoxicated he actually was. Trained in Indian warfare from the time he was knee-high, he usually sensed a person's presence before they got within twenty feet of him. He peered through the darkness, trying to focus. Not that Hunter Wolf's large frame was difficult to home in on. Tossing aside his cigarette, Chase proffered the bottle, not really expecting his father to accept. "It's fair to middling, I guess. Want a swig?"

With the ease of a much younger man, Hunter took the jug and sat Indian fashion beside him. Even in the dimness, Chase could see the stern set to his harshly carved features—features that he knew mirrored his own. Lecture time. Just the way he wanted to spend his evening.

Because of the heat, his father wore no shirt. In the moonlight, his bare chest and shoulders gleamed like polished bronze, his long dark hair a silken curtain that shifted each time he moved. Even after living among the whites for well over twenty years, there was a wildness about him that couldn't be ignored, a dangerous edge that, in Chase's opinion, made other men seem pallid in comparison. Comanche to his core, his father. Always had been, always would be. Not that he had a problem with that. He just felt it unfair that he should be expected to live by the same set of rules simply because he was his son and had inherited his Indian looks. In the logging camps, a man scrabbled just to survive, to hell with his heritage and all the rot that went along with it.

His brain numbed by liquor, Chase found himself expressing those sentiments before he quite realized what he was saying. "You all find it so damnably easy to judge me, don't you? Ever since I've been home, all of you have been noting how much I've changed, all to the bad. But have any of you wasted a single minute wondering why?"

Hunter swallowed a mouthful of bourbon and whistled through strong white teeth. Handing the jug back to Chase, he said, "That burns clear to the gut." He cleared his throat and shuddered. "And to answer your question, yes, I have wondered."

"Well, you sure as hell couldn't prove it by me. And I'll tell you, I'm fed up with being criticized. As if the rest of you are so goddamned perfect you have room to talk."

"Perhaps we only seek to understand you, Chase."

"Right," he scoffed. "If you really wanted to understand me, you'd have tried talking to me about it instead of passing judgement."

"I am here now to talk."

Chase supposed that was true enough, albeit a little late. "Maybe Jake's right. Maybe none of you really know me anymore. I know I've changed. What pisses me off is that none of you give's a rat's ass why." He took another long pull at the bottle. "How could I keep from changing? That's the question. Things haven't exactly been a bed of roses for me, you know. For the last seven years, I've been living in the worst conditions you can imagine, working my ass off from first light until dark, saving every penny I could to invest in land. During the rainy season, I've seen the time I was wet to the skin for days on end, and at night, I crawled into an equally wet bed."

Hunter gazed off into the darkness, saying nothing. His silence encouraged Chase to continue.

"Indigo says I'm hard. You and Ma haven't openly criticized me, but I've seen it in your eyes. You disapprove of what I've become, and don't deny it."

"I will not deny it, for to say we don't disapprove of some of the things you think and do would be a lie. That does not mean we have stopped loving you, Chase, or that we cannot still find much about you to admire."

Despite the gentle delivery, the criticism stung. Chase swallowed the hurt with another mouthful of whiskey. "Well, understand something. I didn't get hard because it sounded like a fine idea."

"No? Then explain to me why."

"I'm a breed, in case you've forgotten, a quarter Comanche."

"Yes. A breed. My blood flows in your veins."

"No offense, but according to white folks, that makes me not quite human."

The words hung like a pall between them. Chase no sooner said them than he wished he could call them back. "I'm sorry, my father. I didn't mean that."

"Yes, I think you did," Hunter said softly. "And it lays my heart upon the ground to know you feel that way."

Chase tightened his fist around the neck of the bottle. "It's not how I feel. You know that. But it's a truth we can't escape, nonetheless. Beyond these mountains, folks take one look at me and know there was a redskin in my mama's woodpile somewhere. That automatically makes me dirt under their feet. I'm not considered to be as good as a white man on all counts. The only way I can ever overcome that is to have power. Money is power."

"I see."

"No, you don't see, more's the pity, and you never will. You and Ma created your own little world here, a safe place where you're pretty much sheltered. You've never faced what I've had to, not to the same extent. Maybe I have become hard, but to survive, I had to."

Hunter sighed. "Chase, if your mother was out here, she would say you are sitting on the great pot of pity."

"The pity pot," Chase corrected. Then it struck him what his father had said. "Jesus. Do I have to listen to this?"

"No, you can close your ears."

"You think I'm feeling sorry for myself, do you?" Chase hesitated a moment, wondering if perhaps he was. "Well, if anyone ever had reason, I do."

"Tell me of these reasons."

That was a request Chase could deliver on. "When I first went to the camps, I tried to live by all your pure ideals, doing unto others as I wanted them to do unto me."

"Oh, yes? That makes me very proud."

"Yeah, well unproud yourself. I got shit on in every conceivable way, and when the bastards weren't shitting on me, they were beating the hell out of me."

Hunter shook his head. "And you such a little fellow?"

The unveiled sarcasm forced Chase to back up a few sentences. Maybe he was on the pity pot. Or perhaps it would be more accurate to say he was crying in his whiskey. Leave it to his father to point that out in such a way that he couldn't get mad. He narrowed an eye. "Do you want to hear this story or not?"

"I will need a blanket to sop up my tears. But, yes, I want to hear your story."

Chase frowned. "Where the hell was I?"

"You were at the part about getting the hell beaten out of you all the time."

"Ah, that's right. Anyway, they kept it up until I fought back, until I got as mean or meaner than they were." He gave his parent a mock toast with the half empty jug. "And now here I am, metamorphosed, a person you can't stand."

"I love you, Chase. With every breath I take."

"Right. But you don't like me much." Chase punctuated that with another swig of whiskey. "Funny, that. You're all so determined not to judge that little whore. But what about me?"

"Franny is a victim."

"And I gather I'm not?"

"Only if you choose to be." His father turned to regard him. "By your own words, the men in the camps were cruel to you only until you fought back. I trained you to fight, if you will remember. I know that when you finally struck back, you did so with great vengeance, as is the way of the People."

In that, at least, Chase had to admit he was his father's son; he fought to win and usually did, even if it took his last ounce of strength. Surrender was not a word Hunter Wolf included in his vocabulary and had never taught it to his children.

"The Frannies of this world have no weapons," his father went on huskily, "and no strong arm with which to wield a weapon if they had one. Heartless men use them, and in order to survive, they must yield. It is their only choice and their greatest shame. One from which there is no escape. Victims, Chase, one and all."

"I disagree. If that were true, they'd accept help when it was offered, and I know from experience they don't. You can't help a person who won't help herself."

Silence settled again, a pained, uncomfortable silence. He supposed that was a bitter dose for his father to swallow, he who had so selflessly shared all that he believed in hopes that his son would embrace the same values. Now they had come to a fork in the road.

As if his father read his thoughts, he said, "I know you walk a path toward dreams, Chase."

"Yes."

"Do not lose your way."

The gentle warning made Chase's heart catch.

"These dreams of yours. Are they worth all that you must sacrifice to attain them?"

"Owning timberland, it's what I've always wanted for as long as I can remember. Even as a boy, I had these plans. You know that."

"But not for the same reasons. And in the end, what will you have? Full pockets, great power, and an empty heart?"

"Sneer if you like, but power is the only way I'll ever amount to anything. I already own one sizable tract of land, and I've saved nearly enough to buy another. One day soon, I'll be richer than anybody you've ever known. So rich that nobody—nobody anywhere—will be able to look down on me."

"Ah, yes. And you will have this power you speak of." Hunter spread his hands palms upward and gazed at the lines etched there. "Just remember that money isn't everything. Look at all Jake gave up to be here with Indigo, to raise his children here."

"What're you asking, that I give up my dreams and settle for a petered-out mine here in Wolf's Landing?"

"The mine still provides a steady yield."

"You barely eke out an existence for two families. And when it's all panned out? Then what? Will we dig another tunnel and pray we find color? Maybe you can live that way, not knowing where your next meal will come from, but I want more than that out of life."

"More? I do not think so." Hunter gestured toward the rambling log house behind them, then swept out his arm to indicate the surrounding property. "How can any man have more, Chase? There is love here, and peace. Those things cannot be bought with coin."

"I'm not a miner. You love it, and so does Indigo. But it's not for me, never has been. You know that." Chase rubbed at the toe of his boot. Never mind that he couldn't see the damned thing. "You've always known that."

"I do not ask you to be a miner, just the best man that you can be. I worry about your dreams, not because I disapprove of them, but because of who you are becoming while you follow them. You are Chase Wolf, my son, and you are forsaking that."

"To be your son, I have to be perfect?"

"A little bit perfect would be very good."

"A little bit? Surely I'm not that bad." Bleary-eyed, Chase focused on the dark woods at the other side of the creek. He tried to take stock of his faults, which in his opinion were damned few. "I cuss a little. So shoot me."

Hunter fixed him with an exasperated look.

"What else? I suppose you think I drink too much? Excuse me all to hell. I keep forgetting I'm back home, living with a bunch of puritans."

"Do you?"

"Do I what? Live with a bunch of puritans?"

"No, drink too much."

"Hell, no." Chase stabbed the cork at the mouth of the jug. It took him two tries to hit his mark. Hunter snorted in disgust. Chase snorted back. "So, I've had a little too much tonight."

"Yes, I'd say you have."

"But I don't make a habit of it."

"That is good."

After a lengthy silence, Chase relented. "Okay, if you want the unvarnished truth, I suppose I could make do with a little less whiskey."

"I always want the truth, Chase. If we speak in lies, why bother to talk?"

Chase supposed that observation had merit. But sometimes it was a lot easier to lie. "On Saturday nights in the camps, there isn't much else to do but drink and play cards. Practically all the loggers are heavy drinkers. I'm no worse than the rest."

"But no better."

"Damn it. I can't win, can I? Why in hell do I have to be better than everyone else? Answer me that? Why can't you be satisfied with my being just as good?"

"Because most of the men in this world are not good, and to stand only as tall as they makes you a man of small stature."

"I stand tall enough to suit me."

"No, you do not. Which is why you drink."

Chase gave a bitter laugh and lifted the jug in a mock toast. "You brought that back around full circle. Back to my drinking, are we? All right, let's address that. As a general rule, I buy a jug on Saturdays and no other time. Sometimes I drink it all, sometimes I don't, and during the week, I can take it or leave it. Is that what you call overindulgence?"

"It is not what goes into your mouth that worries me."

"What then?"

"What I hear coming out of it."

"My cussing, you mean?"

"Cussing means nothing to me. Your angry words do. Sometimes my heart is laid upon the ground at the things you say. And when I look into your eyes? Ah, Chase, I die a little."

"And sometimes I die a little when I look into yours," Chase blurted. Another well of hurt rose inside him. "After all my work to make something of myself, how do you think I feel when I see how disappointed you are in me? When you find fault with me every time I so much as turn around?"

"I do that?"

"Yes, you do that."

Hunter smiled slightly. "I think you are looking in a pool of water at your own reflection."

"Don't start. It never fails, you always turn everything I say all around."

"Why do I do that?"

"I suppose you're trying to make me search for answers."

"That is bad?"

"It is when I don't have any."

Hunter grasped Chase's shoulder. Feeling the warm heaviness of his hand nearly brought tears to Chase's eyes. He had an unsettling urge to press his face against his father's chest and cry like a kid. The most awful part was, he didn't know why. He only knew he felt incredibly lost. And lonelier than he ever had in his life.

"Sometimes I'm not sure what it's all about," he whispered raggedly. He didn't really expect his father to understand what he meant by that because he wasn't sure he knew himself. "Nothing you taught me counts for shit out there."

Hunter gave him a kindly pat. "No," he agreed. "The things I taught you count for nothing anywhere, Chase. Only in your heart."

"The standards you set—only a saint could live by them, and I'm no saint. Not anything close."

"They are a map I drew for you, Chase, nothing more. I tried to mark the way clearly, but as with all maps, there is more than one route. You must choose the way you will go."

Taking a deep breath, Chase said, "Yeah, well . . . I've done my choosing. I guess I'm making a hell of a mess of it, aren't I?"

"Are you?"

"You know damned well you think so. If not, you wouldn't be talking to me."

"What I think doesn't matter. What do you think?"

"That I'm making a hell of a mess of it."

"Perhaps it is time that you set your feet in another direction."

"And give up everything I've ever dreamed of?"

"Not away from your dreams. But toward them by another path."

"Maybe." Chase grew quiet for a moment, thinking. "You know, the funny thing is, I felt perfectly content with myself before I came home. Now I'm suddenly turning every damned thing inside out and upside down. I'm not sure I even like myself anymore, let alone any of you. In fact, if we're dealing in the brutal truth, sometimes I think I actually hate all of you."

At that admission, Hunter chuckled and gave him a slight shake. "You do not hate us, my son. When you look at us, you see a reflection of yourself, and it is a self you would deny if you could. That is all."

Chase didn't see what was so damned amusing about that.

"It is an odd thing that happens when a man returns to the place of his childhood. Instead of looking always at others, he is forced to look carefully at himself. It is an unsettling thing when he discovers he has traveled a great distance, only to go nowhere."

Since that observation made little sense to Chase, he sidestepped it. "I feel trapped in the middle between the life I have now and the way things used to be," he whispered. "And I'm being pulled both ways. A part of me wishes things could be as simple for me as they seem to be for you. But another part of me knows they can't."

"Life is like a blanket you draw around yourself. You make your own weave."

"That's easy for you to say."

"You think all that I have has come to me on the wind?" Hunter shook his head. "I set out from Texas with a pregnant woman and traveled over two thousand miles, more than half on foot because we lost one horse. I didn't know where I was going or what I might find when I got here, only that it had been spoken in the prophecy that I should go west to find a new place where the *tabeboh* and Comanche could live in harmony."

Chase had heard this tale before—so many times he knew it by heart.

"Right after we got here, you were born, the fulfillment of that promise. My son, part Comanche, part *tabeboh*. Since the first time I held you, I have sung to you the songs of my people so you could sing them to your own son someday, and he to his. I did the same with Indigo."

"And now I'm turning away from those songs, is that what you're saying?"

"I'm just asking you not to forget the words. You were born to pass them on, Chase. Through you and Indigo, the People will continue to live even though their bones have turned to dust."

"I can't sing words to songs I no longer believe in."

"If not the songs of your ancestors, what do you believe in?"

"Nothing," he whispered raggedly. "Not a goddamned thing."

After another long silence, Hunter said, "Perhaps you should uncork your jug then and have another drink. With nothing left to believe in, liquor will be your only solace."

Lord, how true that was. "Sometimes, my father, you can draw blood with that tongue of yours."

"So you came by your vicious tongue naturally?"

Chase huffed at that. "I knew you'd get around to it eventually."

"Around to what?"

"You came out here to ask me to go apologize to Fanny or Franny or whatever in hell her name is."

Hunter nodded. "I told Indigo I would speak to you about that, yes. You choose to walk your own way. Yet you feel Indigo should not? Her friends are her concern, not yours, not mine."

"Point taken."

"Your anger about her friendship with Franny worries me."

"I'm not angry. At least that wasn't what prompted me at the start. I was just trying to protect my sister. Was that so wrong?"

"Protect her from what?"

"Open your eyes! The woman is after something. Why else would she be hanging around Indigo?"

"You are so bitter. Why, Chase?"

The temptation was great to tell his father why, but the old hurts ran too deep to exhume them. "I'm not bitter, I just know her kind, and trust me, she's pure poison. Don't believe she's all that she pretends to be, not for a minute."

"What is it she pretends to be?"

Chase wiped his mouth with the back of his hand. "Hell, I don't know. Innocent! She pretends to be innocent, and I know damned well she can't be."

"Has she said this to you? That she is innocent?"

"No, of course not. It's just a look she has. You know, all wide-eyed and—" He broke off. "She has the act so perfected, you'd swear she was fresh out of the schoolroom."

"And you say you saw this in her eyes?"

Chase sensed where this was heading and stiffened.

"There was a time," Hunter said softly, "when you put more stock in the things you read in a person's eyes than you did all else."

That had been before he had looked into lying eyes. "Yeah, well, I learned the hard way not to be a fool."

"And you fear that what you see in Franny's eyes will make a fool of you?"

The question gave Chase pause. If he were honest, perhaps what he saw in her eyes did frighten him. And for damned good reason. There was something about her that drew him, haunted him, and no matter how he tried, he couldn't erase her from his mind.

His father clasped his shoulder again. Then he pushed to his feet. "When your head tells you one thing and your heart another, listen to your heart. It tells no lies."

Chase squeezed his eyes tightly shut. Damn him. Damn him to hell. "I'll go over and apologize to her," he whispered hoarsely. "I won't mean a damned word of it, but I'll do it. I hope that'll satisfy you. Tell Indigo it's as good as done."

"Tonight?"

"Yes, damnit, tonight."

Chase heard the guffaws and whistles before he drew close enough to the saloon to see what all the ruckus was about. When he did get close enough, he couldn't believe his eyes. He had seen a number of strange things while under the influence of whiskey, but never a pair of shapely legs dangling off the edge of a roof.

He reeled to a stop and blinked, convinced he had to be imagining things. But if he was, two other men were conjuring the same vision. By the way they were staggering, Chase knew they must be as drunk as he was.

"Hey, baby, spread them legs wider and give us a show!" one hollered. The other saluted the glorious apparition with his whiskey jug and cackled in agreement. "Whooee!"

Chase focused on one slender foot, from which dangled a pink felt slipper. In his dazed mind, he could come up with only two explanations; either heaven was raining angels or a woman was hanging off the roof of the Lucky Nugget. Since he no longer believed in angels, he decided the only logical conclusion was that the shapely legs were of the mortal variety. He stepped a bit closer, still incredulous.

"What's going on here?"

"What's goin' on?" one of the drunks cried. "Franny's givin' us a free peek, that's what!"

"Help me! Please!"

Chase tipped his head back to get a better look, and sure enough, it was Franny hanging off the roof. From the looks of it, by a hope and a prayer. Even as he watched, her grip slipped on the shingles, and she slid a few precarious inches toward the edge. Through the liquor-induced fog that surrounded him, he slurred, "One of you better catch her, or she's going to break her damned fool neck."

One of the drunks staggered closer, but he seemed more interested in the view than in lending assistance. Chase placed a hand over his ribs, acutely aware that he was in no condition to catch a falling female. Irritation rose in him when the man beneath her made no attempt to give her a hand. Instead he grabbed a fistful of lace, lifted it for a better look, and emitted a suggestive whistle.

"Please!" she cried. "Won't one of you help me?"

"Hell, no. I'm havin' too much fun watchin'!"

With one foot, she groped frantically for one of the overhang support posts, presumably so she could shinny down it to the ground. The shift of her weight loosened her hold on the shingles even more. Looking helplessly on, Chase began to fear that she might indeed fall. At a quick guess, it was only a distance of about eight feet from the roof to the ground, less than that if one measured from her dangling feet. Chase had jumped that far dozens of times without sustaining an injury. But she wasn't built the way he was. The closer he got to her, the more apparent that became.

He had never seen such a lovely display of leg. Mesmerized, he stepped nearer, and what he saw beneath the silk and lace was enough to drop a sober man to his knees. He was a mile shy of sober. "Jesus Christ!"

"Ain't she somethin'?"

"Something" didn't say it by half. Chase could scarcely credit that any man who called himself a man could just stand beneath her and partake of the view. It was obvious even to him she was frantic for help and that she hadn't gotten herself into this position to entertain passersby. If it were any other female in town, these fellows would be breaking a leg to lend her assistance. But because she was a whore, they were taking advantage of her predicament, not caring if she got hurt in the process.

"Don't just stand there gawking! Help the girl down!"

"It ain't my doin' that she's up there. If she had any sense, she wouldn't be."

Chase didn't figure now was the time to debate whether or not the girl had good sense, or to ask why she was on the roof. The fact that she was had to be dealt with. And quickly. He seized the other man by the arm. "If you don't mean to help her, get the hell out of the way."

"By whose say-so?"

"Mine," he bit out. Giving the man a shove, Chase added, "As far as that goes, make tracks. If she wanted a crowd, she would've sold tickets."

"I don't see you wearin' no goddamned blindfold."

Praying Franny could hold on a few more seconds, Chase turned to confront both men. "I said get out of here."

The two miners stiffened, and for a moment, Chase thought he might have a fight on his hands. But in the end their gazes wavered from his and they shuffled away, muttering angrily under their breath about "two bit whores" and "crazy Injuns." Chase figured they were right on both counts. She was without question a whore, and the fact that he was taking up for her was irrefutable evidence that he had bats in his attic.

Shaking off the confrontation, he turned back to help Franny. He grabbed a slender ankle and stepped beneath her flailing legs. Broken ribs or no, he couldn't just let her fall. Looking up to get himself centered beneath her, he tried his best to ignore the view. "Franny?"

"What?" she replied in a thin wail.

"I'm going to catch you, okay? Just turn loose and slide down."

He felt her slip a notch and groped for her other foot, which was slipperless. As his fingers curled around her ankle, he noted rather dazedly how fragilely she was made. If she fell, she would surely break a bone, or worse. Chase took a deep breath, hoping his ribs wouldn't kick up a fuss at her extra weight.

"I've helped Indigo out of trees this way a dozen times."

"Chase?"

"Hell, no. It's the goddamned preacher. Who do you think?"

"Oh, my God . . . don't look under my wrapper."

The truth was Chase was afraid to look too closely for fear he'd drop her. Never in all his life had he seen such a display. Lace and silk and beautiful legs that stretched to heaven. Her hands lost purchase on the shakes, and she slid a few more perilous inches. By way of small clothes, all she had on was a voluminous silk chemise, garters and hose. As pure as driven snow, was she? His ass.

"Jesus Christ," he muttered again. Releasing one of her legs to grapple with her diaphanous lace gown and silk wrapper, he tucked the layers between her splayed thighs. Swearing again, he said, "I know it's no time to ask. But what the hell are you doing on the goddamned roof?"

"Just help me down," she cried. "I'll explain later."

Chase doubted that. There was no explanation for such insanity. He slid his hands up to her calves and tightened his grip. "Okay, I've got you. Just let go and slide down onto my shoulders."

"It doesn't feel like you've got me."

Chase tugged, and she squeaked. "Would you turn loose?"

"I don't trust you to catch me."

"Son of a bitch."

"Well? It's not as if you—" She scrambled for purchase. "Please, Mr. Wolf, don't let me fall."

"Dammit, would you just let go?"

When she persisted in clinging to the roof, he glanced up again in irritation. With the view, however, only a eunuch could have remained disgruntled for long. "Drop onto my shoulders, Franny. I won't let you fall, I promise."

"Swear it."

"I swear it. On a stack of goddamned Bibles. Is that good enough for you?" He got a better grip on her calves. "You think I want you to get hurt?"

"The last time we"— she slipped slightly toward him —"spoke, you weren't exactly friendly."

Steeling himself for her weight, Chase tugged her downward. She cried out in dismay, her nails rasping against the wood as gravity won out. He guided her onto his shoulders. The lace of her gown fluttered over his head. He'd never seen a whore covered in so much cloth. Damn it to hell. None too steady on his feet, he staggered and tried to bat away the material so he could see.

"Oh, dear! You're drunk!"

Oh, dear? The girl didn't even talk like a proper whore. He tore the lace away from his face and swore again. As he settled his hands over her thighs, she gasped. "You can't—! Don't put your hands *there!*"

"Where in hell do you suggest? I might drop you."

"Then kindly put me down. This is"— she swayed and grabbed handfuls of his hair to hold on —"indecent!"

"Fanning your bare backside on Main Street wasn't?" Chase craned his neck to look up at her and immediately regretted it. The lower half of his face connected with silken inner thigh. "And, for your information, I can't put you down." He sputtered to get another bit of lace out of his mouth. "I have three broken ribs, remember. I'm not exactly in the best of shape to be catching crazy women from falling off the roof!"

At the sound of the saloon doors squeaking open, he felt her stiffen. Her hands knotted into fists, making his scalp sting smartly. "Oh, my God. It's them! It's *them!* You can't let him see me."

At the terror in her voice, Chase started to turn and look. "Let who see you?"

"Oh, *please!* Run. Around the side of the building. Please, Mr. Wolf. Please!"

At any other time, Chase would have confronted whoever it was she seemed so terrified of, but this wasn't another time, and the circumstances weren't exactly ideal for him to play hero, not with three broken ribs and a woman astride his shoulders. Left with little choice, he did as she suggested and lurched none too gracefully around the side of the building, trying his best to ignore the fact that she was about to relieve him of his hair and was spurring him forward with sharp little digs of her heels.

"Into the trees," she cried. "Oh, please, Mr. Wolf. It's Frankie. I can't let him see me. Oh, please!"

Chase staggered along the alley between the two buildings, the Lucky Nugget on one side, the livery on his other. His night vision was usually exceptional, but between the whiskey he had drunk and the white lace fluttering over his eyes, his perception wasn't quite what it should have been. Too late, he saw a looming shape, ran squarely into it, and nearly fell.

A barrel. The damned thing tipped and rolled, making a din to wake the dead. Chase skirted around it. As he did, his boot hit something slick and shot out from under him. It was all he could do to keep his feet. Grease. The cook at the Lucky Nugget had been disposing of his drippings in the barrel. As Chase struggled to stay upright and not drop his burden, he tensed the muscles over his ribs. The pain that lanced through him nearly buckled his legs.

Somehow, he made it to the trees. But that was all he was capable of doing.

"I can get down now," she whispered shakily.

Feeling as if he might vomit, Chase stood perfectly still. "Don't move," he gritted out through clenched teeth. "My ribs. I pulled them pretty hard back there."

She unfurled her fists from his hair and leaned slightly forward. "Oh, my stars. Are you badly hurt?"

My stars? No question about it, he had to talk to this girl about her language. "Don't—move. Please."

She froze with her small face hovering above his. "Oh, my. You are hurt. Can I do something?"

Chase swallowed, hard. "Yes. You can sit the hell still until it eases up." He took a shallow breath. "I just need a minute."

Apparently it was beginning to dawn on her that getting down from her perch might prove to be a problem. "Could I just slide off down your back?"

Chase blinked away spots of blackness. "Unless I let you drop like a rock, I'd have to bend forward, and I can't. My ribs are too sore. I might as well have let you fall from the roof. It'd be about the"— he winced — "same distance. Land wrong, and you'll bust an ankle."

She quieted for a moment. "A tree limb. If we could find a tree limb, I could grab it and swing off. That wouldn't stress your ribs."

It was an idea. The problem was spotting a suitable limb and mustering the strength to reach it. Some rescuer he was proving to be. He drew another breath, relieved when the resultant pain was more bearable. "Give me a couple of more minutes. Then I'll think of something."

As the pain slowly diminished, Chase became increasingly aware of what an absurd situation this was. The silken softness of her inner thighs bracketed his jaws. His hands were curled over her lace garters and the tops of her hose. There had been a few times in his life when he had found himself in a headlock between a woman's thighs, but never in exactly this fashion.

He sniffed. She smelled faintly of lavender. He gave a pained laugh. "I know it's probably a stupid question, but do you make a habit of climbing around on the roof?"

"No, of course not. I didn't remember until I got out there that Indigo's tree was cut down last summer."

"Indigo's tree?"

"The one she always used to get up on the saloon roof."

Chase dimly remembered that a tree had once stood at the right rear corner of the saloon building. "My sister climbed up on the saloon roof? To do what?"

"To visit me."

She said that as though it made perfect sense. "Why in hell not use the door?"

"Well, because. Someone might have seen her. Her reputation would have been ruined."

That made sense. He guessed. Finally feeling as if he could move without tearing his ribs loose, he turned in a slow half circle and searched for a low-hanging tree limb. When he spotted one, he moved in that direction, taking care not to lose his footing on the uneven ground. When he reached the limb, she looped her arms around it and swung clear. Afraid she might fall, Chase stood at the ready, praying all the while that she wouldn't need his assistance. He breathed a sigh of relief when she dropped agilely to the ground beside him.

Moonlight dappled her wildly curly hair. He stared down at her heavily painted features. She looked nothing like the sweet, angelic green-eyed girl he had seen twice before. Beneath the silk wrapper and lace gown, he saw that she wore a knee-length silk camisole. Each piece of the ensemble by itself might have been suggestive, but layered as they were, very little of the woman underneath was revealed. Unless, of course, you happened to be looking at her from the ground up.

She glanced uneasily toward the alley between the saloon and livery. Chase saw that she had begun to shake with delayed reaction and realized that whoever Frankie was, she was scared to death of him. Nasty images flashed through his mind of a perverted man mistreating her. He nearly assured her that she had nothing to be afraid of, at least not while he was there, but old resentments made him bite back the words.

When it came to rescuing soiled doves, he had learned his lesson.

Still . . .

Chase scraped the back of his hand across his mouth. "If that Frankie character is giving you a hard time, Gus will probably take care of him for you."

"Gus?"

"Gus, the saloon owner." Chase studied her in puzzlement. "Surely he takes up for you and May Belle when there's trouble. If you're afraid of this Frankie fellow, just tell Gus."

She shook her head. "Afraid? Of Frankie? No. I just—he came into the saloon with some friends, and by chance, I was on the landing speaking to May Belle. When I glanced down—well, Frankie was the last person I ever expected—" She broke off. "I'm not afraid of him. I just couldn't let him see me."

"Oh." Chase rubbed his mouth again. Who the hell was Frankie, and why was she so determined to stay hidden from him? "Is he an old lover or something?"

"Frankie?" She gave a shaky, half hysterical laugh and cupped her hands over her eyes. "Oh, God. When I think of what could have happened. If I hadn't been going to May Belle's room—if I hadn't glimpsed him through the balcony railing and recognized him—he would have come upstairs. Don't you see? In the dark, I wouldn't have known it was him. He might've—oh, God."

Her voice trailed off to a thin wail and she started to cry. Not just a few tears accompanied by delicate sniffs, but racking sobs and unladylike snorts.

"Hey, now," he tried. "Nothing can be that bad."

That was clearly the wrong thing to say. It made her cry all the harder.

Shit. How did he get himself into these situations?

5

Having grown up with a younger sister close to his own age, Chase had more experience at wiping up a woman's tears than most men, but he felt inept with Franny. A female of her profession was supposed to be hard and unflappable. Not that Franny was true to stereotype. Even as upset as she was, she kept fidgeting with the lapels of her wrapper as if she feared parts of her might be exposed. A seasoned prostitute shouldn't give a flip.

Feeling as though he were wading in way over his head, Chase settled a hand on her shoulder. He had every intention of drawing her into his arms, but at his touch she jumped as if he had stuck her with a pin. Chase was as startled as she. The reaction of a soiled dove? He bit back a dozen questions.

"Whoever this Frankie fellow is," he said soothingly,

"all's well that ends well, right? You saw him in time and got out of there."

"You d-don't underst-stand. He could c-come back!" Looking up at him, she caught her lower lip in her teeth in an obvious attempt to silence the sobs tearing up from her chest. In the moonglow, her tear-filled eyes shimmered like quicksilver, kohl streaming down her cheeks in rivers. "What if he comes again next Saturday, and I never even know it's him?" Her face twisted, and she emitted a low wail. "Oh, God, what if he's already come, and I didn't know?"

The question hung between them, obviously a torment for her, but a complete mystery to Chase. Surely the girl knew who her customers were. No one could do the sort of work that she did and not retain some impression of the men with whom she consorted.

Or could she?

Chase remembered Jake's explanation, that Franny lost herself in conjured dream settings while she worked, arising the next morning untouched by the night's experiences.

"Franny . . ."

She cupped both hands over her eyes again. "I wish I were dead."

"I reckon everybody feels that way sometimes. But nothing can truly be that bad. Not once you think about it."

"Oh, yes, it can. *This* is that bad. If I could, I'd shoot myself!" Balling a hand into a fist, she rubbed at her cheek and smeared kohl under one eye. "I-I'm sorry. I don't usually cry. At least not in front of anyone."

Her throat convulsed on another stifled sob. Clearly

uncomfortable with her display of emotion, she turned her gaze toward the woods behind him. Her face was such a mess that Chase couldn't bear it a second longer and fished his handkerchief from his pocket. Feeling clumsy, he dabbed at the black streaks. His touch startled her again, and she reared back, grabbing at his wrist. The frantic clutching of her small fingers caught at his heart as nothing else might have.

"Easy . . . I'm just mopping up a little," he explained and continued to scrub at her cheek. "You can't go back inside like this. Not unless you can afford to scare off customers."

"Don't I wish."

The comeback told Chase more than she could know. He tried to imagine what her profession must be like. The endless submission. Letting filthy strangers paw her body. Who could blame her for trying to block it all out? Just the thought made him feel sick.

As he searched the handkerchief for a clean spot, she regarded him with a disgruntled look on her small face, clearly oblivious to the train of his thoughts. "I'm perfectly capable of mopping up by myself."

"If you could see yourself, you wouldn't say that. The stuff you use around your eyes is smeared everywhere."

"It is?" She scrubbed ineffectually at her cheek. "Where?"

Chase couldn't help but chuckle. "You're just making it worse. Be still."

Resigned, she turned up her face. Looking down at her, Chase knew he was lost. Prostitute or no, only a hard-hearted bastard could resist those eyes of hers. She huffed softly when he pinched the cloth over the tip of her nose. Chase bit back another smile, recalling all the times he had performed the same service for Indigo over the years. Was this girl really so very different? Just the fact that he was asking himself that question told him he was in deeper than he wanted to be, and what was worse, he no longer gave a diddly shit.

"What are you doing here, Franny?"

"I told you. I stepped over to see May Belle and—"

"No, no." He gestured at the saloon. "Not out here, but *here*. You know, at the Lucky Nugget. How did you end up working the upstairs rooms?"

Her lashes swept low. "I . . . um . . . that's really not any of your business."

"Maybe I want it to be my business."

As he said those words, it struck Chase that he sincerely meant them. The change seemed to have come from out of nowhere, so suddenly that he felt like a pendulum making radical swings from one extreme to the other. But when he thought about it, he knew that wasn't actually the case. From the first instant he had clapped eyes on this young woman, he had been fighting the feelings that were welling within him now. Possessive feelings. Protective feelings.

Jesus. He needed a couple of gallons of Ma's coffee, and fast.

She finally lifted her lashes again to look at him, her bewildered gaze revealing far more than she probably realized—confusion and a fear he couldn't quite fathom. His interest in her terrified her, he realized. Life had clearly dealt her some cruel blows.

Chase couldn't help but remember another pair of eyes that had been filled with pain and fear—lying eyes, he had believed then. Now, years later, here was Franny, with a face so sweet it caught at his heart and eyes that flashed messages her every action belied. Whore or angel?

Though he had difficulty admitting it, even to himself, Chase knew the answer to that question. The naked emotion he read in her expression couldn't be feigned. A victim, his father had called her, and Chase realized, almost too late, that she could be nothing else. Looking into her haunted eyes, only a fool would believe she had chosen this life.

Once, so long ago that now there was no rectifying it, he had turned his back and walked away from eyes like hers. If he did the same again, he had a feeling he would be as doomed as she.

Her face was fairly clean now, but loath to release her, Chase cupped a hand under her chin and continued to lightly dab at her cheeks as he studied her features. Finely arched brows, a small, fragilely bridged nose, a jaw so delicate that one blow from his open hand might shatter it. And her mouth. He had never seen such a vulnerable mouth. Even now, it still quivered slightly with suppressed tears. Hers was one of the sweetest countenances he had ever had the pleasure of regarding.

Searching her expression, Chase remembered what his father had said to him, that a man could leave the place of his childhood and travel forever only to discover he had actually gone nowhere. Earlier this evening, that hadn't made much sense to him. But now he thought he understood. He had been raised to be one of the People, and he could never escape that. If he tried, he would only run into a brick wall, in this case Franny.

Looking down at her, he felt a little silly comparing her to a brick wall. But damn if she wasn't exactly that. An obstacle he couldn't shoulder his way through.

As if she sensed his thoughts, she suddenly said, "I-I think I'd better go now."

Dropping his hand, he glanced toward the saloon, his mind racing for a reason to keep her there, if only for a few more minutes. "Do you think Frankie is gone?"

Her face fell. "P-probably not. I flipped the sign over to *Occupied,* but it'll take a while for Gus to realize I've closed up for the night. I usually receive callers clear up until one."

Callers? That was a polite name for them. And she usually worked only until one? That was the time of night when most saloon-goers were just getting into the swing of things. "I'll wait with you then. This is no place for a woman to linger alone at night."

He no sooner spoke than he recalled to whom he was speaking. Franny entertained drunks nightly. One chance encounter more or less shouldn't be a point of concern, to him or to her. As though she didn't see the absurdity in his comment, she shivered and hugged her waist, for all the world as if she had envisioned what might happen to her if left alone and found the thought abhorrent.

Feeling inexplicably weary, Chase leaned back against the tree, taking advantage of the silence to study his companion. She looked about twelve years old standing there, chin aquiver, her slender frame swallowed in silk and lace. Like a small girl who had raided the attic trunks and dressed up in her mother's discarded boudoir finery, a tad lopsided because she wore only one slipper. He noted that she seemed uncommonly nervous in his presence, yet another mysterious revelation to bewilder him. He had the same equipment other men did. Wherein lay the threat?

Chase smothered a grin. He supposed standing out behind the saloon with a man wasn't her usual routine. In these circumstances, it must be a little difficult to transcend reality by dreaming, a fact he determined to remember. If—no, when—he was with her again, he wouldn't allow her to escape into oblivion. Which probably meant he was destined to become the bane of her existence.

That thought gave Chase pause and forced him to step back and analyze his intentions. A futile exercise. Damned if he knew what his intentions were. He had marched over here—well, maybe staggered was a better word—to offer an insincere apology to please his father and sister. Now they were the least of his concerns, and he was thinking ahead to when he might see Franny again.

Crazy, so crazy. Hell. Maybe insanity ran in his family.

"How long do you think we've been out here?" she asked suddenly.

Chase jerked himself back to the moment. She wasn't the only one who could get lost in daydreams. Fumbling for his pocket watch, he withdrew it and peered at the shadowed face. "Ten minutes, maybe?"

She heaved a disgruntled sigh. "It seems like longer."

Not to Chase. He touched a knuckle to her sleeve and smiled. "You cold? I've got heat to spare if you are."

She cast him a startled look and withdrew a step. "I'm not in the least cold."

"Then why are you shivering?"

She fiddled with her wrapper sash and then hugged herself again. "I didn't realize I was."

Her voice was pitched so low, her enunciation so hesitant, that Chase wondered how often she actually spoke with men. Not that he could conceive how she could be in her profession without conversing with customers. "Are you bashful, Franny?"

Another startled look came his way. "Pardon?"

Chase graced her with the grin he'd been practicing in front of a mirror since adolescence. His rakish best, lopsided and mischievous, designed and precisely executed. "You *are* bashful. I haven't seen a girl blush so pretty in a coon's age."

She blinked. It wasn't the reaction he'd been aiming for.

"I frighten you, don't I?"

"Yes."

Again, it wasn't his aimed for response. Surprised at how freely she admitted it, he said, "Why?"

She gazed up at him for a long moment, her eyes a mirror of confusion. "I-I'm not sure. You just do."

"I'm Indigo's brother, remember. What better recommendation do you—"

"You aren't sweet like Indigo."

Disgruntled, he retorted, "Says who?"

She rolled her eyes. "Don't be silly. You know you're not. Indigo is—" She broke off, and her expression softened. "Indigo is like no one else I've ever known."

Chase gave it up. "She is a very special person."

"Yes," she agreed in that same hesitant way. "Very special. She's the best friend I've ever had. I would trust her with my life. Even the wild animals love her."

"They like me just as well." Chase felt ridiculous for having said that. He sounded like a boastful child. "At least they used to."

She looked dubious.

"Hey—I used to have hordes of them hanging around when I was a kid. Coons, deer. I even had a pet rattler once."

She shuddered.

"He didn't bite." Mustering the good grace to laugh at himself, Chase added, "And neither do I." He shrugged. "I know I gave you a hard time this morning. I'm really sorry about that. I hope you won't hold it against me forever. If possible, I'd like us to be friends."

"Friends?"

She clearly found the prospect alarming, which rankled. "Yes, friends. What's wrong with that?"

Her gaze darted to his. Chase wanted to reassure her, to tell her she had nothing to fear from him, but judging by the things he read in her eyes, he might be more of a threat to her than he cared to think.

"I-I think I'd better go now," she said shakily.

He drew out his watch again. "It's only been twenty minutes, tops. Do you think Frankie will be gone?"

"Probably. Boys that age aren't long on patience."

Boys? Chase raised a questioning eyebrow, which she ignored. "You'll be taking a risk."

"I'll check before I go in. Those horses out front belonged to him and his friends. I recognized Moses."

Chase didn't remember seeing any horses, but then he hadn't had eyes for much of anything but Franny's legs. "Moses?"

"Our hor—" She broke off. "Moses is Frankie's horse."

Because he obviously made her so nervous she couldn't think clearly, she had nearly divulged information she didn't wish to reveal. A good indication, that. When it came to digging information out of her, he might have an edge.

Stepping back to give her the space he sensed she needed, he said, "Well, I guess this is good night then."

She nodded, clearly at a loss for anything else to say. After a moment, she whispered, "Thank you for helping me down from the roof."

"My pleasure." And he realized it had been a rare pleasure indeed.

As she started to move, she glanced down, and even in the dim light, Chase saw the dismay that swept across her face. Fastening horrified eyes on the saloon building, she clamped both palms over her chest. "Oh, lands!"

"What?"

"I've been so preoccupied thinking about the close call with Frankie, I never even thought! How shall I ever get back to my room?"

Chase could see she was distressed, but for the life of him, he couldn't figure out why. "The same way most folks do? By the door?"

"Like this?" She indicated her apparel. "Oh, what a pickle."

Doing his best to keep his expression solemn, Chase regarded her clothing. The girl was wrapped in enough layers to be mailed long distance. He supposed it was the type of garments she wore that concerned her, not the lack. Reaching to his waist, he untucked his shirttails. "You can borrow this."

Wincing, he drew the shirt off over his head and

held it up in front of her. The tails reached nearly to her knees. "See? It'll cover you."

She gave him an incredulous look. "Truly? But then you'll be—" She jerked her gaze from his bare shoulders. "I can't take your shirt."

"Why the hell not?"

"Well, because. You'll have nothing to wear."

"Hey, my father goes without a shirt half the time. I'm Indian, remember?" That was a new twist, his reminding a woman of that fact. "Besides, I've only got to go as far as home. It's dark. If anybody sees me, I'll stagger a little, and they'll just think I'm drunk."

"You *are* drunk."

She had him there. Chase pushed the shirt into her hands. "Yeah, well, I had a rotten day." As he spoke, he recalled his reason for approaching the saloon in the first place and decided he hadn't said nearly enough by way of apology. "Which reminds me, Franny. When I ran into you, I was on my way over to talk to you."

She looked wary. "About what?"

"I wanted to apologize."

"You already did."

"Not the way I should. Those things I said—about me getting folks up in arms against you if you kept seeing Indigo. I didn't mean it."

"She sent you, didn't she?"

Because he didn't want to hurt her any more than he already had, Chase was tempted to lie. For reasons he had no time to analyze, he resisted the urge. "Actually, it was my father who sent me."

"Your father?"

"Yeah." His throat felt raw with an emotion he

couldn't quite identify. He only knew he wished he had decided to come on his own accord. Or better yet that he hadn't said such vile things to her in the first place.

"You needn't apologize," she said softly. "I know you were only watching out for Indigo. If it had been me, I would have done the same." She gave a little shrug. "Truth to tell, I'm surprised Jake hasn't run me off. I'm not exactly fitting company for her and the little ones. I know that."

The pain in her expression made Chase feel ashamed. By good measure, he was responsible, but for the life of him, he couldn't think of anything to say that might undo the damage he had wrought. "Ah, Franny. I'm sorry."

She flashed a shaky smile. "Don't be. I love Indigo, too. Feeling protective of her is one thing we have in common."

The way Chase saw it, Franny was the one who needed protection. From heartless assholes like him. "I want you to forget what I said and visit her all you like. Seriously."

She gnawed her lip, eyeing him suspiciously. "I'm afraid I don't understand your change of heart."

That made two of them.

"You're sure you won't change your mind?" she pressed. "I don't want any trouble. For reasons I don't care to divulge, it's very important that I keep gossip about me at a minimum."

"I'm positive. You won't get any trouble from me, I promise you."

Her gaze clung to his for a long moment. Then she finally nodded. "All right then. Heaven knows I would have missed seeing Indigo and the children. They're a bright spot in my days."

Chase had a feeling they might be the only bright spot. "Am I forgiven?"

A fleeting smile touched her mouth. "Yes. Of course you are."

That smile. As hesitant as it was, it warmed him clear through. He inclined his head at the shirt she held. "You'd best get that on before you forget."

"Oh."

She gave a nervous laugh and drew the garment over her head. Chase helped her get it turned right then fished her arms down the sleeves, tugging on the cuffs of her wrapper so they wouldn't be bunched above her elbows. Her long hair was caught under the neckline, and he gathered handfuls to free it. The curls he grasped felt like wire.

"Jesus Christ. What's on your hair?"

She sputtered to get a stiffened tendril out of her mouth. Wrinkling her nose in distaste, she said, "Starch."

A chuckle escaped him before he could swallow it back. "Starch?"

"Laundry starch. My hair won't stay curly without it."

Chase wondered how she kept from poking out her customers' eyes, but he didn't voice the question. Starch? He could use that hair of hers to string fence. "I see," he said, only, of course, he didn't, not at all. If her hair wouldn't hold curl, why didn't she just leave it soft and natural?

He bent to tug the tails of his shirt down over the multiple layers of lace and silk. "There. You could attend Sunday meeting now."

"Hardly." She gave the shirt a final tug. "But thank you all the same. At least it helps." Looking up at him, she caught her bottom lip between her teeth again. Even in the moonlight, he noted the slight flush that touched her cheeks as she extended her hand to him. "I'm indebted to you, Mr. Wolf."

"Chase."

"Yes, well." Her flush deepened. "You have my eternal gratitude."

He grasped the tips of her fingers and slanted his thumb lightly across her knuckles. "Like I said, the pleasure was all mine."

She withdrew her hand from his and turned to go. With the first step, she lurched. Remembering that she wore only one slipper, Chase smiled. Watching her cross the yard to the saloon, he marveled that she maintained any semblance of dignity, but somehow she did, lopsided gait and all. Dressed as she was, his oversized shirt over the lot, she should have looked ridiculous, especially with that hair springing like coiled wire in every direction.

She stopped at the front of the saloon to peek around the corner. Apparently satisfied that the mysterious Frankie was gone, she waved good-bye and disappeared.

6

For a long while, Chase gazed after Franny. When he finally roused himself enough to walk home, he could see dim light spilling from the downstairs windows of his parents' house. Beacons of welcome. His mother, bless her heart, had left the lantern lit for him. Because he had missed supper, he knew he'd probably find food set out on the table. No matter that he had missed the meal only because he'd been too busy getting sloppy drunk in the backyard to join his folks at the table.

Sometimes he wished his parents would be a little less forbearing. It'd be easier that way. As it was, he felt guilty as hell for the way he'd behaved tonight and even worse about the lousy things he'd said to his father. He needed a good ass-kicking sometimes. But that wasn't Hunter Wolf's way, never had been, never would be.

Home. As Chase closed the front door behind him, he leaned back and surveyed the room. To his left sat his mother's prized Chickering piano, shipped from Boston around the Horn and hauled from Crescent City by his father in a wide-tread wagon. The well-polished rosewood shimmered in the lantern light, testimony to the hours Loretta Wolf had spent protecting its finish with wax.

It was a house that was well-loved, as were all those who dwelled within it. Everywhere he looked he saw evidence of his ma's busy hands, from the braided rugs arranged colorfully on the bleached puncheon floors to the crocheted scarves on the horsehair furniture. On the wall above the settee hung their family portrait, taken years ago by a photographer named Britt in Jacksonville.

Filled with nostalgia, Chase moved to stand before it. He and Indigo had been so little when the picture was taken he could only dimly recollect the day. Scarcely more than a child herself, his aunt Amy stood behind him with her hands on his shoulders, her blond head tipped as if to catch something the photographer was saying, her large eyes filled with laughter. It never ceased to amaze Chase how much she resembled his mother. They weren't actually sisters, only first cousins, but to look at them, a body would think them twins.

To the left of the portrait was a photograph of Amy and her husband, Swift Lopez, a Mexican by birth but adopted by the Comanches as an infant. He was one of Chase's favorite people. Below the picture of Aunt Amy and Uncle Swift were likenesses of their two sons, little tykes with huge, soulful eyes and pitch black hair. On the opposite side of the family portrait hung a picture of Indigo and Jake with their children.

Only Chase hadn't married. He felt certain his

mother had a spot all picked out on the wall where she hoped to someday hang a picture of him with his wife and family.

He moved along the wall to peer at the mementos she had framed under glass over the years. There was a Christmas picture he had drawn when he was about eight. He had printed "I love you" under it and "happy Krissmus." In another frame were the first teeth he and Indigo had lost, little kernels yellowed with age. Chase couldn't help but wonder if his mother wasn't missing a screw or two. Who else would hang her children's teeth on the sitting-room wall?

As Chase studied the other keepsakes, his sense of belonging here deepened. So many memories, and so much love. He supposed that was what family was all about—the memories, the unbreakable bonds.

Closing his eyes, he let the familiarity of everything embrace him. Maybe, as he had speculated earlier, liquor was doing his thinking, but he felt as if he'd been wandering for the last seven years in a maze and had just found his way out. Home and its simple pleasures. Somehow he had forgotten how very good life could be, and now that he was remembering, he wanted that for himself.

Over the last few days, being forced to stay here had chafed him at every turn. But now he was inexplicably glad that he had come home for a prolonged visit. As much as Hunter's lectures sometimes rankled, he was usually right. From now on, maybe he should lead with his heart, the devil take the consequences.

*   *   *

Nearly the first thing Chase saw the next morning when he looked out his bedroom window was Franny's pink slipper lying on the roof of the Lucky Nugget. With a sleepy grin, he sloshed water into the basin and quickly performed his morning ablutions. The instant he was dressed, he hurried down the ladder from the loft.

His mother stood at the cookstove, her blond head agleam in a shaft of sunlight coming through the window. The gigantic green mixing bowl she held cradled in one arm was the same one she had mixed griddle cake batter in for twenty years, its edges chipped, its baked finish cracked with age. Before ladling batter onto the hot griddle, she turned to smile at him, her blue eyes as clear as the polished window glass behind her. Startled, Chase froze mid-stride and stared at her. The sensation that he could see straight to her heart was one he hadn't experienced in a very long while. For an instant, he stiffened. Then a feeling of rightness washed over him.

She touched a curl at her temple. "I did a quick job on my hair so I could get started on breakfast, but surely I don't look that bad."

Chase felt a smile tugging at his lips. "You look beautiful, Ma."

It was true. For a woman of her age, she was still incredibly lovely, trim as a young girl in her blue shirtwaist, her hair barely touched with silver, her delicately sculpted face unlined. But his observation went deeper than the surface. Far deeper. The love for him that he saw shining in her eyes struck him the most powerfully. He had a sneaking hunch it had been there ever since his homecoming, and he simply hadn't looked for it. Or perhaps it would be more accurate to say he had insulated himself from it.

The thought gave Chase pause, and he turned his thoughts inward, trying without success to determine exactly what had changed within him during his talk with Franny last night. He only knew that he had awakened this morning for the first time in years feeling lighthearted and eager to face the day. When he remembered Gloria, the pretty little whore who had cleaned out his pockets as well as his heart, he no longer felt angry. Or bitter. Just inexplicably sad, no longer for himself, but for her. If only he had been a little older and wiser back then, maybe things wouldn't have turned out as they had. Maybe if he hadn't given up on her, if he had refused to take no for an answer, she would have come around eventually. That was something he'd never know, he guessed. The important thing—the thing he had to remember—was that only a fool made the same mistake twice.

The back screen creaked open, and Chase turned to see his father stepping into the kitchen, eggs from the henhouse resting in the crook of one muscular arm. Their dark blue gazes locked. In that moment of visual contact, Chase felt stripped, and he realized his reacquired intuitiveness could be a double-edged sword with this man and probably with Indigo as well. Hunter hesitated a moment, the fragile burden he carried forgotten as he looked deeply into Chase's eyes. A wealth of messages passed between them with that one look.

"It is a fine morning," he finally offered by way of greeting.

Chase knew he referred to far more than just the

weather. Not that his father's perceptiveness came as any surprise. Hunter had always seemed to understand him better than he understood himself. "Yes, a fine morning," he agreed huskily.

Hunter continued on his way to the dish board where he began rinsing the eggs. "We have fresh honey for the griddle cakes. Indigo found a honey tree last week and robbed the bees' nest."

"Without a single sting," Loretta put in. "I swear, that girl and her antics will be the death of me one day. Yesterday she was telling me about an article she read about an antivenin of some kind that's being made for rattlesnake bites. She wants to start catching snakes and milking them." With an expressive roll of her eyes, Loretta cast her husband a meaningful glance. "Not for the money! Lands, no. But to save the dratted snakes. And did your father try to discourage her? Not by so much as a word."

Chase gulped back a chuckle. "Save the snakes, you say? From what?"

"Being killed, of course. She figures if they develop a cure for the bites, people won't fear them so much and will stop killing every one they see."

"Folks do tend to hate rattlers. She's right that an antivenin could change that."

"She could also end up dead."

"She hasn't been bit by a snake yet, Ma."

"Hmph. It only takes once. That's my worry. With the wild creatures, that young lady thinks she's invincible. Besides, making pets of snakes is a different thing from catching the poor things and milking them. It can't be a very pleasant experience for the snake, and one might bite in self-defense."

"Not Indigo. If she can't milk them gently, she won't do it." Judging by his mother's expression, Chase figured it might be a good idea to change the subject. He had eccentricities enough of his own without championing his sister's. He looked at the jar sitting on the table and rubbed his hands together. "Mm, honey on hot griddle cakes. Makes my mouth water just thinking about it. A man can't ask for much better than this."

His father nodded, clearly recalling, as Chase intended, their conversation of last night. Once again, their gazes locked, and during the exchange, Chase felt certain not only that his parent understood how sorry he was for the things he had said to him, but that he was forgiven. It was all Chase needed to make his morning perfect.

His mother ladled batter onto the griddle. The hot grease sizzled, and the smell of cooking dough filled the kitchen. "If you're planning to shave before you eat, you'd best get hopping. It's Sunday, and I've got a peck of things to do before two."

Chase rubbed his chin. "Oh? Is Father O'Grady in town to say Mass?"

His mother sent him a look. "If he were, I would've been after you yesterday to go to confession. We're just having Sunday meeting and potluck over at the community hall. There'll be a social tonight. Maybe you'd like to go?"

"Uh . . . maybe." Chase envisioned his mother arranging for him to dance with every unmarried young woman in town and cringed at the thought. He knew when to retreat and started across the kitchen. The last thing he wanted was for her to start grilling him about his social life and the women he kept company with. Next, she'd start on church and how long it had been since he'd attended Mass regularly.

"After breakfast, would you like to walk up to the mine with me?" his father suddenly asked. "We've got plenty of time before the meeting starts. Or are your ribs healed enough?"

Since his arrival, Chase hadn't been to the mine, nor had he wanted to go. Now he wished he could. But that pink slipper on the roof of the saloon beckoned to him more strongly. "My ribs are healed enough, but I have something I have to do this morning. Can I take a rain check?"

Hunter nodded. "Whenever you are ready, I will be here."

A lump rose in Chase's throat. "I know you will be."

Oblivious to the undertones in their exchange, Loretta asked, "What must you do this morning?"

Chase felt a flush creeping up his neck. "There's a little filly here in town I'm interested in."

Hunter's gaze jerked to his. Chase bit back a grin. Loretta looked perplexed. "Why on earth do you want another horse? I'd think one would be enough of a worry, working as you do at the logging camps with no proper shelter for it. And a filly? You don't have time to break a horse, not working the hours that you do."

"But, Ma, this is a special filly. Prettiest little thing I ever clapped eyes on. Gentling her may be time-consuming. But I think she'll be worth it."

"Burning your candle at both ends, I'd say. And what about saving for that tract of land? Buying another horse will set you back."

Chase shrugged. "Looking can't hurt."

"I didn't realize anyone in town had a filly for sale," she added thoughtfully as she turned the griddle cakes.

Flashing his father another smile, Chase said, "I heard tell of her over at the saloon."

"Oh." Loretta wrinkled her nose. "Lands, I hope her owner isn't some drunk you fleeced at cards."

Chase stepped into the water closet his father had erected in one corner of the room. Leaving the door ajar, he drew water to shave. As he splashed his face to soften his whiskers, he chided, "Ma, what do you take me for? Would I fleece a drunk at poker and take his horse?"

His mother turned troubled eyes on him, her expression saying more clearly than words that here lately she wouldn't put much of anything past him. After studying him for a moment, her frown disappeared, and she smiled. "No, of course you wouldn't. It's just that I can't feature you turning loose of money for a horse right now, and I thought maybe—well, it makes no never mind."

Unfolding the razor, Chase said, "I guess maybe I'm rearranging my priorities a little. Turning loose of some money now and again won't stop me from buying the land. It'll just take me a little longer, that's all."

Hunter carried the wire basket of rinsed eggs to the stove and, as was his habit, began cracking them into the waiting skillet. Unlike many men, he didn't hesitate to help his wife inside the house.

As Chase dabbed his jaw with bergamot-scented shaving compound, he watched through the open doorway as his parents worked, each tucking in an elbow to make room for the other, both at ease with the closeness. The unity of their movements put him in mind of a couple dancing, each following the other's slightest lead. Such a simple thing, yet to Chase there was a beauty in it that he envied. Last night his father had asked him what more in life a man could want. The answer was nothing.

Chase winced as he stooped to look in the mirror his mother had suspended from a nail on the wall. Damned ribs, anyway. Or maybe he should be cursing the mirror. The oval of glass had been hanging in that exact same spot, at a perfect height for his ma to see herself, ever since his father had erected the water closet, yet another sign of the give and take between his parents. He had never heard his father complain about having to stoop to see himself in the mirror. Not that Hunter, being half Comanche, found it necessary to shave very often. But he did wash up morning and evening.

Chase grimaced. When he chose a wife, he'd have to be sure she stood taller than his mother, or he'd find himself stooping to shave for the next sixty years. Unlike his father, he was cursed with a white man's heavy beard.

A picture of Franny flashed in his mind. Definitely too short, he decided. Thinking of the slipper lying on the saloon roof, he recollected how she had looked hanging from the eaves last night. For what she lacked in stature she definitely compensated for in curves.

Smiling to himself, Chase decided a man could always hang two mirrors in the water closet.

*　　　*　　　*

Chase slapped the pink slipper down on the bar. After the considerable effort it had taken to lasso the damned thing to fetch it off the roof, he was in no mood for nonsense. "What in hell do you mean, I can't see her?"

Gus, the plump saloon owner, jerked the ever-present white towel from off his shoulder. Bending over the bar, he polished intently at a water spot on its varnished surface. "Just what I said. She don't accept callers 'til after dark, no exceptions."

Chase didn't intend to take no for an answer. "Look, Gus," he said reasonably. "I'm not just any caller. Franny's a friend of my family."

Gus arched a querulous eyebrow. "That's one I ain't heard before."

"It's true. She and Indigo are like this." He held up two fingers pressed tightly together. "I just want to return her slipper, for Christ's sake."

Gus dumped an ashtray. "Leave it with me. I'll give it to her."

Chase decided it was time to try another tack. "Can I go up to see May Belle then? I'll leave it with her."

Gus jabbed a thumb toward the stairs. "Be my guest. Second door on the right. But no detours, Chase. Franny's real peculiar about her rules, and I don't want her quittin' on me."

Rules. Chase had never heard of such. How could an upstairs girl expect to make a decent living if she accepted callers only after dark and worked only until one in the morning? She was losing money hand over fist. Not that he gave a fig. If he had his way, she would quit this kind of work entirely.

He climbed the shadowy stairway and paused on the landing, his curious gaze fixed on the first door, which he knew had to be Franny's since Gus had said May Belle's was the second. A large sign hung on the portal. He focused on the bold black lettering. *OCCUPIED*, it said. Then below, in smaller letters, it read, *Please flip the sign back over as you leave so the next person in line may enter.*

Curiosity got the better of Chase and he stepped closer to flip over the sign and read the other side.

> *It's not necessary to knock. Simply turn over the sign to "Occupied" as you enter. Ten dollars for thirty minutes. The rules are as follows:*
> *(1) No callers before dark*
> *(2) Leave the lamp unlit*
> *(3) No conversation*
> *(4) No extras*
> *(5) No refunds*
> *(6) Deposit your ten dollars on the bureau before you leave.*

The note ended with a thank-you and Franny's signature, the handwriting graceful and precise, exactly as she was. After flipping the sign back over, Chase knotted a fist, tempted to knock on the door, for he knew she must be inside the room.

"Damn it, Chase!" Gus yelled. "That ain't the second door, and you know it."

Seeing another way to get Franny's attention, Chase raised his voice to call over the banister, "Don't get in a dither, Gus! I won't bother her. Though I can't see what the big deal is. All I wanted to do was return her slipper and give her a message from my sister."

As Chase hoped, a second later the doorknob rattled. At the sound, he turned and watched the door inch open. A portion of Franny's face appeared in the narrow crack. "Indigo sent me a message?" she asked softly.

Chase relaxed his shoulders and leaned close to whisper, "Yeah, she did. But I wouldn't want anyone to overhear. Can I step in for a minute?"

One green eye stared at him suspiciously. Chase realized he wasn't the first man who had tried to breach her daytime sanctuary. "Only for a second," he assured her and held up the slipper. "Remember me, the fellow who helped you off the roof last night? Come on, Franny. Let me in. I'll be gone before you can blink."

"All right," she finally relented, "but only for a minute."

To his surprise, the door closed. He thought he heard furniture being moved about inside. When the door opened again, Franny was nowhere to be seen. His neck tingling, he stepped cautiously across the threshold. The instant he was entirely into the room, the door closed, and he turned to see her standing behind him, her back pressed to the wood, her white-knuckled hands folded at her waist.

Her wariness of him was evident in the lines about her mouth and the shadows in her beautiful green eyes. Chase was dying to ask why he made her so nervous. But he'd cover that ground later. He had a suspicion that somewhere along the line, she'd been badly mistreated by someone. Maybe by a customer. Possibly by more than one.

"Is Indigo all right?" she asked.

Feeling a little ashamed of himself for telling such a whopper, Chase hastened to reassure her. "Oh, she's fine. She . . . um . . . " He offered her the slipper. "I just came from her place, and she told me to say hello when I saw you."

"What?"

"She said to tell you hello."

"That's the message?"

He tried a grin. "Pretty lame, I know. But I really wanted to return your slipper in person. That Gus is quite the watchdog, isn't he?" She wasn't smiling. "I tried to tell him you and I are friends, but he wouldn't make any exceptions."

"Friends?" she repeated in much the same tone she had used last night. Incredulous, startled. "You and I, friends?"

Chase tried his best to look harmless. "Well, yes. I consider us friends. Don't you? Not to mention that I've got your slipper, and you've got my shirt." He pushed the shoe toward her again. "Care to make a trade?"

"I intended to wash and press your shirt before returning it to you."

"Oh." Chase nearly assured her that wasn't necessary, but then it struck him that he'd have another excuse to come see her if he left the garment behind. "That'd be nice."

Now that he thought about it, he liked the idea of her ironing his shirt. Imagining her small fingertips smoothing and straightening every inch, he decided that after she returned it to him, he'd wear it more often than any other. Crazy, so crazy.

Because she hadn't accepted the slipper, he opted to keep it. She'd no doubt show him the door the instant he relinquished it. Smiling, he turned to regard the room. A privacy screen concealed one entire end, and he suspected that was the piece of furniture he had heard her moving. What lay behind the screen? Things she didn't want him to see, obviously. He wanted to take a peek, but that would have been unforgivably rude.

Instead he settled his gaze on the small round table near the window. A partially eaten piece of toast rested on the edge of a saucer there, a half-empty mug of coffee beside it. He surmised that she must order her meals from the saloon kitchen. Gus had remodeled the Lucky Nugget shortly after purchasing it and, among other things, had added on a small restaurant so his patrons didn't have to go clear down the street to the hotel for a meal.

"Nice," he commented even though his true reaction to her quarters was just the opposite. He couldn't help but think how lonely her life must be, the sum total of her existence confined within these four walls where she ate, slept, and worked. Now he could better understand why Indigo had been so upset with him yesterday. Without a friend, would Franny ever escape this prison?

Returning his attention to her, Chase decided that in the prim little shirtwaist she wore she looked more like a schoolmarm than a fallen woman. Perversely, the drab gray complimented her ivory skin and the blush of rose at her cheeks and lips. The cream appliqué lace collar that encircled her slender throat matched the platinum streaks in her golden hair, bound in a sleek braid at her crown this morning, no laundry starch in evidence.

Chase's gaze caught on the frayed cuffs at her wrists. The percale shirtwaist had seen better days. Peeking out from under the floor-length hem, the scuffed toes of her kid boots gave further testimony that she spared little coin to dress herself. Clearly uncomfortable under his regard, she rubbed her palms on her skirt.

"Well . . ." she said, leaving the word hanging.

Chase knew an invitation to leave when he heard one, but he was in no hurry to oblige her. Victory seldom went to a faintheart. He gave her what he hoped was a reassuring smile and shifted his attention back to her room. To the left of the privacy screen, nearly concealed by its wooden frame, he saw a black, two-quart capacity water bag hanging on a wall nail, the attached length of rubber hose sporting a vaginal irrigator at its end. On the washstand beneath it was the usual pitcher and bowl, plus a jar of sponges and a jug of Knight's vinegar. There was also an apothecary jar of brown globules, probably a homemade concoction to prevent pregnancy.

Imagining Franny using such things—having a need to use such things—made Chase feel sick. Yet there sat the evidence. What he had expected, he didn't know. A roomful of religious paraphernalia, maybe? As sweet and innocent an air as she emanated, this girl sold her body for a living. If facing the ugly reality of that was going to make him queasy, he'd best stir dust while he still had the chance.

He turned back to her. A scarlet flush flagged her ivory cheeks, and he knew by her high color that she was painfully embarrassed that he had been staring at her personal things. Embarrassed and ashamed. In the harsh light of morning, there were no dream worlds for her to escape into.

Chase swallowed and met her gaze. God, how he wanted to steal her away from here. She didn't belong in a place like this, and if it was the last thing he did, he'd help her find a way to leave. It was something he had to do, not just for her, but for himself. And maybe, in some abstract way, for Gloria. He wouldn't turn his back this time.

Without thinking how she might interpret it, Chase rubbed the embroidered toe of her pink felt slipper along his jaw. Her pupils dilated until her eyes looked nearly black. An electrical awareness arced between them. An awareness that Chase didn't dare acknowledge. Not yet.

He hated himself for what he was about to say. But from here on out, things weren't going to be easy, and he'd probably be doing and saying a number of things that would seem cruel to her. "I noticed on your sign outside that you charge ten dollars for thirty minutes? How many customers do you generally get each night?"

She went pale at the question. Glancing at the dresser, she drew her fair brows together in a frown. He could see that she was as rattled as she was humiliated. He surmised she was trying to recall how much money was usually left on the dresser each night, further proof that Indigo was correct; as much as Franny possibly could, she held herself apart from this whole ugly business.

"I . . . um . . . " She gnawed her lip and lifted one

shoulder. "Three, sometimes four, I guess. Why do you ask?"

"So fifty would cover a whole night?"

"A whole what?"

He nearly chuckled at the horrified expression in her eyes. "A whole night," he repeated. "If a fellow desired your company for that long, fifty would more than cover what you might lose in other business?"

For an endless moment, she stared at him as though he had lost his mind. And Chase wondered if maybe he had. No woman on earth was worth fifty dollars a night. Except maybe a fragile blonde with startled green eyes and a mouth so sweet all he could think about was kissing her.

"I don't work all night," she hastened to remind him. "Only until one, no exceptions, ever."

"I see." Chase extended the slipper to her again. "I'll bear that in mind then and have you back by one."

"Back?"

He pressed the slipper into her hand and curled her fingers around it. "Yes, back. If I pay for the night, there's nothing to say we have to stay here. It'd be more fun to go out and do something."

Clearly suspicious, she said, "Like what?"

Chase knew she generally avoided the townspeople, so he couldn't very well expect her to attend the dance that night. Not that the self-righteous people there would have accepted her anyway. "I don't know. A picnic, maybe?"

"After dark?"

"If the moon isn't bright enough, we could always take a lantern."

She shook her head. "No. I'm sorry. I don't accept all-night customers."

Chase arched an eyebrow. "Really? I didn't notice that rule posted outside."

"An oversight."

"An oversight that isn't posted."

"I shall remedy that."

Chase angled a finger beneath her chin and lifted her face slightly. "I hope not."

There was no mistaking that the anxiety in her eyes was genuine. He supposed she felt safe entertaining men in her room where Gus could hear if she screamed for help. If she left the saloon with someone, she would have no protector. Not that she would need one while she was with him. But she had no way of knowing that.

"I'll be looking forward to seeing you again, Franny," he said as he released her and stepped around her to the grasp the doorknob. "I hope you'll do the same?"

If her expression was any indication, she would look forward to the moment without about as much enthusiasm as she would a case of influenza.

Chase was grinning as he let himself out.

Franny was shaking. The instant the door closed behind him, she whirled to stare at it, her mind racing almost as crazily as her heart. A new sign. She had to make a new sign and tell Gus about the change immediately. *No all-night customers.* That decision made, Franny felt a little better, but not by much. She didn't know what it was about Chase Wolf, but the man could make her heart skitter with nothing more than a look from those piercing blue eyes. He spelled trouble. She felt it in the marrow of her bones.

He wanted to see her again? The idea was so ludicrous, she almost laughed. He actually believed she would leave the saloon and go cavorting off into the dark with him? No way. Any man who wanted to spend a whole night with a sporting woman had a board loose in his upper story. She'd be a fool to trust him, and experience had cured her of being a fool long ago.

7

Freshly bathed and shaven, Chase sat on his parents' porch that night waiting for it to get dark. Five ten-dollar gold pieces weighed heavily in his pocket, which would seriously deplete his ready cash, but as he perused the upper story windows of the Lucky Nugget and envisioned himself spending the entire evening with Franny, he decided the expenditure would be worth it.

Tomorrow was Monday. The bank would be open. Come morning, he could sign a draft and withdraw enough money to carry him through next week. Depending on how tonight went, he might be withdrawing enough to monopolize Franny's evenings until the weekend. That would raise eyebrows, especially Mr. Villen's, the bank president. Chase could almost picture the look on his face.

Sighing, he gazed at the sky, willing it to darken. Jesus. Did he even know what he was getting himself into? Was he even thinking straight? Or, for that matter, thinking at all? Rescuing a soiled dove—it sounded good. But to do it, he had to have something to offer Franny as an alternative. There weren't many good-paying jobs for women, and he wasn't certain what Franny's financial needs were. What if she had to make as much money as she did now? Chase couldn't think of a single occupation for females, other than prostitution, that would pay as well.

And wasn't that a sorry fact? As Indigo said, men in the white world hadn't given their women many options when it came to supporting themselves. Those females who met with misfortune received no help. Instead they became prey. Victims, his father called them, and maybe he was right. Society was full of men who stood in line to victimize.

The possibility that he might be second in line outside Franny's door tonight was enough to tie his stomach into knots. The very idea of some filthy, half-drunk bastard putting his hands on her. Christ. He felt sick when he thought of it. Which was absurd. Franny had been doing business in that upstairs room for far longer than he cared to contemplate. One more customer shouldn't make a difference. But it did. He didn't want another man so much as touching her.

When he tried to analyze his feelings and interpret them, all he felt was confused. By definition, Franny was public property, available to anyone who had the coin to rent her favors, and until she chose to change that, there was very little he could do.

A picture of her guileless green eyes and expressive face flashed through Chase's mind, and his hands curled into throbbing fists. What was happening to him? He had to get his thoughts sorted out before he went to see her, but the more he tried, the more jumbled they seemed. One thing seemed clear; he wanted to help her. Had to help her. It had become an obsession. Maybe he was trying to purge himself, lay old demons to rest. Or maybe his feelings for her went deeper than that. He didn't know. All he knew was that he had to go see her and he didn't intend to back off until he got her the hell out of that place.

When Chase entered the Lucky Nugget a few minutes later, piano music throbbed against his eardrums. He tried to block out the sound, but as he started toward the stairs, Gus's voice brought him up short. Turning, he peered through the lantern lit gloom, his eyes smarting from the clouds of tobacco smoke. Waving his white towel, Gus motioned Chase to the bar.

Weaving his way between the tables, Chase tried not to bump the elbows of any poker players with the basket he carried. The overwhelming smells of cigars, cigarettes, and unwashed bodies made his stomach turn. He couldn't help but think of Franny, working in this place, night after night. The thought made him all the more impatient to see her. As he drew up near the bar, Gus slid a mug of ale to him.

"On the house."

In all the years Chase had known Gus Packer, he had never heard of him giving away drinks. Something was up, and if a free ale was attached, Chase had a gut feeling he wasn't going to like it. He hooked the handle of the mug as it went sailing past, then shook the spill of suds off of his hand. "Thanks." Hesitating for emphasis, Chase added, "I think."

Gus had the good grace to look embarrassed. "Look, Chase, I don't want any hard feelings, but we got us sort of a situation."

Setting down the basket, Chase propped a bootheel on the brass foot rail. "Out with it, Gus."

The barkeep scratched at a flake of dried food on the edge of the counter. "It's Franny," he began softly. "For some reason, she's real determined to steer clear of you."

"I see."

Gus finally looked up. "She asked me to keep you out of her room."

Chase took a slow drink from his mug. After wiping his mouth with the back of his wrist, he set the glass on the bar with a decisive thump. "I'm going up to see her, Gus."

"Do that, and I'll have to send someone for the marshal."

"I guess that's your prerogative."

"You don't wanna tangle with the law, Chase."

"It won't be the first time and probably won't be the last. I come from a long line of renegades, remember?"

"She ain't worth it. No woman is."

"That's for me to decide."

Gus set his jaw. "If you start trouble in here, there's not a man in the place that'll hesitate to jump in and help me out."

Chase turned to regard the ragtag collection of individuals in the room. As weary and disreputable as the miners looked, he didn't underestimate them. A man couldn't eke his living from a hole in the ground without developing hard edges. By the same token, loggers weren't exactly soft, and Chase knew for a fact they were a hell of a lot meaner. These fellows had nothing to offer that he hadn't been up against before, and in spades. He was tender across the midriff, no doubt about it, and that put him at a disadvantage. But once the first punch was thrown, he knew his temper would take over.

When he slid his gaze back to Gus, he smiled slightly. "Destructive business, saloon brawls. Tends to tear hell out of a place. If I start a scuffle, I have a standing rule that I always pay for the damages. But I'm not so accommodating if someone else takes the first swing. You reckon these fellows have the coin to pay for broken tables and chairs, not to mention all the glasses, pitchers, and jugs that are bound to get shattered?"

"I don't want trouble, Chase."

"Trouble's my middle name."

"You talk mighty tough for a man with cracked ribs."

"Fact or brag, that's the question, and I don't think you want to find out."

"Oh, I've heard the stories about you," Gus admitted. "A regular hell-raiser, ain't you? But that's when you're away from home. I got me this sneakin' hunch you'll think twice before you start anything in here that might get back to your folks and make your mamma cry."

At any other time, the threat might have forestalled Chase. But tonight it was Franny's tears he was concerned with, not his mother's. If worse came to worse, he felt certain his parents would understand that. "Gus, I'm warning you. Don't try me."

"You're pappy should've beat the meanness out of you while you was still small enough to whup."

"Probably so. But beating his kids regularly wasn't one of his strong points."

"Never laid a hand on you, or I miss my guess. If he had, you wouldn't be such a cocky ass." Gus's gaze wavered. "Franny don't want to see you. Why can't you just respect her wishes and stay clear?"

"Because I don't think she knows what's good for her." Chase returned the nearly full mug to the saloon owner in much the same fashion that it had been served, roughly and slopping ale. Dealing with Franny would be difficult enough without clouding his judgement with drink. "You haven't got a leg to stand on when it comes to denying me access to the upstairs rooms, Gus, and neither does she. I may be a breed, and I sure as hell won't deny being ornery when the mood strikes, but no matter how you portion it out, I'm usually one hundred percent a gentleman with the ladies. You won't find anyone in Wolf's Landing or elsewhere who'll say different."

"Gentleman or no, she don't want no part of you."

"I'd say it's the nature of her business to accommodate paying customers she doesn't particularly like on occasion. If there's trouble tonight because you and she disagree, and I end up in jail for brawling, that point will be brought up by my defense lawyer. A whore can't turn a man away without just cause, and I haven't given her one."

"Yeah? Well, just remember this, partner. While you're waiting for the judge to show up here at the landing, you'll be resting on your laurels in jail."

"And you'll be shut down for repairs," Chase retorted. "Repairs I won't have to pay for. If you start something, you'll eat the cost of the damages."

Gus's face went crimson.

Chase arched a challenging eyebrow. "By the way, by the letter of the law, is prostitution even legal? Or does the law hereabouts just turn a blind eye?"

"There ain't no prostitutes in this establishment, just dance girls."

"My ass." Chase chuckled and shook his head. "And you're going to sic these yahoos on me then have me tossed in jail for asking her to dance? Explain that one to the judge, Gus."

With that, Chase pushed away from the bar and started toward the stairs. So this was how the wind was going to blow. Well, he had news for Miss Franny; this time around she had seriously underestimated her opponent. He didn't bluff quite that easily. And when it came to fighting dirty, he was a master.

Anger made his stride brisk, his movements clipped. Not wishing to intimidate her in his present mood, he considered waiting downstairs for a few minutes until he calmed down, but he feared that if he did another man might beat him to her door. Proof in point, at the banister he bumped into a miner who was heading in the same direction, a whiskey bottle in one hand, money in the other. Chase clamped a hand over the fellow's shoulder and drew him to an abrupt halt.

"Sorry, chum. The lady's not accepting callers tonight."

"Says who?"

"Says me," Chase informed him softly.

Despite the loud piano music, Franny heard her door-knob rattle. An instant later, the noise from downstairs, a decibel higher for lack of a barrier, floated in on a draft of air, which told her the door was opening. A narrow shaft of anemic light spilled across the floor to splash against the wall, illuminating the daisy pattern of her wallpaper. As always with the first customer of the evening, tension filled her, but with the ease of long practice, she separated herself from it.

Daisies, a meadow of daisies.

Trying to ignore the sound of the man's boots approaching her bed, she closed her eyes. Concentration, that was the trick. She didn't just see the meadow but immersed herself in it, feeling the light brush of grass against her skirt as she walked, the sun's warmth on her shoulders. She could even hear the breeze whispering. And the scents. Ah, the wonderful scents. Nothing smelled quite so sweet as a meadow full of flowers. One by one, she engaged her five senses in her dream world until she had no awareness to spare for reality.

She wasn't sure how much time passed before she began to sense something was wrong. Slowly, measure by measure, she resurfaced, intensely aware that she lay alone on the bed, as yet unaccosted, and that her imaginary sunlight had somehow become real. Its golden warmth pressed against her closed eyelids.

Confused, she lifted her lashes slightly. Had she fallen asleep? Was it morning already? As she studied the light, it occurred to her that its tint was too golden to be sunshine. Then she heard the soft, sputtering hiss of the lantern.

All of her customers knew that lighting the lamp was strictly forbidden, and with the exception of only two men several years ago, they had always honored that rule.

Alarm coursed through her. She pushed up on her elbows and blinked to clear her vision. "May Belle?" she said hopefully.

Her gaze shot to the table where a dark-haired man sat. She recognized Chase Wolf almost instantly. With his feet crossed at the ankle and propped on the table's edge, his posture was insolent, the chair beneath him rocked back onto its hind legs. Instead of his usual lumberman pacs, tonight he had on black, high-heeled Montana boots, serviceable but rather dressy for Wolf's Landing. In addition, he wore black denim pants and a store-bought teal shirt of plain-weave silk with an attached collar and gold-plated studs on the front placket and pockets. Because she had recently ordered some clothing for her brother Frankie, she knew an overshirt like that cost at least $2.50 in the Montgomery Ward catalog, an extravagant price when something in domette flannel or Melton cloth could be had for 45¢. He had clearly dressed for an occasion, and judging by his intent expression, she was it.

Stiffening, she gazed into his piercing blue eyes, uncomfortably aware that the burnished features encompassing them were set in harsh, relentless lines. There was no mistaking the fact that Chase Wolf was angry. The emotion radiated from him like electricity before a lightning storm, making the air so heavy it tingled on her skin. Worse yet, she knew why he was so furious. So much for Gus playing watchdog and keeping him away from her.

"What are you doing in here?"

With an unhurried, deliberate movement, he set a short stack of ten dollar gold pieces on the table, his gaze never releasing hers. "Why do men usually come in here?"

Unnerved and determined to camouflage that fact with anger, she made sure her wrapper sash was tied and sat up. Swinging her legs over the side of the bed, she slipped her feet into her felt slippers. "Get out."

He gave a low chuckle that fairly dripped with martial arrogance. "Well, now, darlin', why don't you try and make me?"

"What I lack in muscle, Mr. Wolf, I more than make up for in reinforcements. Give me any difficulty, and all I need do is call for Gus. Why don't you save yourself a heap of trouble and leave before I feel it's necessary to do so."

He didn't look intimidated. Indeed, if anything, he appeared amused. His dark blue eyes slowly swept the length of her, lingering boldly, first at her hips then at her breasts. "Trouble, now there's a word that keeps cropping up this evening. Funny how everyone seems to think I'll walk a mile to avoid it." He lifted the stack of coins then began to drop them, one by one, onto the table. "I'm a scrapper, Franny. Have been since I was knee-high. There's nothing I like better than a good brawl, unless, of course, we're counting women and booze."

Franny averted her gaze. "I have every right to refuse

service to anyone, no explanations. I'd like you to leave."

"And I'd like to stay. Since I have you outweighed by a good hundred pounds and outflanked at every turn, I reckon I'll do just that." He punctuated that statement by dropping the last coin onto the stack. "Fifty dollars. You said you usually get three to four customers a night? I figure fifty should cover what you usually make, plus extras."

"No extras," she retorted in a quavery voice. "If you had bothered to read the sign, you'd know that."

"Oh, I read it. But I'm a firm believer that the only thing rules are good for is to break them."

His eyes glinted with mischief as he pushed slowly to his feet. Stretched out to his full height, he seemed all the more intimidating. Franny retreated a step and threw a glance at the door. To her horror, she saw that the dead bolt had been shoved home. She didn't stand a prayer of escaping onto the landing before he caught her.

She hugged her waist and hid her trembling hands by tucking them inside the roomy sleeves of her wrapper. Twice before she had faced a situation such as this, and she knew revealing weakness would be a costly mistake.

The memories. They leaped into her mind with frightening clarity. She knew firsthand how much damage a man of Chase Wolf's size and strength could inflict on a woman. She also knew how quickly it could happen.

"I've asked you nicely to leave," she finally managed.

"And I've refused. Nicely."

Help was only a holler away. She knew Gus would be up the stairs in a flash if she needed him. But with the piano music throbbing against the walls, would her screams even be heard? She knew from experience that she would have time to yell only once, twice if she was lucky. After that, he would be upon her, and with only one of those large, leathery hands, he could muffle her cries.

A slight smile quirked the corners of his firm mouth, and he lifted one coin from off the stack, flipping it in a flashy arc before palming it. "You're selling, honey. And I'm buying. Isn't that how it goes?"

That stung. And it was cruel of him, heartlessly cruel. But it was also a truth she couldn't deny. "I don't do business in the usual way. No guarantees, no refunds. And I reserve the right to refuse service to anyone." She turned toward the door and prayed with every step he wouldn't physically detain her. "You have to the count of three. If you aren't gone, I'm calling for Gus."

"I don't think you want to do that."

His tone made her freeze with her fingers on the deadbolt. She looked over her shoulder at him.

He tossed the gold piece carelessly onto the table and hooked his thumbs over his hand-tooled leather belt. With one hip thrust out and a long leg slightly bent, he looked as if he were spoiling for a fight. Despite that, he was undeniably handsome with the teal of his shirt bringing out the darkness of his skin and the lantern light glistening on his mahogany hair.

Gentling his expression, he said, "You have nothing to fear from me, Franny. I promise you that. Not if you cooperate with me."

"And if I don't?"

"Then all hell's going to break loose. Gus will come

upstairs, probably with reinforcements, and there's going to be a ruckus like you've never seen."

"You're bluffing. With three broken ribs, you're in no shape to engage in fisticuffs."

"True. But before I go down, I'll take a few men with me. And in the process, this place will be demolished." He narrowed an eye as if in thought. "The railing around the landing will go, for sure. And the door will be kicked in. The window will definitely get broken." He shrugged. "That's the way it goes when a bunch of men start throwing punches. Another thing you shouldn't discount is the contagion of fights inside saloons. There's every possibility that what starts upstairs will spread downstairs, and the whole saloon could suffer serious damage."

Detesting herself because her voice quavered, she said, "You'll either pay for those damages or be thrown in jail."

He flashed her a lazy grin. "Not if I don't start it. That's the kicker, darlin'. You don't have a reason in hell to refuse to *dance* with me. If Gus and the others come up here, I'll be a perfect gentleman until someone smacks me. That'll make me the injured party. If it goes before a judge, what're you going to say, that you didn't like my looks? Sorry. But women in your line of work can't be that choosy."

"I'll lie. I'll say you got out of line. That you were rough and obnoxious."

He shrugged again. "Your choice."

"The damages you described will cost more than you can afford. Mark my words, you'll be put in jail, and they'll throw away the key."

"No. That's where you're wrong. I have plenty of money to cover the damages. As far as that goes, I could cover similar damages tomorrow night. And the next. Any way you look at it, Gus will be forced to shut down while he makes repairs." Withdrawing his thumbs from over his belt, he placed his hands lightly on his hips. "If I keep coming back, which I promise you I will, and you persist in refusing me service, there'll be more trouble. And more trouble after that. Sooner or later Gus is going to start asking himself who is at the root of all his miseries."

"You."

"And you. As much as he probably likes you, business is business, and you're not indispensable. Before he'll watch his saloon go under, he'll hand you your walking papers, sweetheart. When that happens, you're out of a job."

"That is despicable."

"I know it is. I'm real slick at being despicable when I want to be."

"I need this job."

He smiled slightly. "I'm banking on it."

"You, sirrah, are beneath contempt."

"I know that, too. But until I get my way, I can't afford to be charming." He inclined his head at the deadbolt. "Your choice. Either open the door and call for Gus or admit I've won this round."

Trembling so badly she could scarcely stand, Franny dropped her hands from the bolt and turned to press her back to the door. "Why are you doing this?"

"I'm not sure I can explain that."

"I can't lose this job."

"Cooperate with me, and your job's perfectly safe."

"I don't work with the lights lit. I won't, not for you or anyone else."

"I don't expect you to."

On wobbly legs, Franny started toward the bed. "Then douse the lamp and get to your business."

"The lamp stays on."

She froze. "But you just said—"

"All I want is to spend time with you. To talk, nothing more." He bent and retrieved a basket she hadn't noticed from under the table. "A picnic, remember?"

Franny gaped at him. "Are you mad? You're willing to spend fifty dollars to take me on a picnic? In the dark? I'm not quite that stupid, Mr. Wolf. Any man willing to spend that much money has things besides talking and eating on his mind. I'd be a fool to leave here with you."

"The name is Chase. And by the same token, I'd be a fool to harm a hair on your head if you do leave with me. Everyone downstairs will see us leave together. If anything happens to you, it'll come to roost on my doorstep."

Franny supposed that was true enough. Filled with indecision, she studied him, wondering if she dared to call his bluff. For reasons beyond her, she had the awful feeling that he had meant every word. If men came upstairs, he would go down swinging, and cause as much damage as he possibly could while he was at it. It made no sense. Absolutely none. And yet the gleam of determination in his eyes was unmistakable. He wanted something from her, and he meant to get it.

What, that was the question.

As if he read her mind, he smiled again, his expression more friendly now. "Honey, I've never laid a hand on a woman, and I don't plan to start with you. I only want to spend the evening with you. Where's the harm in that if Gus knows who you're with? I get what I want, and you get your night's wages. It sounds like a fair deal to me."

"If you wanted to take me on a picnic, did it ever occur to you to simply ask? You might have saved yourself fifty dollars."

His eyes filled with a knowing glint. "If I asked, would you go?"

He clearly knew the answer to that. Rather than look at him, Franny regarded the toes of her slippers. Her mind raced for an explanation for his insane behavior, but there was none.

Was he curious about her? Was that it? Maybe he'd never known a woman like her, and he was fascinated. Sneaking a glance at him, she scotched that thought. Chase Wolf had been in plenty of brothels. She would bet money on it.

Did he fancy himself in love with her? Franny had received her share of proposals from men, some simply because they were lonely and could find no one else, some because they wanted to play hero and rescue a fallen woman from her tawdry existence. Thanks to May Belle's recounting of her past, Franny knew how that fairy tale ended. The hero awakened one morning and realized he was married to a whore, end of fairy tale. The game got ugly after that. Very ugly. And it was one she had no intention of playing.

Except that she had no choice. Gus would ask her to

leave before he suffered irreversible financial losses. Franny couldn't blame him for that. This saloon was his livelihood.

"Well?" Chase said in a low voice.

She slowly nodded. "I guess I'm going on a picnic."

"There's my girl." He set the basket on the table and turned to the window, presenting her with his back. "Wash your face, brush that starch out of your hair, and get dressed, hm? It's a beautiful night. It'd be a damned shame to waste any of it."

While Franny dressed, safely hidden behind the privacy screen, Chase began to quiz her, subtle questions at first, which she managed to ignore, then blunter queries, to which she gave vague replies. He finally became frustrated with her evasiveness and said, "Tell me about yourself."

There was nothing to tell him. Franny of Wolf's Landing led a pretty boring life, and Francine Graham didn't exist unless she was in Grants Pass visiting her family. She doubted he would be satisfied with that as an answer, however, and even if he would have been, she had no intention of opening a can of worms. No one knew about Francine Graham, not even Indigo. "I'm not a very interesting person."

"I'll be the judge of that."

With trembling fingers, she buttoned the high collar of her white blouse. "Truly, there's nothing much to tell. I work, I visit with Indigo, I sleep, I eat. That's it."

"Secrets, Franny?"

The mocking tone in his voice made her skin prickle.

"No secrets. Nothing interesting enough to keep secret."

"What's your surname?"

She straightened her waistband. "I haven't one."

"Found under a cabbage leaf, were you?"

"No, in a strawberry patch." She sat on her rocker to don her high-top shoes. Retrieving her buttonhook from off the table, she bent forward and nearly impaled her ankle when his shadow fell across her. She glanced up, angry beyond expression that he had dared invade her inner sanctum. "And you? Found in the barnyard, maybe? Under a petrified chip of cow dung?"

At that, he laughed. Hunkering before her, he wrested the buttonhook from her rigid fingers and lifted her foot onto his knee. "You're a danger to yourself with this thing," he said, then deftly began pulling through buttons.

Franny thought he represented the greatest danger. To her wary eyes, he seemed uncommonly broad across the shoulders, a play of muscle in evidence under the silk of his shirt every time he moved. In the dancing shadows, his face looked all the more burnished, like a sculpture in rubbed mahogany, his glistening hair several shades darker, his lashes incredibly long and casting spider-etchings onto his cheeks. His mouth was entirely masculine, the lower lip sensually full, the upper narrow and sharply defined. His distinctly squared lower jaw made his face seem rugged and frighteningly invulnerable. The knot along the bridge of his nose, compliments of a break that had never mended properly, belied that. Yet the imperfection only enhanced his maleness.

Unable to look away, she wondered what his plans for her were. His lashes swept up in a silken arc to his sharply arched brows, and his dark blue eyes pinned her. After studying her for a moment, he ran a hand under her skirt and petticoats, his warm fingers curling over her calf as he lowered her foot back to the floor. Even through the leg of her drawers, the heat of his touch made her stomach lurch. Apparently unaffected, he drew her other foot onto his upraised knee. Deftly, he inserted the hook into an eye, snagged a shoe button, and popped it through the hole. He was no stranger to dressing a woman.

"I see that you sew," he noted in a silken voice. "Who's the clown pillow for? Hunter or Amelia Rose?"

Franny shot a glance at her sewing table. This was her private place where she could forget her life in Wolf's Landing and be herself. Having him in here made her feel violated.

When she didn't answer his question, he looked up at her again. "I like that dress you're making. Pink will go nice with your fair coloring, not to mention that it's high time you had some pretty gowns with ruffles and lace. The ones you wear now are better suited to an impoverished widow twice your age."

How dare he criticize her wardrobe? Franny clenched her teeth.

"And these shoes?" He harrumphed with disgust. "They've seen better days. How much of a cut out of your wages do Gus and May Belle take, for Christ's sake? At thirty or forty a night, I'd think you could afford decent footwear."

"My income is none of your concern."

He conceded the point with a low laugh, which infuriated her. Nothing she said or did seem to ruffle him. He lowered her foot to the floor and leaned slightly forward to trace her cheekbone with the buttonhook. Her heart skittered at the contact. As if he sensed his effect on her, he gently snagged her lower lip with the hook, his gaze riveted to her mouth. For a moment, he seemed to stop breathing. Franny knew that she did.

"You are so sweet," he whispered. "How can that possibly be?"

It was a question that didn't deserve an answer. And so much for his only wanting to talk, she thought bitterly. She'd seen that look in men's eyes before, and she knew what it portended. Freeing her mouth, she said, "Mr. Wolf, is there anything I can say to change your mind about this picnic idea? I'd really prefer—"

"Chase," he corrected, "and no, there's nothing you can say to change my mind. Accept it and enjoy the evening, that's my advice to you."

He pushed abruptly to his feet and returned her buttonhook to the table. She saw his dark blue eyes scan the pages of her Bible, and she wanted to kick herself for having left it open.

"The story of Mary Magdalene, Franny?"

To comfort herself, she read those passages at least once every day. But she would never admit that. Not that she had to. The knowing look in his gaze told her he had guessed her reasons for reading that particular story. "I'm ready to go."

He caught one of her starched curls between his fingers. "Not quite." Stepping to her washstand, he moistened a cloth and picked up her brush. After returning to her, he set the brush aside to scrub her face. At the first touch of the cloth, Franny sputtered indignantly, which seemed to amuse him. "Don't be difficult. "

She batted at his hand. "You're taking hide and all."

He gentled the pressure. "Then stop putting this shit on your face. You look more like a clown than that pillow face you're embroidering."

Franny refused to be baited. After cleaning her face, he reached for her brush before she could forestall him and began running the bristles through her stiff curls. He was surprisingly careful and took great pains not to tug on her scalp. "It really does brush right out," he said in obvious amazement.

No man had ever brushed her hair. It seemed a highly personal thing, something a husband might do for his wife. Franny had difficulty breathing, a condition that became more pronounced with each passing second. After he had brushed out most of the starch, he ran the brush the length of her tresses with sensual slowness. She watched in frozen fascination as he let the strands escape the bristles. In the amber-touched shadows, her hair rained toward her lap like spun fibers of gold.

"Beautiful," he whispered. "Like liquid sunshine with splashes of silver."

Franny wrested her hair from his grasp and shoved the brush away. "I shall braid it, and then I'm ready to leave."

Given the close quarters, escaping outdoors would be a relief. At least then she might have room to breathe. She stood, forcing him to rock back on his heels. She wished he'd fall flat on his arrogant posterior, but Chase Wolf was more agile than most, even with sore ribs. She didn't miss the grin that flashed across his mouth.

So he found her amusing, did he? Deciding to forego

a braid, which would take too much time, she gathered her hair and gave it several twists. Stepping to the mirror above the washstand, she picked up the scattered hairpins next to the basin and stabbed viciously at the coil atop her head, missing her mark more times than not. Liquid sunshine? Men. They were all the same. Fetching her bonnet from off its nail, she drew it on, jerking hard at the strings as she tied them. The result was that her chin hurt.

He regarded her with a mischievous grin. "Afraid of getting freckles?"

Franny snorted in answer to his question and swept grandly past him. Let him laugh. She didn't care. She wasn't about to explain why she planned to wear a sunbonnet after dark. He could think whatever he liked.

8

The moment they were outside the saloon, Chase switched hands on the picnic basket, untied Franny's bonnet strings and removed her hat. He didn't miss the panicked expression that entered her eyes, and she made a wild grab for the sunbonnet, clearly determined to have it back.

"It's dark, for God's sake. You don't need to keep your face hidden now."

By her expression, he knew he had hit closer to the truth than she might have liked. She hesitated and then dropped her hand, her gaze still fixed on the bonnet.

"I paid fifty dollars to spend this time with you," he said softly. "I'll be damned if I'll stare at the side of your hat all night."

Determined to ignore the frightened look on her face, Chase folded the cloth bonnet and tucked it over his belt. That done, he grasped her elbow to guide her along the boardwalk, his mind racing with questions he knew would probably go unanswered. Why did she fear recognition? Was she hiding from someone?

Studying her pale profile, Chase had to hand it to her. The starched curls and garish paint she wore while working altered her appearance so much that only a very close observer might make a connection between this prim, ladylike young woman and the prostitute who worked at the Lucky Nugget.

Determined to make the evening as productive as he could, Chase pushed all his questions aside and released his hold on her elbow to take her hand. She looked incredulous, which made him wonder if she had ever had a beau. She was so pretty he had difficulty believing she hadn't. This couldn't be the first time a young man had escorted her out.

At this end of town lay the community hall. A bit farther north was Indigo's house and the school. Chase had a destination in mind and quickened his pace as they left the boardwalk. The sound of laughter and low voices drifted to him on the night air, and he glanced up to see several couples leaving the hall. The dance must be ending. He wished he could have taken Franny to it. He could almost feel her floating in his arms to the tune of a waltz, her cheeks flushed, her eyes sparkling with pleasure.

Glancing down at her, he couldn't miss the look of yearning in her expression when she saw the young ladies in their finery, all escorted by attentive young men. Nor did he miss the fact that she increased their pace in an obvious attempt to hurry so no one would see her. He ached for her, unable to understand why she continued in a profession that brought her such pain. There had to be a way out for her. All he had to do was help her find it.

Only when they drew near the schoolhouse did she relax a little, and even then only by a negligible measure. Chase chose to ignore her uneasiness and led her to the playground. When she realized he meant to seat her on one of the swings, she clutched her skirt and shook her head.

"I haven't been in a swing for years. I really don't—"

"It's high time, then, isn't it?"

After setting aside the basket, he pressed her down onto the seat. "Grab hold," he ordered, and then gave her no choice by grasping the ropes and hauling her back so her feet couldn't touch.

She squeaked when he released her. Her skirt caught the wind. With one hand, she grappled to tuck its folds under her knees. God forbid that she should flash any ankle. Chase smiled to himself and settled his hands at her waist when she swung back to him. God, how he wanted to retain his hold and nuzzle the nape of her neck where those silken blond curls lay in such tempting tendrils.

He resisted the urge and gave her another light push. Watching her, he felt a certain measure of satisfaction when he saw some of the tension drain from her shoulders. He knew damned well she wasn't always so serious and withdrawn. He wanted to work his way past those defenses of hers until she was as at ease and quick to laugh with him as she was with Indigo and the children.

Catching her by the waist again, he held her suspended for a moment, her fanny pressed against his abdomen. The back of her neck was at a perfect height for him to kiss, and he was once again sorely tempted. He imagined her skin there would feel as soft as velvet against his lips, and recalling her scent last night, he guessed she'd smell sweetly of lavender.

But Chase had a mission in mind, and startling her with sexual advances wasn't part of his plan. He released her and followed up with another push to send her sailing higher than before. She squeaked in alarm again, but the little laugh that followed told him she was more exhilarated by the height than afraid.

"You're pushing me too high. What if I fall?"

"I'll catch you."

"What about your ribs?"

Chase had nearly forgotten his ribs. "They're better."

"They can't be that much better."

"Would you let me worry about my ribs? Relax, Franny. Have a little fun for once."

She gave a startled giggle when he gave her another push. "It seems a peculiar way for a man to waste fifty dollars."

"I'm a peculiar fellow."

He continued to push her until she did as he suggested and enjoyed herself. When he finally grew weary and drew the swing to a stop, she angled her head to look up at him, her large eyes filled with questions and more than a little bewilderment. That was just how he wanted her: guessing.

"Why did you bring me out here?" she finally asked.

With every minute he spent in her company, his

motives became more and more confusing, even to him. Evading the issue, he left her sitting there and went to fetch the picnic basket. She watched him warily as he spread a lightweight blanket under the sprawling oak at the edge of the playground. Sitting cross-legged upon the flannel, he patted a spot beside him.

"Come on. I don't bite. At least not hard."

She remained in the swing for a moment, clearly leery of him and suspicious of his intentions. Chase pretended not to notice and began setting out the food. Not very exciting fare, but the best he had been able to manage without asking his mother to prepare something special. Corn muffins, melon, cold chicken, and a bottle of wine he had purchased especially for this occasion. He poured a measure of burgundy into each of the mugs he had brought along, acutely aware that she was finally walking in his direction, albeit slowly.

"I hope you like cold chicken." He sank his teeth into a drumstick and fell back on one elbow, smiling at her as he chewed. "Are you hungry?"

In truth, Franny was starving. She seldom ate an evening meal. Until that first customer came through the door each night, she was always half sick with tension, and she had learned long ago that her stomach rebelled if she ate anything before her shift began. "I suppose I could have a snack."

He gestured for her to sit down. Though she knew how swiftly he could move, having something between them, even so inadequate a barrier as a wicker basket, made her feel better. Gathering her skirt close, she sank to her knees. He watched her speculatively. Taking care to modestly cover her ankles, she cast a curious glance into the basket, spied another chicken leg, and hesitantly reached for it. Crisp breading. She took a small bite.

"Mm. It's delicious."

"My ma can flat cook."

Shifting on his elbow, he leaned closer to the basket to search through its contents. She heard eating utensils clatter. An instant later, his hand emerged holding a fork with a cube of melon speared on its tines. With no warning, he pressed it upon her, leaving her little choice but to part her lips. Cantaloupe. The sweet juice from it filled her mouth, and the taste was absolutely exquisite. Gus seldom bought fresh fruit. it wasn't something his intoxicated customers generally liked to eat. She sometimes had fruit at Indigo's house, of course, but otherwise she went without.

After swallowing, it occurred to her that the melon was not yet in season. Surprised, and momentarily forgetting her wariness, she asked, "Where on earth did you get cantaloupe?"

"Jeremy, Indigo's brother-in-law. You know, Jake's brother? He was just down in California, and he stopped off here on his way back to Portland. He brought Ma a whole crate of melons. They weren't quite ripe, so she wrapped them in paper to sweeten them up. Now we've got cantaloupe coming out our ears."

That sounded heavenly to Franny, and she wished she had some to take home to her mother the following weekend. Cantaloupe was Mary Graham's favorite fruit. "Melon nearly two months early? I can scarcely believe it, and it tastes so good. Who'd think it would ripen wrapped in paper?"

"California has a much longer growing season.

Sunshine, and tons of it. Folks down there have tanned faces year around, practically."

"And Oregonians rust," she put in.

"Spoken like a native webfoot, or I miss my guess. Where were you born, Franny? Anyplace close?"

Heat flooded to her cheeks. He was clearly waiting for her to make a slip, and she couldn't allow him to lull her into forgetting that. "A strawberry patch, I told you."

"But not a patch here in Wolf's Landing. If so, you would've gone to school here, and I don't remember you."

"Perhaps I never went to school."

"My ass. You're too well-spoken for that to be the case. I've got an ear for poor grammar. My aunt Amy was hell on greased runners about our using proper English."

"I've done a lot of reading."

"And who taught you to read?"

Franny sighed. "A teacher, of course. I attended school until my thirteenth year. Then I had to quit."

Chase's throat tightened. Thirteen. Little more than a baby. Christ. "Is that when you became a working girl?"

"Shortly after that."

"At thirteen?"

"Yes."

"Son of a bitch." Chase threw away his drumstick. He wanted to throw more than that. The picnic basket, maybe. A child selling her flesh to men. "Where the hell was your father? Didn't you have one?"

"No. He died in an accident."

"And left you an orphan?"

She hesitated. "Yes. An orphan."

An accomplished liar, she wasn't. "And no one offered to take you in?"

She averted her face. After a long moment, she said, "I've said all I'm going to say. If you brought me out here to ask me questions, I'm going back."

Chase knew she meant it. He went back over their conversation, trying to recall what they'd been talking about before he'd gotten off track. California. Webfeet. Safe ground. "Would you like some more cantaloupe?"

"No, thank you."

He'd spoiled her pleasure in it, and he wanted to kick himself. Eventually he'd learn all he wanted to know about her, but the process couldn't be rushed. "You ever been to California?"

"No. I've met people from there." Clearly striving to regain her composure, she took a deep breath, exhaled shakily, and then forced a tremulous smile. "They all look rich. I know they can't be, of course, but there's something about them—an air of sophistication. And they all wear store-bought clothes. Have you noticed that?"

"Not all of them. Maybe all the ones you've seen. Folks who can afford stage fare are usually well-heeled, I reckon. I saw poor folks down there as well as rich. The only thing most of them had in common, to my recollection, was faces as brown as raisins."

"Even the ladies?"

His mouth tightened slightly. "No, not the ladies, of course. They protect their skin." Touching her hat where it was still tucked under his belt, he added, "With sun-bonnets, mostly."

"Far prettier ones than that, I'd venture."

"Some of them. Truth to tell, I didn't have much truck with ladies while I was there."

Something in his expression and the way he said "ladies" told her his visit there had been unpleasant. She couldn't resist asking, "What took you down that way?"

"Timber. I logged in the redwoods for a spell. During a layoff, I went farther south looking for other work. If you think it gets hot here, you should be down there in the summer. Eggs'd fry on a wagon seat."

"Well, all that sun certainly makes for wonderful-tasting melon."

"It's even sweeter if it ripens on the vine." He took a sip of wine and winked at her over the rim of his cup. "Kind of like strawberries."

Franny seldom allowed herself more than a few sips of liquor, wine included, but tonight she decided to make an exception. Chase made her tense. She couldn't block him out as she did other men. Not in these circumstances, at least. She took a taste of the burgundy and gazed longingly at the basket, wishing for more melon. As if he read her thoughts, he speared another cube and offered it to her. This time she didn't demur. Leaning forward, she seized it with her teeth. To her dismay, juice spurted.

He groaned and wiped his eyes. Horrified, Franny gulped the mouthful of fruit. "Oh, dear! I'm sorry."

Parting his fingers, he peeked out at her, his smile laced with devilment. "Gotcha."

She gave a startled laugh. "You're impossible."

"Ain't I just?"

He chuckled and returned his attention to his chicken.

Franny did likewise. A comfortable silence settled over them, which she found difficult to credit. She took another sip of wine, wondering if its lulling effects could be the reason she was beginning to feel so relaxed.

Chase devoured two more pieces of chicken before she finished her first. She noticed that he left half the bowl of melon cubes for her. While she finished eating, he rolled onto his back to regard the starlit sky. Franny lingered over the meal, dreading the moment when her mouth would no longer be full and he would expect her to start talking again. She had no idea what more she might say to him. One could only discuss cantaloupe and Californians for so long.

Eventually, though, her stomach began to feel full, and she knew if she kept eating, she'd make herself sick. After tossing the scraps into the darkness for the wild animals, she began wiping the plates with a napkin and putting the food away. When she reached for the wine jug, he said, "Leave that out. I don't know about you, but I'd like some more."

Franny wasn't at all sure she should join him. But when he sat up to refill their mugs, he didn't extend her the courtesy of a choice. He simply poured her more wine and handed her the cup. She accepted it without comment. Crossing his legs and tucking his heels snugly under his thighs, he winced and leaned forward slightly, elbows on his knees. Though his ribs were clearly paining him, he was surprisingly agile for so tall and well-muscled a man. He looked so comfortable she spread her skirts and assumed the position herself.

His eyes warming on hers, he said, "You would have made a real pretty little squaw with that silver-blond hair and those big green eyes. In my father's day, some enterprising young warrior would have stolen you. With that hair, he could have gotten a hundred horses for you, and that's low bid."

"The fifty dollars you spent tonight is outrageous enough."

Franny immediately wanted to call that back. But the words were out before she thought. Silence descended. A tense silence. For the night, she belonged to this man, and her thoughtless comment had reminded them both of that.

Searching for something, anything, she might say to move beyond the moment, she rubbed her hands on her skirt. "Cross-legged. Is that the way all Comanche women sit?"

"Sat," he corrected. Then he shrugged. "Not all, I guess, but a fair number. They seldom had chairs, you know, and sitting any other way would have gotten hard on the back."

She couldn't help but note that he referred to his father's people in the past tense, and she wondered how he felt about that. An entire society, destroyed. Since taking up her profession, Franny had often found solace between the covers of a book, and because of her friendship with Indigo, reading about the Plains Indians had interested her for a short time. Only for a short time. It soon became apparent to her that most of the books in print about the Comanches or any other tribe had been written from an extremely biased point of view.

"It must be very difficult for you and your father, knowing that those few of his people who survived are all on reservations now. The way of life he once loved no longer exists."

"He doesn't look at it that way."

Franny wondered how else one could look at it. Because his talking relieved her of the necessity, she decided to ask.

"It's my father's belief that his people live on in us," he explained softly. "As long as we sing their songs, they will never die. The Comanches were a wonderful people, and wonderful people always leave a mark that can never be erased."

It was a beautiful thought. Franny sighed and took another sip of wine. Following his example and bracing her elbows on her knees, she allowed herself to relax a little more, beginning to believe, even though it was against her better judgment, that perhaps all he truly did want from her was friendship. He had made no other move toward her.

"The People maintained that there was no yesterday, only tomorrow," he went on, "so my father never allows himself to mourn what was. He keeps his gaze fixed always on the horizon. What happened a minute, or a day, or a year ago doesn't matter. Who he was then doesn't matter. Only now and the way he plans to go forward has importance."

"That's very idealistic."

"But true." In the moonlight, his eyes glittered like blue velvet studded with diamonds. "Think about it. Right now, try to concentrate on this very moment." He grew quiet for an instant then smiled at her. "You see? Before you could even capture it, the moment was gone. Forever lost to you, and you can never reclaim it.

When you think of it like that, it's sort of ludicrous that so many people dwell on what happened to them yesterday. It's done, over, dust on the wind."

"But a vivid memory, nonetheless."

"If you let it be."

"Sometimes our yesterdays control our todays and tomorrows, no matter how much we might wish otherwise."

He shook his head. "The past counts for nothing because the moment something happens, it's behind you."

It made a wonderful kind of sense. She smiled wistfully. "If only life could truly be so simple."

"Life is like a blanket you draw around yourself. You make your own weave."

As he spoke, he chuckled as if at a private joke. Fascinated, Franny studied him. He was more like Indigo than she had first thought, she realized. As recently as yesterday morning, she could never have imagined his saying such lovely, profound things. But gazing into his eyes, she knew he sincerely meant them. Just as Indigo always did. She also knew his words were aimed directly at her, that he was trying to tell her she wasn't bound forever to be who and what she was right now, that she could change if she wished.

If only it could be that easy.

Wishing. Sometimes it seemed to her that she had spent her whole life wishing, and always for impossible things. No matter what he said, circumstances often created the weave of your life, and there was nothing one could do to alter that. "Leave here with me," he whispered.

The words slipped softly into Franny's mind. For a moment, she thought she imagined them. But when she refocused on Chase's face, she could tell by his expression that she hadn't.

"Leave here with me," he repeated. "When my ribs heal and I go, come with me. No obligations. Just as friends. I'll help you find a job somewhere. You can put all of this behind you and forget it ever happened. Wolf's Landing is a small place, and even if you run into familiar faces on down the line, yours will never be recognizable. With your face washed and your hair up, you look nothing like Franny from the Lucky Nugget."

She knew she looked nothing like Franny from the Lucky Nugget; she had gone to great lengths to be certain of that. Trying to think of a way she might explain her circumstances to him without giving too much away, she gazed off into the blackness of the woods that bordered the schoolyard. She realized now that she had sorely misjudged Chase. His relentless pursuit of her stemmed from philanthropic motives, not carnal ones. He sincerely wanted to help her, not as a hero who swept her off her feet and into his arms, but as a friend. The thought brought tears to her eyes.

"If thinking about leaving here frightens you," he whispered, "don't let it. Until you're on your feet, I'll stay around. If things go wrong, you'll have me to lean on."

Franny blinked. Oh, God. It was so unfair. To have someone offer such a thing and not be able to accept. The most awful part of it was, she doubted she could ever make him understand, not without revealing too many secrets.

In a tight voice, she said, "I appreciate the offer, Chase, but there are reasons I can't accept."

He studied her for a long moment. "What reasons? Maybe I can help."

"No. Perhaps you'd try. But some difficulties can't be solved."

"My family isn't like most. You know Indigo would be there for you. And my parents are exactly like her. Between them and me, somehow we can iron out the tangles for you."

That would have cost a fortune, not to mention that it would take a miracle. "My tangles are a bit worse than most, I'm afraid."

"Tell me."

He looked so earnest that for the first time in nine years, she was tempted. But common sense returned before she gave in to the urge. Even with the best of intentions, Chase might accidentally repeat something she told him. If the truth of her identity ever became public knowledge, it would be disastrous. As far as that went, it would cause irreversible harm even if people only suspected who she really was. Grants Pass, her hometown, was far enough to provide a buffer as long as she was careful, but not far enough to guarantee against gossip if she let her guard down. There were too many people she loved who could be badly hurt.

"Please don't misunderstand," she said shakily. "I'll always be grateful that you've offered to help me." She managed a smile. "I've had offers before, of course, but always with strings attached. You're the first man ever who didn't want something out of it for himself."

His mouth tightened. "That's not exactly true. There is something in it for me."

"Oh."

He grimaced. "Nothing like you're thinking. And don't take that to mean I don't find you extremely attractive. I do. It's just that—" He took a deep breath. "I'd like to help you start over without anything like that entering into it. You understand? No obligations, nothing messy. Just as a friend. I need to do that."

Franny frowned slightly. "You *need* to? I'm afraid I don't understand."

He scratched his nose and gazed into his mug of wine. In the darkness, Franny knew he couldn't see anything, that he was focusing on the contents of the cup only because he found looking at her unsettling. "Once, a long time ago, I could have helped someone, but in the end I turned my back and didn't. Since meeting you, I've realized how wrong that was." He finally glanced up. "I can't go back and change the past. I can only go forward. But if I can help you, maybe I can at least stop feeling guilty."

"I see."

"Probably not. It's a poor explanation, I know. But about the best I can do."

"If rescuing a soiled dove is your plan, I'm afraid you've chosen the wrong woman. There is no way out for me. In several years—" She waved her hand. "I'm hoping that in time my circumstances may become a bit more manageable, that perhaps then I can choose another means of making a living, but until then, I have no choice but to keep doing what I do."

"Everyone has a choice, Franny."

"No," she said simply. "Some of us don't."

His frustration was evident in his expression.

"This has been lovely," she told him. "But now I think I should go back. If you'll walk with me, I'll return that fifty dollars. There's still plenty of my shift left. I can make up for the lost time."

"You're backing me up against a wall here. I can't leave you in that hellhole. If I can't get you out of there one way, I'll do it another."

"You may need a stick of dynamite and several pry bars," she said lightly.

He shook his head. "I won't walk away this time. Make up your mind to that."

That determined glint was back in his eyes. He was dead serious, she realized. Come what may, he intended to get her away from here. If he had been any other man, Franny might have been amused. But from the first she had sensed Chase Wolf had a dangerous edge. He wasn't a man to take lightly, and she had a feeling he seldom failed to accomplish something he set out to do.

"If I have to, I'll take a page out of my father's book and kidnap you," he said teasingly.

Despite the levity in his voice, Franny couldn't discount the threat. Like everyone else in town, she had heard the rumors about Chase Wolf. He was a rebel, no question of it. If he decided to kidnap a woman, he'd probably do it, the devil take the consequences. It wouldn't be the first time he had thumbed his nose at authority.

Something in her expression must have told him what she was thinking, for his own softened. "Don't start feeling afraid of me again, Franny. I'm harmless, really."

Steel wrapped in velvet, she thought nonsensically. Not exactly what she would term harmless. She threw the remainder of her wine away and stowed her mug in the basket. As she rose, she said, "It really is time I was getting back."

She expected him to argue. Instead, he pushed to his feet, put his mug and the bottle inside the basket, and then helped her to fold the blanket. Stepping close to even the edges, Franny accidentally brushed her knuckles against his. The contact electrified her, and she glanced up only to find herself unable to look away. For an awful moment, she thought he might kiss her. And what was worse, she wanted him to. So badly that she ached.

There was no question; Chase Wolf was dangerous.

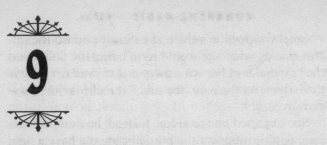

9

Long after Chase escorted Franny back to
the saloon and went home to seek his own bed, he lay
awake remembering the incredulous expression in her
eyes when she realized he had no intention of accompanying her back upstairs to get his money's worth out
of her in the traditional way by making love to her.

Not that he believed for a minute that Franny thought
of the sexual act as making love. If indeed she thought
about it at all.

A sad smile settled on his mouth as he recalled her
hobby area, separated and hidden from the rest of the
room by a screen. Franny, with her true self walled off
and hidden from prying eyes.

One question ate at Chase. Why? What string of
events had led Franny to her present life, and what prevented her from putting it behind her? He recalled the

whimsical clown face she had embroidered on the pillow, the lacy dress on her sewing table, the collection of sketches and flower art upon her walls, and her well-read Bible, left open at the story of Mary Magdalene. A young woman like her didn't belong in the Lucky Nugget. She should be married and embroidering pillows for her own babies. She should have a man to love her, shield her and provide for her.

Closing his eyes, Chase tried to imagine himself filling that role, and the image took shape in his mind all too easily. The pictures filled him with a sense of rightness and contentment. Recalling her innocent-looking green eyes and the way her mouth dimpled at the corners when he wrung a smile from her, he couldn't shake the feeling that his footsteps had been leading him toward her all of his life.

Crazy, so crazy. Or was it? According to his father, every man had his own personal destiny, a purpose he was born to fulfill, and until he found it, he wandered through life, always searching, never satisfied. Chase had experienced that feeling, but now that he'd stumbled upon Franny, it was gone. Maybe he was destined by fate to be the man who plucked her out of her present circumstances to give her the home she deserved.

The yearning within him to do just that was undeniable, and as he drifted to sleep, a tiny seed of determination found fertile ground. During the course of the night while he slept, that seed took root, and by morning when he awakened, he was filled with purpose. Immediately upon opening his eyes, he began planning his strategy.

That evening, the moment it turned dark, he went

back to the Lucky Nugget with another fifty dollars in hand. Within thirty minutes, he had spirited Franny away from the saloon to go walking with him in the moonlight again.

"Are we returning to the playground?" she asked a bit nervously.

"Not tonight." Glancing down at her, Chase couldn't miss the way she gnawed at her lower lip, and he smiled in spite of himself. "There's nothing to worry about, Franny. Gus knows you left the saloon in my company. My ass'll be grass and he'll be a hungry goat if anything happens to you."

She shook her head. "It's not that. After last night, I'm convinced you're harmless."

"Harmless, am I?" He couldn't resist teasing her. "Never tell a man he's harmless. He'll set out to prove you wrong every time. Trustworthy, maybe."

She made an exasperated little sound. "This is no laughing matter."

"What isn't?"

"This entire situation."

"And what situation is that?"

"You paying such an outlandish amount of money two nights running to monopolize my time. You can't continue to do this, you know."

"Do what?"

Her voice rose an octave. "Waste your money this way."

"Care to see me for free?"

She rolled her eyes. "I have to make a living."

"Then I'll keep wasting my money. Not that I think it's a waste."

"At this rate, you'll soon go broke."

Despite the sharpness of her tone, Chase saw the genuine concern in her eyes. He couldn't help recalling how convinced he'd been that she was a gold digger. How wrong he had been. "Why don't you let me worry about my money," he told her gently. "I won't spend more than I can afford."

In truth, every cent Chase had in the bank was already targeted, and if he meant to attain his goals on schedule, he could ill afford to spend much more seeing Franny. But, the way he saw it, it was a matter of priorities. He already had one sizable tract of timberland, and if he couldn't afford to purchase more right away, he was still young. Franny needed him now.

Lost in thought, it took Chase a moment to notice that she was nervously wringing her hands, a habit that he found endearing because it was something his mother often did when she was upset. It was a purely feminine gesture, he thought, one that conveyed anxiety far more eloquently than words.

He leaned forward slightly to see her face as they walked. "A penny for them?"

"You can't afford to give me a penny for them."

Chase laughed in spite of himself. Then he sobered because he could see that she was truly distressed. "Franny, I wouldn't spend the money if I didn't have it to spare."

"No one has that much to spare." She came to a stop and took a deep breath. "We must have a talk about this, Chase."

"All right. So talk."

"I've been friends with Indigo for a number of years.

I know all about your aspirations to be a timber baron one day."

"So?"

She lifted her hands. "So? If you spend money high, wide, and handsome, you'll never accomplish your goals. I know you must be dipping into your savings. You worked very hard for every cent of that money, and I don't want to be responsible for your spending any of it frivolously."

"I'll bear that in mind."

"Then take me back to my room. I'll return the fifty dollars you gave me tonight, and you can stop this foolishness before you've piddled a large sum away on nothing."

"On nothing?"

"Whatever it is you want from me, I can't give it to you. Don't you see? Your bringing me out here, pushing me on the swing last night and holding my hand! And tonight, taking me for a stroll in the moonlight." She touched her throat, her gaze fixed on one of his shirt buttons. "What point is there in it? You're behaving as if you're . . . as if you're courting me."

"And what's wrong with that?"

"There's no future in it, for one thing. And for another, why would any man want to? Find yourself some nice girl, Chase. Take *her* for walks in the moonlight. It won't cost you a penny."

"Maybe I don't want to be with another girl."

"That's silly." With an obvious effort, she raised her eyes to his. By her expression, he knew what it cost her to say what she did next. "I'm a . . . a prostitute. Brushing the starch out of my hair and washing my face doesn't change that. I don't know why you're doing this, but whatever your reason, it's useless. I am what I am, and that can never change."

"Why can't it?"

"It just can't, that's all. If you have some crazy notion of saving me from myself and turning my life around, forget it. I'm a lost cause."

"Franny, no one is a lost cause." As he said the words, Chase realized how sincerely he meant them. "And there's always a way out. For you, maybe it's me. Let's at least give this a chance, hm?"

"No." She gave her head an emphatic shake. "I don't want to see you again. I mean it. Take me back to the saloon, get your money, and smarten up."

Chase took her arm and guided her back into a walk. "We came out here for a walk, and we're taking one."

With a weary sigh, she pressed the back of her wrist to her forehead. "All right, fine. But don't tell me later that I didn't warn you. There's no future in this, period, and nothing you do or say can change that."

"Fine. No future. But we have tonight and as many other nights as I can pay for before my money runs out."

"You're crazy."

"Probably. But it's my money, and I can spend it any damned way I like."

Chase took her to one of his favorite places along Shallows Creek. A great gnarled old oak grew there, its heavily laden branches fragmenting the moonlight so it lay upon the green grass below it like scattered pearls on velvet. Instead of sitting beside him on the bank, Franny remained standing and leaned against the tree trunk, her hands primly folded and held tensely at her waist. She stared fixedly at the water as it gurgled past, giving Chase the eerie sensation that she was with him only in body.

He decided to allow her to escape him in that fashion for a couple of minutes, for he sensed how genuinely upset she was. In a way, her attack of conscience amused him. She took money from men nearly every night of the world, yet she balked at taking his. He supposed she must feel that theirs wasn't a fair exchange, but the way he saw it, it was far more equitable than the other way around. There was nothing right about a woman being reduced to selling herself to men for coin. Nothing right about it, and nothing fair.

After several minutes, Chase broke the silence. "It's a beautiful night, isn't it? I love the sound of the wind in the trees. My father says it's God whispering His wisdom, and that if one listens, the words will become clear."

She made no reply, and Chase turned to look at her. The vague expression on her face told him that she had immersed herself in images he couldn't see. The realization both infuriated and saddened him, the first because she could separate herself from him so easily, the second because she seemed to feel it was necessary. He wasn't a threat to her. At least not in the usual way.

The thought gave Chase pause, and he began to wonder if perhaps he didn't threaten Franny in other ways he couldn't fathom. He pushed to his feet and slowly approached her. She seemed unaware of his movements. Coming to a stop before her, he nearly cupped her chin in his hand, then thought better of it. Physical touches wouldn't force her back to reality. In the darkness of her room, she endured much more and successfully blocked it out.

"How old are you, Franny?"

Something flickered in her eyes, and Chase smiled slightly. To respond to direct questions, one had to think.

"Yoo-hoo. How old are you?"

The blankness slipped slowly from her expression, and she focused on him, looking mildly irritated. "How old do I look?"

"About sixteen."

She wrinkled her nose. "I was never sixteen. I went from thirteen to ninety with no birthdays in between."

Chase had the awful feeling she truly had. "And before, when you were thirteen?"

Her mouth twisted in a forlorn smile. "I was a little girl who still believed in fairy tales."

Feeling a little sick, Chase swallowed. What kind of men could slake their lust on the body of a child? What kind of a world allowed the innocent to be victimized?

"What happened, Franny? Can you tell me that much? Last night, you mentioned your father dying, that you were left orphaned. Was there no one to help you? Were you forced into this profession by hunger?"

"No, I wasn't starving," she said hollowly. "I suppose if I had been, then you could excuse me? Find what I did justifiable?"

There was such bitterness in the question. Chase hadn't meant to sound judgmental. "I'm not condemning you, Franny, just trying to learn more about you."

She pushed away from the tree. "There's nothing to learn. I have no past." After putting some distance between them, she turned back to face him, her gaze touching on the tree trunk behind him. The unmistakable longing in her expression caught at his heart. He knew she had seen all the initials that had been carved in the tree's bark by young lovers of years gone by. This spot along Shallows Creek was a favorite trysting place, had been for decades, and probably always would be. As she regarded the many hearts and cupid's arrows that had been carved by zealous young lovers, she added in an oddly hard and expressionless voice, "No past, and no future."

That was really the way she saw it, he realized. These weren't well-rehearsed histrionics in a bid for his sympathy. Drawn to her, Chase ate up the ground between them with measured strides, not at all certain what he meant to do when he reached her. He only knew there was a yearning in her eyes he couldn't ignore. When he drew to a stop, he became aware of two things, that she was of more diminutive stature than he had realized, and that his nearness unsettled her.

Chase smiled slightly as he cupped her small chin in his hand. A prostitute whose mouth quivered when a man cornered her? What an enigma she was. There should be nothing about men to alarm her, yet he had the feeling just the opposite was true.

That mouth. It was perfectly shaped, the upper lip delicately etched in a bow, the lower pouty and full, the color of pale rose petals unfurling to gentle spring sunlight. It was the kind of mouth a man fantasized about and yearned to taste. Standing as closely as he was, the tips of her breasts grazed his shirt, and he could feel the heat of her searing through the layers of linen that bandaged his ribs. Not relinquishing his hold on her chin, he settled his other hand at her waist.

Dipping his head, Chase sought that sweet mouth with his own, having every intention of kissing her. But just before their lips touched he looked into her eyes and saw nothingness. Just that quickly, and Franny was no longer there with him. He froze, feeling as if someone had buried a fist in his guts.

"Franny," he whispered.

Lifting her face slightly, he studied her expression, amazed at how adept she was at separating herself from reality the moment she felt threatened. Her chin lifted easily in his grasp. Beneath his hand where it rode at her waist, he felt no tension. Chase knew he could divest her of her clothing, lay her on the grass, and do anything he wished to her lovely body. She wouldn't resist. He doubted she would even be aware of him. But he wanted more from her than physical acquiescence.

"Tell me about the dream pictures you see," he whispered huskily. "Where is it you go?"

She didn't respond, so Chase repeated the request more loudly. She blinked and her breathing altered, much as it might have if she had been surfacing from a deep sleep. "Pardon?"

"Just now," he repeated, "what were you imagining?"

Her eyes fastened on his, bewildered and shimmering in the moonglow. Such beautiful eyes, he thought. He could lose himself in them for forever.

"What kind of things do you dream about?" he asked more specifically.

"I . . . I don't know what you mean."

She knew exactly what he meant, and he knew it.

"You escape into images. Indigo mentioned it to Jake, and Jake told me. It's how you survive the nights, isn't it? How you live through being used by the men who visit your room."

She tried to twist away, but Chase was prepared for that and held her fast. As he tightened his grip on her chin, her mouth puckered invitingly under the pressure of his fingers. He yearned to taste those lips, to settle his own over them, to stake a claim she couldn't deny. But he wanted her aware of him when he did it, not off somewhere in her blasted dream visions.

"You can't escape me quite that easily," he told her.

Looking up at him, Franny knew his warning was double-edged, that he was not only telling her she couldn't slip from his grasp but that he wouldn't let her escape him into unawareness, either. Tall, dark, and whipcord lean, he filled her vision, his shoulders broad, his arms tensed to forestall her if she made any sudden moves. That alone would have alarmed her. The determined glint she saw in his eyes unsettled her even more. Chase Wolf wasn't a man who did anything by halfway measures, and when he possessed a woman, he would possess her completely. His expression told her more plainly than words that he had decided he wanted her.

Franny's pulse accelerated. In her panic, she hatched a dozen plans of escape, all of which she discarded as absurd. She couldn't outrun the man, and even if she could, she had only one place to go, the saloon. He would simply intercept her there. In her room on the table sat fifty dollars in gold, the price he had paid for an evening in her company. She could spend the time with him here, or risk having to spend it with him in her bed. Normally she wouldn't have found the latter alarming, but she sensed that Chase would demand her close attention while he joined with her physically. There would be no escaping into dreams, no separateness from reality as this man's hands claimed her body.

He angled a thumb lightly across her parted lips, his mouth tightening slightly at the corners as he measured her rapid intake and expulsion of air. She could feel her pulse slamming beneath his fingertips where they pressed beneath her jaw. The signs of her fear didn't escape him; she could tell that by his mildly amused expression.

Releasing her so suddenly that she was caught off guard, he turned back toward the tree. Shaken, Franny hugged her waist and watched as he drew his knife from the scabbard at his hip. The weapon's blade glinted bluish silver in the moonlight as he applied it to the tree bark. With flicks of his strong wrist, he removed bits of bark. Watching from behind him, Franny felt tears begin to sting her eyes as her name took shape.

It was so silly. She knew it was. But having her name carved in a tree by a boy had been one of the things she had missed as a girl and had long since accepted would never come to pass. Without realizing it, Chase was fulfilling a dream. Except, of course, that the raw gouges he was making in the bark would stand alone. No man in his right mind would link his name with hers, on an old tree or anywhere else.

Incredulous, Franny watched as Chase finished off her name and began carving another beneath it. A *C* was quickly followed by an *H.* By the time he finished and began carving the heart to encircle both their names, she was shaking. When he finally straightened and smiled at her, she was convinced he had to be mocking her.

Franny, the whore, who would never be loved.

All rationality fleeing her mind, she reacted instinctively and ran. As she cut through the moonlit forest, she heard Chase, his tone unmistakably bewildered, call out to her. She didn't stop or slow down for fear he might catch up with her. She was nearly to the saloon before it occurred to her that he must not be chasing her. With those long legs of his, there would have been no contest, and she knew it.

Left alone in the woods, Chase gazed after Franny in confusion, uncertain what he had done to offend her. Carving their names in the tree? Surely not. He had meant it be symbolic of the feelings he was developing for her, not as an insult. Yet that was how she had acted, as if he had somehow humiliated her.

Patience, he admonished himself. He had to be patient. It might be a good idea if he backed off for a few days and gave her some breathing room. As abhorrent as the thought was to him of her working again, he knew he had to move more slowly with her. He couldn't expect her to capitulate overnight. Maybe if he gave her some time to think things over, she'd be more receptive the next time he went to see her.

10

As she had once a month for eight years, Franny rented a buggy the following Saturday morning and headed home for a visit. Though the roads were well maintained and easily traversed during the summer months, the trip was still long and grueling, taking her nearly the entire day. Ten miles outside of Grants Pass, there was a deserted miner's shack where she always stopped to wash away the road dust and change her clothes. When she emerged from the dilapidated cabin, Franny from Wolf's Landing no longer existed. Francine Graham, a fashionably dressed, well-coiffed young woman, had taken her place. Franny's face-concealing sunbonnet was carefully hidden at the bottom of her satchel along with all her secrets.

Seeing her family didn't fill Franny with the joy that it usually did. Chase Wolf had opened old wounds within her and forced her to look at how lonely and meaningless her life was. Spending time with him had rekindled a longing within her for things she had long since abandoned all hope of having, and the ache inside her couldn't be assuaged.

While she was home, Franny tried to banish Chase from her thoughts, she truly did, but it seemed there were reminders of him everywhere she turned. The following week was Alaina's sixteenth birthday, and the girl could scarcely contain her excitement. Had Francine gotten her a pretty present? The question called to Franny's mind the lacy dress on her sewing table and the way Chase had studied it.

And so it went.

Studying the beloved faces of those in her family, Franny reminded herself that her purpose in life had already been decided. She had no choices, and she never would. Chase Wolf was dangerous to her. And whether he intended to be or not, he was also cruel. For reasons she couldn't fathom, he was trying to make her believe he wanted to court her. The very notion was absurd. Men didn't court whores. Or respect them. When they fell in love it was with chaste women, good women, pure women. Never with prostitutes. She would be a hundred times a fool if she began to think it could be otherwise.

Besides, she scolded herself, even if, by some strange stroke of fate, Chase did fall in love with her, she came with an extremely large, ready-made family. The sum of money needed each month to support them and see to their special needs precluded any possibility of a young man assuming financial responsibility for them. It would certainly take more than love to convince him to do it. He'd have to be out of his blooming mind.

During her visit home, Franny caught her younger brother, Frankie, watching her at different times with a speculative look in his eye. She couldn't help but recall the night he and his young friends had shown up at the Lucky Nugget. When she thought of how close she had come to being discovered, she trembled. Had Frankie somehow connected her with the whore in Wolf's Landing?

At moments, Franny had to bite her tongue to keep from scolding Frankie. She knew why he and his friends had traveled so far from home to visit a saloon. The scamps. Though she realized her brother was reaching a manly age now that he had turned seventeen, she wanted to castigate him for seeking out the company of a loose woman. True, by going so far afield he had at least tried to be discreet. But the fact still remained that he had visited Wolf's Landing to procure the services of a sporting woman. In her estimation, he was not only too young for such assignations, but had been raised to know better. It would break their mother's heart if she found out, and Franny couldn't help but fear that the way a young man stepped forward into life might be the way he continued to go. She wanted her brother to be a good, God-fearing man who lived a clean life, not the sort who visited saloons and consorted with prostitutes.

Unfortunately, Franny couldn't very well confront her brother about his transgression without exposing herself.

* * *

When Franny got back to Wolf's Landing Monday evening, she stopped by May Belle's room and found her friend crying. Alarmed, Franny stepped into the bedroom and drew the door closed. "May Belle, what is it? What's happened?"

Clearly embarrassed at having been caught at a weak moment, May Belle turned her tear-swollen face into her pillow. Her shoulders jerked on a sob. Concerned, Franny sat on the edge of the bed and lightly touched her friend's brassy hair. "Is there something I can do?" she asked gently.

"Yeah," was May Belle's muffled reply. "You can knock some sense into this empty old head of mine."

Franny patted the woman's shoulder. "Oh, now. I don't know a single soul with more sense than you have."

"Not here lately."

With a loud sniff, May Belle rolled onto her side. Now that advanced years prevented her from entertaining gentlemen, she no longer painted her face. Franny thought she was far prettier without the heavy makeup. The lines in her skin were less noticeable, and her natural rosy complexion lent her a healthy glow that the powder had hidden.

"Oh, Franny," she whispered shakily. "As many times as I've warned you against it, you'll never believe what I've gone and done."

Perplexed, Franny tried to think what it might be that her friend referred to.

"I've fallen in love," May Belle blurted.

For an instant, Franny felt joyful. Aside from her

mother, there was no woman on earth more kindly or loving than May Belle, and it was Franny's fondest wish to see her find peace and happiness in her retirement years. But a man? Retired or no, love interests were risky for a prostitute. May Belle herself had always espoused that belief and had been very outspoken to Franny in defense of it. The sporting girl who gave a man her heart was begging for trouble, usually more than she could handle.

Years ago May Belle had fallen in love with a gambler and believed in his promises of a wedding ring, a cottage, and a white picket fence. She had begun traveling with him. One night when the gambler was down on his luck, he sold May Belle's favors to strangers in the saloon below their rented quarters. Reformed and determined to remain so, May Belle had protested his actions. In retaliation, the gambler beat her nigh unto death and left her behind with no money and no one to tend her while she recovered from his abuse. May Belle had been forced to prostitute herself to survive, and eventually she had ended up here in Wolf's Landing, wiser for having endured what she had. In all the years since, she had never allowed herself to grow fond of another man, and she frequently cautioned Franny against doing so.

"Who is he?" Franny asked.

"Shorty," May Belle replied forlornly.

Franny nearly giggled. Shorty? The old miner was the farthest thing from a Romeo she could imagine, short, potbellied, and missing more than half of his teeth. Safe in her work disguise, Franny had ventured downstairs a few times when Shorty was there. He had always been polite and kindly to her, and she knew him to be a good friend of Indigo's. But the sort of man one fell in love with? Not in her estimation.

"Oh, I know he doesn't look like much," May Belle admitted. "But when you get to be my age, honey, a man's appearance isn't what matters. He's got a big heart, and the way he treats me—" Her voice caught. "He makes me feel like I'm somebody special, you know?"

"So what's the problem?"

"I ain't fool enough to swallow that hook again. That's the problem."

For all his shortcomings, the old fellow didn't strike Franny as the sort who might use and abuse a woman, then leave her. When she voiced that sentiment, May Belle gave a derisive snort. "In the end, honey, they're all that kind. At least when it comes to gals like us. I've been a whore for over half my life, and being retired don't change my colors. Even someone like Shorty would eventually regain his senses and remember that. I don't want to be tangled up with him when it happens. He's been after me to marry him. Can you believe it? Says we'll build us a pretty little house along the crick somewhere, that he'll plant me climbing roses all along the porch, and we can sit out there of a summer evening and listen to the crickets sing."

"It sounds lovely," Franny whispered wistfully.

"Yeah, and while it lasted, it probably would be. But sooner or later, one way or another, I'd come out a loser."

Franny could think of nothing she might say. After a moment, she murmured, "Maybe he doesn't care what you did for a living, May Belle. Maybe he—"

"It's the rare man who doesn't care," the older woman snapped. "They might claim they don't, but in the end it always comes back to haunt you. When I was still working, I tucked away money to build myself a nest egg. If I married him, he could take my money and tell me to go whistle Dixie. I'm not that big a fool."

Neither was Franny. There was a parallel to be drawn between May Belle's problems with Shorty and her own with Chase. If she was smart, she'd take the old woman's warnings to heart and not let herself believe, even for a second, that Chase Wolf might have a sincere regard for her. Once a whore, always a whore. Only a miracle could change that, and God surely had far more important things to do than make miracles for prostitutes.

Her visit with May Belle still fresh in her mind, Franny was pleased when Chase showed up at her door that evening right before dark. His brisk knock told her who it was. None of her other customers came before the sun was completely down, for one thing, and they never announced their arrival. It was against the posted rules.

Emboldened by May Belle's warnings, Franny let Chase in, then turned to open her top bureau drawer, drawing out the one hundred dollars in gold he had previously paid her. The coins were bundled in a lace-edged handkerchief, and she guessed by his expression that he had no idea what was inside until she put it in his hand.

Avoiding his intense blue gaze, Franny swept around him to open the door and gestured for him to leave. "I don't want your money," she informed him politely but firmly. "I didn't earn it, and I don't accept charity. Now, if you'll be so good as to leave, I have to dress for my shift."

"Franny, can we talk for a minute?"

His gentle, cajoling tone made fear chill her spine. He was breaking down all the carefully erected walls that she had been hiding behind for so many years. In doing so, he was shattering the insulation she kept between her and reality. When he looked into her eyes, she felt naked in a way that she had never felt with another man, yet she knew he had no intention of using her body. He wanted something more, and she had nothing else to give. He was trying to make her believe in impossible dreams. If she let down her guard, he would destroy her in the end.

"I want you to leave," she insisted. "Men don't pay me to talk, which is just as well because I'm not much good at it. They want one thing when they come to see me, and that's all I'm interested in providing." She gestured toward her sign which was visible with the door open. "From now on, abide by my rules, Mr. Wolf, or don't darken my threshold. No lights, no conversation, no all-night customers. Well intentioned though I know you are, if I allow you to monopolize my time, I may lose all my other customers, and I can't afford to do that."

"Franny, I—"

"Go ahead!" she said shrilly. "Cause a big ruckus and make me lose my job. I can earn my living as a whore anywhere. On down the road, there's another town, another saloon, another room just waiting for me to claim it. If I have to leave here, it won't be pleasant, but it won't be the end of the world. I have a little money set aside to tide me over until I can find other work."

That familiar glint entered his eyes. A muscle sprang up along his jaw, pulsing with his every heartbeat. "Fine," he said evenly.

Franny jumped when he slapped the bundle of money down on the bureau. Loosening the knots in the handkerchief, he drew out a ten-dollar gold piece and set it aside. "By the rules," he said softly, inclining his head toward the sign. "I'll take whatever I can get."

Feeling frozen inside, Franny tightened her hand on the doorknob. "I don't start my shift until after dark," she reminded him, "and as you can see, I'm not completely ready for work yet."

He regarded her face, which was devoid of paint, then glanced downward at her silk wrapper. "You'll do. I don't like your hair starched, anyway."

With that, he closed the distance between them with slow, measured strides. After flipping her sign over to read *Occupied*, he curled his strong fingers over her hand where it was clenched around the doorknob. With a relentless but gentle pressure, he pried her fingers away and pushed the door closed. Holding her gaze with those glittering, midnight blue eyes, he whispered, "I assume that you do work on the bed?"

Before Franny guessed what he meant to do, he bent toward her, catching her with steely arms at the backs of her knees and around her shoulders. She gasped as he swept her up against his chest. By the way his teeth were clenched, she knew his ribs were screaming with pain.

"What're you—" She pushed ineffectually at his shoulders. "Put me down this instant."

"You're talking," he reminded her. "That's against the rules. Remember?"

"Put me down!" she repeated furiously.

After taking two long strides, he obliged her. Franny fell with an ungraceful plop onto the bed. The support ropes creaked in protest. She tried to fling herself to one side, but he was too quick for her. Following her down, he seized her shoulders and pressed her back onto the pillow. Supporting himself on one knee, his chest mantling hers and barring her escape, he whispered, "Going somewhere?"

"It isn't dark yet. I don't work before dark."

"You're talking again. I didn't think that was part of your services. Can I take that to mean we can dispense with that rule?" Before she could form a reply, he said, "Good. Sex just wouldn't be the same without a little conversation."

Never had Franny felt such strength in a man's hands. When she tried to move, he tensed his arms against her and held her fast. The complete ease with which he did it frightened her.

"I do not appreciate your manhandling me, Mr. Wolf. You're behaving like a barbarian."

"My wild side coming out, I guess." He released her and sat on the bed facing her. Leaning toward her, he said, "I'm not manhandling you now. Is this better?"

"Your leaving would be better yet."

He laughed softly. "What's the matter, Franny? Are you afraid your dream images won't save you this time?"

That was exactly what she was afraid of, what she had always been afraid of when she was with him.

From the beginning, she had sensed a relentlessness in him.

With his free hand, he touched her cheek. The contact was searing and nearly took her breath away. Franny squeezed her eyes closed, frantically trying to conjure a picture into which she might escape. All she saw was blackness. The calloused tips of his fingers were textured like raw silk, eliciting an unwelcome response from her sensitive nerve endings.

Raw silk against satin. A breathless, electrical stillness settled over Franny. She was not only completely aware of him, but acutely so. She could have sworn she even heard her blood rushing. His hand skimmed a burning path to her throat. Then lower. She felt his fingertips lightly trace the V neckline of her wrapper.

Shame welled within her, a shame so thick it nearly strangled her. Holding herself rigid, she tried to stifle the sob that pushed up from her chest. In her mind's eye, she saw his piercing blue gaze trailing over her. The palm of his hand swept with agonizing slowness over the silk bodice of her wrapper, his touch so light she had to concentrate to feel the contact, yet staking a claim she couldn't ignore or deny. The peak of her breast went hard and thrust upward in anticipation.

He gave a low, satisfied laugh. "No pictures, Franny? No dream places to hide inside?"

Her stifled sob broke free and came upward in a ragged rush. Tears of humiliation squeezed out from under her tightly closed eyelids. In that instant, she hated Chase Wolf as she had never hated anyone—for making her feel.

Unable to bear it a second longer, she flung herself

away from him and scrambled off the bed. Making a dive for the bureau, she snatched up the bundle of money and threw it at him. "Get out!" she cried. "Other men can buy me. You cannot! I don't ever want to see you again. Never, do you hear me?"

Coins hit the wood floor and rolled in all directions. His gaze fiery and relentless, Chase pushed slowly up from the bed. "Keep the money, Franny. You obviously need it a whole lot more than I do." He laughed again, but this time the sound was harsh and cut right through her. "Some people just never learn. And I guess I'm one of them. The bottom line is, you don't want to be helped. You like your life just as it is."

She cupped a trembling hand over her eyes, aware of him in every pore of her skin as he stepped past her to the door. Another sob welled up from her chest and tore free. She hated herself for that. But she hated him more.

At the door, she heard him pause. A long silence stretched between them. As surely as if it were a tangible force, she could feel his gaze resting on her.

"No woman has to sell her body," he told her softly. "There are always other options. Always. I'm willing to help you." He hesitated for a moment, then plunged on. "If you want no part of me, which you obviously don't, then I'll give you money. No strings. You don't have to pay it back. Just take it and quit this life. Go to another town, find some other sort of work, and never look back."

Another silence fell. She knew he was waiting for her to reply, expecting her to acknowledge his offer, perhaps to accept it. Only she couldn't, and because she couldn't, there was nothing else to say. Franny knew what he must be thinking. That she didn't want his help or anyone else's. That she liked playing the whore. Nothing could have been farther from the truth.

"Well," he finally said, "I guess that settles that." She heard him sigh. "I'll leave the sign flipped over to *Occupied* as I leave so you can get ready for work." He emphasized the last word, lacing it with syrupy sarcasm. "Enjoy your evening."

A moment later, she heard the soft click of the door as it opened and then closed behind him. Unlike the other men who visited her room, Chase moved so quietly his footsteps couldn't be heard on the stairs. Holding her breath to control the sobs, she waited until she felt fairly sure he was gone. Then she sank to her knees. Arms vised around her waist, shoulders hunched, she moaned and started to cry.

Outside in the hall, Chase pressed his forehead against Franny's door. The stifled sound of her sobs cut through him like knives.

The following Sunday was Franny's little sister Alaina's sixteenth birthday, and Franny made an extra trip home on Saturday so she could be there to celebrate the occasion. The festivities, which were to begin after their Sunday dinner, were anxiously awaited by everyone in the family, and it was all Franny could do to get the excited younger children to gather around the table. She had just accomplished that and was about to ask her mother to say the blessing when someone knocked at the front door.

"Oh, bother," Franny muttered under her breath. As she always did when she was home on Sunday, she had cooked a large midday meal, the preparations for which she had begun directly after morning church services. After putting in so much work, she hated to see the meal get cold before they could eat. "Excuse me while I answer that."

"Hurry, Francine!" the children called out in unison. "Tell whoever it is to go away!"

"Hush!" she whispered. "It may be Preacher Elias. Do you want to offend him?"

Pasting a bright smile on her face, Franny scurried to the door, fully prepared to invite the minister to join them for the meal. There was always plenty to eat at the Grahams' house; Franny saw to that. Her smile froze when she saw who stood on the porch.

One long leg slightly bent, the other bearing most of his weight, Chase Wolf's stance could only be described as insolently masculine. Large hands bracketing his lean hips, he also had the look of a man ready for trouble. He wore his black shirt unfastened to mid-chest, the sleeves rolled back to reveal his thick forearms. At her startled expression, he flashed a slow grin and drew off his black riding hat, politely inclining his head in greeting. "Hello, Franny," he said softly.

Franny nearly fainted. Evidently he feared she might, for he moved quickly forward to grasp her arm. She fastened horrified eyes on his handsome face, scarcely able to believe he was standing there. Why? The question reverberated in her dazed mind. He had obviously followed her. But for what reason? Oh, God.

Her first thought was that he had come to expose

her, and the moment she regained a shred of her composure, she whispered, "How *dare* you?"

For all the world as though she'd expressed pleasure at seeing him, he flashed another dazzling grin. "I told you I could find my way here without getting lost. You give better directions than you think."

Directions? Franny's legs wobbled.

Glancing past her at the members of her family gathered around the table, he nodded politely. Franny didn't miss the hitch in his smile or the startled expression that flitted across his face when he saw what a crowd there was. Eight was no small number.

"Francine, dear, do we have a guest?" her mother called.

Taken off guard as she was, Franny could think of nothing to say. To her horror, Chase took his cue from that and stepped across the threshold as if he'd been invited in. She saw his eyes narrow slightly as his gaze routed through the dimness. The fact that her mother couldn't see for herself if they had a guest clearly hadn't escaped him, and he shot a questioning glance at Franny.

"You must be Franny's—Francine's mother," he observed warmly. "What a pleasure to finally meet you. I've heard so many nice things about you."

Franny gulped. Chase took another stride into the room. Under his breath, he whispered to her, "It'll be your funeral."

Franny knew he was giving her fair warning. If she didn't play along with him, she would be risking exposure. She hurried to come abreast of him and plastered what she hoped was a charming smile on her mouth as they crossed the sitting area rug together. Upon entering the kitchen, she said, "Mamma, I'd like you to meet my friend, Chase Kelly Wolf. Mr. Wolf, my mother, Mary Graham."

"Pleased, I'm sure," Mary Graham replied graciously.

Though Chase had made scarcely any noise, her sightless blue eyes turned directly toward him. He realized that she must have developed an acute sense of hearing to compensate for her blindness, a phenomenon he had heard of but never witnessed. Her smile was nearly as sweet as Franny's, her delicate face almost as lovely. Now Chase could see where Franny had gotten her looks.

Chase's voice was husky with sincerity when he rejoined, "The pleasure is entirely mine."

Frankie, whose privilege it was to sit at the head of their table, cleared his throat to get his eldest sister's attention. Nerves still jangling with alarm, Franny pressed a hand to her waist and said, "Oh, Chase, I'd like you to meet my brother." She hesitated only for a heartbeat before she added, "Frank Graham."

Frankie scooted his chair back, placed his napkin beside his plate, and rose. Extending his arm, he said, "My friends call me Frankie."

Chase stepped forward to shake his hand. "And I'm Chase. I've heard a lot about you, Frankie." He glanced quickly at Franny. "It's good to finally make your acquaintance."

Smiling slightly, Chase settled his attention on the rest of the children. Starting with Alaina, the next eldest, Franny went through the formalities until each of her siblings had been formally presented to him.

Chase's head was swimming with names by the time she finished, and he knew he would have difficulty keeping the youngsters straight. Blond, fine of feature, with blue or green eyes, they all resembled Franny. Even the child named Jason with his vapid expression and slack mouth was a handsome boy.

Alaina, who was feeling full of herself because it was her sixteenth birthday, graciously said, "We'd be honored if you'd join us for my birthday dinner, Mr. Wolf."

"Oh, no, really. I couldn't," he said.

Franny was about to say how sorry she was to hear that when her mother intervened. "Nonsense, Mr. Wolf. Any friend of Francine's is a friend of ours. Please pull up a chair. We've plenty of food on the table."

With a quick glance at the heaping serving dishes, Chase ascertained that was true. Franny was obviously doing quite well by her family. And a very large family it was. His throat felt tight as he accepted the extra chair Frankie drew up. The three children on that side of the table moved their places down to make room for him. Her face flushed, her green eyes unnaturally bright, Franny got him a plate and silverware before she reclaimed her seat across from him. To her right sat the slack-jawed, vacant-eyed child named Jason in an oversized, homemade highchair. Judging by the boy's size, Chase guessed him to be about ten years old.

Jason grunted with impatience and reached toward the food, his mouth aglisten with drool, his tongue limp and protruding slightly from between his lips. Instead of scolding him, as some might have, Franny crooned softly and pacified him with a piece of bread while the family bent their heads for the blessing. Instead of attending to Mary Graham's prayerful words, Chase heard only the wet smacking sounds Jason made as he clumsily devoured the bread. With a sick sensation in his lower belly, Chase realized he had finally unveiled Franny's secrets—all eight of them, seven siblings and a blind mother. When he recalled how he had judged her, how arrogant and self-righteous he had been, accusing her of liking her life just as it was, he felt smaller than he ever had. Sometimes, just as Franny had tried to explain, circumstances dictated and you did what you had to do because there was no choice.

After grace was completed and the serving dishes began to make their rounds, Mary Graham fixed her sightless gaze on Chase with unnerving accuracy and said, "So, Mr. Wolf, are you a friend of Mrs. Belle's?"

"Excuse me?"

"Mrs. Belle, my employer," Franny quickly interjected. "May Belle."

"Oh! Yes, of course. May Belle." Chase gave a nervous laugh. "A friend of mine, yes."

When Chase spoke, Mary Graham tipped her head as if to hear better, the first gesture he'd seen her make that bespoke of her affliction. A shaft of sunlight came through the window behind her and played upon her platinum-colored hair, which she wore in a braid encircling her head. If she had gray, which at her age she surely must, Chase couldn't detect it.

"Ah," she said in a musing tone, "so that's how you made Francine's acquaintance."

"Um, yes." It wasn't exactly a lie. Though she didn't formally bear the title, May Belle was, for all practical purposes, the madam at the Lucky Nugget, and over-saw Franny's enterprise. "That's how we met, yes. Through Mrs. Belle and my sister, who's Francine's good friend."

"Indigo?" Mrs. Graham asked.

"Yes."

"Oh, Francine speaks so highly of her. So you're her brother. How nice."

Mary Graham's thoughtful smile was radiant. Like his mother, she was still a lovely woman, the sort who had acquired a different kind of beauty with the years. As Franny grew older and her blush of youth faded, she would be just as lovely. If the hardships of her life didn't destroy her. The thought made Chase's stomach knot.

Mary Graham wore a blue day dress of raw silk, the detailed bodice finely embroidered and edged with ecru lace to match that at her cuffs. Chase had already taken note of the children's clothing. All of it was homemade, compliments of Franny and her new Wheeler-Wilson sewing machine, he felt sure. Looking across the table at her, the magnitude of her responsibilities struck him. Just to keep all these people well shod, which they were, would cost a small fortune each year. It hadn't escaped Chase that Franny's own shoes were scuffed and badly worn at the soles.

"Chase is a timber faller, Mamma."

"Oh, my. Just the thought of felling those huge trees makes my pulse quicken."

Chase grinned. "Once you learn how, it really isn't that dangerous."

"Hard work, though."

"Yeah, it keeps a man's muscles toned." Chase looked at Franny. "I've been recuperating this summer from a slight injury, which is why I was in Wolf's Landing and had an opportunity to meet your daughter."

"What sort of injury?"

"Cracked ribs. I was walking logs, slipped, and got crushed."

"I thought you said it wasn't dangerous," Mary reminded him.

Chase cleared his throat. "Yes, well . . . I wasn't using good judgment when it happened. One might say I asked for it."

Franny's green eyes sharpened. "How is that?"

"I was well into a jug of bourbon," Chase admitted.

Mary Graham arched a delicate eyebrow. "You're a drinking man, Mr. Wolf?"

By her imperious tone, Chase knew she didn't approve of those who imbibed. Luckily, Jason spilled the milk Franny was giving him at that exact moment and the distraction saved Chase from having to explain himself. To ensure that he wouldn't, Chase took a large bite of bread.

"How long have you known Mrs. Belle?" Mary queried.

Chase gulped to empy his mouth. "I, um . . . for years."

"A generous woman, that. If not for her having hired Franny as her companion, I truly don't know what this family would have done. In a very real sense, she has been our salvation."

Chase studied the blind woman's face, wondering how she could believe that anyone could earn the sums of money Franny did by working as a gentlewoman's companion. She served as a companion, all right, but not in the way her mother clearly believed. Chase's gaze shot to Franny. Two bright spots of color flagged her cheeks. In his peripheral vision he saw Jason grinning at him. Jason—one of Franny's many well-kept secrets. It occurred to him, suddenly, that the young woman across from him was surrounded by secrets, that neither of her identities was totally honest. Here with her family, she played one role, in Wolf's Landing another. Where in all of this was the *real* Franny?

As the meal progressed, the children, who were remarkably polite, joined the conversation. Though all of them seemed genuinely fond of Franny, Chase couldn't help but notice that much of their interchange concerned things she had or might yet provide for them. Alaina and little Mary wanted dancing slippers. Theresa, a precocious thirteen-year-old, wanted rhinestone hair combs. Matthew, a year Theresa's junior, had high hopes that Francine would get him a hunting rifle. Even Frankie put in a bid, describing a ready-made wool suit jacket and vest he had seen at the mercantile. He was "old enough for store-bought clothes," he said. In Chase's opinion, he was also old enough to get himself a job and help support the family, but his thoughts on the subject weren't solicited.

Another thing that troubled Chase was that Mary Graham gave him the impression she was somewhat concerned that her eldest daughter had a gentleman caller. Nothing blatant, just nuances in her expressions, so subtle he doubted anyone else would have noticed. Franny was a lovely and personable young

woman. She was also twenty-two, which was uncomfortably close to being considered an old maid. Any
mother in her right mind would be pleased that she
had attracted the interest of a young man. But Chase
got the distinct feeling that Mary Graham was not.

Though he knew it was uncharitable of him, he
couldn't help but wonder if Mary Graham wasn't worried that her daughter might marry and cease contribut-
ing to her family's support. Could it be that the woman
suspected the truth? That she not only knew what Franny did to earn their living, but approved? The thought
niggled its way into Chase's mind, and once there
refused to be banished. Gazing at the filled plates on
the table and the number of elbows bending, he
couldn't see how the woman could fail to be suspicious
of her daughter's income source. There weren't many
jobs that paid a woman enough to feed and clothe eight
people. From the looks of things, Franny had not only
managed to provide the necessities, but a few luxuries
as well. Mary Graham was blind, but not stupid.

The gay atmosphere and lively conversation at the
table didn't leave Chase much time to ponder those
thoughts. Before he knew it, he had been sucked into
the birthday spirit. Despite Jason's affliction and their
mother's blindness, the Grahams were a jovial lot and
seemed to enjoy one another's company. From tidbits
of the conversation, Chase ascertained that Frank Graham, Franny's father, had been killed in a carpentry
accident over nine years ago. Without asking, Chase
guessed that Franny, the eldest child, must have been
about thirteen at the time of his death.

"It was a tragic loss," Mary said softly, casting a pall

over the festive mood. "For reasons I shan't get into"—
she cast a sweet smile toward Franny —"measles were
brought home, and our whole family came down sick.
Jason and—" Her voice caught as though she were nearly overwhelmed with emotion. Swallowing as if to
regain her voice, she continued. "Jason and I suffered
permanent effects, and the medical bills were exorbitant.
Frank, God rest his soul, took every job he could get and
worked himself into a state of exhaustion. If not for
that—well, he was very agile and always so careful." She
smiled again, but with sadness. "He had so many who
depended on him, you see. He knew he was desperately
needed and took great care. If not for our family tragedy,
he would never have been roofing a church steeple when
it had begun to sprinkle rain. It was slippery and dangerous. But he wanted to finish the job so he could be paid.
Because of that, he continued working."

Chase couldn't miss the stricken expression that came
across Franny's face. His heart caught, but before he
could look deeply into her eyes, she bent her head.

"Well, enough of that!" Mary said with forced brightness. Placing a hand over her chest, she said, "How I
got off on that subject, I shall never know. As if it matters
now. My wonderful, precious Francine has seen to our
needs very nicely. Though we shall always mourn my
Frank's senseless death, none of us can say we've ever
gone without necessities. Francine has taken care of us,
bless her dear heart."

Chase swallowed a dry wad of meat. Searching Mary
Graham's lovely features, he assured himself that he
was misreading this entire situation. For a moment, it
had seemed to him that Mary Graham had revealed the

circumstances of her husband's death, not to inform Chase, but to remind Franny of her familial obligations. Perhaps even to prick her conscience? As if it could have been her fault that her family caught the measles? The very notion was absurd. Chase decided that, while he could usually read a person pretty well by looking into the eyes Mary Graham's blindness must be giving him false signals.

After the meal, Mary Graham was ensconced on a stool to crank the ice cream machine while Franny and the girls washed the dishes. Frankie invited Chase outside and promptly began rolling a cigarette the moment they were on the porch. Recognizing the logo on Frankie's pouch as that of a fine tobacco, Chase had to swallow back questions and more than a little outrage. Frankie was plenty old enough to assume the responsibilities of a man, yet he was still attending school, taking advanced mathematics in preparation for college under the guidance of a special tutor, which left the support of his mother and siblings to his sister. Something about this picture left a bad taste in Chase's mouth. Did the boy have any inkling of how much his sister had sacrificed to provide the money he so thoughtlessly squandered? Expensive tobacco, indeed. If the boy wanted to indulge, he should pay for his own habit.

Chase couldn't help but recall the threadbare dresses and scuffed shoes Franny wore for everyday back in Wolf's Landing. Yet her family wore only the best? The house was modest of structure, but the interior was nicely done, the furnishings far from shabby. Something about all of this seemed way off plumb to him. Way off plumb. He was dying to get Franny alone so he might ask why she didn't insist Frankie and Alaina quit school and work so she might seek other employment.

In a family the size of the Grahams', Chase soon realized that moments of privacy were a commodity in short supply. The moment the ice cream was ready, Franny cut and served birthday cake, which got the party festivities off into full swing.

Spying a horsehair chair in one corner, Chase retreated to it so he might observe without intruding.

Franny . . .

Seeing her in this setting with her family, Chase could scarcely believe she was the same reserved young woman he had come to know. Here, she had no fear of being recognized, a paranoia he now understood was to protect her family from scandal. Her laughter came easily and rang through the house as sweetly as a melody. Her gentle patience with her mother and Jason told Chase more about her than she could know, not only that she was as sweet within as she was without, but that she was loving and loyal to a fault.

Those two qualities had obviously led her into a life as a prostitute, the ultimate sacrifice any young woman could make. But what other recourse had there been? Mary Graham, for all that she clearly loved her children, was blind and unable to shoulder the responsibility for their care. Unlike many widows, she hadn't been in a position to remarry. Not many men were willing to take on a blind wife with a ready-made family this size. The financial burden alone would be a deterrent.

That thought made Chase's stomach tighten. How blithely he had pursued Franny, thinking to rescue her from the life she led. Now he realized it wasn't quite that simple. To assume responsibility for Franny, he would also have to assume responsibility for her family. The monthly outlay for food and lodging alone would be considerable. Chase suspected a child such as Jason probably incurred extraordinary medical costs. The man who took on this challenge would do well to make ends meet. Things like buying tracts of timberland would be out of the question.

In that moment it struck Chase how impossible a situation this was. On his own, with only himself to worry about, his future looked bright. He could reach for the moon and stood a damned good chance of attaining it. If he married Franny, he could kiss his dreams good-bye.

One life in exchange for eight; that was the sacrifice Franny had made. As noble as that was, it was also a shameful waste. Leaning over Alaina as the girl opened her gifts, Franny looked so sweet and beautiful, every man's dream, with her gentle smile and shimmering green eyes. She deserved so much more than she had, so very much more. And Chase yearned to give it to her.

When Alaina opened her gift from Franny, Chase instantly recognized the pink lacy dress as the one he had seen on Franny's sewing table. The girl gave a squeal of delight and danced about the parlor, holding the gown pressed against her.

"Oh, Franny, it's so beautiful! I just love it."

Chase's gaze shifted from Alaina and her new dress to Franny's attire. Her rose pink, lightweight cotton blouse had stylish ruffled caps at the sleeves and ruffles at the waist. Her wool skirt, cut on the bias to flow gracefully from her hips to the floor, was a deeper rose. In contrast to her golden hair, the blend of colors put him in mind of rose petals and sunlight. It was a pretty outfit and of the latest fashion, unlike the drab, threadbare rags she usually wore. Chase suspected that she set aside special clothing to wear only at home so her family would never guess the truth, that she did without herself so none of them would be deprived.

After Alaina finished opening all her gifts, Chase was once again invited to join Frankie outside on the steps for a smoke. Though he enjoyed his tobacco as much as the next man, Chase had been raised by a father who usually helped with kitchen chores, and he found Frankie's aversion to "woman's work" irritating. Despite his grown-up airs, the boy had a lot of maturing to do, in Chase's estimation, and the sooner he got that behind him, the better for Franny.

Unable to resist having a little fun at Frankie's expense, Chase regarded the youth's handsome profile for a moment. "You know, Frankie, I'd swear we've met before today."

The boy's blue eyes filled with puzzlement. Taking a deep drag from his freshly rolled smoke, he exhaled and said, "Really? If we have, I don't recollect it."

Enjoying himself immensely, Chase pretended to ponder the past. Finally he shook his head. "I know I've met you. I guess it'll come to me sooner or later."

A few minutes after that when he and Frankie reentered the house, Chase waited for a lapse in conversation, snapped his fingers, and said, "I have it!"

"You have what?" Turning from the sink, Franny fastened curious green eyes on him.

Chase clapped Frankie on the back. "Where I met Frankie." He gave a knowing laugh. "You young rascal, you. It's quite a ride to Wolf's Landing for a Saturday evening at the saloon. I'm surprised you ventured that far afield."

The ensuing silence that fell over the room seemed deafening. Frankie's face turned scarlet. "Wolf's Landing? I'm afraid you're—"

Interrupting him, Chase said, "I knew it'd come to me eventually. Where I'd seen you, I mean." At Frankie's agonized expression, Chase cast a quick glance toward his mother. "Oh, say, old man. I didn't mean to—well, you know. I thought that—" Chase cleared his throat and did his best to look embarrassed. "What with you being the man of the house and all, I figured you were past having to—hey, I didn't mean to let the cat out of the bag."

"Frankie?" Mary said softly. "What were you doing in Wolf's Landing? The only reason I can think of would be to visit your sister, and you know very well Mrs. Belle forbids her to have callers at her home."

Frankie squirmed. "I, um, went to Wolf's Landing with some friends of mine, Ma."

"To the saloon?"

"Yes, ma'am."

"With which friends?"

"Just some fellows from school."

Chase sneaked a glance at Franny. To his relief, her eyes were twinkling, and he could see she was struggling not to laugh. Pressing her lips together, she assumed a disapproving expression as she folded the dish towel and hung it on the rack. "The saloon in Wolf's Landing is no place for boys your age, Frankie," she scolded. "I've heard the gossip about that place, and I happen to know there are women of ill repute in residence upstairs."

Mary gasped. Frankie's face flushed a deeper shade of crimson.

Chase decided now would be a circumspect time to make his exit. Giving Frankie another apologetic pat on the back, he bid Mrs. Graham a polite good-bye, thanking her for including him in the birthday festivities and expressing his regret that he couldn't stay longer.

"It's a long ride back," he explained, "and I'd like to get most of it behind me before it turns dark."

Like a queen from her throne, Mary Graham held out her hand for Chase to take. He smiled slightly at the gesture, aware that it was born more from necessity than any illusions of grandeur. The woman couldn't see and had learned ways in which to compensate. By extending her hand expectantly, she prompted people to grasp it and thereby avoided any clumsy groping. Chase found her manner endearing, the earmarks of a woman who hadn't been beaten by her affliction and probably never would.

"I'll walk you out," Franny said as he drew his hat from off the rack. "Please excuse me for a few minutes, Mamma. I shall be back shortly."

Chase had tethered his horse at the water trough. Franny fell in beside him as he descended the porch steps and struck off in that direction. She waited until they were well out of earshot of the house before speaking.

"Well, are you finally satisfied?"

Chase heard the bitterness in her voice and knew he had it coming. Now that he had met her family, he could better understand her penchant for secrecy. "I'm sorry, Franny. When I saw you leaving town again yesterday, I couldn't resist following you."

"Did you spend the night in Grants Pass?"

He put on his black hat and nudged back the wide brim to regard her as they walked. "I'm accustomed to sleeping outdoors. I just shook out my bedroll under a tree."

"And waited until early afternoon to come calling?"

He shrugged. "I couldn't show up too early without it looking suspicious. If I had ridden all the way from the landing, it would have taken me most of the morning."

"I see."

Only, of course, she didn't see, not at all. Chase could tell that by her expression. "I guess you think I'm incurably nosy."

"I'm more concerned about what you intend to do with your knowledge of me."

Chase spun to a stop. "What in hell does that mean?"

"I'm just having a very difficult time understanding why discovering the truth about me was so all-fired important to you."

"Franny, I wanted to help you. That's all."

Shadows filled her eyes. "And now? Are you still so anxious to help me, Chase?"

They both knew that the answer to that was no longer quite so simple. He swallowed and glanced away, wishing to God he could just say yes. But the truth was he needed time to think. Franny came wrapped up in a bow with a family of eight. Any man who assumed that kind of responsibility better be damned sure what he was getting into before he took the leap.

When Chase finally looked back down at her, he saw a suspicious shimmer in her eyes that he guessed was unshed tears. Oh, God, he had never meant to hurt her. By the same token, he couldn't make any rash promises, not even to save her feelings. As much as he was coming to care for her, he had dozens of unfulfilled dreams beckoning that he'd never in a million years accomplish if he made a commitment to her.

It was selfish, and he knew it. Unforgivably so. But it wasn't easy to kiss everything he'd always wanted good-bye. Since childhood, he had yearned to own timberland one day. For years now, he had been working his ass off and saving nearly every dime he made to buy forest land. If he allowed himself to love this girl, he would have to give all of that up.

"Franny, I need time to think all of this through."

Her mouth twisted in a bitter little smile. "I tried to tell you there was no way out for me, but you refused to listen." Her chin came up a notch. "Don't feel bad on my account. My obligations may come as a surprise to you, but I've been shouldering them for a good long while and have long since accepted that I must continue to do so."

"Now there's where we differ in opinion," Chase ventured hopefully. "Frankie and Alaina are both old enough to contribute to this family's support. You should insist they do so and get yourself another type of job."

"I see," she said softly. "And what of Frankie and Alaina? I don't suppose either of them should marry and have a chance for normal lives?"

"Why not? You've sacrificed everything. It isn't fair that you should continue to be the only one to do so."

The breeze lifted and caught a stray curl at her temple. With trembling fingertips, she brushed the hair from her eyes. "There, you've said it. I've sacrificed everything. There isn't any turning back for me, Chase. From that first night, my fate was sealed. I can't pretend it never happened. And even if I could, what chance have I of leading a normal life?"

"With the right man, a damned good one."

"While Alaina and Frankie grow old taking care of our family? By the time the other kids are old enough to support themselves and there are only Jason and Mamma to care for, Alaina will be an old maid and Frankie will be a poor catch with a blind mother and idiot brother to shackle him."

"Ah, I see," he said with a touch of sarcasm. "Better that you make the sacrifice."

"Yes."

That simple answer drew his gaze to hers and forced him to look deeply into those green depths. He read a wealth of pain there. "Why, Franny? Don't you deserve a little happiness? It isn't as if it's your fault that your mother and Jason have afflictions."

"Yes," she whispered again. "It is my fault. Entirely my fault."

"What?" he asked incredulously. "Blindness and idiocy? Come on, Franny. How can you take the blame?"

"It's a long story. Just trust me when I say they would both be normal if not for me. As an extension of that, I was also responsible for my father roofing that steeple in the rain." She lifted her hands in a helpless little gesture. "So, you see? I made the decision long ago that it was my duty to look after my family. When the other children are adults, it should still be me who makes the sacrifices necessary to care for Mamma and Jason. Better one life be ruined than three. I want Alaina and Frankie to . . ." Her voice trailed off, and she swallowed, hugging herself as if against a chill. "I want them to have a chance for happiness, that's all."

Chase knew she had nearly said she wanted her brother and sister to have a chance at all the things she had missed.

"What about your happiness?"

She lowered her lashes slightly so he couldn't read the expression in her eyes. "It isn't important."

"Not important?"

Dropping her arms to her sides, she dredged up a shaky smile. "Good-bye, Chase. I trust that what you have learned about me today will remain a secret between us. It would cause untold pain for my family if the truth about me were ever revealed."

With that, she turned toward the house. Chase grasped her arm. "Franny, wait."

She glanced back over her shoulder at him. "Don't you see?" she asked him in a hollow little voice. "If you truly want to help me, stay away from me. All you've managed to accomplish is to make me wish for things I can never have."

With that, she jerked free of his hold and spun away.

11

Chase spent the following day agonizing over the discovery he had made about Franny. Even though he saw her return to Wolf's Landing in the rented buggy late that afternoon, he didn't visit her at the saloon that night. As sweet and lovely as she was, she came in a package with eight others, and if he married Franny, nature was bound to take its course. Eventually babies would come. Before he knew it, he'd have two large families to support. That was a frightening thought. True, he had done well in timber. He already owned one tract of land, and with what he had in the bank right now, he could buy a bit more. Harvested carefully, the trees would yield him a steady and respectable income for years to come.

The problem was, he had dreamed of a dynasty, not a modest income. His feelings for Franny threatened that.

In the end, Chase did what he had always done when

he grew troubled; he laid the problem before his father. Without mentioning names, he explained that he had come to care very deeply about a young woman who had eight people dependent upon her for their support.

A knowing look came into Hunter's eyes. "This young woman must have a very good job if she earns enough to support eight people."

"Anyway," Chase finished gruffly, "if I married her, I'd have to assume responsibility for her family, and in doing so, I'd see all my dreams of building a timber empire turn to dust."

They were sitting on the bank of Shallows Creek. Moonlight gilded the night, spilling in a silver mist over the rushing water and dappling the whispering leaves of the trees. Somewhere in the darkness, a bird, disturbed from its rest, chirped frantically, making Chase wondered if an animal of prey had found its nest. It was a harsh old world they lived in, he thought sadly. The helpless always seemed to be victimized. His thoughts turned to Franny, and an ache filled him. Why was nothing in life simple? Why did he have to choose between his dreams and the woman he wanted? It wasn't fair. It just wasn't, no matter how he circled it, not to Franny or him.

Hunter startled Chase by slapping at a mosquito. Afterward, he rubbed his muscular shoulder and grinned, flashing white teeth in the darkness. "They like this Comanche, eh?"

Chase slapped at one of the bloodsuckers himself and chuckled. "They like this Comanche as well."

Hunter shifted his moccasined feet and rested his powerful arms atop his knees. Chase assumed the same position, aware as he did that his bent leg reached as high as his father's and that his folded arms were as well muscled. Another wave of sadness washed over him, for as a boy he had believed he would be all-powerful and all-knowing when he had grown to be as large as his sire. Unfortunately, that was not the case.

Silence settled between them, broken only by the occasional cries of the bird and the rushing sound of the water. A musty, moldy scent from the forest floor behind them floated on the moist night air to blend with the fresh smells of summer and rebirth. Chase took a deep breath, comforted by the sense of timelessness. God's earth produced life in an endless cycle; things were born, they died, and life replenished itself. It made his own concerns seem smaller and less important when he fitted himself into the greater circle.

When Hunter finally spoke, he provided no answers to Chase's dilemma, but asked a question. "When you are a rich timber man, my son, with whom will you share the joy?"

Chase smiled slightly. Trust his father to come at a problem from the wrong end. "I haven't considered that. Until I have the timber, it's kind of getting the cart before the horse. Isn't it?"

"Ah," Hunter said. "That is one of your mother's wise sayings, no?"

"I think that's where I heard it, yes."

Hunter nodded. "She is a very stupid woman sometimes."

Chase arched an eyebrow. Never had he heard his father refer to his mother as lacking in intelligence. "Come again?"

"Her stupidness—it is not because she has no brains," Hunter elaborated, "but because she was raised with the *tabeboh* within wooden walls, and she was not taught simple truths. Ignorant, I think she calls it. I call it stupidness."

"I was raised within wooden walls."

"Yes, and you are very much stupid sometimes." His father turned to gaze at him, his midnight blue eyes nearly black in the darkness and as polished as jet. "If you have no cart, why would you need a horse to pull it?"

Caught off guard, Chase considered that and then chuckled. "In other words, if I have no one to share all my riches with, why bother to get them?"

Hunter shrugged. "Will you turn away from true love to fill your pockets? One day, your pockets will be heavy, but so will your heart. The true riches in life are love and laughter. With this woman who has eight people to feed you will have much love and laughter within your lodge. When babies come, the love and laughter will be multiplied a hundredfold. You will be rich in all the ways that matter, and you will be happy. A happy man has no need of money."

"Money is a necessary evil."

"Having enough to get by is necessary. More than that is not. Follow your heart, Chase, not foolish dreams. When winter comes to your hair and wisdom to your eyes, money will not soothe your loneliness. A woman who loves you will."

"Why can't a man have both wealth and love?" Chase argued.

"Love springs up from a hidden place. We do not choose the woman, the place, or the time. Walk away to seek dreams, and the chance for love may be forever lost to you."

Chase sighed. "Sometimes, my father, you are an incurable idealist."

"Only sometimes? I am disappointed to hear it. I try to always be."

With that, Hunter pushed to his feet. Chase looked up. "You're not leaving? We only just started talking."

"I am finished. I have no other words inside me."

Chase shook his head. "Just like that. You've said your piece, and now it's my problem?"

"It is your heart and therefore your decision. You must reach it by yourself. I can point the way, but you must choose which way you will walk. Just be sure to fix your eyes far ahead of you, my son, and see where it is that you go."

Shadows swallowed Hunter as he turned and walked away.

Left alone to make his decision, Chase oscillated, convinced he should choose Franny one moment, reluctant to relinquish his dreams the next. Wrestling with his tangled emotions, he avoided Franny yet another full day, hoping that the problem and its solutions might become more clearly defined for him if he gave himself more time to think things through.

Meanwhile Franny believed the inevitable had occurred. Chase Wolf had finally come to his senses. There was no other explanation. As May Belle had always said, once a whore, always a whore. Franny had known that from day one. For a brief while, Chase had nearly convinced her she might have a chance for something else, and the hard landing back in reality hurt more than she cared to admit.

Foolish. So very foolish. Hearts carved on gnarled old trees. Walks in the moonlight. Those things weren't for her. She had relinquished all hope of them when she was thirteen years old. What point was there in mourning things that had never been hers to begin with?

No point, she assured herself. None at all. Even so, Franny found herself sitting near her window all that morning and afternoon, her gaze fixed on the sprawling log house at the end of town. The Wolf home. Chase's home. She imagined him sitting with his parents in the soft glow of lantern light the evening before, joining them for supper at the table, then retiring to a cozy bed to slumber the night away under colorful patchwork quilts. Franny had never seen the interior of the house, but knowing Chase and Indigo had painted it golden within her mind, a place where there was love and warmth in abundance.

The ache of loneliness inside Franny was so acute, she almost felt sick. At breakfast, she was unable to take a single bite of her egg, and she only nibbled at the toast. Even that much food had made her stomach rebel. Lovesickness, she scoffed. Here she was, twenty-two years old and mooning over a man. At lunch she put forth a more determined effort to eat, but managed to consume only about a third of what was on her plate.

A few minutes after setting the uneaten plate of food outside her door in the hallway, May Belle paid her a visit. Resembling a ship in full sail in her voluminous white wrapper, she swept into the room, bringing with her the overpowering scent of roses, her favorite perfume. "Feeling puny?" she demanded to know. "Gus says you're off your vittles."

Franny turned her chair from the window and motioned for May Belle to join her at the table. "A little puny, I guess. Mainly just blue."

May Belle looked relieved. "Thank God. The first thing I think of when a girl gets off her food is that she's pregnant."

"Bite your tongue." Franny laughed and shook her head. "Not this girl. I use the vinegar-soaked sponges faithfully, I never forget to irrigate, and I take a nightly dose of your powders."

May Belle smiled. "Yeah, but even my remedies aren't surefire, honey."

"They've served me well for eight years. Truly, May Belle, I'm just feeling out of sorts. It'll pass."

"It isn't like you to feel out of sorts. Why don't you go visit Indigo? Get out of here for a while. It might do you a world of good."

"I was gone all weekend."

May Belle repositioned the tortoiseshell comb in her brassy hair, her tired blue eyes filled with concern. "Is everything okay at home? How's Jason doing?"

Franny sighed. "He's doing great. The doctor found a new elixir for him. It's expensive, but Mamma feels he's really perked up since Alaina started giving it to him."

"And the other kids?"

Franny realized how gloomy she must look and gave herself a hard mental shake. Her path had been clearly marked the day her father died, and she was being utterly foolish to wish things might have happened differently. "Everyone at home is fine, May Belle," she assured the older woman with a smile. "I'm just having one of those white-picket-fence days. We all do on occasion, don't we?"

In the business, "a white-picket-fence day" was an expression prostitutes used to describe the yearning that sometimes struck them for a family and children, home, and hearth. May Belle's mouth tightened. "Jesus, not a man. Give me one guess. Tall, dark, and so handsome the women drop around him like falling trees."

Franny plucked at a loose bit of yellowed lace on her cuff. "Stupid of me, isn't it? He could snap his fingers and have any woman he wants. It's insane to think he might be genuinely taken with me."

"He's a Wolf. Like father, like son?"

Franny met her older friend's gaze. "Meaning?"

May Belle shrugged. "His pappy marches to a different tune. Always has, always will. Maybe Chase is like him." Her eyes gentled. "Honey, you know I've always warned you not to go swallowing any of the lines men might try to feed you. And I meant every word I said. But that doesn't mean there isn't a rare bird or two out there. If any fellow on earth is a straight shooter, I'd put my money on Hunter Wolf. Chase could be like him in that."

Franny's heart caught. "He knows about my family. I haven't seen hide nor hair of him since."

May Belle seemed to consider that. "Backing off until he gets things sorted in his mind, you reckon?"

"Running scared, more like." No longer able to bear sitting, Franny pushed to her feet and began pacing. "Oh, May Belle! No man in his right mind would want me. I'm a whore. If he could get past that, then there's my family. The two things combined are just too big an obstacle."

"We'll see. Who knows? Maybe God looked down and said, 'That little Franny girl, she doesn't belong in that life.' Maybe he's making a miracle, hm?"

Afraid to let herself believe that, even for a moment, Franny drew the bitterness around her like a cloak. "God doesn't make miracles for whores, May Belle. If you believed that, you'd accept Shorty's proposal and get the heck out of this place."

"You've got me there."

Fighting off a wave of nausea, Franny hugged her waist. "I can't afford to get my heart broken," she whispered miserably. "All I want in the way of a miracle is for Chase Wolf to stay away from me. He's like a magic potion. One taste and I was under his spell. He's walking, talking trouble. The minute I forget that, I'll be a goner."

The next afternoon, Franny cracked her door to answer a light knock and found walking, talking trouble standing in the dim hallway. With one eye, she regarded him through the narrow opening, her heart skipping beats like a schoolgirl's.

"I've seen your face," he said softly. "I know your real name. Is it really necessary to look out at me through a crack?"

Ever aware that someone downstairs might glimpse her face if she wasn't careful, Franny stepped back from the doorway to allow him entry. When he had stepped into the room and closed the door behind him, she relaxed slightly. But only slightly. "What do you want, Chase?"

In answer, he stepped to her bureau and plunked down a stack of gold pieces. She didn't need to count them to know they stood five deep. As he turned to regard her, he arched one dark eyebrow. "The same thing I wanted from the first, you."

Folding her arms, Franny spun away. "I asked you to stay away from me. If you want to play games, find someone who knows the rules. I have enough trouble following my own."

"Your rules stink," he shot back. "From here on out, you're going to start observing a different set, namely mine."

"Go away," she said weakly.

"Only if you come with me."

"I can't do that, and you know it. I have a family who depends on me. I—"

"Let me worry about your family."

"You?"

"That's a husband's job."

Franny could only stare at him, quite sure she hadn't heard him correctly.

"You're going to marry me," he inserted gently. "We can take care of it today, or you can put me off until later. I don't care which. But from this moment on, you will no longer sell your wares in this hellhole to support your family. No ifs, ands, or buts."

Stiffening her spine, Franny forced herself to meet his gaze. "What do you take me for, a fool? Since learning about my family, you haven't darkened my doorstep."

"You don't have a doorstep. That's one of the things I intend to rectify."

She opted to pretend he hadn't said that. "Now, here you are, suddenly demanding I marry you?"

"That's right."

"I'm sorry. But I know how that fairy tale always ends." Gazing at his burnished features. she decided that his Comanche heritage had never been more apparent than now, in the way he stood, in the leashed strength of his body, in the bold way he met her accusing stare. There was a wildness in him she couldn't ignore, bred into him by blood. She couldn't help but fear that the wildness made him impetuous, that what he decided to do on the spur of the moment today might become ashes on the wind tomorrow. "You may tell yourself right now that what I am doesn't matter to you," she said gently, "but a few months down the road, you'd wake up to reality."

"Reality being?"

"That I'm a whore!" she cried shakily. "Once a whore, always a whore, Chase. There is no changing that. I appreciate your philanthropic bent, but the day would come when you'd look into the faces of other men in this town and wonder how many of them had been with your wife. The answer would probably be dozens. Knowing that would eat at you until you detested the sight of me."

Moving so quickly she couldn't react, he closed the space between them and made a fist in the bodice of her dress. Franny felt the anger emanating from his body and knew he was mere inches from tearing her clothing off of her. "Once a whore, always a whore? Is that engraved somewhere on your flesh, Franny? Some sort of indelible mark that brands you? That's bullshit.

You can walk away from this life. All you have to do is turn your back on it. And, by God, that's exactly what you're going to do. With me. As my wife. There won't be any looking back, not on my part. It goes against everything I was ever taught."

The sting of tears washed over Franny's eyes.

"You're a beautiful woman, that's what you are," he whispered raggedly. "Any man would be proud to have you as his wife, to bear his children."

"No." Her protest rang out thin and tremulous. "No man in his right mind, at any rate."

"I would, and in this instance, how I feel is all that counts."

"No. How I feel counts as well. I can't gamble the lives of eight people on pretty promises, no matter how sincerely you might mean them now. If I gave up this job, someone else would move in to take my place. If things didn't work out between you and me, which they probably wouldn't, I'd have to go elsewhere to find another position and then build up an entirely new clientele. Meanwhile my family would have to suffer the consequences. I can't take that risk, no matter how much I might wish I could."

"Life is full of risks, Franny. You have to trust me."

Recalling her recent vow not to let him make her believe in foolish dreams, she said, "No, I don't have to trust you, or anyone else for that matter. And I won't. I can't. It's too big a gamble, and the stakes are way too high."

"I guess that means I'll have to prove myself to you, doesn't it?"

"And how do you hope to accomplish that?"

"By spending time with you. Once you get to know me a little better, you'll realize I don't make pretty promises unless they're ones I can keep. The only risks involved here are inside your head."

"I can't spend that much time with you. I have a job, remember?"

He hooked a thumb toward the bureau. "That fifty dollars covers what you would earn tonight. Grab your bonnet. Let's go for a walk."

Never in all Franny's life had she wanted so badly to say yes. "I can't do that."

"Why the hell not?"

"Because, I told you. My family counts on the money I earn from this job. If I allow you to monopolize my time, I'll lose all my regular customers."

That familiar glint of determination crept into his dark blue eyes. "Don't fight me on this, Franny. If you do, I won't play fair, and in the end, you'll lose."

"Fair or foul, that's entirely up to you, I suppose. I only know what I must do."

"That's debatable."

"To your way of thinking, perhaps. But that's beside the point."

"Really? And if I disagree?"

"That's your problem."

"Not if I choose to argue my case in your mother's parlor the next time you go home for a visit."

Franny felt the blood drain from her face. "You wouldn't."

"Try me."

"That'd be despicable. If she learned the truth, it would break her heart."

"Then humor me so she won't learn the truth."

"You'd actually resort to blackmail to get your way?"

"Like you said, I'm despicable."

"And you actually believe that with this sort of behavior, you can win my trust?"

His mouth slanted into one of those dazzling smiles. "Quite a charmer, aren't I?" Inclining his head toward her privacy screen, he said, "Get your bonnet."

12

That afternoon was the beginning of a very expensive courtship. Always with fifty dollars in hand, Chase began coming to collect Franny from the saloon far earlier in the evenings. He took her for walks. They picnicked along Shallows Creek. Sometimes they went riding. Once he even accompanied her home to visit her family and attend the circus that was being held in Grants Pass. On that occasion, he was wonderfully patient with Jason, which earned him Mary Graham's favor.

Franny knew it was his aim to make her see how much she was missing and want the life they could have together. And he was more successful in that than she dared to reveal. The yearning he kindled within her was more frightening than anything else she had ever experienced. She was convinced it would end in heartache.

How else could it end? Chase might pretend not to care about her past. But no man could pretend forever. Sooner or later, he would turn away from her. It was as inevitable as the stars coming out on a cloudless night.

Only he didn't turn away, and the days swept past, taking them deep into July and the lazy heat of summer. Franny tried to hold herself apart from Chase. She truly did. But Chase wasn't easy to evade, not even for an expert like herself, well practiced at escaping into fantasy.

As she had sensed from the beginning, Chase wasn't a man to allow a woman to hold herself aloof from him. Little by little, he chipped away at the walls she had erected around herself, delving into her deepest secrets, forcing her to lay bare emotions she had never revealed to anyone.

One evening after attending the circus in Grants Pass, he caught her off guard by saying, "It's such a shame about Jason. He's such a perfect child in every other way. Handsome, beautifully proportioned. What a cruel joke of nature for him to be born with a flawed mind."

Before she thought, Franny replied, "But he wasn't born that way."

The instant she spoke she realized he had baited her. They were just approaching Shallows Creek, and to cover her discomfiture, Franny hurried on ahead. Spying a large boulder on the sandy bank, she went to lean against it. Pretending to enjoy the starlit sky and the summer night, she smiled nervously. "It's lovely out here. Now I'm glad you asked me to come."

In truth, the invitation had been more an ultimatum,

but Franny could see little to be gained by arguing the point. Chase would have his way. If she had learned nothing else about him these last weeks, she had learned that. Here lately, though, the thought filled her with dread. She had begun to suspect he would win in the end, that she would eventually marry him, not because she felt it was wise, but because he would maneuver her into a corner and allow her no choice. He had a ruthless streak when it suited him.

Her nerves leaped when he drew up beside her and leaned against the boulder. Dressed all in black, which seemed to be his favored attire, he looked sinister and impossibly large in the shadows. Pale moonlight glanced off his sharply bridged nose and squared jaw. His dark hair caught the illumination in shimmers that winked out and reappeared with each motion of his head. Broad shoulders, powerful yet lean legs that seemed to stretch forever, muscular arms that could offer a woman solace or become her worst nightmare, depending upon his whim.

Franny toyed nervously with a button on her bodice, acutely aware of the man beside her and his intent regard. She could almost feel the net closing over her, almost predict his next move.

"That's right. I had nearly forgotten. Jason wasn't born with his affliction, was he? Measles, didn't your mother say?"

There it was, the subject she had known he would circle back to eventually. She was only surprised he had waited this long. Stupid, so stupid. Why had she opened herself up for this? It should be a simple matter of watching her tongue. But around Chase, with him constantly waiting for her to make a slip, it was almost impossible never to make one.

"Yet you take the blame for his idiocy? Measles sort of strike at random. Don't they? How could a person be held accountable for someone else's catching them?"

Electrified and feeling panicky, Franny pushed away from the boulder. At this point in the stream there was a bend, and the water eddied against an outcropping of stone that impeded its rush. She walked to the lapping edge of the still pool. "Oh, look. Minnows."

Watching her, Chase's heart broke a little. He knew Franny blamed herself for Jason's affliction, just as she assumed the responsibility for her mother's blindness. He had known that since the first day he had visited her home and met her family. She had alluded to her feelings of guilt then, but had carefully avoided the subject since.

He knew it was merciless of him to press her. The very way she stood betrayed her reluctance to discuss it, and there was no missing the nervous, almost frenetic plucking of her fingers at her dress. He had a feeling there was a whole lot more roiling beneath the surface than even Franny realized.

"What happened, Franny? Did you come down sick first, or what?"

God, how he hated himself for being so relentless. But he had to be. The more layers he peeled away from Franny, the more she fascinated him. With her, little was as it seemed on the surface.

"It wasn't a simple matter of my getting sick first," she finally admitted in a thin, quavery voice. "It was my fault, and afterward he was never right again."

Her fault? There it was again, an admission of guilt for something she couldn't possibly have caused. Chase stared at her slender back, now held so rigidly straight, as if in anticipation of a physical blow. How could she possibly hold herself to blame for an illness? It made no sense. Absolutely none. But there was no doubt it made perfect sense to her.

"How was it your fault, honey?"

"I brought—" Her voice turned shrill and cracked. He saw her take a deep breath before trying again. "I brought them home. The measles. I brought them home to everyone. It was because of me they all got sick."

Chase closed his eyes for a moment. He and Indigo had caught the measles as children and suffered no ill effects, but to this day he could recall how frantic his mother had been. In some cases, the disease was treacherous, leaving its victims blind, sometimes deaf. And in the very young, the raging fevers sometimes destroyed the mind. But to be blamed for infecting one's family because you caught them first? It was madness.

Before he considered the impact on her, he swore and said, "How in hell can you blame yourself for giving everybody the measles, for Christ's sake?"

She jerked as if he had slapped her. "Because, just because."

Chase wasn't willing to settle for that as an answer. "Bullshit to just because. The disease strikes at random. If you're blaming yourself for that, it's crazy."

She whirled to face him. In the wash of moonlight, her eyes were huge splashes of darkness in contrast to her pallor. Her mouth twisted and quivered as she strove to form words that tangled in her throat and erupted as incoherent little *blurps* of sound.

"An . . . an epidemic," she finally managed. "A measles epidemic. Jason was just a baby."

"You can't be held responsible for an epidemic, honey."

"Yes."

In her eyes, he saw a world of pain. He yearned to go to her, to draw her into his arms, to hold her so nothing else could ever hurt her. But he knew she wasn't ready for that and would panic if he tried.

"I started it," she blurted. "The epidemic? I was the one who spread the disease."

Chase circled that, much as he might have a coiled snake, uncertain of his next move, fearful of making the wrong one. "Can you explain that for me, how you were responsible?"

"What's to explain? And besides, I can tell by your tone that you're sneering. You don't understand at all."

She had him there. He was sneering, and he sure as hell didn't understand. "Well, explain it so I can." He threw up his hands. "I'm sorry. But where I come from, sickness chooses its victims. It's nobody's fault. I can't comprehend how it was different in your family's case."

Still rigid with tension, she rubbed at her temples then spun away as if she couldn't bear looking at him. "I attended the academy in Jacksonville back then. My parents could barely afford the tuition, and I really didn't want to be away from home, but they insisted because they wanted me to have the best education possible."

Obviously entrapped in the memories, her voice took on a faraway tone, and she paced aimlessly around him, stopping to nudge a rock with her toe, then moving on to touch the shiny leaves of a drooping laurel limb.

"I was a headstrong child," she murmured.

Chase smiled sadly at that revelation, for it was no news to him. She was equally headstrong as an adult. No one knew that better than he.

"I resented their sending me away to school. I was horribly homesick during the week, and every weekend when Papa came to fetch me home for a visit, I begged not to go back. They turned a deaf ear, and I grew rebellious. Nothing serious. I was only twelve, so my transgressions were harmless enough." She took another deep breath. "Only in the end, they weren't harmless after all."

Chase sensed that she was lost in the past and didn't risk speaking.

"There was this family who lived at the outskirts of Jacksonville by the name of Hobbs. The father was a heavy drinker, and the mother had an unsavory reputation. One day when I sneaked away from the academy, I met their daughter, Trina, and we became fast friends. When my parents learned of it, they were concerned and forbade me to associate with her. Not because she was a bad girl, but because they feared I might come to harm. Her father was renowned for his drunken rages."

She ripped off a handful of laurel leaves and made a tight fist over them. When she unfurled her fingers, her expression revealed a pain that ran so deep Chase ached for her.

"Resentful as I was, I didn't obey my parents and met with Trina every chance I got. One day she wasn't at our meeting place, and I went to her house to see what kept her. One of the younger children answered the door, and when I stepped inside, I could smell the sickness. Taking a page from my mother's book, I did what I knew to help." She lifted her hands in helpless appeal. "Unfortunately, I was far too inexperienced a nurse to recognize the symptoms or to know the risk I was taking. A few days later, Trina recovered, and she and I began meeting in secrecy again."

Chase sensed what was coming.

"When I started feeling poorly, I never even thought of those few short minutes I had spent inside the Hobbs house. I was scarcely there for any time at all!" She turned an agonized gaze toward him. "It was a Friday evening when the sickness struck me. Only at first I just felt cranky and a little flushed. Papa came to fetch me home, and I went, never dreaming I was coming down with an illness that would nearly kill my little brother and my mother."

"Oh, Franny."

Moonlight shimmered on the tears that welled in her eyes. "Everyone at the academy who wasn't already immune fell sick as well, and they took the sickness home to their families, too. The measles. It hit Jacksonville and Grants Pass with a vengeance, sparing only those who were immune. Not everyone suffered lasting effects. But in my family the disease was devastating."

A hard knot forming in his throat, Chase swallowed, hard. The sensation didn't go away. "Franny, it probably would have happened anyway. You can't—"

"Yes, I can. It was my fault. I disobeyed my parents. I went to the Hobbs house. I caught the measles and took them home to all the people I loved the most. How can I not blame myself for that?"

"You never intended any harm."

"Tell that to Jason," she shot back tremulously. "He was a bright baby. He was just learning to walk when it happened. Afterward he couldn't even hold his tongue in his mouth. Tell Jason I meant no harm, Chase. With my willfulness, I destroyed his life and made my mother go blind." She gave a shrill, wet laugh. "And what was worse, I finally got my wish. After that, Papa no longer sent me away to school. I stayed at home to take care of my mother and brothers and sisters while he worked trying to pay all the bills." Her small face twisted with pain. "He died trying to pay them."

"Dear God, Franny. It wasn't your fault."

"Yes. Color it any way you like, all of it was my fault. The Hobbses didn't mingle much with the townspeople in Jacksonville. If not for my contact with them, the disease might have run its course within their family."

"That's highly unlikely."

"We'll never know, though, will we?" She pushed angrily at a stray curl that had fallen across her forehead. Then, as if the dam within her had burst, words began to pour from her. "Only a few months later, Papa fell off the steeple. There was no more money. My mother was unable to work. I was the eldest and the responsibility of feeding my family fell to me. Jason was unwell, and he needed a special elixir to build up his system. It was horribly expensive. The doctor gave me several bottles for free, and several of the neighbors pitched in to buy a few bottles after that. To keep food on the table, I worked doing laundry and mucking stalls at the livery. We scraped by for a while."

Chase pushed away from the boulder. For weeks he

had been trying to dig all this out of her, but now that she was willing to tell him, he almost wished he didn't have to hear it. "Franny, honey, things happen. Things we can't help."

"One of my best laundry customers was the madam at the brothel," she plunged on. "At church on Sunday, Preacher Elias talked about the sisters in sin and the burning fires of Satan that would engulf the unwary who ventured near the establishment. I never would have solicited laundry business from there because I was afraid to go close. But one day on the street, this painted woman stopped me. She said she'd heard about my laundry service and wanted to become a customer. Her business meant a substantial increase in my earning capacity, so I couldn't bring myself to say no. The next week, I was afraid to knock on the back door to collect the linens, but I needed the money so badly, I forced myself to."

"The madam seemed like a kindly woman, and every time she saw me, she said I could earn far more money being nice to a gentleman than I ever could doing laundry. She told me to put on a pretty dress and pay her a visit any Saturday night. She promised I'd make at least seven dollars. Seven dollars sounded like a fortune to me."

Chase took a step toward her then hesitated. She held herself so tautly he was afraid she might shatter if he touched her.

"The neighbors couldn't continue to help me buy Jason's medicine for long, and eventually the time came when I had to choose between putting food on the table or keeping him supplied with the elixir. A few days after we stopped dosing him, he started losing strength, and soon after that, he started getting sick. The doctor said he might die without the blood builders." Her quivering mouth twisted in a tearful smile. "I knew how I could make seven dollars. All I had to do was put on a pretty dress and be nice to a gentleman. One Saturday night, I did just that." She made a vague gesture. "I . . . um . . . The gentleman was very polite and kind until I went upstairs with him. By the time I realized what being 'nice' to him entailed, it was too late. He had paid the madam for my company, and he wouldn't take no for an answer."

"Jesus Christ."

Shaking violently, she hugged her waist. Though her gaze seemed to be fixed on his face, Chase had the feeling she no longer saw him.

"He paid thirty dollars to be the first," she whispered. "Innocent young girls bring top dollar in those places. My cut was supposed to be half. Fifteen whole dollars! Only I couldn't collect it until morning. When the gentleman left the room, I couldn't move, let alone get up. The second man found easy pickings, and so did the third. I quit counting then and closed my mind to what was happening. At dawn I got twenty dollars for my trouble." She gave a hysterical sounding laugh. "After all that, and the madam cheated me. I was supposed to get half of everything, and no matter how I figured it, twenty wasn't nearly enough."

Chase wished he could close his mind. Better yet, he wished he could go back in time and kill the bastards with his bare hands. What kind of monsters could use a child in that fashion? What kind of woman could lure her into such a trap?

If you
have a passion
for great
historical
romance,
here's an offer
you'll love...

4 FREE NOVELS

SEE INSIDE.

Introducing
The Timeless Romance

Passion rising from the ashes of the Civil War...

Love blossoming against the harsh landscape of the primitive Australian outback...

Romance melting the cold walls of an 18th-century English castle —— and the heart of the handsome Earl who lives there...

Since the beginning of time, great love has held the power to change the course of history. And in Harper Monogram historical novels, you can experience that power again and again.

Free introductory offer. To introduce you to this exclusive new service, we'd like to send you the four newest Harper Monogram titles absolutely free. They're yours to keep without obligation, no matter what you decide.

Free 10-day previews. Enjoy automatic free delivery of four new titles each month — up to four weeks before they appear in bookstores. You're never obligated to keep a book you don't want, and you can return any book, for a full credit.

Save up to 32% off the publisher's price on any shipment you choose to keep.

Don't pass up this opportunity to enjoy great romance as you have never experienced before.

Reader Service.

Yes! I want to join the Timeless Romance Reader Service. Please send me my 4 FREE HarperMonogram historical romances. Then each month send me 4 new historical romances to preview without obligation for 10 days. I'll pay the low subscription price of $4.00 for every book I choose to keep--a total savings of at least $2.00 each month--and home delivery is free! I understand that I may return any title within 10 days and receive a full credit. I may cancel this sub-scription at any time without obligation by simply writing "Canceled" on any invoice and mailing it to Timeless Romance. There is no minimum number of books to purchase.

NAME

ADDRESS

CITY   STATE   ZIP

TELEPHONE

SIGNATURE

(If under 18, parent or guardian must sign. Program, price, terms, and conditions sub-ject to cancellation and change. Orders subject to acceptance by HarperMonogram.)

"A couple of weeks later, the twenty dollars was all gone," she said hollowly. "We had credit at the store, and I'd fallen behind paying the bill. Jason's medicine cost dearly. Before I knew it, we were broke again, and he was nearly out of elixir.

"The pretty dress I wore the first time was all ruined, but I had another. When Jason began to get sick again, I put it on and went back to be nice to the gentlemen. I was afraid, but it was that or watch my baby brother die. So I went."

Chase wanted to weep for her and for the child she had once been. "Oh, honey . . ."

"It wasn't so bad," she assured him. "As I climbed the stairs with the first customer, I wasn't as ignorant as I'd been the other time. I was so scared my knees knocked. To keep myself from running, I thought of my papa. In the summer on Sundays, he always took us to a meadow for a picnic after church. I always loved it there. So I imagined it up. As clear as a picture in my mind. A beautiful hiding place inside my head where nothing could reach me. It wasn't as bad that night. And the next time, it was even easier. I got really good at imagining up pictures in my head, mostly of the meadow, but sometimes of other things. Pretty soon, those places seemed so real, I didn't want to come back out of them and face reality. Isn't that crazy? I just wanted to stay in my secret places and pretend none of it had ever happened."

"No," he whispered hoarsely, "it's not crazy at all, sweetheart. I just thank God you found a way to hide."

She blinked, as if giving herself a mental shake. "Anyhow, I had to come back when the nights were over. My family needed me."

"How long did you work in the brothel in Grants Pass?" he asked.

"A few months. Because I lived in constant fear that my family might learn what I was doing, eventually I came to Wolf's Landing to work under May Belle. I've been here for nearly eight years now, I think. But who's counting?"

"I am," he said softly and closed the remaining distance between them to grasp her by the shoulders. "I am," he repeated. "And wish I could set the clock back, Franny. I wish I could go back in time and undo everything that's been done to you."

"No one can do that," she said faintly.

"No," he admitted. "But I can change things from this moment on, if you'll only give me a chance. Will you trust me enough to do that?"

Her gaze lifted to his. Seeing the pain there, it was small consolation to Chase that he saw awareness as well. He was touching her, and she wasn't trying to hide from him. A secret place inside her head, she called it. And she was right; it did sound crazy. But Chase knew it was also the absolute truth. This woman who called herself a whore, who no longer believed anything good in life would ever come her way, was still a child in some ways—a little girl, hiding from an ugliness her mind couldn't accept. It would be his job to show her that the ugliness could be something indescribably beautiful in the arms of the right man.

He was that man. He had felt certain of that for a long while now, and all that remained was to convince Franny of it.

"I'd like to trust you, Chase. Truly I would," she whispered.

Chase smiled sadly. "So what's stopping you?"

"I'm afraid."

Her voice shook on that last word, which told him just how horribly afraid she actually was. "Of what, Franny?" he asked gently. Thus far, it had been a night for honesty, and he prayed she would continue in the same vein. "Of me? Of my touching you?"

"The touching part, yes."

He nearly smiled again at that. Her expression said more clearly than words that the mere thought of anything physical between them appalled her. Only it was nothing to smile over. Nothing that caused her such pain could be taken lightly, even if he saw it as absurd. "I'd never do anything you didn't like," he assured her.

"I don't like *any* of it."

"I see." And he did. All too clearly. The problem was that Franny didn't. "Franny, with the right man, it can be magical."

She gave a slight shudder. "Yish."

There was no help for it; in spite of his efforts to the contrary, he grinned. "Yish?"

"I *hate* it. All of it. That's why you frighten me, because I know you won't let me hide inside the dream places. You'll make me—"

Chase touched a fingertip to her sweet mouth. "You're wrong, Franny. I'll go with you into the dream place."

Her eyes widened, and she freed her mouth to say, "It's *my* place, my private place. I don't want you to go there with me. I don't want anyone to."

"I see."

"No, you don't see." She jerked out from under his grasp and put several paces between them. "It's how I survive. Can you understand that? It's the only way I can live with all of it. And you'd ruin it if I let you."

She spun to look at him, her heart in her eyes. "If I let you, you'll destroy me as well. Why can't you see that?"

"Maybe you should explain it to me."

She threw up her hands. "Explain it to you? You dangle dreams in front of me like candy before a child. You make me want things I can never have. Have you any idea how that hurts? I was content with my life until you came along. Now all I do is think about the things I *could* have if only a miracle happened. The problem is, miracles don't happen for women like me. We're standing in the back row, and when God gets time to work wonders, He puts forth the effort for worthy people, not whores."

"Worthy people? Honey, there's no one more worthy than you."

"How can you say that? People switch sides of the street when they see me on the boardwalk! I'm dirty in their eyes, and in God's as well. How can you even consider marrying me? Having children with me? I'm a pariah! And that will never change. You can't wish what I am away."

"We'll leave here," he assured her. "I work the timber, Franny. The land I bought is clear up near Canyonville. No one there would even know you. As for the people here, who gives a shit what they suspect? If they've glimpsed your face, it was only that, just a glimpse. The only people who'll know for sure who you are are May Belle and Gus. The others may whisper and speculate and accuse, but if we're only here for occasional visits, who cares? We'll have a life elsewhere among people who have no idea."

"You're dreaming."

"Life is dreaming. Without dreams, what have we got? Dream with me. Take a chance with me. If Canyonville isn't far enough away, we'll go someplace else."

"What about my family? They need me."

"They need the money you provide. I'll continue to support them."

"And what of your dreams of being a timber baron?"

Chase sighed and raked a hand through his hair. "It'll just take me longer, that's all."

"Forever, maybe? Oh, Chase, it wouldn't work. You'd end up hating me. Don't you see that?"

"No. I'm in love with you, Franny."

She averted her face as if he'd slapped her. "Oh, God!"

"It's true. I think I fell in love the first time I saw you, and it's been downhill ever since. I want a life with you. Is that so impossible?"

"I'm afraid it is. You aren't being realistic."

"And you? Are you being realistic? We can make it work if you'll just give it a chance. I promise you that. At least think about it." He scrubbed his mouth with the back of his hand. "Goddamn it! You're the stubbornest woman I've ever known, and that's a fact. I can't stay here forever, you know. My ribs are long since healed. I have to go back to work. How long are you going to shilly-shally?"

"Shilly-shally? You're upending my whole life."

"What life?" he shot back. "Do you call that room above the saloon a life? Stolen moments with my sister and her kids, is that a life? Hell, no. Isn't it about time you grabbed a handful of happiness for yourself? The excuse of your family is gone, Franny. The only thing holding you in Wolf's Landing now is fear. Are you too big a coward to take a chance on me?"

She stared at him for an endless moment. "Maybe I am. Maybe I'm afraid to believe it's possible because I want it so much. I don't know."

"Find out."

"Oh, Chase. You make it sound so simple."

"It is. All you have to do is go away with me. Take the gamble. I swear to you, Franny, you'll never regret it. At least tell me you'll think about it."

She took a shaky breath and finally nodded. "All right. I'll think about it. But I want some time, Chase."

"A day."

"A week," she shot back.

"A week?" He swore under his breath. "All right, a week."

"And I want you to stay away during that time."

"For a week? Hell, no."

"Yes. When you're around, I can't think straight."

"Dammit."

"A week isn't that long."

"No customers in that time," he warned. "I'll give you money to cover what you would earn, but no working."

"No working," she acquiesced.

The instant she agreed to that stipulation, Chase knew he had won even if she wasn't aware of it yet. A few weeks ago, her precious clientele had meant everything to her, and now she was willing to jeopardize it. Whether she realized it or not, she was beginning to trust him, if only a little. It wasn't exactly what he would term a giant stride, but at least it was in the right direction.

Toward him.

13

When Franny returned to the saloon later, she found May Belle waiting in her room. Going to join her friend where she sat at the table, Franny studied her face. May Belle so seldom invaded Franny's inner sanctum that she couldn't help but be concerned.

"Is something wrong?"

May Belle turned twinkling blue eyes on her and smiled joyously. "No, honey. For once in my misbegotten life, I think everything's actually going right." She squirmed in her chair, clearly so anxious to share her news she could scarcely contain herself. "Oh, Franny. I know you'll think I'm nuts, but I'm going to do it. I'm actually going to do it!"

Even though Franny had a fair idea what this was about, she decided to err on the side of caution.

Nonetheless, May Belle's happiness was contagious and she smiled in spite of herself. "You're going to do what?"

"Marry the old coot!"

"Shorty?"

"Who else? Gus, maybe?" May Belle hugged herself. "I can't believe it. He actually serenaded me at my window earlier! Oh, Franny, it was so romantic. He said if I didn't say yes, he'd sing all night. Can you imagine that?"

Franny could only shake her head in stunned amazement. Shorty had to wear suspenders to hold his britches up. She couldn't imagine him serenading anyone.

"He said I'm beautiful," May Belle said on a sigh. "Dressed like this, and he thinks I'm beautiful? The silly old fool."

On that point, Franny agreed with Shorty. Even in her threadbare, white cotton nightdress with her brassy hair tousled and her face devoid of make-up, May Belle cut a fine figure for a woman her age. But Franny thought it was more than that. There was a goodness that shone from within May Belle, a sweetness that had never been destroyed, not even after years of working in the world's oldest and ugliest profession.

"Oh, May Belle, you *are* beautiful. Shorty's absolutely right about that."

A flush of pleasure touched May Belle's cheeks, and a mistiness came into her eyes. "I'm so happy, Franny. After all these years, I finally found me a Prince Charming. He doesn't look like much, I know. At least not to other folks. But to me, he's about the handsomest fellow who ever walked. I suppose you're going to remind me how foolish an idea it is, me marrying him. That he'll probably bleed me dry financially and take off."

"No," Franny said softly. "I'm not going to do that. Indigo loves Shorty like family. That's good enough for me." As she spoke, it occurred to her that Chase was actually Indigo's brother. "I think you should get married and never look back."

May Belle shook her head. "I hate to leave you, that's the only thing."

"Don't worry about me." A flutter of nerves attacked Franny's belly, and she gulped on a sudden wave of nausea. Since meeting Chase, her constant state of agitation had made her feel queasy quite a lot. "In fact, I'm thinking about leaving myself."

"To go where?"

"Somewhere up around Canyonville." Franny could scarcely believe it was her speaking, but as she said the words, she knew how sincerely she meant them. "I've found my own Prince Charming, and he's asked me to marry him."

"Chase?"

Fighting back tears, Franny nodded.

"Praise be!"

"I'm so scared, May Belle! I've never been so terrified. Not just about him taking me off somewhere and then leaving me. But about—well, you know. I *hate* being touched. I don't know how I'll bear it. Chase won't let me think about my meadow filled with daisies, I can guarantee you that."

The older woman burst out laughing. "Thank God!" After her mirth subsided, she leaned forward to place a hand over Franny's. "Honey, you've never been with a man you love. It's a whole different kettle of fish, believe me. And with a handsome devil like Chase Wolf?" She rolled her eyes. "To hell with daisies."

"My daisies have kept me sane."

"I know, honey, but you won't be needing them from now on." May Belle's eyes were cloudy with understanding. "Trust me on that. It'll be nice for you with Chase. He's a fine young fellow. So much like his pappy it's scary sometimes. But Hunter's a fine, honorable man. If Chase is half the man, he'll treat you like a queen."

"You aren't going to caution me about making a mistake?"

May Belle smiled. "If it was any other man on earth, yes, I'd be raising sand. But not with him. He knows about your family, and he's still dogging your tracks. He wouldn't be if he didn't truly care about you."

"I've asked for a week to think about it."

May Belle whooped with laughter again. "Me, too! Ain't that peculiar? I was playing hard to catch. How about you?"

"Don't I wish. I'm just scared to death." Franny glanced at her window. The glass was an oily black from the darkness beyond, and the soft glow of the lantern on the table threw her reflection against the pane. She stared at herself for a moment. "I just hope I'm not making the worst mistake of my life."

*   *   *

Without Chase to fill up her hours, Franny found time to do all the things she'd been neglecting these last weeks. One afternoon, after finishing a shirt for little Hunter and a summer dress for Amelia Rose, she went to visit Indigo. The four of them escaped the July swelter by going down to the creek. Indigo took a picnic basket along. Franny took one look at the venison sandwiches Indigo drew out and felt as if she might be sick.

"None for me, thanks."

Indigo flashed her a concerned glance. "What's wrong? You always loved my venison sandwiches."

Franny touched a hand to her rolling middle. "Nerves, I think. My stomach's been going end over end a lot lately."

Indigo's eyes widened. After a moment of stunned silence, she said, "You aren't—I mean, you couldn't be—you aren't in the family way, are you?"

Franny laughed. "No, of course I'm not. I had my complaint right on schedu—" She broke off, trying to recall her last menstrual cycle. Because she hadn't been working recently, she hadn't been watching the calendar as carefully as she usually did. "I'm sure I'm not late, Indigo. I always get my complaint like clockwork. I just forgot to watch for the date this month. With Chase monopolizing so much of my time, I haven't been keeping up with much of anything. Matthew has a birthday the last of August, and I'm supposed to make him a shirt and trousers. I haven't even picked out the yardage yet."

The troubled frown vanished from Indigo's forehead, and her lovely blue eyes filled with curiosity. "How's it going with Chase, by the way?"

Hunter, who was playing in the creek, sent up a splash. Franny giggled and wiped a droplet of water from her cheek. Feeling embarrassed, she watched the children for a moment. Amelia Rose was tottering bare-foot along the bank, collecting curiosities, most of which she tasted before tossing them down. "Things are going fairly well, I guess. That's why I'm so nervous." She slanted a look at her friend. "How would you feel if I became your sister-in-law?"

Indigo whooped with joy. Venison sandwiches went in every direction as she sprang to her knees to hug Franny. "How would I feel? Oh, Franny, I'd be over the moon! You mean he asked you? He asked you to marry him? Oooh! I'll kill him when I get my hands on him. He came over for coffee this morning and never said a word."

Still feeling a little nauseated, Franny extricated herself from Indigo's enthusiastic embrace. "That's because I haven't given him an answer yet. But I'm thinking about it." She met her friend's gaze. "I have to admit, I'm a little frightened. It's a big step to take."

"Yes, it is," Indigo admitted. "But, oh, Franny. What a joy it could be. Chase is a good fellow, truly he is. He'd be a kindly husband, I'm sure. And he'd never, ever, not in a million years, ask a woman to marry him unless he loved her. I'm stunned that someone's finally snagged him. I should have guessed. He's had a bee in his bonnet since the first time he clapped eyes on you, and that's a fact. Oh, I can't wait to tell Jake. Will he ever laugh. Chase used to swear up and down he'd *never* get married."

"I haven't said yes yet," Franny reminded her.

"But you surely will. You love him, don't you?"

Franny's stomach turned another slow revolution, which convinced her more than ever that nerves were responsible for her queasiness. "Actually, Indigo, I'm not sure. I like him a lot. And he's very attractive."

Indigo leaned forward, avidly curious. "How does he make you feel?"

Franny considered the question. "Do you promise not to get mad? He is your brother."

"Of course I won't get mad."

"Well . . ." Franny nibbled her bottom lip. "The truth is, Indigo, he makes me feel kind of like I swallowed a bucketful of garter snakes."

Indigo threw back her tawny head, shrieked with laughter, and fell prostate on her back, completely oblivious to the sandwiches scattered around her. Franny couldn't see what was so funny and only stared at her. "It's love!" her friend finally managed to say between gasps for breath. "I felt exactly that way with Jake, only I thought it felt kind of like a bunch of minnows swimming around in my belly."

"That's close enough."

Indigo burst into giggles again. "It passes. And it's ever so nice when it does."

"I hope so. It's not a very pleasant feeling." Franny touched her waist again. "I feel a little squiggly just thinking about him."

"The only cure is marriage." Indigo sighed and sat up. She smiled as if she knew a wonderful secret. "Oh, Franny, you'll be so happy. I just know it. I'm so pleased for both of you. My two favorite people, and you've fallen in love. It's a dream come true. My best friend will be my sister. Just think! For the rest of our lives, our families will gather together for holidays and special occasions. Your kids, and our kids. Won't it be wonderful?"

It not only sounded wonderful, it sounded incredible. But for once, Franny dared to dream. Of children and Christmas trees. Of tables laden with food. Of love and laughter. Of belonging. Tears filled her eyes. "Oh, Indigo, do you really think it could happen for me? I'm afraid to believe it might for fear it won't."

"Of course it can happen! Why not? Just tell Chase yes, you silly. That's all there is to it."

That's all there is to it.

Franny hugged those words close as she walked back to the saloon. She tried to imagine what it would be like to walk along a boardwalk like this and look into the shop windows without wearing her broad-brimmed bonnet. To greet the other ladies and have them nod politely. To feel a part of a community. Mrs. Chase Wolf. Franny Wolf. Francine Wolf. It had a wonderful ring to it.

As she ascended the stairs to her room, the greasy smells from the kitchen made Franny feel a little queasy again. Once closeted in her quarters, she stepped over to her calendar where it hung on the wall. She had already turned to the month of July, and she quickly scanned the squares for the little X she always drew to mark the beginning of her cycle. How odd. There was no X. Had she forgotten to count forward from her last cycle to pinpoint her due date?

She supposed that had to be it. She smiled slightly

at the oversight. With Chase hounding her, day in and day out, it was a miracle she hadn't forgotten her head someplace. Intending to rectify matters, Franny flipped back to June to find the days of her last complaint, which she always marked with a line drawn horizontally through the squares. Her heart felt as if it dropped to her knees. There was no line to mark the days of her complaint last month.

There was only a lone X to mark her due date.

Franny stared at it. An X with no lines. June 24th. She should have had her complaint then, and here it was past the middle of July. She was over three weeks late.

Shaking, Franny went to sit on the edge of the bed. She had never been late. Not ever.

The next afternoon, Franny went a few doors up Main to see Dr. Yost. Convinced he would provide a perfectly reasonable explanation for her nausea and skipped period, she was stunned when he looked so gloomy after examining her. Franny sat up on the edge of the table and rearranged her dress. She was so distressed at his expression that she scarcely thought about his seeing her face. Usually, when she needed medical care, she saw the doctor in Grants Pass.

"What is it? A flu of some kind?" she asked hopefully.

"You're May Belle's girl, aren't you?"

Franny felt heat wash up her neck. May Belle's girl. It sounded so ugly. "Um, yes. I work at the saloon."

He nodded and scratched alongside his nose. "Well, missy, I wish it was a flu ailing you. I know news like this isn't exactly welcomed by a sporting woman."

Franny closed her eyes. It couldn't be. Not now. Not after nine years of never getting caught. In three more days, she intended to tell Chase she would marry him. In three more days, this life would be behind her. She was about to get her miracle. Didn't God understand that? Her one and only chance at a miracle.

"It's hard to say for sure this early along, but my guess is you're well over two months gone. Definitely pregnant, judging from the feel of things."

Franny shook her head. "Are you sure you're not mistaken? I'm only about three weeks late. It being so early and all, couldn't you be wrong?"

His kindly gray eyes rested sadly on her face. "Honey, I wish I was. But in forty years, I've never missed yet. You're pregnant. The only question is exactly how far along you are." He regarded her with a thoughtful frown. "Only three weeks late, you say? And what was your last showing like? Normal? Or light and spotty?"

With a sinking feeling of resignation, Franny thought back. "Light and spotty."

He nodded. "Yes, I figured as much. That happens sometimes. Why, I've had women go as high as five months not realizing they were in the family way, and all because they had some spotting and a light show each month."

"I see."

The doctor said nothing in response to that. After a long while, he cleared his throat. "If you're thinking about asking me to help you out of this fix, I can't. And I won't recommend anybody who can. I don't care who tells you differently, it's dangerous. I won't be a part of it."

Feeling numb, Franny slid off the table and tugged on her bonnet. The doctor kept talking, but the words swam around her in a confusing jumble. She felt as though she were moving through a haze of cotton. Out the office door. Onto the boardwalk. Instinctively she turned toward the saloon. One foot in front of the other. She scarcely saw, scarcely heard, scarcely felt. Pregnant. She was pregnant.

When she reached her room, she sat on the edge of the bed and stared blankly at the floor. Pregnant. Chase would never marry her now. Taking a whore to wife, that was one thing. Wedding a woman pregnant with another man's child was quite another.

Franny didn't know what she was going to do. She couldn't continue in her profession pregnant. The flow of money she'd been receiving from Chase would stop the instant she told him. What of her family? What would happen to her mother and Jason now? Frankie and Alaina might find employment in Grants Pass, but neither could earn enough to keep their little brother in elixir and their family fed. The costs were exorbitant.

For just an instant, Franny considered not telling Chase. She could marry him and pretend the baby was his. Couldn't she? She was in the early stages of pregnancy. Only two months. When the child was born, she could make out as if it had come early. He'd never know. All she had to do was live a lie for the rest of her life.

A lie. Franny closed her eyes, knowing even as she toyed with the idea that she could never do that. Especially not to Chase. It was a despicable thing to even think about doing. But, if not that, then what?

Another possibility slid icily into her mind. Her gaze shifted to her clothing rod and the wire hangers there. Over the years, she had heard talk. She knew how some sporting women took care of problems such as this. The thought made her want to weep. All her life, for as long as she could remember, she'd wished for a baby of her very own. Now she was thinking about getting shut of it. Turning her gaze to the wall, Franny stared at the intricate pattern of daisies. A heavy, relaxed feeling entered her limbs.

She didn't have to close her eyes or be surrounded by darkness this time to find her meadow. Sunshine and daisies. A sweet breeze blowing. In a twinkling, she was there, all the problems and heartache far behind her. Her papa was sitting on a blanket with Ma, and the two of them were taking food from a picnic basket. Jason was toddling near them, his blue eyes dancing.

"Franny?" a voice called.

Breaking into a run, she went toward her parents. Papa looked up, his green eyes and red hair glinting in the sunshine. "Franny? Honey, what's wrong?"

Confused, Franny missed a step and turned in her dream world to see who was speaking. Not her papa. It was a woman's voice. May Belle? Ah, yes, May Belle. She smiled slightly, wondering how May Belle had found the meadow.

"Franny, stop this. You're frightening me. Come on, love."

Franny heard someone snapping their fingers. Then there was a stinging sensation on her cheek. She blinked and frowned.

"Dammit, Franny. Don't do this. Hey, girl. Wherever it is you've gone, you get right back here. Franny?"

May Belle. Franny could hear her clearly, but she couldn't see her. And she didn't want to. There was nothing bad here in the meadow. She could stay here if she wanted. The world where May Belle called from would move away, and this one could become her reality. She walked closer to her parents, and May Belle's voice grew more distant. Franny tensed to break into a run, but the frightened note she heard in May Belle's entreaties made her hesitate.

She looked over her shoulder. Saw May Belle's anxious face. "No," she whispered. *"Let me go, May Belle. Please let me go."*

May Belle reached through and cupped Franny's face in her trembling hands. "Oh, honey, you scared the sand right out of me. Are you all right?"

At the touch, Franny's meadow shattered like a crystal bubble. She blinked and gazed at the room in confusion. Never before had she slipped away so easily, nor had it ever been so difficult to make herself come back.

Pain filled Franny as she recalled her reasons for escaping to the meadow in the first place. She closed her eyes, wishing with all her heart that she could have stayed there. She was so tired. So horribly weary of it all. In this world, all there was for her was pain, and more pain. Every time something good almost happened, God prevented it. Like marrying Chase. There'd be no cottage and a picket fence for her. She was pregnant. Not even Chase Wolf could overlook that.

"Oh, May Belle," she whispered raggedly. "It's happening again."

"What is, honey?"

"God won't let me have anything or anyone to love. I'm bad, and He doesn't want me to be happy. Not even a little bit. That's my punishment. Don't you see? Every time I love something, he takes it away."

May Belle crouched before her and took her hands. "Oh, now. If that isn't the silliest thing I ever heard, I don't know what is."

"No, it's not silly. I loved my cat, Toodles. Remember? And he died."

May Belle winced at the reminder. "Oh, honey, that wasn't God. That was two mean-hearted drunks being cruel." She rubbed Franny's hands. "Lord, you're like ice, girl. What put you in this state?"

Franny had difficulty saying the words. "I'm pregnant."

The older woman blanched. Releasing Franny's hands, she pushed to her feet and paced in agitation. "Are you sure?"

Franny gulped down a sob. "Yes, I'm sure. I just visited Dr. Yost, and he says I'm pregnant."

"Oh, dear God."

May Belle's appalled reaction cemented in Franny's mind the seriousness of the situation. "What on earth am I going to do, May Belle?"

No reply. For what seemed forever, May Belle just stood there. Then she heaved a weary sigh and came to sit on the edge of the bed. "If you don't have the most miserable luck, Franny, I don't know who does. How can this happen now? Right when everything was looking up for you?"

Franny fought off another urge to weep. "He won't want me now."

May Belle didn't ask who. It was obvious to whom Franny referred. "Not unless he's a saint," she finally admitted. "And those are in short supply in this old world, I'm afraid. Ah, sweetie, what a pickle."

May Belle's plump arm curled around Franny's shoulders. The warmth of it was her undoing. With a sob, she hid her face against the other woman's bodice. "I can't work while I'm pregnant, May Belle. What'll happen to my family? To Jason and my mamma? They're so helpless. I've always taken care of them. What will they do without the money I've always taken home each month? How will they survive?"

May Belle patted her back. "We'll think of something, honey. We'll think of a way. I've got some money set aside."

A pocket of air snagged in Franny's throat, and she nearly gagged on it. "I can't take your savings, May Belle. How would I pay it back? I can't stay here at the Lucky Nugget and raise a child. How can I continue working and raise a child anywhere? What sort of life would it have?"

No answer. Just a heavy silence that spoke more eloquently than a thousand words.

"We both know what I have to do," Franny whispered.

"Let's not get hasty. There has to be another way. Just let me think on it for a bit."

"What other way, May Belle? Name me a single one."

"Maybe a couple who wants a baby? Let me do some asking around, hm?"

"A whore's baby? Oh, May Belle, you're dreaming.

People are afraid of disease and defects. You know it as well as I. And who can blame them? They'd have no way of knowing if I was healthy."

"That doesn't mean we can't find someone."

"And if we do? You and Shorty were counting on your money to build a house along the creek. I know you were. It might be years before I can pay you back. If I have the baby, I'll start back to work straight away, but most of what I make goes to support my family. The little bit that's left doesn't amount to a lot."

"I'll think of something," the older woman vowed. "You just promise me you won't do anything rash until I get it worked out. Promise me, Franny. What you're thinking about—honey, more often than not, gals die doing that. They miss their mark and end up bleeding to death. You can't take that kind of chance."

Franny wasn't sure she was going to have a choice, but rather than worry May Belle, she reluctantly promised not to do anything right away.

"Listen," May Belle said. "I'm gonna walk down to the church and—"

"The church?"

"Of course, the church. What better place to start than with the preacher? He's sure to know a childless couple. And if he doesn't, he can ask around. There's bound to be someone who'd love to have a baby, Franny. Someone who'd be willing to take a chance on its being healthy. We just have to look till we find them, that's all."

Franny didn't share in her friend's optimism. When May Belle finally left, Franny lay on the bed and stared at the ceiling. No matter how she circled it, she could see no conceivable way that she could carry this child. May Belle had been saving all her life for her retirement years. Franny couldn't allow her to squander that money. Unexpected pregnancies were a part of this profession. A woman grew hard and did what she had to. It was as simple and horrible as that.

14

Chase was in the barn oiling tack when Gus came bursting through the open doorway. Hair wind-whipped, eyes wide with fright, he was panting so hard it took him a moment to speak. Chase dropped the harness he held and pushed slowly to his feet, his heart slamming with dread.

"Gus, what is it?"

Still heaving for breath, the plump barkeep gulped and rubbed his mouth with the tail of his white apron. "May Belle. She says—it's Franny—you'd better come—quick."

Franny. Chase had suspected it the moment he saw Gus. Without pausing even so much as to wipe his hands, he ran out of the barn. The Lucky Nugget was only a short distance up Main, but in that moment, it looked like a country mile to Chase. Lengthening his stride, he cut up the center of the thoroughfare, zigzagging to miss a wagon, then a horse. Franny. Something terrible had happened. May Belle would never have sent Gus to fetch him otherwise.

Franny. Oh, God. Oh, God. A dozen possibilities raced through Chase's mind, each more awful than the last. That she'd fallen on the stairs. That a customer had gone berserk. He pictured her beaten and unconscious. Weeks ago, he had decided that he loved the girl. But it took the thought of losing her to make him realize just how much. Franny, his little green-eyed angel. Jesus. If someone had hurt her, he'd kill him. With his bare hands, he'd squeeze the life right out of the son of a bitch.

Chase hit the boardwalk outside the saloon, his boots impacting on the wood, the sound a hollow resonation. Shoulder first, he shoved through the swinging doors into the dimly lit saloon. At so early an hour in the afternoon, there was only one customer, a faceless miner who sat in the shadows, one hand curled around a whiskey jug. Chase barely spared him a glance. Veering right, he raced for the stairs, using the banister to swing his weight and lend himself impetus.

"Franny!" He hit the landing. Her door stood open. "Franny."

Chase wasn't sure what he expected to see as he plunged into the room. Chaotic disarray, perhaps. Instead everything appeared to be in perfect order. May Belle stood near the bed, her face white and haggard, her eyes dark with worry. Chase staggered to a halt.

"Where is she?" he demanded.

"I was hoping maybe you could tell me that. She isn't with Indigo, and I'm worried, Chase. Real worried."

After the fright her summons had given him, Chase felt more than a little irritated. "You're worried because she went somewhere? She comes and goes all the time."

May Belle gestured at the bed. Chase turned to look. The spread was a bit rumpled, as if Franny had been lying on it. But otherwise— His gaze landed on a long piece of wire. He stepped closer to get a better look and saw that it was a coat hanger someone had untwisted and straightened. Not understanding the significance, he glanced back at May Belle.

May Belle's eyelashes fluttered to her cheeks. After drawing a tremulous breath, she said, "She saw Dr. Yost a couple of hours ago. He told her she's pregnant."

Chase tried to assimilate the words. Pregnant. Understanding finally dawned, and he shot another look at the coat hanger. "Oh, my God."

"She was going to accept your marriage proposal, you know," May Belle said with a wobble in her voice. "She was so happy." She raised her hands then slapped her ample hips. "And now this. I swear, that girl's never had a fair hand dealt to her in her whole life, and now this."

Chase felt as if his legs might fold. From living in the logging camps, he'd come to know more about the shady side of life than he cared to. It wasn't necessary for May Belle to explain how Franny had intended to use the wire, or for what. The thought terrified him. Pray God Franny hadn't gone through with it. Women who did such things often ended up dead.

"We have to find her," May Belle said shakily. "God

knows where she might have gone or what condition she's in. If she used that hanger, she could be—" Her voice broke and she cupped a hand over her eyes. "I'll never forgive myself for leaving her alone. Never. I knew she was upset, that she didn't know what she was going to do. I just didn't realize how desperate she was feeling. Old fool that I am, I left her alone—only for a few minutes, mind—but when I came back, she was gone."

Gone. Oh, sweet Jesus. Chase spun and ran from the room. When he exited the saloon onto the boardwalk, he stopped to glance wildly in every direction. If not to Indigo's, where might Franny have headed? The possibilities were endless.

Acting on instinct, Chase cut across the street and went down an alley. If he had just received devastating news and were feeling desperate, he would find a secluded, peaceful place to lick his wounds. In his estimation, there was nowhere more peaceful or secluded than the shady banks of Shallows Creek, one spot in particular. He was convinced Franny might have gone there.

His heart slammed like a sledge as he raced through the maze of trees. Undergrowth loomed in his path. He didn't waste time trying to go around it. What he couldn't jump over, he plowed through. The pictures inside his head terrified him. Franny lying along the creek, her life seeping steadily from her body in a crimson flow. Oh, God. And May Belle blamed herself? He was the one to be held accountable. He should have insisted Franny marry him weeks ago. Failing in that, he should have at least made sure she believed how much he loved her. Nothing could change his mind about that. Nothing. Certainly not a pregnancy. Loving Franny as he did, how could he fail to love her child?

He found her sitting beneath the sprawling oak tree whereon he had once carved their names. It seemed to Chase that a lifetime had passed since that night. Arms encircling her ankles, she sat on the grass, her face pressed against her upraised knees. Beside her on the grass lay her sunbonnet. She wore a faded blue shirt-waist, which he quickly scanned for signs of blood. Nothing. Physically, she looked perfectly fine. As perfectly fine as a person could be when her heart was breaking. Like a lost child, she rocked rhythmically back and forth. Above the rush of the water, Chase could hear her sobbing. Deep, tearing sobs.

His first impulse was to rush over and gather her into his arms, to assure her that he would take care of everything and that she needn't worry, but the sound of her sobs, the utter hopelessness they expressed, held him back. No child, this, but a woman. Since the age of thirteen, life had forced her along a path she never would have chosen for herself otherwise. Now Mother Nature had finally put her in checkmate. She could no longer continue in the way she had always gone, but neither could she retrace her footsteps, and for a woman in her profession, there were few detours.

In that moment, Chase ached for her as he never had for anyone. Life had robbed her of so much. Not only of her girlhood, but all the other things people took for granted, not the least of which was a right to walk with her head held high. Now he was about to rob her yet again by rushing to her rescue and offering to make her his wife? His intentions were good, and God only knew he loved her. The problem was, did *she* know it?

Franny. Tears stung Chase's throat as he regarded her. If any woman on earth deserved to be properly courted and wooed, she did. Flowers, an engagement ring, a romantic proposal on bended knee, a fancy wedding with all the trimmings. Other young women took those things for granted, expected and even demanded them. For Franny, those things were dreams that could never be.

As Chase moved slowly toward her, he felt impotently angry. Not with her, of course, for none of this could be laid at her door. And certainly not with himself. After seeing that wire hanger on her bed, the way he perceived it, he had one choice, and that was to marry the girl as quickly as he could. He didn't dare do otherwise. But damn if he didn't want to shake his fist, if not at God, then at fate, for pushing her into yet another situation over which she had no control.

Granted, Chase had been hoping she would marry him for quite some time, and if left to his own devices, he might have pressed his suit by fair means or foul. But he never would have forced her. Now he had no alternative. If he had to, he'd use blackmail. If she detested him for that, so be it. Anything was better than what she obviously had in mind, which was to end her pregnancy, consequences be damned.

A baby. In all the rushing about, Chase hadn't spared more than a second to think about the child, and now he couldn't allow himself to. According to the beliefs of his father's people, if a man claimed a woman, he also claimed her children, and in the claiming, they became his as though by birth.

As if she suddenly sensed his presence, Franny jerked her head up and fastened aching eyes on him. With trembling hands, she quickly wiped her cheeks. "Chase," she said weakly.

He knew she wished he'd go away, but he wasn't about to oblige her. Lowering himself to the ground beside her, he draped his arms over his upraised knees. To give her a moment to recover her composure, he pretended to be intensely interested in something at the opposite side of the creek. In his side vision, he saw her make a frantic attempt to straighten her hair. He knew it wasn't vanity that prompted her. Despite all the rotten hands life had dealt her, she still clung to her dignity. She didn't want him to see her like this. Beaten, with nowhere to turn. No, not Franny. If he allowed it, she'd try to put a bright face on things and finish shedding her tears after he was gone. Fat chance of that. From now on, he was sticking to this girl like a goddamned cocklebur.

Because there was no way he could think of to ease into the subject, he decided to live up to his name and cut right to it. "May Belle found the wire hanger. Not knowing where you'd gone or what you might have done, she panicked and sent for me."

Her voice thin and reedy, she said, "You mean she told you?"

"That you're carrying a child?" He fixed her with a relentless gaze. "Yeah, she told me."

Clearly ashamed, she averted her face. Plucking a handful of grass, she unfurled her slender fingers and stared at the green blades that striped her palm.

"Franny . . ."

Still not looking at him, she held up her other hand to silence him. "I know. Please don't say it. Just go away. Okay?"

Chase could only guess what she thought he meant to say. "Honey, I—"

"I understand. Really, I do." She made another odd little sound and shrugged. "It never would've worked anyway, Chase. I was—" She gulped and strained to steady her voice. "I . . . um . . . think you're a fine fellow for even trying to explain. Truly I do. Most men wouldn't have asked me in the first place, and they sure wouldn't bother to feel bad when something like this . . ." She gestured limply with her hand. "Anyhow, it's happened, and you don't have to say a word. I understand."

"Maybe I want to say a word. If I can get one in edgewise."

"Well, please don't." She scrubbed at her cheek with trembling fingers, then cut a glance at him. "Let's leave it unfinished. Okay?" She gave a breathy, tremulous little laugh. "I know it probably sounds silly coming from someone like me, but you're the only beau I've ever had. I'd like to keep the sweet memories and not end with sad ones."

The only beau I've ever had. By his measuring stick, he'd given her damned few sweet memories. Yet the way she saw it, there had been a wealth of them. "Franny . . ."

Her mouth quivered at the corners. Making a visible effort to fight back fresh tears, she said, "Before you came, I was sitting here wondering about—well, about dumb stuff, I guess. Like what color its eyes will be."

That she would confess such a thing to him told Chase more than she could know, most importantly that all his efforts to woo her hadn't been in vain. If nothing else, she had at least come to trust him as her friend. He felt as if she'd just handed him a large chunk of her broken heart. And, oh, God, how he wished he could mend it.

She lost the battle against the tears, and more welled over her lashes and onto her cheeks. Caught by a shaft of sunlight coming through the trees, they sparkled against her pale skin like diamonds. "Isn't that absurd? With everything else that I should be worrying about, all I can think of is the color of its eyes."

Digging deep, Chase found his voice. "I don't think it's absurd at all."

Her throat worked again as she struggled to swallow. "I . . . um . . ." She lifted one fragile shoulder. "Growing up as I did in a large family, one of the things I dreamed about as a little girl was some day having a baby of my own. Now God has sent me one, and no matter how I circle it, I can't see a way to keep it." She sniffed and shivered. "I guess that's the way it goes for some people."

"A wire hanger isn't a solution, Franny."

"No," she admitted shakily. "I meant to go through with it. I truly did. But at the last second, I began to wonder—" Her voice cracked and she swallowed to regain it. "Silly things, like whether it was a boy or girl. And suddenly it was no longer just a problem I had to get rid of. I . . . um . . . couldn't do it. I just couldn't."

When she glanced at him, her beautiful eyes were dark with shadows and struck a startling contrast to her pallor. Spiked like the points of a star and sable black with tears, her eyelashes enhanced their color, making them seem impossibly green. A shaft of sunlight cut through the trees behind her, creating a golden nimbus around her tousled hair. Never had she looked more like an angel to him. Chase wanted nothing more than to take her into his arms.

"Anyway," she continued in a wobbly voice, "I've decided I'll go ahead and have this baby. May Belle seems to think we can find adoptive parents, and she's offered to loan me some money to support myself and my family until I get through the pregnancy. I'm handy at sewing and good at crafts. I've been thinking that I might earn the wages to pay her back by putting things on consignment in stores. Not just here, but maybe in Jacksonville and Grants Pass as well. Do you think people would buy my stuff?"

Her resilience amazed Chase. But only for a moment. One of the things that had made him love Franny in the first place was that she had found a way to survive. She wasn't a very large woman, and her fragile features and large eyes made her seem all the more delicate. Thinking back to the first time he had clapped eyes on her, he recalled wanting to fight mountain lions for her and win. What he hadn't realized then and was just coming to accept now was that Franny didn't need anyone to fight her battles for her. It didn't necessarily take strength of arm to stand up against adversity.

"Well," she pressed. "What do you think?"

"I think," he replied slowly, "that you are the most amazing woman I've ever met."

She turned incredulous eyes on him. "Pardon?"

"You heard me."

A blush flagged her pale cheeks. "Oh, go on."

"No, seriously." She clearly didn't believe herself to be admirable, or anything close to it, which was all the more reason he felt he had to tell her. "You are one in a million. Beautiful, sweet, desirable. Being with you makes me feel ten feet tall."

He trailed a finger along the hollow of her tear-streaked cheek. The bone there felt incredibly fragile beneath his blunt fingertip, and he yearned to explore further, to feel the delicate structure of her jaw, the V of her collarbone. Loving her as he did, he cringed every time he remembered that wire hanger on her bed and what might have happened had she used it. As courageous as she obviously was, there were still no guarantees that she wouldn't do something desperate in a moment of panic. All it would take was for her to think her family might be left destitute, and she would probably risk anything to prevent it, including her life. As much as he hated to force her into anything, that was a chance he wasn't willing to take.

"Franny, what would you say if I asked you to marry me and let me be this baby's father?" he asked softly.

She threw him another incredulous glance.

"Please think about it before you answer. I love you, you know. That has to count for something."

"You're having me on, right?"

"Lord, no. This is nothing to joke about." Chase looked deeply into her eyes, trying to convey the depth of his regard for her. In his heart, he prayed, "Please, God, let her believe me and say yes. Don't make me do something that'll make her despise me." Aloud he said,

"I love you, Franny. Make me the happiest man alive and say you'll marry me."

What little color remained in her face drained away. "You can't marry me."

"Oh, yes."

She shook her head vehemently. "Have you lost your mind? You can't marry a pregnant prostitute."

God, how he detested that word. Prostitute. She referred to herself as though she were a scrap of excrement in a dung heap. It made him angry, impotently angry. She was so incredibly lovely, so infinitely precious to him. How could she look in a mirror and not see herself as he did? "The instant you agree to be my wife, you won't be a pregnant prostitute," he whispered. "You'll be my woman." Reaching to lay his hand over her waist, he added, "And this child will be mine."

She jerked at his touch as though he had burned her. Shoving at his arm almost frantically, she cried, "Don't be absurd. I don't even know who fathered this baby."

Seeing her panic, Chase drew his arm back, allowing her the space because he sensed she desperately needed it. "It doesn't matter."

"Yes! It does matter. It matters immensely!" She lifted her hands. "I can't even *guess* who the father was, Chase."

"Then my claim will be uncontested."

She stared at him as though he were insane. "If we sat in front of the general store and watched the men in this town walk by, I couldn't point to a single one and swear he had been to my room. I kept the lights out. Talking wasn't—"

"I know all about your rules, Franny," he inserted

gently. "I understand you weren't familiar with the men, that they . . ." It was his turn to gesture with his hands. "Jesus Christ. What difference does it make whether you know or not? The truth is, I prefer you don't. I want it to be *my* child. Only mine."

"Oh, Chase." Her chin started to quiver, and in an effort to control it, her lips drew down at the corners. "Don't do this to me."

He could tell by her shattered look that the plea was heartfelt. "Do what to you, sweetheart? Ask you to be my woman? To be at my side for the rest of your life? It's where you belong. Don't you see that?"

"Go away," she whispered raggedly. "Please, just go away. You're catching me at a weak moment. I can't be strong right now. Go away. Before I do something totally insane and say yes. Please?"

If not for the stark terror he saw in her eyes, Chase might have whooped with relief. She was about to say yes. Praise be to his mother's God and his father's Great Ones, she was about to say yes.

"You're bent on making me love you," she blurted. "You just never quit, do you? And it'll be a disaster if I do. Why can't you see that?" She turned away, as if she couldn't bear to look at him. "Do you think I'm made of stone? Right now, I'm more frightened than I've ever been in my life. And I've never felt so alone."

Aching to hold her, Chase settled for lightly touching her shoulder. She shrank from his hand. "Honey, you don't have to be alone. Never again. Let me take care of you, hm? Of you and your baby. Of your family. All it'll take is one word. Yes. And you won't have to feel afraid anymore."

A tearing sob caught in her chest. "Oh, Chase. Do you know what I nearly did?" She squeezed her eyes shut. "When I learned I was pregnant, I thought about marrying you and pretending this baby was yours. I thought about lying and saying it was yours. That's how desperate I am right now."

"Then do it." He caught her chin in his palm and forced her to meet his gaze. "Marry me, sweetheart, and tell me this baby is mine. That's what I *want*. Don't you see? I can't think of anything that I'd love more. Say it now. 'Chase, this is your baby. And, yes, I'll marry you.' Say it, Franny."

She scrambled away from him and shot to her feet. "Stop it! Just stop it!" Pressing rigid fingers against her temples, she whirled to present her back to him. "You've gone mad, and me right along with you. If I married you and you claimed this child, you'd end up despising me for it. Sooner or later, you'd begin searching the faces of the men in this town, looking for a resemblance to *your* child. You'd look in their faces and wonder how many of them were intimate with your wife, and the answer would be dozens. I can't do that to you, or to myself, and least of all to an innocent baby."

"Franny—"

She pressed her palms over her ears. "Shut up! Don't say another word, Chase Wolf! If you do, I might—" She broke off and shook her head. "It'd be madness."

"What might you do? Say yes?" He pushed to his feet. "Then, honey, do it. Follow your heart and do it."

"My heart?" She turned a stricken gaze on him. "Oh,

Chase. What of your family? Your parents? They'd never forgive you, and they'd hate me. They'd never accept this baby in a million years. It'd be a pariah."

"You know nothing about my parents," he admonished. "They'll love you and my child, I promise you."

"It's *not* your child."

Chase took a deep, bracing breath. "Yes. My woman, my child. Enough of this. Marrying me is what's best for both of you, and that's exactly what you're going to do."

"Don't tempt me."

"I'm telling you."

She fastened disbelieving and wary eyes on him, clearly alarmed at the firmness in his tone. "I just explained to you why I can't."

Chase planted his hands on his hips. "You're obviously too upset right now to make the decision. Either that or you're afraid to. So I'm taking the decision away from you. No choices. How's that sound? You *will* marry me. If everything turns to shit later, then it won't be your fault. I'm making the decision. If it's not the right one, I take full responsibility."

She regarded him through shimmering tears. "Oh, Chase, it's a lovely gesture. But I have to think about my baby."

"It's not a gesture, it's an order. And from this second on, you aren't allowed to think. Not when it involves this. You're going to marry me, end of conversation. So, let's go and get it done."

She hugged her waist. With her nose red from crying and her eyes widened with wary astonishment, she looked about twelve years old to him. He imagined she must have looked very like she did now on that fateful night nine years ago. Small, frightened, exhausted from crying. How any man who called himself a man could have forced himself on her, Chase didn't know. The thought literally sickened him. Even now, she wasn't much bigger than a minute. He knew he'd have no contest if he wrestled her to the ground. He could easily grip both her wrists in one fist and hold down her legs with one of his. Her struggles might be an irritation, but nothing more. He could help himself and linger over whatever part of her he fancied, taking her first with his mouth and hands, then by invasion.

Only, in the taking, he'd be gentle, and he doubted the bastard who'd done the honors had bothered. A man who paid top dollar to bust a little girl's maidenhead was the kind who got his jollies by overpowering someone helpless, by terrorizing, and by inflicting pain. It was inconceivable to Chase that other men had gone into that room afterward, seen a torn, bleeding child on the bed, and used her battered little body. What kind of monsters did such things? How could they reassume a cloak of respectability after and go home to their own children without feeling vile?

Moving toward Franny with slow, measured steps, Chase held out a hand to her. "Come with me, honey. It's over. No more agonizing. I've made the decision for you."

She regarded his outstretched hand in much the same way she might have a snake about to strike. "I can't."

"You don't have a choice."

"Of course I do."

His pulse kicking into high speed, Chase drew his

one big gun, angry with himself for using it against her, yet convinced all of this would be easier on her if he did. "No, Franny, you don't. If you want to continue this argument, we'll do it in your ma's parlor."

Her body stiffened and she fixed accusing eyes on his. "You wouldn't! I know you now, Chase. You wouldn't be that cruel."

"Try me."

"She's blind. It'd be absolutely ruthless to drag her into this."

Chase hardened himself to the plea in her eyes. "Franny, ruthless is in my blood. I'm Comanche, remember? I come from a long line of men who set their sights on women and were ruthless in the taking. It's kind of like the first time I climbed on a horse. It just comes naturally. I want you, and I'm going to have you. Simple as that." He shrugged. "As for ruthless, your mamma could give lessons."

"Lessons? What on earth do you mean?"

"That she's pretended to be a lot blinder than she actually is these last nine years, that's what."

She flinched as though he had struck her, which made Chase wish he could call back his words. He hadn't intended to get off on that subject, not now, maybe not ever. Some truths were too painful to face, and he sensed that for Franny, this was one of them.

"How dare you imply my mother knows," she cried brokenly. "How dare you?"

Chase could have implied a hell of a lot more, but his aim here was to protect the girl, not destroy her. Prepared for her to try and resist, he grasped her arm. "It's nigh on four o'clock. If we're going to see the justice of the peace and get this finished, we have to get cracking."

She tried to jerk her arm free. He held her fast.

"You can come on your own steam," he said softly. "Or I can carry you tossed over my shoulder. And, please, don't make the mistake of thinking I'm bluffing. I was raised on the stories of how my father took my mother captive. When I was a kid, I used to daydream about catching myself a pretty little gal someday and carting her off, just like my father did my ma. Throwing you over my shoulder would fulfill all my pubescent fantasies."

Her eyes widened. "That's barbaric."

"Ain't it just?" He smiled to take the edge off the threat. "All in fun, of course, albeit at your expense. Come on, honey. The second mode of transportation is going to draw a lot of stares once we reach town."

Her mouth quivered at the corners and a muscle beneath her eye twitched. "You wouldn't."

Chase feinted as if to grab her around the legs. With a startled squeak, she pressed her hands against his shoulders. "No, wait! I-I'll walk."

He slowly straightened. When she tried to step away, he tightened his hold on her arm.

"My bonnet," she said shakily.

"Leave it," he replied firmly. "From here on out, you won't be needing it."

15

Feeling as if she were flotsam being carried forth by a wave, Franny lived through the next hour in a daze. Brooking no further arguments, Chase hauled her back to town, searched out a justice of the peace, and demanded they be married immediately. Franny could scarcely assimilate what was being said. When the brief ceremony commenced, Chase had to nudge her with his elbow to prompt her to say "I do."

Just that quickly, she became Mrs. Chase Wolf. Chase sealed their vows with a gentle kiss, the first he had ever given her, and Franny was so numb, she couldn't feel it. Unfortunately, the numbness didn't extend to her stomach, and when they emerged from the justice of the peace's office onto the boardwalk, she felt a little nauseated, whether from nerves or her pregnancy, she didn't know. Swaying slightly, she clamped a hand over her waist.

"You okay?" he asked gently, his tone completely at odds with his martial arrogance of a few minutes ago.

Afraid to take chances, Franny muttered, "Sick," and gulped, afraid she might humiliate herself, and him, right there on the boardwalk. Splattering his black Montana boots wasn't exactly a champion way to begin their life together.

Their life? The words resounded in her mind. They didn't have a prayer of building a life. A circus, more like, with everybody gaping at them. The only difference would be that folks wouldn't have to pay to buy tickets.

"Ah, honey." With husbandly solicitousness, he slipped a strong arm around her waist. "Let's get you home then. Ma'll know something to give you. She's good with home remedies, especially for things like this."

Home. His ma. Franny had a hysterical urge to run. To where, she didn't know. Anywhere would suit, just as long as it was away from him. He couldn't just take her home, as he might a stray puppy he'd found. What would he tell his parents? That he'd married the local prostitute? And, oh, by the way, she was pregnant? The very thought made her skin shrivel. They would detest her on sight. How could he do this to her? Or to his parents?

Very simply, he did it by placing one foot before the other and hauling her along beside him. Through town. To his parents' house. Up the steps. Across the porch. The entire time, Franny was gulping to make her stomach behave and frantically thinking of ways she might escape.

Too late. He opened the front door, drew her inside, and hollered, "Ma! I've got a surprise for you!"

A surprise. Oh, God. Oh, God. No maybe about it, she was going to vomit. Dimly she was aware of the surroundings. A horsehair sofa, crocheted doilies, a gleaming wood floor and colorful rag rugs. Beyond the sitting room area, she saw a friendly-looking kitchen divided by a long plank table, the cooking area to one side, storage on the other. It was the kind of house that said "welcome" and warmly embraced all those who entered. Polished window panes winked at her from behind pristine white and crisply starched curtains.

From a distance, Franny had seen Chase and Indigo's mother, Loretta Wolf, at least a dozen times, and as she remembered her, she was a small woman with honey gold hair who always seemed to be smiling. When she sailed out of a room to the left, however, she looked like Franny's most dreaded nightmare, a lady from the tips of her black high-topped shoes to the coronet atop her head. Her lightweight alpaca shirt-waist, nearly the same shade of blue as Franny's, was beautifully appointed with intricate bodice pleats, a sheer frill of white at the collar and cuffs, cording and ruffles at the waist. Instead of walking like a normal person, she seemed to glide. When she spotted the woman at her son's side, she hesitated for an instant, then recovered from her surprise, her large blue eyes warming with welcome.

"Ah, a guest. How nice. I just put on some tea."

Franny felt Chase's arm tighten around her. "Is tea good for morning sickness?"

The floor disappeared. At least that's how it felt to

Franny. She threw a horrified look at her new husband. He was grinning as if he had good sense.

"Morning sickness?" Loretta frowned slightly. "Ginger tea would be just the thing for that. Or some raspberries." Her friendly blue eyes filled with concern as they shifted to Franny. "Are you feeling ill, dear?"

Ill didn't say it by half. She was going to faint. "I . . . yes, a little."

"Ma," Chase said huskily. "Prepare yourself for a startle."

Loretta's eyes widened. Then she shot another look at Franny.

"We just got married," Chase said gently.

To Loretta Wolf's credit, she didn't reveal the shock she must have felt by so much as the batting of an eyelash. Her lovely face immediately burst into a joyous smile, and she pressed her palms together as if having her son drag home the local whore was the answer to her lifelong prayer. "Married? Oh, lands, how wonderful!"

Franny decided the poor woman didn't have a clue who she was. It was either that, or she was tetched. Loretta hurried to close the remaining distance between them and clasped Franny's cold hands. "Oh, Chase, she's absolutely lovely."

Chase seemed a tad disappointed. "You don't act very surprised."

Loretta kissed Franny's cheek in welcome. "Of course not. Your father told me which way the wind was blowing well over a week ago. We'd begun to think you'd changed your mind. Oh, I am so pleased. Franny, isn't it? Indigo has nothing but wonderful things to say about you. Come in, come in. I'll put some ginger tea on to brew. It'll settle your tummy in nothing flat, I assure you."

In a whirl of skirts, she was off for the kitchen. Franny was so stunned, she forgot all about feeling sick. Chase gave her a jostle and winked when she looked up. "What did I tell you? There's nothing to worry about. Next to you, my ma is the sweetest woman who ever walked."

"I heard that!" Loretta called from the stove.

Chase laughed and led Franny toward the table. After seating her, he stepped across the kitchen to sweep his mother into his arms. She squeaked in surprise then chuckled. "Scamp!"

"Nobody'll ever take your place. You know that."

She gave him a thump on the forehead. "I was only teasing you. If you don't think she's the sweetest woman on earth, you need your head examined for marrying her." Loretta flashed a warm glance at Franny. "I'm just pleased you've finally gotten some sense about you. I was beginning to think you'd never give me a grandbaby."

"Fooled you, didn't I?"

"Yes, well, you never did do anything in the conventional way." Loretta extricated herself from his embrace to sprinkle ginger into a small pot of water. "I have no fresh," she commented to no one in particular. "But the dried works just as well."

"Where is Father?"

"He'll be home shortly. He's still at the mine." The teapot at the back of the stove began to whistle, and she grabbed a potholder to remove it from the heat. "I have dried raspberries, Franny. Once the ginger has settled your stomach, you can have a bit of supper and seeped berries for dessert. We'll have you feeling fit as a fiddle in no time."

Franny could only hope. Now that she was sitting down, her stomach had started to roll again. She guessed she must look as green as she felt, for when Chase turned to regard her, his eyes darkened with concern. "I think maybe you should lie down for a bit. I can bring you the tea in bed."

"No, I'm fine, really." Franny felt out of place sitting at his mother's table. Going to bed in her house was out of the question.

Chase was having none of that. Before Franny guessed what he meant to do, he scooped her up off the bench into his arms. The next thing she knew, he was carrying her up a loft ladder. Built on a slant, the ascending stairway might not have seemed so treacherous if he had gripped the rails to steady himself, but his arms were filled with her. With his every step, Franny feared they might plunge to the sitting room floor below, and she clung to his neck in terror.

"Remind me to carry you up to the loft more often," he teased.

Franny had a vague impression of a center wall that divided two sleeping areas. Chase veered toward the one on the right. A sunny window over the bed filled the room with brightness. Not releasing her, he somehow managed to flip the colorful quilt and sheet back before he lowered her onto the edge of the bed. Too sick to resist, Franny sat there like a lump while he removed her shoes. When he reached for the buttons of her shirtwaist, she was galvanized into action.

"No, please, I—"

"Don't be a goose." Brushing her hands aside, he began unfastening her bodice with expert fingers. "I'm your husband now, remember? Undressing my wife is one of the many privileges that comes with the honor."

Her husband. Her hands fell numbly to her lap. Two buttons, three. She closed her eyes, too ill to resist the situation and to frightened to contemplate how far he might take it. If he chose to strip her to the skin, what could she do? Insist he not? She felt sure his mother could probably hear every word that passed between them.

With the mastery of a man well practiced at disrobing females, he drew her shirtwaist down over her shoulders and peeled the sleeves off over her hands. Pulling her gently to her feet, he quickly untied her petticoats and bloomers, then skimmed the lot, along with her stockings, down her body. Franny shivered. As familiar as she had been with men, none had undressed her since her initiation into the profession. Nor had a man looked upon her when she wore nothing but a chemise.

Chase didn't linger over the chore. The instant she was stripped to the one undergarment, he pressed her back onto the bed and helped her to lie down, fluffing the feather pillow for her head and pulling the quilt up under her arms. It would have pleased Franny more to have it tucked to her chin. But she supposed that was asking a bit much of a newly married man. Naturally he wanted to regard his wife.

Which was exactly what he proceeded to do.

Franny felt like a bug pinned to velvet. She started

to close her eyes, but Chase forestalled her by touching a fingertip to her cheek. She settled her gaze on his dark face. Leaning over her as he was, he looked immeasurably broad across the shoulders, and his mahogany hair fell in glistening waves across his high forehead. The dark planes of his handsome face hovered scant inches from hers, making her feel breathless. Their marriage had taken place with dizzying speed, and she felt trapped. It was rather like testing cold water with the tip of one's toe, only to have someone shove you in from behind. Shocking. She felt as if she were about to go under for the third time.

Not entirely sure where the words came from, Franny blurted, "Oh, Chase, I'm so scared."

She half expected him to mock her for being so utterly absurd. She was a prostitute, and intimacy such as this should have been old hat for her. But instead of pointing that out, he smoothed the hair at her temples and said, "I know you are, sweetheart. I wish Ma had a cure. If she did, I'd brew it up myself and feed it to you by the spoonful."

The concern in his voice brought tears to Franny's eyes. "It won't work. I know it won't."

He leaned closer and held her gaze with his dark blue one. "Franny, have I ever lied to you?"

"No."

"Then believe me when I say it *will* work. You shouldn't be all upset like this. It isn't good for our baby. You should have happy thoughts, and you can if you'll only trust me."

"Do you have pockets full of magic or something?"

"Maybe," he said softly. "I'm a quarter Comanche,

remember. We have spells and talismans and incanta-
tions. I'll fish around inside my pockets and see what I
can come up with. The question is, if I work us up
some magic, will you believe in it with me? I don't
think it works otherwise."

Franny wanted to believe. With all her heart, she
wanted to. But instead she was filled with dread. He
had forced her to enter his world. And, oh, God, it was
everything she had dreamed it might be. His mother
was wonderful. His boyhood home had walls that
emanated warmth. And when she looked into his eyes,
she read a hundred promises she was terrified to
believe in. A wonderfully handsome husband, a baby, a
family of in-laws who welcomed her with open arms. It
was the dream of her life. An impossible dream.

"Chase? The ginger tea is done!" his mother called
from downstairs.

His eyes still holding hers, he straightened. "Be right
back."

As he disappeared around the dividing wall, those
three words rang in her ears, a simple assurance. She
was afraid to believe even in that. *Be right back.* She
knew in her heart that eventually he'd no longer want
to come back, that the time would come when he left
her and kept going.

The heartbreak of it was, she wouldn't blame him.

The ginger tea worked wonders. After drinking it,
Franny felt worlds better and closed her eyes, aware
that Chase held her hand and watched her, but too
exhausted to care. It had been an endless day. Her

world had been tipped upside down, then righted again, but nothing was the same. Nothing would ever be the same again. All she wanted was to slip away so she didn't have to deal with it all right now.

A meadow filled with daisies, sunlight, a sweet summer breeze, the sound of water gurgling over rocks. Reality or dream? The defining line between the two was becoming blurred, but Franny didn't care. She felt so safe in her meadow. Nothing could touch her there. Nothing bad could happen. Nothing could hurt her. It was a good place to fall asleep. A safe place.

When she awoke, the window above her looked out onto twilight. Startled, Franny shot up in bed and cocked an ear. The Wolfs' house was quiet. The appealing smells of their evening meal drifted upstairs to her from the kitchen, and in response, her stomach growled. Easing her legs over the side of the bed, Franny reached for her clothes.

After she had dressed, she crept down the loft ladder. The house was quiet and empty. The lanterns positioned strategically throughout the rooms to provide illumination after dark had not been lit as yet, and shadows fell across the polished wood floor. More at ease in darkness than light, Franny relaxed slightly as she drew to a stop in the center of the sitting room. Her gaze fell on a beautiful Chickering piano, its surface highly polished. Nearby, the horsehair sofa held court beneath an assembly of frames, some of which displayed pictures, some mementos. She stepped closer to study them, smiling slightly when she saw photographs of Chase as a boy. He had been good-looking even then, his eyes alight with mischief, his smile impish.

"My woman has all her memories on the wall," a deep voice commented from behind her. "This is because she believes she has a very small brain, yes? Most white people are the same. They think they have room in their heads for only the here and now."

Franny leaped and swung around. After peering through the shadows for a moment, she made out the dim shape of a large man sitting in an overstuffed chair near the hearth. Hunter Wolf. From her window above the Lucky Nugget, she had frequently watched him from afar as he walked about town. That was different from finding herself alone with him.

Bare-chested and sinister-looking with his long, dark hair, he seemed to loom as he rose and moved soundlessly toward her. She saw that he wore leather pants, fringed along the outer seams and tucked into knee-high moccasins.

"I frightened you. I'm sorry."

He halted within arm's reach of her. Looking up at him, she guessed he was about Chase's height, broad of shoulder and narrow of hip. Franny could see where her husband had gotten his dark good looks and air of wildness. At Hunter Wolf's hip rode a huge knife, its hilt worn smooth and darkened with age. She couldn't help but wonder how many people he might have scalped with it years ago.

"So . . ." His dark blue eyes slid slowly over her. "You are Franny. I have seen you, of course." He made a circular motion near his temple that made her wonder momentarily if he questioned her intelligence. "Always with the hat and—what are the wide ruffles called?"

Relieved that he had been referring to her bonnet, she said, "Ruching?"

"Ah, yes, ruching." He nodded thoughtfully. "I saw you many times, but didn't. Yes? The small woman with no face." He studied her for a long moment. "Now that the ruching no longer hides you, I can see why my son's footsteps led him always to the saloon."

Franny felt a burning flush creep up her neck. Bending her head, she stared blindly at the floor. "I'm sorry for inflicting myself on you and your wife like this. I know how you must—"

"Inflict?" he cut in.

She was so startled when he cupped her chin in his hand that she nearly parted company with her shoes. Before she recovered, he was lifting her face. "In this house, you will always look up, never down."

"But I—"

He slanted a thumb across her mouth to silence her, which was just as well, for Franny had no idea what she intended to say. "No buts." A slow smile crossed his firm lips. In that instant, he reminded her very much of Chase. "Around here, no one will trip you, so you need not watch your feet. If you stumble, one of us will catch you from falling. So look up, yes? The best things in life are ahead of you, daughter. If you hang your head, you may miss them."

With that, he released her and settled his gaze upon the wall. Inclining his head at the family portrait, he said, "I'm sure you know most of those homely people. The one standing behind Chase is my woman's sister, Amy."

Franny smiled to herself, for the Wolfs were a handsome lot, not a homely countenance among them. "Amy looks very like your wife."

"Yes. And some say my son is like me." He seemed to consider that for a moment. "I think I'm much better looking."

Franny gave a startled laugh. He chuckled with her. Then, catching her completely off guard, he draped a strong arm over her shoulders and pulled her close. There wasn't time for her to feel trapped or suffocated. Before she could completely register the sudden closeness, he pressed a fatherly kiss to her forehead and released her.

"Welcome, Franny. Into my house and into my heart."

With that, he turned away. Franny stood there rooted, her startled gaze fixed on his muscular back as he moved into the kitchen. "Chase has gone to collect your things," he called over his shoulder. "My woman is at Indigo's making woman talk. You slept through supper, and she left strict orders that I was to feed you if you woke up. Are you hungry?"

Franny pressed a hand to her rumbling stomach. "A little."

He arched a questioning glance her way. "And the sickness in your gut? It is gone?"

She gave another startled laugh. "Gone, yes."

He struck a match and lit a lantern on the dish board. The sudden flare of light played across his dark, sharply chiseled features. He looked even more like Chase under close scrutiny. His teeth flashed white as he smiled. "I go backward with my tongue sometimes. You will soon get used to it."

Franny hadn't meant to offend him. "I don't think you talk funny."

He narrowed an eye. "We don't speak untruths in this house, not even to be polite." His fleeting smile told her he was only teasing, but Franny had the distinct impression there was also an underlying note of seriousness. "I have odd expressions. Mostly I talk like everyone else, but my strange way of putting things has never completely gone away." He shrugged a shoulder. "Perhaps it is because I cling to my own ways, yes? To remain one of the People and not become one with the whites?"

Franny sat at the table and nervously folded her hands atop it. "Are you prejudiced?"

He narrowed an eye again. "You tell me."

"Considering the company you keep, I would guess not."

"That is good. It sounds like an awful thing to be."

She giggled again. The sound just burst out before she could stifle it. "You don't know what prejudiced means?"

"I know many twenty-dollar words, but not that one."

Trying to think of a simple way to put it, she explained, "It means to dislike a person because of his color or race."

"Ah. You are right. I am not prejudiced. My woman has pale skin, and I like her very much."

Franny smiled. "She's a very warm, lovely person."

"You have not felt her feet."

Franny gulped down another startled laugh. His twinkling eyes sought hers.

"That is why she keeps me, yes. To keep her warm? And I do not mind, for as you say, she is lovely. With her, I am like the bear to a honey tree, drawn by her sweetness."

"Chase says you took her captive," Franny blurted. "That isn't true, is it?"

"Ah, yes. Many winters ago, I stole her away from her wooden walls."

"And kept her against her will?"

"For a little bit of time."

He didn't seem in the least remorseful. Franny studied him, not at all envious of Loretta Wolf for having found herself at the mercy of all that muscled power. "It seems an odd way to begin a marriage."

"What begins very badly can only get better." He finished adjusting the lantern wick and fitted the globe into its base. He turned to regard her with suddenly solemn eyes. "Do I hear alarm in your voice? Do you fear that my son walks in his father's footsteps?"

Franny bit down on her inner cheek. Her first impulse was to lie, but Hunter Wolf's gaze was too compelling. "He's very determined to have his way in certain matters. I find that a bit unsettling."

"His way, or the way? He is my son. He stands tall above his brothers and sees into tomorrow with eyes like the midnight sky. Trust him to know where he is going, Franny. And to get you both there safely. He will find a path wide enough for you to walk beside him."

Franny lowered her eyes. Hunter Wolf made this situation sound like poetry. In truth, it was a tangled mess. And she was mightily afraid she and her baby would be the ones who suffered for it.

The front door swung open. With a bundled sheet slung over his shoulder, Chase elbowed his way inside. Upon seeing Franny, he said, "Oh, good. You're awake. I was starting to worry that you'd sleep through our whole wedding night."

Hunter winked at Franny. "Why should she not? You run off and leave her with only an old man to keep her company."

"I was only gone a half hour, and knowing you, you kept her entertained." Setting the bundle near the loft ladder, Chase raked a hand through his wind-tossed hair as he strode toward the table. Like his father's, his feet made little sound, even encased in boots. "Don't believe any of the lies he tells you about me. It was Indigo who filled the sugar bowl with salt and put the frog in Ma's water pitcher." He leaned over Franny and kissed her cheek. "Feeling better?" he asked softly.

"Much."

To Franny, the small house suddenly seemed overly full of masculine presence and she felt a little breathless. She was relieved when Chase moved past her into the kitchen. He investigated the pot on the stove. "Plenty of stew left. You want some?"

"I . . . um . . . yes, that would be nice."

Chase plucked a bowl from off the shelf and began ladling. His father stood beside him, slicing cornbread inside its pan. Lifting out a piece, he plopped it on the edge of the filled bowl. Grabbing a spoon out of a drawer, Chase came toward her. With a flourish, he plunked the offering on the table in front of her. "Lay back your ears and dig in."

Franny picked up the spoon. Both men watched her

expectantly. She hoped they didn't plan to stare at her as she ate. She took a bite. Chase seemed to be counting how many times she chewed.

"Would you like some milk?" he asked.

"No, thank you."

"Some butter for your bread?" Hunter offered.

Franny's mouth was full again, so she mutely shook her head.

"Jelly?" Chase asked. "Raspberry preserves!" He swept by her to investigate the cupboards along the wall behind her. "I remember Ma saying raspberries are good for morning sickness." Jars clanked. "Here we go."

Coming to the table, he sat the jar near her elbow and began working out the paraffin with the tip of his knife. Franny could only smile at the solicitous behavior. They clearly wanted her to feel at ease and in their eagerness were accomplishing just the opposite. Her throat tightened as her gaze shifted from one man's dark face to the other's. Like father, like son. Now she knew where that expression had originated. Chase piled preserves onto her square of cornbread. Apparently satisfied on that score, he stepped to the sink and wiped his blade clean.

"You should probably have some more ginger tea."

Franny nodded and sank her teeth into the slathered bread. It was delicious. So delicious that it caught her off guard and momentarily made her forget her self-consciousness. "Mmm."

"Good, huh? Ma's preserves are fantastic. She took the blue ribbon three years running at the fair."

"Really?" Franny took another bite. "I can see why. I

truly don't think I've ever tasted preserves to compare."

The door to the firebox creaked as Hunter opened it to stir the fire. Chase moved the pot of ginger tea over the heat.

"It doesn't have to be piping hot," Franny offered. "It's so warm an evening. I wouldn't want everyone to suffocate for the sake of tea."

"We get a nice breeze from off the creek," Chase assured her. "At night I open the window over my bed, and the draft keeps me as cool as a long, tall drink."

Because she supposed she would be sharing his bed later, Franny could think of no polite rejoinder. A sudden panic welled within her. Bed. Wedding night. She filled her mouth and immediately regretted having done so. The chunk of stew meat became larger and larger as she chewed. In Chase's loft bedroom there was no daisy wallpaper to stimulate her imagination. When he came to her, there would be no posted rules he'd be obliged to follow. Gus wouldn't be downstairs if she needed him. And worst of all, there'd be no limit to the time Chase could spend with her. At one o'clock, her shift wouldn't be over.

She was in up to her neck, and the shift would last a lifetime.

Franny shot to her feet. The bench scraped loudly across the floor at her sudden lurch. Chase and his father both turned to stare at her in puzzlement. "I . . . um . . . need a breath of air."

With that, Franny made her way blindly out of the house. Once on the front porch, she gulped greedily at the coolness, feeling dizzy and clammy. On legs that felt none too sturdy, she moved to a porch rail and grasped it for support. She wasn't afraid of Chase. She truly wasn't. So why did the thought of being intimate with him panic her so?

"You okay?"

The sound of his voice startled her. Between him and his father, she would be lucky if she didn't die of heart failure. She shot a frustrated glance over her shoulder. "Must you sneak up on me?"

"I didn't sneak. I just—" He broke off and sighed. Moving to stand beside her, he bent and braced his arms on the rail. Gazing off into the shadows of early evening, he said nothing for several seconds. To the east, the moon hovered, shimmering like a silver dollar against dark denim blue. Lofty pine trees stood in silhouettes of charcoal against the sky. "I'm sorry, Franny. I guess in our eagerness to make you feel at home, we did just the opposite."

His apology caught at her heart. No one could have been made to feel more welcome. "Oh, Chase, it isn't your fault. I'm just tense, that's all."

"I know, and we just made it worse." He laughed softly. "I hate it when people watch me while I eat. I don't know what I was thinking. We ran you off before you got much of anything down."

Franny dragged in another deep breath. "I'll eat more. I just needed a breath of air, that's all. Truly."

He shifted his weight and bent the opposite knee. After studying the palms of his hands a moment, he sighed. "I can understand your being a little nervous. About tonight and all. Especially after the way I railroaded you into it. My father believes you're feeling a little apprehensive about what I may pull next."

Franny started to feel breathless again. "Yes, well . . . I am, just a little."

He turned his hands and hooked his thumbs. Regarding his spread fingers, which suddenly appeared enormous to Franny, he said, "I'd never hurt you. You do know that?"

"Of course."

"And rabid dogs don't bite, either. Correct?"

She gave him a startled look. "Chase, I don't—"

"Let's not circle this, Franny. You're nervous. Because you're nervous, I'm nervous." He straightened and leaned a hip against the rail. "I know the few times with men that you didn't blank out weren't pleasant, and I don't blame you for feeling apprehensive. Really. It doesn't offend me."

"It doesn't?" she said with some relief.

The corners of his mouth quirked. "No. Why should it? Just trust me when I say you have nothing to dread."

"Thank you. I appreciate that."

"The question is, do you believe it?"

"I want to."

He caught her chin on the edge of his finger and lifted her face. "Sweetheart, if I could go back nine years and stomp the hell out the bastards who hurt you, I'd do it in a shot. But I can only go forward from here and try to make being with me as sweet for you as I can."

"Oh, Chase. I'm not comparing you to anyone. I haven't even thought—"

"Don't."

"Don't what?"

"Lie. I've caught the looks you've given me," he said huskily. "And I've read what was in your eyes. You've measured my strength a dozen times—no, a hundred—and you've shivered at the thought that I might use it against you. Don't pretend you haven't. It's an insult to my intelligence."

Franny twisted away and grasped the rail again. "I've earned my living making my body available to men for nine years. It would be absurd to dread doing the same with you."

"So you're absurd?"

"No, I—" She broke off and swallowed. "All right, yes, I'm being absurd. It's just that—"

"Just that what."

"It isn't the same with you."

"Thank God."

"You want more from me than those men did. Far more."

"Yes."

"And I'm afraid that—" She glanced over her shoulder at him. "I've always slipped away. I know that sounds incredible, but—"

"At first, yes. I couldn't fathom how you did it. Or why you'd bother. Sex is supposed to be—" It was his turn to break off. He laughed softly under his breath. "Anyway, I doubted at first. But I don't now. Not after you told me about your first experience. It makes perfect sense to me that you blocked it all out. It's the way you've survived, and I understand that."

"It's what I've always done. I'm very good at it now—at slipping away. Only with you, that night when we argued?" She pressed her fingertips to her throat. "I tried to—to leave, and I couldn't. Instead I was horribly aware of everything, of every touch, every heartbeat." Her voice went shrill. "I know it sounds stupid, but I'm nervous about being with you because I'm afraid I'll have to st-stay in my body. It doesn't even make sense, does it?" She gave a high-pitched laugh. "People can't leave their bodies. But somehow I do, and I—"

"Franny . . ." He stepped up behind her and encircled her waist. Tensing, he turned his arm to bunched steel around her, splaying his hand over her midriff, his thumb and a fingertip grazing the underside of her breasts. "Feel that?"

Her heart thumped wildly against her ribs, so wildly she felt sure he must feel it.

"It's yours," he whispered. "My strong arm is yours." He bent his head to nuzzle her hair. "It's your shield against harm. When you need support, it will be there to hold you up. When you're cold, it'll draw you close to my heat. But never will I raise it against you. Never. Do you understand me?"

"Oh, Chase."

"As for being with me, there won't be a need to slip away, I promise you. If you feel horribly aware, or horribly anything else when my hands are touching you, then you just tell me."

"And?"

She felt his chest jerk on a smothered chuckle. "We'll dispense with the horribly, of course."

"It may not be that simple."

"Sure it will. I love you, Franny, and I believe you love me, whether you're ready to admit it yet or not.

When people who love each other touch, there's no room for horrible. Only indescribable sweetness. That's how it will be between us, indescribably sweet. If it's not that way for you, I'll relick my calf and start over."

"Pardon me for saying so, but if you relick your calf, it'll just make it last longer."

At that, his chest jerked again.

"You can laugh at me all you like."

"Honey, I'm not laughing *at* you but with you."

"I'm not laughing. I'd prefer quick and horrible to endless and horrible while you're trying to accomplish the impossible. I don't *like* it, Chase. None of it. It's revolting to me."

"We'll see how you feel once I'm finished with you," he said smugly.

That was exactly what Franny was afraid of. "If it's awful and disgusting, I'll slip away," she confessed. "I won't be able to stop myself. And I'm afraid I'll hurt your feelings if I do."

"You won't hurt my feelings," he assured her. "If you can slip away while I'm making love to you, I'll be the one at fault, not you. It's my job to see to it you don't want to slip away. If I can't handle that, my name isn't Chase Wolf."

Marvelous. Now she'd become a challenge. Franny closed her eyes in dread. She immediately opened them again as Chase moved his hand up from her midriff to her breast. Through the cloth of her dress, his fingertips glided over her as softly as a whisper, searching for her crest, then tantalizing its peak with light strokes. Her breath caught behind her larynx. She felt her flesh begin to swell. The tip of her nipple hardened and became elongated to accommodate him. Lowering his head, he caught her earlobe between his teeth as he lightly pinched the flesh he had teased into throbbing erectness. His hot, moist breath rasped in her ear, tickling, sensitizing the skin along her neck into tingling awareness.

Franny's belly writhed and knotted as a thrill of sensation shot deep into her. Suddenly her legs felt weak, and she leaned more heavily against him, afraid she might fall. Angling his other arm across her hips, he held her fast against his chest, his hand still at play on her breast, his mouth waging a separate assault on the sensitive place just below her ear.

"Oh, God," she whispered.

"Mmm."

"Chase, I—"

He grasped the throbbing peak of her nipple and gave it a sharp roll that made her forget what she meant to say. Made her forget everything. A tremor ran the length of her body, and she moaned low in her chest, letting her head drop back against his shoulder so his wonderful mouth could make tantalizing forays lower along her throat.

"Sweet Jesus," he said in a raspy whisper.

Abandoning her breast, he clamped his large hand back over her ribs. His hand was shaking, and by the placement of his fingertips, she knew he was taking measure of her frantic heartbeat. Moving his lips in a whisper of kisses up to her temple, he took a deep breath, held it for endless seconds, and then exhaled with a shudder.

Franny came back to earth with a jolt. Still leaning

against him, tension reentered her body, and she fixed her gaze on the treetops. She could scarcely believe how she had responded to him and doubted that any lady would have done the same. Right now, he was probably thinking she had surrendered too quickly, that she was a tart. It occurred to her that she was damned if she did, damned if she didn't. She felt him lift his head. She was too humiliated to meet his gaze and was afraid of what she might see there.

Taking her by the shoulders, he slowly turned her to face him. She stared resolutely at his throat. With a bent knuckle, he caught her by the chin and leaned her head back. His dark eyes, aglitter with moonlight, delved deeply into hers and he smiled. "Ah, Franny, you are so precious." Chuckling, he dipped his head and playfully bit her lip. "Now you're embarrassed. I can't believe you sometimes."

Her lip tingled where he'd nipped it, and she ran her tongue over the spot, not realizing until it was too late that he was watching. A lambent gleam came into his eyes.

"Shit," he said raggedly.

Before she could ask him what was wrong, his mouth settled over hers. Startled, Franny planted her hands on his chest, intending to shove him away, but within a heartbeat, she was clinging to his shirt to hold herself up. His mouth. She'd never felt anything so hot and slick and soft. His tongue against hers made her think of the sweet, ripe center of a plum. It twined around hers, then slipped away to explore the roof of her mouth, tickling, soothing, tantalizing.

He broke away from her with a suddenness that left

her reeling. Vaguely she realized that he was breathing as heavily as though he'd been running, and beneath the heels of her hands, she could feel his heart slugging against the wall of his chest.

"Son of a bitch," he said softly.

Stepping back, he swiped at his mouth with the back of his wrist, freezing mid-motion, his dark eyes fixed on her lips. After a long moment, he spewed a breath and bent his head to scuff the heel of his boot against the porch. Legs trembling, she hugged her waist, afraid he was angry. When he finally looked up, he put his hands on his hips and gazed at the beams of the overhang above him, laughing derisively.

Dragging in another shaky breath, he looked back down at her. "Franny, I apologize. I . . . um . . . " He ran his fingers through his hair, clearly agitated. "I swore to myself I wouldn't do this. It's just—" He shook his head and said, "Whew. That came over me like a house afire. I'm sorry."

"That's all right," she assured him in a small voice.

He regarded her for a long moment, then slowly smiled. Crooking a finger at her, he said, "Come here, sweetheart. Let me see if I can't do it right this time."

Franny couldn't see how he could possibly improve his technique, but his gaze compelled her, and she stepped close, her pulse skittering at the tender look in his eyes. In the moonlight, or otherwise, he was the handsomest man she'd ever clapped eyes on, but in that moment, he was absolutely devastating to her female sensibilities, his dark hair catching silver light, his burnished face bathed in glow and shadow, his teeth iridescent.

Framing her face between his hands, he ran his gaze slowly over her face as though he were trying to memorize each line. "Have I told you how beautiful you are?"

Because he held her fast, Franny couldn't shake her head, and for the life of her, she couldn't speak.

"You're beautiful and so incredibly, unbelievably sweet. I think I'm the luckiest man alive."

With that soft avowal ringing in her ears, he moved his thumbs over her cheeks and bent his head to reverently touch his mouth to hers. It was a shy kiss. A hello kiss. The kind Franny had once dreamed of receiving when she was a flibbertigibbet twelve-year-old who still dreamed of romantic assignations with handsome young men who worshipped at her feet. It was sweet, so wonderfully sweet, to finally experience the feeling. He moved his mouth to her eyelids, pressing them closed. Then he kissed her forehead and the tip of her nose.

"I love you," he murmured. "God, how I love you. I'm sorry for going after you like a thirsting man for drink."

Franny slowly opened her eyes.

"It's just that I've waited for this, anticipated." He pressed his forehead against hers. "You have no idea how much I've ached to touch you, to kiss you. Now, knowing you're mine, in the eyes of God and the law, it's a little hard to mind my manners. You know?"

His manners. That brought tears to Franny's eyes.

"I'll try to go more slowly, I swear it," he assured her.

After feeling the way he had trembled, Franny

doubted his success. She only wished it could all be as nice as what had already passed between them.

"I'll bet your tea is done," he said suddenly. "What do you say we go inside before I make a bigger ass of myself than I already have?"

She nodded.

"So you agree, I've made an ass of myself."

She gave a startled laugh. His rumbled low in his chest. Slipping an arm around her, he hauled her close for a quick hug, then released her.

"Let's go get that tea down you before you start feeling queasy again."

16

When they reentered the house, Franny was surprised to find Loretta had returned from Indigo's, evidently through the back entrance. The presence of another woman might have helped Franny to relax had she been anyone other than her new mother-in-law. As it was, Franny couldn't feel at ease. She was afraid of saying or doing the wrong thing and retreated into silence, which in itself worried her, for she feared they might think her rude.

Ginger tea and its amazing properties in the treatment of morning sickness was the initial topic of conversation among the other three adults. As Franny sipped the brew in question, they sat around her at the table, watching her expectantly and relating to her their knowledge of the plant: how quickly they had seen it settle an expectant mother's stomach, the flavorings that could be added to make the taste more palatable. What Franny couldn't forget was that her pregnancy was on all their minds. Self-conscious and dreading the moment when they might begin to speculate on dates, she could scarcely swallow the sips of tea she took and wasn't at all surprised when Loretta paused in the conversation to ask her how far along she was.

His dark features beaming with pride, Chase replied, "Over two months, according to Dr. Yost, and I doubt he's wrong very often."

Franny threw him a horrified look. Though he sat right beside her, he pretended not to have noticed, which made her want to grind her teeth. How could he just blurt out the truth? Did he think his parents were imbeciles? He'd only been in Wolf's Landing a month and a half. Anyone with ten fingers and an ability to count could easily figure out that he hadn't been around when her child had been conceived.

To Franny's dismay, Loretta Wolf didn't even try to conceal her finger counting. "Let's see. We're well into July." On the tips of her slender fingers, she counted off the months, and her blue eyes widened. Franny fully expected her to say, "Wait a minute. How can that be?" Instead, her cheeks flushed with obvious delight, and she cried, "Oh, how lovely. It may be a February baby! What an ideal time, Franny. Right before spring. Warm-weather babies don't soil nearly as much laundry."

"Trust a woman," Chase said with a snort. "Worrying about laundry. This is my son we're discussing. He can soil all the laundry he wants." Curling a muscular arm around Franny's shoulders, he gave her a quick hug. "I'm handy with a scrubboard. I'll help with the wash."

"This baby could be a girl, and I don't expect you to do my chores," Franny inserted thinly. She was so humiliated, she wanted to die. What must his parents be thinking? If she were in their shoes, she'd be appalled. And angry. They couldn't help but feel she was using their son, and in the worst conceivable way.

"*Your* chores?" Loretta set down her coffee mug with a decisive click. "My dear girl, get that thought right out of your head. In this family, the men do their fair part. It takes two to make a baby, and two should share the burden of rearing it." She smiled fondly at her handsome husband. "Hunter washed nearly as many diapers as I did when the kids were small, and when he was at home, he practically took over the care of them. I was the envy of every woman in town. Too many men abhor any form of household chore. They think it makes them less masculine. Hunter never worried about such silliness, and neither does Jake. Of a Saturday morning, you'll see him out in the backyard, helping Indigo wash the laundry. I'm sure Chase will be as helpful."

"Is there a doubt?" Chase asked. "Franny isn't interested in mining like Indigo, but she does have plans to sew and do crafts, I think." He flashed her an admiring look. "Just wait until you see her handiwork, Ma. She makes beautiful things. Clothing, dried flower designs under glass, children's toys. She could earn really good money if she put some of the stuff on consignment."

"Really?" Loretta's eyes reflected genuine interest.

Franny shot Chase another questioning look. As

much as she loved creating things with her hands, it had never occurred to her that she might expect cooperation from her husband so she might have time for such pursuits. "Just small projects," she said hesitantly to her mother-in-law. "Nothing quite so grand as Chase makes them sound."

He grimaced in exasperation. "They are so grand. I'd buy our baby a clown-face pillow like the one you're making for Jason, and I'd be willing to part with good money for it."

Our baby? Hearing him say that—offhandedly, as if it were so—filled Franny with an intense yearning. If only. Oh, she wanted so badly to believe that her life could so easily be set aright, that Chase could just step in and wave a magic wand, transforming all that had been so tawdry into something beautiful.

"Have you a sewing machine, Franny?"

With a guilty start, Franny jerked herself back to the conversation. "Yes. A Wheeler-Wilson."

"Brand spanking new," Chase elaborated. Grinning at his father, he said, "Watch out. Ma'll turn green when she sees it. First thing you know, she'll be wanting to order herself one."

"A Wheeler-Wilson!" Loretta dimpled a cheek. "Ah, well, as old as mine is, it still does the job. I can't wait to see yours, Franny. Where is it?"

"I haven't brought it over from the saloon yet," Chase replied.

Franny cringed. She waited for one of his parents to make a disparaging remark, but neither did. The fact that they refrained amazed her. It didn't take a genius to put two and two together and come up with four. The remainder of her belongings were over at the saloon. She was pregnant with a child that couldn't possibly be their son's. These were either the stupidest people who had ever walked, or they were the kindest. Franny was afraid to let herself believe they were the latter.

"With two sewing machines, we can have your wedding gown whipped up in no time," Loretta commented cheerfully. Leaning forward over her coffee mug, she fixed twinkling eyes on Franny. "I can't wait to go shopping for the yardage. Hunter says he'll hitch up the buckboard and take us to Jacksonville. We'll make a day of it."

"Ma," Chase tried to cut in.

Loretta kept jabbering. "The selection there is so much nicer. Are you fond of seed pearls?"

"Ma?"

"Ever since Chase told me that you two are planning to have a formal wedding, I've been envisioning a gown literally dripping with seed pearls."

Franny choked on a sip of ginger tea. She could only stare at her mother-in-law in speechless amazement. A formal wedding? This was the first Franny had heard of it. And the idea was sheer nonsense. A white wedding gown? For her?

"You deserve to have a beautiful wedding," Chase inserted quickly. "While you were asleep, we were all visiting, and I happened to mention that we might—" He broke off and directed a searing look at his mother. "We just discussed it in passing, that's all."

Franny could see by Loretta's expression that she had perceived Chase's mention of a wedding much differently.

"We'll talk about it. You really should have a nice wedding, honey."

"Well, of course she should!" Loretta seconded. "It's the most important day of a woman's life, and it should be something she can always remember. Getting married in front of a justice of the peace simply isn't the same."

Hunter settled dark blue eyes on Franny's pale face. "There must be a wedding, yes? Promises made before God and the Great Ones? Without them, it is not a proper marriage."

Chase cleared his throat. "Franny and I, we need to discuss this privately, Father."

Hunter smiled. "What comes after is for private. The wedding belongs to everyone. You do not mind being married by a priest, I hope? Father O'Grady is very kind, and he will not insist you become—" He looked to his wife for help. "What is the word?"

"A convert," Loretta supplied. "It's the usual thing, of course, that the spouses of Catholics convert to the faith. But in our family, we're a bit unorthodox in our worship. Father O'Grady's given up on us, I think." She touched her chest. "I am a traditional Catholic to the marrow of my bones. But Hunter has his own religious convictions, so we raised our children to believe in both doctrines. Chase and Indigo are—" She broke off and smiled at her son. "Actually, I think Father O'Grady would say they're hopeless. He's content just to see their faces in church on occasion and doesn't insist they do things in the traditional way. That includes marriage. Jake is Methodist, and so far, he hasn't taken instruction. He says he's afraid his first confession would make Father's heart malfunction."

Everyone but Franny laughed at that. Chase cleared his throat and said, "I think we're overwhelming Franny, Ma. I don't think she had a church wedding in mind. We're kind of taking her by surprise."

"Oh, I see," Loretta said softly.

Only she didn't see, Franny thought. None of them did. She couldn't have a church wedding. She could see they were all set on it, but the idea was utter madness.

"I really would like to have a nice wedding," Chase told her softly. "I want to see you in a beautiful wedding gown and walking down the aisle to me on Frankie's arm. I'd like all your family and mine to be there. Your ma and all the kids. My folks, and my uncle Swift and aunt Amy. And Indigo and Jake, of course. I bet Indigo would love to be your matron of honor."

Frozen in mute denial, all Franny could do was stare at him.

He smiled slightly. "A hasty legal ceremony just doesn't—well, you know. Until we say our vows in a church, I won't feel properly married. Will you?"

Franny felt as though her heart were shattering into a million sharp little fragments. A beautiful wedding gown. Being escorted to the altar by her brother. Of course she wanted those things. She yearned for them. What woman didn't? But those were dreams, not reality. These people were out of their blooming minds. She was a prostitute. A pregnant prostitute. If she dressed all in white and walked down the aisle of a Catholic Church, or any other church, for that matter, it would be blasphemous.

As though he guessed her thoughts, Chase said again, "Maybe we should talk about it later."

Franny's face felt prickly, as though it were smeared with drying egg white. Humiliation surged within her, and she lowered her chin, unable to bear meeting anyone's gaze. A wedding. A real wedding. How could he not know how badly she had always wanted one?

Silence fell over the table. An awful, horrible silence. She knew they were all hoping she might say something. But what? That she'd be perfectly willing to make a laughingstock of herself at a church wedding? If Chase wanted a conventional wedding, he should have married a conventional girl. Perhaps that was the problem in a nutshell. They were all pretending she was something she wasn't because they couldn't bear to face the truth.

Franny pushed up from the table. "Please excuse me," she said shakily. "I'm feeling a little weary and believe I'll lie down for a bit."

The words were no sooner out than she whirled away. She could scarcely see where she was going. The furnishings in the sitting area were a blur as she cut across the polished wood floor.

"Franny?" Chase called.

The ladder to the loft loomed before her. She grasped the rungs and hauled herself frantically upward, her feet a flurry of motion, her skirts tangling about her ankles. Oh, God. She wanted to die. She wished she could. Right now, before her heart could beat again. Because this hurt. It hurt so much, she could scarcely bear it.

A beautiful wedding. How could they? More importantly, how could Chase? If he had set out to shame her, he had chosen the perfect way. Once in the loft, she ran to his room. Throwing herself full-length on the bed, Franny buried her face in his pillow to muffle her sobs. How could he be so blind that he couldn't see how impossible all of this was? The man was crazy. His parents were crazy. She was a whore, and all their pretending that she wasn't would never alter that fact. If Chase wanted a pure, virginal bride, he had married the wrong woman.

After Franny's abrupt departure from the table, Chase simply sat there, stunned. He had thought that a big wedding would be Franny's dream come true, that his willingness to have one would make her indescribably happy. Instead, she had looked—

There weren't words to describe the expression he had seen on her face. Like a dog that had been kicked and didn't know why. On legs that felt too shaky to support him, he rose from the bench.

"Jesus. I must be the stupidest bastard that ever breathed," he said to no one in particular. "Of course she *wants* a big wedding. It's not a case of what she wants. It's never been a case of what Franny wants. Only what she gets dished up to her."

His parents didn't speak, and in their silence, Chase heard the heartfelt regret neither of them could express.

"Well," his mother said tremulously, "we certainly made a mess of that, didn't we? I'm sorry, Chase. I didn't realize you hadn't spoken to her about it."

Chase closed his eyes and rubbed the bridge of his

nose. This wasn't his parents' fault. It was his. This afternoon, he'd taken the bull by the horns and had been ramrodding Franny ever since. It was all too much, too fast. He had scarcely given her a chance to breathe.

Dropping his hand, he said, "I, um, have to go upstairs. Talk to her. Excuse me."

Before he could step away, his mother rose. "Indigo asked your father and me over to her place for dessert and coffee. I think we'll mosey on over and take her up on it."

Chase knew damned well his sister hadn't issued such an invitation. The visiting arrangements between the two households were far more informal than that. "You don't have to leave, Ma. This is your home."

"And yours," Hunter cut in. "We will go. For this little while, yes? It is nothing."

It meant everything to Chase. In that moment, looking back over his behavior toward these two people the last few years, he felt so ashamed. Misdirected rebellion. Anger that made no sense. Obsessions with all the things in life that weren't important. He didn't deserve parents like these. Yet they didn't seem to realize how special they were. No matter how inexcusable his actions, they had continued to love him, waiting, always waiting, for him to finally grow up.

"Thank you, my father." Chase turned his gaze to his mother. "Ma."

"Go," Loretta urged. "We'll see you when we come home."

* * *

Go . . . It sounded simple enough. Only for Chase it wasn't. As he ascended the loft ladder, he thought of a hundred things he might say to Franny and discarded all of them. Lantern light from downstairs seeped up through the planked floor, striping the bare logs with muted amber. Chase paused near the dividing wall, remembering a thousand other times when he had entered this room. As a child. As a young man. In all the years, it hadn't changed. It was home to him, and would always be home. The patchwork quilt. The rag rugs his ma had braided. The clothing rod that hung in one corner. Not much in the way of finery. But there was a lot of love, and that made all the difference. His father would never be a wealthy man. But he had given his family riches beyond compare, all the same.

Moving slowly toward the bed, Chase heard Franny's muffled sobs, and each one sliced through him like a knife. Again, he thought of a dozen or more things he might say. That he was an imbecile. That he was sorry. That he'd never meant to hurt her. But every time he tried to speak, the words became a tangled mess and lay unspoken on his cottony tongue. He wanted her to have all the things life had denied her, and in his mind, she deserved them. The last nine years could be like an autumn leaf blown away on a brisk breeze if only she would allow it. Why couldn't she turn loose of what was behind her? No one could walk forward without falling if they continually looked at the path behind them.

There was so much more to goodness than sinlessness, so much more to God than judgment. But he didn't know how to express those convictions. Not to someone like Franny. His father always drew comparisons between nature and the divine to get his point across, but he doubted she would see the significance if he tried to do the same.

Chase had been taught from childhood that everything had its roots in the mystical. To her, water was wet and ran downhill. To him, it not only sustained all in existence, but whispered of great mysteries and wisdom. To her, sunlight was pretty and warm. To him, it was worthy of worship, the giver of life. Mother Moon, Mother Earth, the Four Directions, the Wind. All were his father's gods. The horizon, the dawning of a new day, the setting of the sun, darkness. Those things were all divine and interwoven with magic. There was no yesterday, only tomorrow. You fixed your gaze ahead and walked forward, never looking back.

There was such a beauty in those simple concepts. Such peace. Only when Chase tried to convey them to someone like Franny, it no longer seemed so simple. Her feet were mired in guilt. There was no horizon ahead of her, only another day like the last, and a reality from which she couldn't escape. How could she hear a song on the wind? It had been all she could do just to survive.

In the end, because words failed him, Chase did the only thing he knew to do, and that was gather her into his arms. He half expected her to resist. Or worse yet to strike out at him in anger. If she had, he wouldn't have blamed her. A wedding. To Chase, it seemed like the most natural thing in the world. But he hadn't been raised the way Franny had. In her mind, she didn't deserve a wedding. She was a lost soul and soiled. A soiled woman couldn't wear white, and once soiled, there was no way for her to become clean.

Her sobs shook her whole body. As Chase closed his arms around her, the enormity of her pain washed over him. When she didn't try to pull away, but clung to his neck instead, tears stung his eyes.

"I'm s-sorry," she managed to squeak. "Your parents. I-I'm so sorry. That was unforgivably rude of me, r-running out like that. Now they'll hate me for sure."

"Oh, Franny, I'm the one who's sorry."

Chase tightened his hold on her, a little amazed when she twisted to accommodate him, pressing close to his warmth like a forlorn child. He pressed his face into the curve of her shoulder and breathed in the scent of lavender he had come to associate with only this woman. It struck him that this was the first time, aside from the briefest of touches, infrequent hugs, and the fiasco on the front porch a while ago, that he'd actually embraced her. And it felt as he imagined heaven might feel. Perfect. Absolutely right.

It was on the tip of Chase's tongue to tell her that he had been wrong to suggest they have a formal wedding in a church when he happened to glance up and see the stars beyond the window. Like a million brilliant diamonds scattered across dark blue velvet, they winked and shimmered, each encircled by a silvery nimbus that made him think of Franny's hair ignited by sunlight.

Dammit. If any young woman on earth deserved a beautiful wedding, it was Franny. If only he could make her believe in that.

Wishing on stars. Chasing rainbows. Foolish dreams. Chase rocked her and smoothed her hair, his gaze fixed on the heavens. Those stars were real. All you had to do was look up, and you could feast on their brilliance. Reality wasn't bleak and dull and hopeless. It was whatever you made it.

Gently rocking her, Chase kept his gaze fixed on those stars and began to talk. He told her stories from his childhood, Comanche stories that had been passed down from generation to generation. They came to his tongue easily, every detail memorized, every word recorded in his mind because his father had repeated them to him so many times. After a while, Chase wasn't even sure what he was saying, or whether he sounded stupid or foolish. The truth was, he didn't really care. What mattered, the only thing that mattered, was that he somehow distract Franny and ease her pain.

Eventually the tension began to slip from her body, and her sobs became soft huffs of breath against his shirt. Chase looked down and saw that her gaze was fastened on the window, her expression dazed and dreamy. For an awful instant, he thought she had escaped into that hidden place inside her mind that she had told him about. But then he saw her gaze shift to another patch of starlight, and he knew she was still with him.

Still with him . . . yet floating in dreams. Not secret dreams within her mind, but ones that he had spun around the two of them with softly whispered stories that were a fanciful but intrinsic part of his heritage. Peacefulness settled over Chase. Dream places could become their common ground. They were something Franny understood. She'd been escaping into them for years. Why couldn't he blur the line between the world around them and the ones she created in her head? After all, he had been walking between two worlds all his life.

"Franny?"

She stirred slightly. "Hm?"

"Tell me about your dream pictures," he requested huskily. "Share what they're like with me."

Her breath caught, then shuddered from her on a weary sigh. A leftover sob, he guessed, but one that had lost its force. Running a hand up and down her arm, he willed her to oblige his request. A handful of her dreams, that was all he wanted. All he needed. It wasn't a lot to ask, yet he sensed that for Franny it was everything. To describe the places into which she escaped was to diminish their magic and make them less sacrosanct. Once she did that, she'd no longer have anyplace completely her own where she might go to hide from him.

In a tremulous voice barely above a whisper, she finally said, "I have lots of dream places, but the one I go to most often is the meadow full of daisies."

Chase closed his eyes on that. Her meadow full of daisies. She spoke of sunlight shimmering through raindrops, of tall grass whispering in the breeze, of water rushing over cascades of stones, of flower scents so sweet she wanted nothing more than to stand with her arms flung wide and breathe them in. It was a magical place, she whispered, where no one could follow, where no one could touch her, where there was no ugliness. It was *her* place. Hers alone, always waiting there for her inside her mind when she needed to separate herself from what was happening around her.

"Papa used to take us to a meadow just like the one I dream of," she admitted. "The times we had there were always so happy. I imagine him there when I go sometimes. Him and Mamma, and all of us kids. Before Jason got measles, before she went blind, before he fell from the steeple. The meadow I imagine inside my head seems just as real to me. Sometimes—" She dragged in a shaky breath. "Sometimes I want to stay and go forward from there. If I could, I'd do everything different. I'd be good and obey my parents. No one would ever get measles. Papa would never die. I'd make it all happen the way it should have happened. I'd never do a single bad thing to hurt all the people I love."

In her dream place, things could happen the way she desperately wished they had, he realized. Chase felt as though he were peeking through a keyhole into her soul, and he wasn't pleased by what he saw there. Guilt. A terrible, overwhelming guilt that he was beginning to suspect had been carefully cultivated. The thought made him feel sick.

"Well," he said softly, "I hope you never follow through on the inclination to stay there. I'd miss you sorely."

He had meant it as a joke. But she stirred as though it made her uncomfortable.

"What?"

She shook her head slightly. "Nothing. It's silly."

"Nothing you think is silly, not to me."

"It's just that . . ." She moved her hands over the quilt, her fingers plucking nervously at the tufts of yarn. "Earlier today, I went there when I didn't intend to, and if May Belle hadn't reached through and grabbed me, I—" She shook her head again. "It's silly."

A shiver coursed along Chase's spine. "What is?"

"Just a feeling I had that the meadow was real. That it was more real than here, and that I could have stayed if I wanted."

"Only May Belle reached through?"

"Sort of. You know how your mind wanders sometimes when somebody's talking to you? And all of a sudden, they talk louder or something and jerk you back? It was like that. She was calling to me, and when I turned to look, she reached through and touched me. It sort of frightened me. I think I almost got lost in there."

Chase didn't like the sound of that at all. Which was all the more reason for him to create a new dream place, one firmly rooted in reality here with him. "If you like it there so much, why would getting lost there frighten you?"

"Because I'm needed here." She arched her neck to give him a slightly exasperated look. "I'm not crazy, Chase. I know the meadow isn't real. I can't go there and turn back the clock. What happened happened, and my family counts on me. It's just . . . well, wishing. I wish I could go there and change it all. I know I can't."

"You heard May Belle calling?"

"Yes. When I'm in my dream places, I can still hear the people here talking." Her mouth tightened. "If they're saying ugly things, I make up dream happenings and pretend my family is saying them."

With a catch in his heart, Chase whispered, "When do people say ugly things?"

Her fingers plucked more urgently at the quilt. "The men."

Chase closed his eyes.

"They said ugly things sometimes, and when I couldn't close my ears, I just pretended the words into my dreams so they weren't ugly anymore."

Trying to conceal the trembling of his hands, Chase crossed his arms over her chest and rubbed her shoulders. If it was the last thing he did, he was going to make damned sure she never had to pretend away ugliness again.

"Don't ever go away and leave me here," he whispered before he thought. Once the words were out, he realized he was afraid of her doing just that. He didn't like the idea that the meadow was reaching through and surrounding her when she hadn't conjured it up. "Promise me that, Franny? That you won't slip away from me into the meadow and not come back?"

She rubbed her temple against his jaw. "It only happened that once. I'd just been to see Dr. Yost and I was looking at the hangers, thinking of what I was going to have to do. I was scared. So awfully scared. And sad because I knew you wouldn't want me anymore when I told you about the baby. It was such a lonely, awful feeling. I looked at the wallpaper and just went in."

"The wallpaper?" Chase didn't see how that related.

"The daisy wallpaper in my room."

"Oh." He tightened his hold on her. "If you ever feel lonely and afraid again, promise me something?"

"What?"

"That you'll find me so I can make you feel unafraid and unalone."

"Oh, Chase," she said tremulously. "I never dreamed then that you'd marry me anyway. That's why I felt so alone. I thought you'd hate me."

"Well, you were wrong. I could never hate you. No matter what."

"There are some things a man can't overlook."

"Where you're concerned, I'm blind in one eye and can't see out of the other. I can overlook anything."

They fell silent for a time. While she gazed out at the stars, Chase tried to think of a way he could best broach the subject of her creating a dream place with him. She had described her meadow so clearly that he could almost see it. What broke his heart was that she had ever needed such a hiding place. He couldn't begin to imagine the horror her nights must have been if the only possible way she could survive them was to separate her mind from her body.

"You know what I'd like?" he asked softly. "I'd like to create a new hiding place, one that belongs to both of us."

She sniffed and rubbed her cheek on his shirt. He saw a bemused smile flit across her small mouth. "A meadow?"

"No," he said with certainty. "The meadow is your special place. A new place, one that we'll make just for us. And for our baby."

"It isn't really your baby, though."

"Ah, but in our dream place, we can make our own rules, right? Everything can be just the way we want. And I want it to be my baby."

She sighed. "Oh, Chase, I wish it were. While I'm wishing, I wish I weren't me, that we had met like regular people and fallen in love and that I wasn't—"

"In our dream place, we can make wishes come true. If not Franny, who would you want to be?"

"You mean I can be whoever I want?"

Chase smiled slightly. "Of course. It's a dream place."

"Then I'd be—" She broke off to ponder the question. "I guess I'd keep the same name. But otherwise, I'd be totally different. I wouldn't have a past. There'd be no Lucky Nugget behind me. I'd have a clean slate and be able to start all over fresh."

Shifting her weight onto his other arm, Chase rested his chin atop her head and gazed out at the stars. "Then we could have a proper wedding?"

Warming to the game, she said, "Oh, yes, a glorious wedding. I'd even let your mother put seed pearls on my gown."

"I take it you don't care for seed pearls."

She laughed softly. "I hate them."

"She'd be disappointed."

"Well, we couldn't have that, not in a dream place."

Chase turned his cheek against her hair, remembering how it had looked touched by sunlight. Gold shot through with silver, as brilliant as the stars, yet warm from her scalp and laced with a scent that was uniquely Franny, a blend of freshly scrubbed skin and lavender. "It'll be a place where we can do whatever we want."

"Yes, anything," she agreed dreamily.

"And we'll be untouchable? No one but us would matter."

"Absolutely."

"God, Franny, I wish we could really go there."

For a moment, she was utterly silent. Then she said, "Me, too."

Tension closed around Chase's throat. "Then let's do."

She twisted to look up. He drew his head back to meet her puzzled gaze. "It's not a real place," she reminded him.

"It's as real as your meadow."

"But my—" She gave her head a slight shake. "My meadow isn't real, either."

"But you went there."

"Well, yes, but that was—" She broke off and stared at him. "This conversation is totally insane. You do realize that. We're arguing about a place that doesn't exist."

"But it could. In our minds. Franny, you've been slipping away to your meadow for nearly nine years. If you could do it alone, why can't we go to another place together that's just as beautiful?"

Her troubled expression made him grin.

"You're entirely too serious. Do you realize that?" he asked. "It's just a game. What harm can it do to imagine?"

"None, I suppose."

"Then imagine with me," he whispered. "Just for tonight." He grinned again and shrugged. "If it's wonderful, maybe we can do it again sometime."

Her shimmering eyes were filled with wariness. "Is this a trick?"

"My mother asked my father that question once. Do

you know how he replied? He said that whatever he wanted from her, he could easily take. He had no need for tricks. Correct me if I'm wrong, but I don't think I need them either." He touched a fingertip to the fragile bridge of her nose. "Point made?"

"Yes," she replied softly. Her eyes took on a mischievous twinkle. "But to stay on the safe side, in our dream place, I want to be stronger than you are."

At that, Chase barked with laughter. As his mirth subsided, he said, "No beating up on me?"

"Only if you need it," she conceded.

He leaned around to regard her. "Well?"

"Well what?"

"Let's go."

She was clearly dubious. "We need to dream up a place to go first."

He pretended to consider that problem. Then he shrugged. "Here will do." He indicated the room. "It's cozy. And look at those stars. Nothing we imagined could be as beautiful as that."

Her gaze shifted to the heavens, and a beatific smile touched her mouth. "You're right. The sky is beautiful tonight, isn't it?"

"Beautiful enough for a dream place?"

"Mmm."

"So, are we officially there?"

She gave a soft laugh. "I've never tried to go into a dream place *with* someone. I'm not sure it'll work."

"Sure it will." He snapped his fingers. "We're there."

She smiled again. "All right. We're there."

He set her gently off his lap. "Since you've only given me tonight, I want to enjoy every minute. My vote is that we lie down to gaze at the stars and talk until we fall asleep."

She brushed a stray tendril of hair from her cheek. "That's all? Just talking?" she asked suspiciously.

Chase held up his hands. "If I try any funny stuff, you can get the hell out of here and go to your meadow."

She gave a startled laugh. "You're crazy, Chase Wolf."

Chase braced a knee on the edge of the mattress and placed his other foot on the floor. She knelt there on the bed, looking wary and uncertain. Slowly, so as not to startle her, he reached for the button at her collar. "I'm crazy all right. Crazy about you," he admitted huskily. "How about going crazy with me?"

"I think we've both already gone, what with all this foolishness about dream places."

As he unbuttoned her dress, he bent to trail kisses over her small face. He loved her nose, so small and fragilely bridged. And her eyebrows. They were the color of honey and finely arched. He'd dreamed of tracing their shape a hundred times and did so now with the tip of his tongue. She tasted lightly of salt and feminine skin, so sweet he could have happily sampled her from her hairline to her toes.

As he slipped her shirtwaist off her shoulders, she shivered slightly, and given the warmth of the evening, he knew it wasn't from the cold. "I'll never hurt you, Franny, and if I do something you don't like, just tell me to stop."

Lightly, ever so lightly, Chase trailed his fingertips down her arms as he peeled away her sleeves. She shivered again, and he smiled, dipping his head to settle his mouth over the pulse point along her slender throat.

Skirt, petticoat, bloomers. As he divested her of each and sent them in a downward slide over her hips, he nibbled lightly at her neck, seeking out all those places he instinctively knew would please her. She sighed and tipped her head back to accommodate his mouth. By that sigh, Chase knew she hadn't fled from him into her meadow yet.

And despite his aching need of her, he was determined not to give her any reason to do so. Especially not tonight. Tonight was for dreaming together. A time to hold her in his arms, to gaze at the stars with her, to show her that for short chunks of time, dreams could be the reality, and reality a dream.

As far as tactical maneuvers went, it wasn't the best one he had ever come up with. But it was all he had. He could only pray God it worked.

Once he had her stripped to her chemise, Chase lowered her to the bed. She watched him nervously as he drew off his boots, then his shirt. Heeding the worry he saw in her expression, he opted to keep his jeans on. After flipping back the quilt and coaxing her between the sheets, he stretched out beside her on his back. She didn't resist when he gathered her close in the circle of his arm.

For a moment, she seemed uncertain where she might rest her head. Then she found the hollow of his shoulder with her cheek. Chase's belly snapped taut when she placed a small hand on his bare chest. He closed his eyes against a wave of longing so intense he ached with it.

"I thought we were going to gaze at the stars," she reminded him.

He opened his eyes. "Yeah, the stars," he said tightly. "Chase? Is . . . something wrong?"

Was something wrong? Everything was absolutely right. He gave a low laugh, focused on the stars, and prayed to become a eunuch.

17

When Franny woke up, it was late morning and Chase was gone. Touching the impression on the pillow where his dark head had lain beside her own, she gazed sleepily out the window at the sun. Its position in the bleached-denim sky told her it was nigh on ten o'clock, an unusually late hour to awaken, even for her.

Her senses slowly sharpening, Franny looked around the room. The log walls emanated the essence of the boy who had slept within them for so many years; the clothing on the rod and possessions lining the shelves showed the man he had become. She studied the teal shirt that hung from the rod, recalling the night she'd seen him wear it. She had been so afraid of him then. Now he terrified her in a totally different way.

On the shelf above the rod rested his black hat. Beneath his clothing sat his lumberman pacs. With a start, Franny noticed that feminine apparel hung at one end of the clothing rod. She blinked and pushed up on an elbow to stare at the assortment of shirtwaists. Looking utterly frivolous, her pink slippers sat beside his pacs, and next to those were her black kid boots. While she slept, he had unpacked her bundle of belongings and neatly organized them beside his own.

As though they belonged there. As if they would always belong there. Silly though it was, Franny found herself wishing that would be the case. She wanted all of this. So badly.

Hugging the quilt to her chest, Franny sat up and swung her feet to the floor. Her stomach gave a sickening roll at the movement, and she swallowed convulsively. Aside from a few bouts with childhood illnesses, she had always been in good health, and she was unaccustomed to feeling poorly.

Morning sickness.

She pressed her hand over her middle and, despite the nausea, gave a weak smile. A baby. Did every woman feel so incredulous when she learned she was carrying a child? To Franny, it seemed impossible. A baby. Her very own baby. So many times she had lost count, she had jealously observed pregnant women walking along the boardwalk, convinced that motherhood was something she would never be able to experience. Now, she was not only pregnant but married.

It was too good to be true.

Franny's smile vanished, and her queasy stomach knotted with tension. She was afraid to let herself believe that any of this could last. The instant she started letting herself think Chase truly loved her—the very minute she began to think they might actually be able to build a life together—all of this would be snatched away from her. All of it. Something would go wrong. It always did.

"Did I hear movement up there?" Loretta Wolf called softly.

Franny jerked with a guilty start. "I . . . um . . . yes, I just woke up."

"Sit tight, dear. I'll bring you some tea. Chase put a chamber pot under the bed for you. While I'm pouring, attend your morning appointments. I'll be up shortly."

Still holding her stomach, Franny leaned over to fish for the chamber pot. Tea in bed? She wasn't an invalid. As quickly as she could, she tended to her business. When Loretta started up the loft ladder, Franny was sitting with her back supported by the pillows, the quilt tucked across her chest and caught beneath her arms. Giving her hair a pat, she pasted on a nervous smile to greet her new mother-in-law. From the sound of her feet on the ladder rungs, she was like her son, surefooted. Franny couldn't feature herself managing the steps with her hands full.

Bustling with energy, Loretta swept around the dividing wall, her starched calico skirts awhirl, her glove-top button shoes flashing with each step. Before her, she balanced two delicate china cups on saucers, both wafting steam. Glancing at Franny, she drew her lips into a moue. "Ah, honey, you look green." Her blue eyes clouding with sympathy, she perched carefully on the edge of the bed. "Well, never you worry, we'll have you feeling right with the world here shortly."

Franny accepted her cup, noticing as she did that two thin slices of crisp bread sat on the saucer's fluted rim. "I'm sorry I slept so late."

"Nonsense. I'm sure you're accustomed to keeping late hours. It follows that you're used to rising later than most. As time wears on, you'll readjust."

Franny flashed her a startled glance, but Loretta was busy tipping a bit of coffee into her saucer and didn't notice. "Chase and Hunter went over to the saloon to get the rest of your belongings." She smiled conspiratorially as she held her cup aloft and blew on the hot coffee in her saucer before taking a dainty sip. "You never saw me do this, you hear?"

Franny smiled in spite of herself. Saucering one's coffee wasn't exactly the height of scandalous behavior. "Your secret is safe," she said softly as she took a sip of tea. Secretly she wished for coffee herself but doubted it would settle well on her queasy stomach. "Your china is lovely."

"Straight from Boston," she said proudly. "So is my piano. Shipped around the Horn, special order." Her eyes warmed with memories. "Right after his first gold strike, Hunter bought me the Chickering, a whole set of dishes, and glass panes for all my windows. That's been—dear, me—well over twenty years ago, now. Goodness, how the time does fly." She settled her gaze on the window. "Hunter brought everything here from Jacksonville in a wide-tread wagon. All but the sugar bowl arrived unchipped."

The love that softened Loretta's features when she spoke of her husband was unmistakable. Franny's throat tightened with an indefinable emotion. She suspected it was envy. How wonderful it must be to love and be loved by a man like Hunter Wolf, to have borne two of his children and raised them to adulthood in this cozy log house. Her thoughts shifted instantly to Chase, who was the image of his father. Oh, how Franny wished this child she carried were his, that one day everyone would comment on its striking resemblance to its father.

"We no sooner got the dishes unpacked than Chase Kelly shattered a plate," Loretta added with a chuckle. "To this day, I wish I could have captured the expression that crossed Hunter's face. After all his care, and there was china scattered all around his feet."

"I'm surprised Chase survived that with his hide intact," Franny murmured.

Loretta smiled. "Oh, Hunter never punished the children—not physically, at any rate."

Franny couldn't conceal her incredulity. "Never? Then how did he discipline them?"

"The same way Chase will discipline this one." Returning her cup to its saucer, Loretta leaned forward to pat the quilt over Franny's middle. "With a look, nothing more." She shrugged. "Well, sometimes he followed up with a lecture. Hunter has always been one to pontificate."

"A look and a lecture? That can't have been very effective with toddlers."

"Very effective, actually." Loretta met Franny's gaze. "Children are more perceptive than we think. Chase and Indigo always knew when their father was disappointed in them, and that was punishment enough. Even when they were tiny." She let loose with a tinkling laugh. "I don't suppose they understood much of Hunter's eloquent lectures. But they seemed to get the message. One nice thing about the Comanches is that they tend to communicate with their hands and facial expressions as much as with words. Watch all of them while they're talking sometime. You'll see what I mean."

Thinking back, Franny recalled instances when Chase and Indigo had conveyed their emotions to her with gestures as well as speech. "I think I know what you mean."

Loretta made a fist of one hand and pressed it against her bosom. Imitating her husband, she said, "My heart is laid upon the ground."

Franny giggled.

Laughing with her, Loretta said, "You see? Say that to a naughty child, and they understand they've done something that"—she pitched her voice to a more masculine tone—"makes you 'very big sad.'"

Franny giggled again. In all her imaginings, she hadn't expected her mother-in-law to be so warm and friendly toward her. The thought sobered her. Balancing her cup and saucer with one hand, she plucked self-consciously at a tuft of yarn. A long silence fell over them. Glancing up, Franny said, "Mrs. Wolf, I want to thank you for making me feel so welcome."

"Mrs. Wolf? Please, Franny. You make me feel as old as Methuselah. Call me Ma or, if not that, Loretta."

Ma? Franny couldn't feature herself being so bold. "Loretta, then. Thank you." She swallowed and took a deep breath. "Despite Chase's reassurances to the contrary, I'm sure you must feel some measure of resentment toward me. Thank you for not giving vent to it."

Loretta's blue eyes darkened. "Resentment, Franny? Why on earth would I resent you?"

"Well, because. You can't help but—" Franny lost her hold on the yarn tuft and bumped her saucer. China clattered, and both she and Loretta shot out a hand to steady her cup. Their fingers brushed, and at the contact, Loretta curled hers warmly over Franny's. Rushing to blurt out what she felt had to be said, Franny finished, "You know what I am. And that my child isn't your son's. You've been so very kind, and I just want you to know that—"

Loretta tightened her grip on Franny's fingers. "Shush," she said softly but with motherly imperativeness. "That's the last I want to hear of such talk." She released Franny's fingers to pick up the spilled pieces of crisp bread. Gentling her voice, she went on. "You're my son's wife. You're expecting my third grandchild. Don't say otherwise, not in my presence. *That,* my dear girl, I will resent, and heartily. When you gave your hand to my son in marriage, you put all that went before behind you."

"But I—"

"No buts."

"But you—"

"No buts!" Sparking with indignation, Loretta's large blue eyes met Franny's. "No one speaks badly about one of mine. That includes you. The instant you married Chase, you became my daughter, and anyone who says aught against you in my presence will be sorely aggrieved for his or her trouble."

Franny could only stare at her. But try as she might she could detect no pretense in her mother-in-law's expression. As impossible as it seemed, she truly meant it.

As quickly as she displayed anger, Loretta gentled her expression. "Now, you really should drink up that tea and eat your toast. If that baby proves to be anything like its daddy, you'll be needing something in your tummy before you get up and start moving about. When I was expecting, I found that it helped, at any rate."

Franny obediently picked up a slice of bread and took a nibble. To her surprise, her stomach, already somewhat soothed by the ginger, welcomed the bit of nourishment. "I believe I'm already feeling better," she admitted.

"You're looking better. Maybe later today, you'll feel up to studying some of my dress patterns. We need to decide on the style of your gown."

Franny nearly choked on her bread. "Gown?"

"For your wedding."

"But Chase and I—we aren't—I thought that—" Franny broke off, feeling helpless. "Franny, every young woman should have a beautiful wedding," Loretta reminded her kindly. "Chase expressed your concerns to us this morning. But Hunter feels very strongly that your fears are groundless. He . . . um . . ." She waved a hand. "How can I explain Hunter? He's very big on ceremony, I guess because of his upbringing. And he absolutely insists there be a religious ceremony. Simple, if you prefer, but a ceremony to mark the day, nonetheless, in the church of your choice. Since he will have it no other way, we may as well make a dress. Don't you think?"

Franny wanted to scream that Hunter Wolf had nothing to say in the matter. It was hers and Chase's decision, their life. Evidently her thoughts must have shown on her face, for Loretta looked distressed. She gazed at the ceiling for a moment. "Oh, Franny. When Chase talked to us, I came to understand how you must feel. Truly. But—" She looked her in the eye. "Hunter simply can't conceive that kind of thinking. To him, there is no yesterday. Does that make any sense at all?"

If she heard that expression one more time, Franny thought she might screech. No yesterday. It was Chase's favorite saying, and he'd clearly come by it naturally.

"At any rate," Loretta went on, "in the Comanche family structure, the father has the final word. Hunter very seldom plays the autocrat, but he won't bend on this. Chase has no choice but to honor his edict, and as his wife, you must as well. It's just the way things are."

Franny gazed into her tea.

"Maybe if you discussed it with Hunter," Loretta suggested. "Just lay it on the line for him, and tell him you absolutely *don't* want a wedding? He might be swayed if he could better understand how you feel. As if is, Chase and I may as well be speaking Greek. He just looks at us as if—well, he clearly can't see what the problem is."

Franny had no intention of confronting her father-in-law about a wedding or anything else. For one, the man was intimidating. For another, it was Chase's place to make a stand, not hers. She intended to bring up that fact to him the moment she could find an opportunity. The very idea that a grown man like Chase had to obey his father? It was absurd.

"I'll speak to Chase," Franny said.

"And to Hunter?"

Never. But Franny wasn't about to say as much.

"Oh, Franny. A wedding won't be so bad. Truly. We could have it in Grants Pass, where there'll be less chance of anyone's recognizing you. And with only family there, what can go wrong?"

Everything. Everything could go wrong. But for the life of her, Franny couldn't put her fears into words.

Loretta gave Franny's leg a kindly pat as she stood up. "Finish your tea, love. I think Indigo's coming over in a few. We'll have a nice little brunch when you're up and dressed. Something suitably bland for your queasy tummy, yes?"

With that, she left the bedroom.

Franny sat there staring after her. A wedding. Deep down, the very thought that she might truly have a wedding filled her with a rush of pleasure. But she quickly returned to earth. Even though no one in Grants Pass suspected the truth about her profession and she could probably get away with having a fancy church wedding, complete with symbolic white, she would know the truth. She couldn't even contemplate walking down the aisle in a pure white gown. It would be a mockery and a lie. God would surely strike her dead if she dared.

Franny needed time alone. Despite the fact that Indigo was expected, she made her apologies to Loretta and escaped the house. Her footsteps led her to the creek. Instead of sitting in one place, she opted to walk off her nervousness and strolled along the bank, seeking out familiar places where she had come with Chase or Indigo.

The exercise didn't help calm her. Her skin felt prickly, and unexpected noises made her nerves leap. Behind her eyes, there was a dull ache that she couldn't soothe away, and there was a heaviness within her chest she knew was from unshed tears.

Why couldn't anyone understand how she felt?

The question made Franny increase her pace, for when she confronted it, she realized she wasn't sure she understood her feelings herself. Panicked. That's how she felt. Like an animal helplessly trapped in a cage while people poked sticks at it.

An insane comparison. But it was the way she felt. Jumpy. Afraid. Convinced something awful was going to happen. She wanted to run, only there was nowhere to go. She wanted to pray, but she could think of no words, and she wasn't sure God would be listening even if she could.

It wasn't just the wedding. Franny wasn't sure what all she was upset about. Just that she felt a sense of doom she couldn't shake.

It was all too neat and easy. Chase loved her. He had insisted they be married. His family was wonderful. She was going to have a baby. Yesterday was behind her, forever behind her. Her family would be well taken care of. It was like a perfect dream. And she knew it couldn't last.

The instant Chase learned that Franny had left the house, he went in search of her. Though she had kept to the rocky creek bank, his skill at tracking stood him in good stead. He fell in behind her, moving as quickly as his eye could lead the way. Worry dogged him. He knew his mother had told Franny that his father insisted there should be a church wedding. That was one of the problems in having a family, not being able to control their mouths. Franny wasn't ready to deal with all of this yet. Chase wanted to move slowly with her, but things seemed to be on a downhill track.

As he trailed her, he toyed with the thought of their

leaving Wolf's Landing immediately. He had hoped to stay, if only for a few days, so Franny might come to realize that his mother and father truly did accept her and the baby. Chase couldn't help but feel that was vitally important to her eventual happiness. But away from here, he would have more control. No one would be telling his wife things that upset her.

Damn. Even in his frustration, Chase smiled slightly. His ma meant well. She had a heart the size of Texas. And so did his father. Both of them only wanted Franny to feel welcome and a part of their family. Chase knew that was the main reason his father insisted there should be a church wedding, because to make an exception in Franny's case was the same as saying she was different. His father was nothing if not perceptive. One look into someone's eyes and, like Chase and Indigo, he could see straight to the heart. Chase knew he had sensed Franny's feelings of unworthiness, and his stubbornness about the wedding was his way of making a statement.

The problem was, there seemed to be more going on inside Franny's head than even Chase could read. Something—and he wasn't certain what—was eating her little heart out. When he looked into her eyes, he tapped into her fear. But for some reason he couldn't get a fix on the cause. It was as if Franny was running scared and wasn't sure why.

Chase caught up with her at a bend in the creek. She had stopped to throw rocks into the water and, he noted, with no little amount of anger. He had never seen Franny in a high temper before, and the sight gave him a moment's pause. After watching her chunk the rocks for a moment, he waded into the fray, deciding that the worst she could do was clobber him. At best she might reveal what was bothering her.

"Mind if I join you?" he asked and stooped to pick up a rock.

She turned toward him, her green eyes fiery. "You!"

Chase nearly looked over his shoulder. As he recalled, they had drifted off to sleep last night with peace in full reign. "Have I done something to get on your bad side that I don't know about?"

She hefted her rock, giving him cause to wonder if she wouldn't throw it at him after all. "It's what you haven't done. When I married you, I didn't realize I was tying up with someone so spineless he still does everything his father tells him."

"Ah." Chase took aim at a tree across the stream and let fly. The stone hit its mark with a satisfying *thunk*. "So that's what has you frothing at the lips."

"You're a grown man. You know I don't want a church wedding! How your father figures into the decision, I can't fathom."

Chase bent to choose another stone, a flat one this time so he could skip it across the water. "Franny, Comanche customs are a little different than white. That doesn't make them bad. It isn't a question of spinelessness but respect." He shot her a look. "He's my father. About once every ten years or so, he *insists* on something, and somehow, I can't bring myself to quarrel with him when he does. Can you understand that?"

"No." She threw a rather large rock into the water near the bank.

The upshot of spray splattered Chase's pants. He slanted her a glance. "Did you do that on purpose?"

"And if I did?"

He grinned. He couldn't help himself. He'd never seen Franny so angry. Her cheeks flamed. Her eyes shot sparks at him.

Her eyes. Chase looked deeply into them, and what he saw behind the flare of brilliance wasn't anger, but pain. And a crawling fear. His heart caught. "Franny, honey, can't you talk to me? This isn't really about the wedding at all, is it?"

She knotted her hands, and in her frustration, she brought them down hard against her thighs. "Yes! I *won't* walk down the aisle pregnant. I won't. Get it through your head! And once you do, make it clear to your father."

"All right."

She was about to say something more, but his reply forestalled her. "What?"

"You heard me. We'll hold off on the wedding until after the baby's born. Then we'll talk about it again and plan a ceremony. Will that satisfy you?"

He could tell by her expression that she figured he'd never bring it up again if they waited so long. The girl had a lot to learn about his father's people, namely that they were the most stubborn that had ever walked.

"You'll inform your father?"

Chase didn't look forward to doing so. But the way he saw it, there wasn't a choice. His first loyalty lay with his wife, and if that meant bucking Hunter, he'd have to do it. "Yes, I'll tell him. But understand that once the baby's born, there *will* be a church wedding. Your church or mine, I don't care. But in a church it will be, with you wearing white. Is that clear?"

She gave a reluctant nod, and her high color began to fade. Looking into her eyes, Chase knew the anger she had felt was the least of his worries. Regardless, he wasn't sure discussing her feelings with her was the answer. He sensed confusion. He wasn't at all sure Franny knew why she was so upset. If she did, she wasn't prepared to vocalize it as yet. He'd have to be patient. She was strung as taut as a piano wire. He doubted it'd be long before she snapped.

"So . . . is that issue settled?"

She nodded, looking like a rebel who'd just lost her cause. "I guess."

Chase smiled slightly. "Good, because I've got a bone to pick now."

Her eyes widened. "What's that?"

"A little matter of your splashing me on purpose."

Her gaze shot to his wet pants. "Oh, that."

He took a threatening step toward her. "Yes, that. Do you know what I do to females who splash me?"

Her eyes went even wider, and she retreated a pace. "No, what?"

There was more than one way to take a woman's mind off her woes, Chase thought, and until Franny was ready to address hers, he could be as inventive as the next man. Spreading his hands and keeping them in constant motion, he assumed a predatory stance. "I throw them in the creek, clothes and all."

He deliberately drew a fierce scowl so she'd know he was teasing her. He saw a tiny smile flit across her mouth, and that was enough to make Chase warm to the game. He growled. She squeaked, retreated another step and held up her hands. "You wouldn't!"

"Oh, but I would."

"But your parents. What will they think if I go back drenched?"

He advanced another pace. "I don't give a rat's ass what they think."

She whirled to run, and the chase was on. He let her get a head start, then leveled out, lengthening his strides. Squealing and laughing, she cut up the bank into the woods. Putting a tree between him and her, she danced about, managing to stay beyond his reach. For a few minutes, Chase was content to allow her to evade him. She was giggling like a young girl. Her eyes sparkled with excitement. He had a feeling Franny had romped and played all too infrequently in her young life.

Feinting to the left, Chase lunged right to intercept her as she fled. She shrieked when he caught her around the waist and lifted her against him. Pumping her feet, she tried to twist free. He spied a grassy spot under a tree, carried her there, and, taking care not to hurt her, lowered her to the ground.

"This isn't the creek!" she cried breathlessly.

Following her down, Chase captured her arms and manacled both her wrists with one hand. Drawing her arms above her head, he slanted a thigh across hers. "Before I drown my victims, I nibble on them a little first."

She gave one last giggle, then sobered, her beautiful eyes searching his. Tears sprang to the pools of green so quickly that Chase was caught off guard. For a moment, he thought she was frightened. But then she sobbed and whispered his name as if her heart was breaking.

Chase released her wrists to cup her face between his hands. He wanted to look into her eyes, but she forestalled him by fiercely hugging his neck and burying her face against his shoulder.

"Hold me," she cried raggedly. "Oh, please, Chase, hold me. Don't ever let go."

He was happy to oblige her. Drawing her tightly against him, he rolled onto his side, carrying her slighter weight along. He felt a shudder go through her. And then, as though the dam burst, she began to weep. Running a hand into her hair, Chase whispered, "Franny, honey . . . what is it? Tell me."

"I'm afraid. I'm so afraid."

She said the words over and over again, a pleading litany. He knew she sought comfort from him, but God help him, he didn't know how to soothe her. She clearly wasn't afraid of him. Yet she was terrified of something. The violent trembling of her body told him that.

Chase tightened his arms around her. "What is it you're afraid of? Tell me, and I'll take care of it. I won't let anything hurt you. I swear it."

At that proclamation, she wailed. "You can't stop it. No one can. It'll be just like Toodles. I know it! I loved him, don't you see? Just like Toodles, only worse, so much worse. I don't think I can bear it."

Completely baffled, Chase ran a hand up and down her back, massaging the knotted muscles in her shoulders and along each side of her spine. "Toodles? Franny, who is Toodles?"

"He's dead." Her sobs gained force after she made that admission. "He died."

Chase closed his eyes, feeling her pain as intensely

as if it were his own. Toodles? Pressing kisses against her hair, he whispered, "Who was Toodles, sweetheart? Tell me."

"A kitty. Just a straggly old cat."

Chase cracked open an eye. "A what?"

"A cat. My cat. I tried not to love him. I truly did. But he was just like you!"

"Like me?"

"Yes. No matter what I did, he wouldn't stay away. I even kicked him once. He was so—" She sputtered as she searched for an appropriate word. "Stupid. He was stupid. I didn't want him. I *never* wanted him. But he wouldn't stay away."

Chase wasn't sure if he appreciated being compared to a cat, much less a stupid one, but she was so upset, he let it pass.

"He kept coming around." Her voice went shrill. "He just kept coming, no matter what I did. And I started to love him."

His stomach dropped as understanding started to dawn.

"He was all mine. Don't you see? Somebody of my very own who stayed with me all the time. Somebody who knew all about me and loved me anyway. And one night they"— she knotted her hands in his shirt — "shot h-him. He jumped up on the bar. Gus didn't care. The regulars bought him b-bowls of milk. But two strangers—they got mad and shot him before Gus could st-stop them."

"Oh, Franny . . ."

"And now I love you. Don't you see? Now I love you." With that, she dissolved into tears again. Chase pressed his face into the curve of her neck and hunched his shoulders around her. She loved him. God, he'd worked like a dog to drag those words out of her, and now that she'd finally said them, all he wanted to do was weep with her.

"Now I love you."

There was a wealth of heartache in those four words. She didn't have to say anything more, for that said it all. Now I love you. Chase groaned, finally seeing and wishing to God he didn't.

The mystery of Franny. Like he might have a beautiful, intricate puzzle, he'd been taking her apart, piece by little piece, studying, analyzing, trying desperately to understand her. Her Christian faith. Her belief in her sinfulness. Yet he'd overlooked what should have been glaringly apparent, especially to a Catholic. Penance. In Franny's mind, she had to be punished for all her wrongful acts, and what better way for God to punish her than to take from her anything she could love and have for her very own.

Toodles and Chase, the two stupid ones who wouldn't stay away, no matter what she did. Who kept coming back, again and again. Who knew all the bad things about her and loved her anyway. Her family didn't qualify, for to keep their love, she felt she had to conceal the truth from them. Impotent rage filled him. But it died as quickly as it came. He couldn't help her if he was blind with anger.

He searched for something, anything, he might say to ease her mind, but there was nothing. He could talk himself blue. Her beliefs were too ingrained to be erased with words. Franny, the prostitute, was by definition unlovable. Anyone or anything who dared to break that unspoken law would be stolen from her.

Toodles and him.

Chase did the only thing he knew to do, and that was simply hold her. With Franny, he seemed to be reduced to that more times than not. She clung to him and cried until she exhausted herself. Until she had no more tears to shed. Then she lay quietly in his arms, running the fingertips of one hand over his hair, down the back of his neck, over his shoulder.

The way in which she touched him broke Chase's heart. For she touched him wondrously, as though she were trying to memorize everything about him. He could better understand her reluctance to have a wedding now. And God forbid that she should wear white. All his life, he'd heard people jokingly say that the roof of the church would cave in if they entered. In a sense, Franny felt the same way. But her paranoia extended beyond that into her life. She was a bad person. And if she dared to forget that, if she presumed too much, the vengeance of God would surely strike.

Loving and being loved was, to her, the pot of gold at the end of the rainbow, something bestowed upon only deserving individuals. He had sensed how deeply she yearned for a wedding, but for her to have one? In her mind, walking down the aisle in white would be tantamount to thumbing her nose at God and inviting His wrath. To accept and be accepted by his family? The same. She wasn't deserving, and if she admitted, even to herself, how much she wanted the life he offered her, God would surely take it away from her.

Chase felt as if he were trapped inside brick walls

that stood twenty feet high. Now that he had identified Franny's problem, he had no idea how to solve it.

No idea at all.

In time, perhaps. Surely she'd eventually get over this. But Chase hated to let her suffer until then. "Franny," he said gently. "How would you feel about talking to Father O'Grady?"

She stiffened. "About what?"

About what. Now that was a damned good question. "Oh, just about things. Toodles, maybe. And me. About how you feel."

"To a priest?"

She said priest as though it were a dirty word. Chase smiled in spite of himself. "Preacher Elias, then?"

That brought her head up. "Are you *mad?* I can't talk about this to Preacher Elias. If I did, then he'd know."

"Know what?"

"That I'm—" She broke off and reared up on an elbow to fix him with an incredulous gaze. "You know very well what!"

"Franny, he's a man of the cloth. He has surely seen and heard just about everything. Do you think he'd die of shock if he found out about you?"

"Probably. And he'd hate me. He might—well, he might tell my mother!"

The way Chase saw it, Mary Graham already knew. "Would that be so bad?"

Her pupils dilated. "Bad? Would it be that bad? She'd never feel the same about me. Never." She pushed to free herself of his hold. "Don't even *think* it. Do you understand? I've gone to elaborate lengths to keep all my family ignorant, and now you'd have me risk exposure by speaking to Preacher Elias?"

Chase caught her arm. Holding her gaze, he said, "You need to talk to someone, honey. Someone you can trust. Someone who can understand your fears and put your mind at rest. Do you know someone?"

"You?" she said thinly.

Chase sighed. "Franny, I can't ease your mind. I've tried. You're carrying around a load of guilt. You believe God's going to punish you. You can't go on feeling this way. It isn't healthy for you or our baby."

"I can't risk my family finding out," she cried. "I won't! They're all I have. Don't you see? They love me."

"And they won't if they learn the truth about you?"

"How could they?"

Chase groaned and released her to drape his forearm across his eyes. "Jesus." Moving his arm slightly to regard her, he said, "The same way I do. It's easy to love you, Franny. And your family *isn't* all you have. Not anymore. You have me. You have my folks and Indigo."

"For now."

"For always! Do you think God's going to strike us all dead?"

She pushed to her knees. "I don't want to talk about this."

"Because I'm making sense, and you know it. Honey, I'm telling you, your family is going to love you, no matter what. Because you're you. And just think. Wouldn't it be a relief if they knew the truth? All those people who would know everything there is to know about you, and who'd love you anyway."

She shook her head. Chase could see talking to her about it was useless. She fixed those big green eyes on him. "Chase, promise me. Promise you won't ever tell Mamma. That you won't even hint. If you do, I'll never forgive you. Never."

"I'd never do such a thing, and you know it."

"You threatened as much just yesterday."

"Yeah. I threatened. And we both knew it was just that, a threat." He sat up, brushing pine needles and parched leaves off his shirt. Leveling a gaze at her, he said, "You knew I'd never make that trip to Grants Pass. Deep down, you knew it. Which brings us to another subject all together. You *want* this marriage, Franny. You want it all. My name, the baby, the life I've promised you. Only you're afraid to reach out and take it. If I know that, don't you think God's probably got it figured out as well?" He raised his hands and looked skyward. "Do you really think He's so damned stupid?"

She bent her head and toyed nervously with her collar.

"Life is a gamble, Franny. We're all born. We all have to die. All there is in between is getting the most out of life that we can. Bad things happen sometimes, and I can't promise you they won't happen to us. But I can tell you this. God isn't up there picking people out as targets because they did something wrong."

She looked up, her eyes filled with uncertainty.

Sensing his edge, Chase pointed to an Indian paintbrush. "Think of your flower arrangements under glass, how you feel when you make them."

"What about them?"

Chase draped his arms over his knees and gazed off into the woods. "How many times have you made one of those arrangements, noticed a flaw, and then thrown it onto the floor to shatter it?"

She eyed him in complete bewilderment. "Never."

"Why?"

"Well, because, I—" She shook her head slightly as if to clear it. "I work really hard to make them. And I think they're pretty. Why on earth would I want to ruin one because it had a flaw? I'd simply lift the glass and rearrange the—" She broke off as though it had just occurred to her what she was saying. "I'd fix it, not throw it away."

She flushed slightly and looked away. But Chase could tell he was making sense to her.

"Let God lift the glass and rearrange things," he said softly. "Think of yourself as a flower that's been misplaced in the arrangement. He's plucked you up out of one spot and put you in another. Here, with me. It's where you should be. Where you belong. Have faith that this is where He wants you."

Chase pushed to his feet and gazed down at her where she knelt before him. "Do you love me?" he asked.

"Yes," she admitted tremulously.

"Do you want a life with me?"

"Oh, yes."

With the toe of his boot, he drew a line in the dirt and held out a hand to her. "Then step over here with me," he said huskily. "Leave the last nine years on the other side. We'll make a world just for us, where nothing can touch us, where we can make our wishes come true. A dream place, sweetheart. Only it'll be our reality."

She gazed with open yearning at his hand.

"Come on."

"But what if—" She broke off and spread her fingers

over her chest. "What if something bad does happen, Chase? What if I let myself love you, and something awful happens?"

"Then it happens. Life doesn't come with any guarantees. Not for anybody. That's why it's so damned important that we don't waste time worrying about yesterday. All anybody's got is right now and hope for tomorrow."

She pushed shakily to her feet, her gaze still fixed on his outstretched palm. Chase wanted to say it was only a stupid line in the dirt. He wanted to reach over and grab her. But it was a step he knew she had to take by herself.

She finally looked up at his face. Her green eyes darkened to the color of water on a stormy winter day. "You won't ever leave me? You won't let me start loving you and then decide you don't love me?"

"As long as there's breath left in my body, I'll never leave you," he said solemnly. "I swear it."

Instead of taking his hand, she launched herself at him. Chase caught her in his arms and spun in a dizzying circle, his face pressed against her hair. She held onto him as though she might never let him go.

He hoped she didn't.

18

As Chase turned with Franny in his arms, she closed her eyes at the sheer glory of sensation that swept through her. His embrace surrounded her like warm silk over steel. His strength buoyed her. Letting her head fall back, she lifted her lashes just enough to see the trees and sky above her.

A dream place. A place where there was only the two of them and their baby, where nothing could touch them. Last night, she hadn't believed it was possible to go with him into such a place. But now they were there. Only it wasn't a place she'd created inside her head. It was real. Absolutely real. And all the more beautiful to her because it was.

Chase. Oh, how she loved him. When he finally stopped whirling and allowed her feet to touch the ground, Franny felt as though the world around her was still spinning, a sensation he amplified with a kiss.

Not a kiss such as they had shared last night, but a deep, soul-searching kiss that made her mind reel.

Without reservation, Franny opened her mouth to him, for to do otherwise with this man was impossible. His lips settled over hers, moist, impossibly hot and silken, his tongue searching, finding. Sensation rolled through her in waves that splintered into molten silver ribbons that warmed every part of her. Shimmering ribbons that combusted into fire. Franny lost all sense of self and sank against him, loving the feel of his hands on her back, on her sides, at her breasts.

She recalled the morning he had walked toward her through the shadows cast by the trees outside Indigo's little house, how lean and powerful he had looked. Now all that lean strength surrounded her. Yet he touched her as though she were made of fragile glass. Her breath was coming in short bursts when he finally drew back to regard her. His midnight blue eyes held a question, and within hers, he must have read an answer, for he started unbuttoning her shirtwaist.

Franny's eyes drifted partway closed.

"Don't leave me," he whispered raggedly. He rained kisses across her face as he drew her bodice open and peeled the cloth over her shoulders. "Please don't, Franny love. I swear you won't regret it. Stay with me."

The sleeves of her dress caught at her elbows and held her arms to her sides like ropes. When his hot mouth trailed from her cheek to her throat and lower, she could do nothing to stop him. The question was, did she want to? A shiver ran the length of her as his tongue began making light circles over the upper swells of her breasts. With every touch, her skin became more electrified. She moaned and whispered his name. *Chase.* It slipped through her mind as sweetly and softly as a breeze. *Chase.*

He tugged on the ribbon of her chemise. The drawn cloth went lax and fell away, baring her breasts. Franny's lungs ceased to function and her spine snapped taut. Memories mantled black wings over her pleasure, and for an awful moment, she surfaced, knowing what he meant to do and dreading it. As if he felt the change in her, he raised his dark head. His blue eyes searched hers, and his firm lips tipped in a crooked smile.

"Do you love me?"

Franny lost herself in his gaze. "Oh, yes."

"Then trust me, hm?"

Her pulse quickened. "Yes. Trust."

Tightening his hold at her waist, he bent her back over his arm and freed her arms from her sleeves. Franny clutched his shirt, rigid, filled with a haunting anguish because the memories were winning the war inside her. She felt flanked on all sides by them. To stay with him while he did these things . . . It was to invite recollection. It was to drown in it. And that was too ugly to face.

As she had for nine years, Franny quailed before the invasion. Only this time, in order to save herself, she would have to hurt this man, and she loved him better than herself. *Stay with me.* The meadow filled with daisies beckoned to her. She could almost hear the water rushing, almost feel the sunlight touching her skin. It would be so simple to slip away, to separate herself from this. But he had asked her to stay, and stay she would.

Moving her hands into his hair, Franny held his head as his mouth moved over her breast. Heat. A wet, drawing heat. With a flick of his tongue, he laid bare every nerve ending in the hardened nub of flesh at the crest of her nipple. His teeth entered the play, closing, tugging, lightly grazing. She shuddered and nearly choked on a low cry. *No.* That was the word she wanted to scream.

"My God, you are so sweet," he whispered. "Oh, Franny, my precious angel. You are so wonderfully, impossibly sweet."

At the sound of his voice, the blackness within Franny's mind began to splinter. When his mouth covered her breast again, she concentrated, not on the memories, but on the sensations he evoked within her. Pleasure, not pain. A sweet, tingling pleasure. His large, strong hands bracketed her ribs, lifting her up to his mouth. She realized that her hands in his hair were guiding him, holding him close. She let her head fall back and closed her eyes for a moment, revelling in the feelings that rocked her.

This was nothing like what she had suffered before. This was— She gasped at a wondrous shock of feeling. "Oh, Chase."

"I'm right here."

And he was. Like a shimmering blanket of magic all around her. The heat of him seared her. Franny opened her eyes and gazed at the sky, drifting with the feelings he evoked, each more wondrous than the last. He bent her farther back over his arm and sank with her onto the grass again.

"My God, I can't believe how perfect you are," he whispered against her breast.

Perfect . . . Tears filled Franny's eyes as his warm, leathery hands slid over her skin, the callouses on his palms slightly abrasive, reminding her of when she caressed the underside of silk against the grain. Chase.

Dark hair. A fierce visage sculptured in a lighter shade of mahogany. Eyes that held hers, fiery with passion. He was as elemental as the earth. With a low curse, he jerked at the front of his shirt. Buttons flew. Groaning low in his throat, he reclaimed her mouth in another kiss and drew her to him. Bare skin against bare skin. The rhythm of his heartbeat slugging against her breast. Sweat, bunched muscle. Yet he held her to him with quivering reverence.

Breathless, they parted mouths to look into one another's eyes again. Messages given and received. His gaze clouded with tenderness. Franny felt as if she had vertigo. The world was upside down, right side up, then tipping crazily. His breath came in deep, ragged gusts, fanning her face with moist warmth. He held her so close to him that his pulse throbbed though her.

"I love you," he whispered.

"Oh, Chase, I love you, too."

Sunlight shafted into Franny's face, touching him and everything around her with gold. He drew her hands to his shoulders. Smiling down at her, he tugged her dress, then her chemise to her waist. Franny didn't protest. Couldn't protest. She felt as if she'd been waiting for this all her life.

Blackness, shifting shadows, strange voices. Those were the things of her nightmares. How right it seemed that Chase was making love to her in sunlight. She felt the kiss of gold against her skin and reveled in the brightness.

No more nightmares. Only dreams. Wonderful dreams that had magically become her reality.

With gentle hands, he drew away the rest of her clothing. Franny felt no awkwardness, not even when he had difficulty unfastening her shoes. When she finally lay naked, he knelt beside her, his gaze sweeping boldly over every curve of her body.

"You are absolutely beautiful," he whispered.

Her breath caught when he reached to lift her breast. Sunlight warmed her nipple, but that was nothing compared to the burning heat of his fingertips. He bent to lave a peak with his tongue, and she cried out at the pleasure that raced through her. Dropping onto an elbow, he stretched out beside her.

Loving Chase. Being loved by him. For Franny, there was nothing beyond that. He became her everything. There, in the sunlight, where there were no secrets, could be no secrets, he taught her how to love and be loved. Sunlight and Chase. It seemed to her that the two combined and became a searing flame. With his hands, with his mouth, with his body, he worshipped her, and in the face of such love, she surrendered all that she was to him.

When he shed his remaining garments and rose over her, splendid in his nudity, she caressed the powerful lines of his bronzed body with a loving gaze. Bracing his weight on his hands, he moved into position between her thighs. Muscle bunched and rippled in his arms and shoulders. His chest gleamed with a film of perspiration. It seemed the most natural thing in the world to lock her legs around his and draw him to her.

Holding her gaze with his, he thrust slowly into her. The planes of his face went taut, and his eyes went glassy with passion. Nostrils flaring, lips drawing away from his white teeth, he rasped, "Oh, dear God."

Franny needed no other words. For she shared in his feelings. With a powerful push of his hips, he completely impaled her. Lowering his upper body over hers, he retreated only to thrust deep again. A glorious, white-hot tingling began within her.

"Oh, yes . . ."

With jarring impact, he set the rhythm, and she lifted her hips to keep measure, sobbing as the need within her built. And built. At last release rolled over her in spasmodic waves, filling her with a feeling she had never imagined could even be possible. As she crested and began her descent, his body knotted with rigidity, his thrusts became violently quick, and he let loose with a husky growl. An instant later, he jerked and froze. Tingling hotness spread through her.

Magic . . . As he collapsed atop her, Franny closed her arms around him, too spent to move, too content to care. Dimly she heard birds twittering in the trees above them. Somewhere nearby, water rushed helter-skelter over a cascade of stones. The sweet scent of wild flowers wafted to her on a gentle, sun-kissed breeze. All combined, the things that assaulted her benumbed senses made her think of her meadow. Only this was better because Chase was here with her. And it was real.

She could stay here, she realized. In his arms, in a dream, for as long as she wished. On that thought, Franny floated into a blissful slumber, protected head to toe by her husband's strong body.

When next Franny opened her eyes, she was cradled in Chase's arms. With a start, she realized he was carrying her somewhere. Hooking an arm around his neck, she raised her head to see.

Water. The cold hit her with a shock. She screamed and bucked, unable to escape his hold. "Chase! What're you—Oh, my God!"

Laughing, he sank into the pool to his shoulders. "I told you what I do to females who splash me."

She gave an outraged shriek and skimmed the surface of water with her palm, sending a spray across his dark face. He snorted and blinked, shaking the droplets from his dark hair. When his eyes met hers, there was no mistaking the mischief in his gaze.

"Oh, ho-ho! You've really done it now."

Franny giggled and twisted out of his arms only to discover her feet wouldn't touch. He caught her at the waist to buoy her, his dark face splitting in a white-toothed grin as he swept her in a slow circle into deeper water. Accustomed to the coldness now, Franny curled her hands over his shoulders, laughing in spite of herself.

"What have you got up your sleeve?"

"I don't have a sleeve. I'm buck naked."

She shot a glance at the dark surface of the water where it lapped against his chest.

"And so are you," he said suggestively.

She fixed him with a startled look. "Not in the creek, surely."

"Why not in the creek?"

"It'd be bad for the baby."

He narrowed an eye. "How so?"

"It might drown."

He threw back his head and howled with laughter.

"Well, it might. I remember hearing that even baths are dangerous."

"Bullshit." He drew her close. "Put your arms around my neck."

She obliged him.

"Now your legs," he said huskily. "Lock them around my hips."

She did so. "Chase, are you certain this is safe?"

He kissed her throat. "No, it's dangerous as hell, but not for the baby, for you. You're fixing to get raped."

She giggled and playfully bit his shoulder. In response, he lifted her and nibbled lightly at her hardened nipples. Franny braced her hands on his shoulders, locked her arms, and arched her back to accommodate him.

"Minx."

"Scoundrel."

With a powerful thrust of his arms, he pushed her high out of the water and settled her knees on his shoulders. Fearful that she might fall, she grabbed handfuls of his hair to hold on. Flashing her a wicked grin, he nuzzled the golden curls at the apex of her thighs. Franny gaped, scarcely able to believe what her eyes were seeing. Precariously balanced, she risked falling if she shifted her position. He locked his strong hands over the backs of her thighs to brace her in the position that best suited his purposes.

"Chase, what are you—don't do that—have you lost—oh, my God!"

His mouth, shockingly hot after the coldness of the water, closed over a sensitive place. She gasped. With a flick of his tongue, he made her jerk.

"Chase? Don't—this is—you can't!"

But, of course, he could.

And he did.

When Franny convulsed and shuddered, he lowered her gently back into the water, drew her close, and thrust inside her. Already limp with pleasure, she didn't believe she could bear any more, or that she could respond.

But, of course, she could.

And she did.

Happiness. Franny realized she had never truly understood the meaning of the word. Loving Chase. Being with him. It was better than her dreams. There, along the shady banks of Shallows Creek, they loved the day away, as greedy for each other as children for candy, neither of them caring that their bellies rumbled with hunger. When they grew weary, they napped, secure in one another's arms. When they awoke, they made love again, sometimes in the water, sometimes on velvety grass, sometimes in shadow, sometimes in sunlight.

Chase observed no rules when it came to lovemaking. In that, he was Comanche to his core. He was not only intuitive to her body's sensitive areas, but skilled at stoking a fire within her, his techniques sometimes shocking to her but effective. By day's end, she felt she had been loved in every conceivable way and found herself anticipating each experience again.

Along about dusk, they dressed and walked slowly home, pausing frequently to embrace and kiss under the canopy of trees. Franny hated for their intimacy to end. If not for the practical needs, such as shelter and nourishment, she might have suggested they stay at the creek all night. As they approached the house through the backyard, she couldn't shake the feeling that her time with him was limited, that she could lose him in a twinkling.

"Don't," he whispered.

Franny glanced up, a little amazed that he could so easily read her thoughts. He smiled and lifted her hand to his lips.

"Right now is all any of us have, Franny."

She nodded, accepting that in her mind, but unable to in her heart.

When they entered the house, the smell of food assaulted Franny's senses, and her empty stomach, which had been solid as a rock all day, took a sickening roll. Loretta had prepared fried chicken with all the trimmings for the evening meal. Usually, Franny loved it. But this evening, the very smell made her feel nauseated. Chase must have seen the look on her face, for he steered her toward the table and set about putting some ginger tea on the stove to brew.

"You've felt so good all day," he observed. "I can't believe one whiff of supper made you sick. I'm starving."

Franny had been. Until she smelled food.

"It's the grease," Loretta commented sagely. "Something about it turns an expectant mother's stomach." She gave Franny a kindly smile. "Never you worry, the ginger will settle it down, honey."

"I hope so," Chase said in a concerned tone. "She hasn't eaten all day."

Franny tried to reassure him, but every time she started to speak, she felt as if she might get sick. Fortunately, Loretta was correct, and the ginger made her feel better. An hour after drinking a cup, she was able to eat a light supper, after which Chase hustled her upstairs to bed.

"I love you," he whispered softly as he helped her undress.

Still a bit woozy, Franny smiled wanly. "I love you, too. I'm sorry I got sick on you. I felt fine until I walked in and got a whiff of that chicken."

Her stomach rolled at the memory. Hearing its growl, he said, "Don't think about it."

"Lands." Still wearing her chemise, Franny sank into the comforting embrace of the feather mattress. Curling an arm over her middle, she sighed. "This baby business isn't nearly as much fun as I thought it'd be."

He stripped off his shirt, then sat on the edge of the bed to remove his boots. When he rose, he shed his pants. Pocket change jingled as he dropped the denim to the floor. Stretching out beside her, he whispered, "The sickness part will pass."

She sniffed, unwilling to be so easily mollified. After sharing such a beautiful day, it didn't seem fair that her evening had to be ruined by a rolling stomach. "About the time the sickness goes away, I'll have a big belly."

At that, she felt him grin. "You'll be adorable with a big belly."

Franny heard the back screen door squeak and slam shut downstairs. She closed her eyes and pressed close to him. "As long as you think so."

"I will," he promised.

Franny could only pray she had that much time with him.

19

The first thing the next morning, Chase suggested that he and Franny should make a trip to Grants Pass to inform her mother and family of their marriage. Because of Franny's pregnancy, Chase hoped to take the wagon only as far as Jacksonville then take the train from that point on, which he felt would be a quicker and less jarring mode of transportation.

Time being of the essence if they meant to catch the train, Franny hurriedly dressed and packed them each a satchel for the trip while Chase went to hitch up the wagon. Loretta had ginger tea brewed by the time Franny came down from the loft. The two women sat at the table together to drink their respective brews, Franny the remedy, Loretta her coffee.

After finishing the first cup of tea and starting on her second, Franny began to wonder where Chase was.

"It seems to be taking an uncommonly long time for him to hitch up the wagon."

"It certainly is."

After draining her second cup, Franny grew impatient and decided to go see what was keeping Chase. When she stepped out onto the porch, she saw him up out in front of the barn. He was bent over the left wagon wheel, which told her something was wrong.

Feeling oddly exposed without her bonnet, Franny lifted her skirts and hurried down the porch steps. Her cheeks felt uncomfortably warm as she made her way toward him. *Stuff and nonsense.* Farther up Main, there were few people out on the boardwalks, and those who were didn't even seem aware of her. She couldn't hide forever. Sooner or later, she had to venture forth without her hat.

Nonetheless, Franny felt conspicuous. Chase glanced over his shoulder as she approached. Upon seeing her, he flashed a smile. "No big delay. I just have to replace a rivet," he explained.

"Will it take long?"

"A few minutes, no more."

Franny hugged her waist and glanced toward the saloon. "Um . . . do you think there's time for me to go see May Belle real quick? At this hour, the downstairs business will be slow, if not nonexistent. I'd like to let her know I'm okay and—" She shrugged. "Well, you know, tell her thank you and say good-bye."

He shot a look at the Lucky Nugget. No horses were tethered outside. "I reckon it's okay with me."

"If you'd rather I didn't—"

"No, no." He stepped close to touch her chin. "I just

wouldn't want you going in when there were customers, that's all." Dipping his head, he kissed her
temple. "You go on ahead. Just don't stay long, okay?"

Sensing that he had reservations about her going,
Franny wanted to kick herself for making the sugges-
tion. Of course he didn't want his wife traipsing over
to the saloon. When a lady passed such an establishment, she stepped across the street and walked on the
opposite boardwalk. "Nah. Now that I think about it,
I'll just wait until you're done."

Noting the high color coming to her cheeks, Chase
narrowed an eye. "Franny, she's your friend. You were
right to want to go see her. If you don't, she'll be hurt.
I really don't mind."

"That's all right. I . . . um—it's no place for a lady. I
just forgot for a minute that—"

"It's fine," he said, cutting her off. "Would you just
go? I've got to go in the barn and rustle up a rivet.
You'd just be standing here, twiddling your thumbs.
When I get finished, I'll go in the house and grab
myself another cup of Ma's coffee."

As he stepped past her, he aimed a playful swat at
her behind. Franny jumped and touched a hand to the
spot. "You'll pay for that."

"Promises, promises," he called over his shoulder as
he went into the barn. "Tell May Belle hello from me."
He disappeared into the cavernous shadows. Then a
second later, he reappeared. "Now that I think on it,
why don't you invite her and Shorty for supper?"

"Supper? May Belle?"

"My ma will make her feel welcome and so will my
father."

Franny couldn't conceive of anyone's asking a known prostitute to their home for supper. "Oh, Chase, I wouldn't want to inflict my friends on your parents. Truly."

"My father's been trying to get May Belle over to our house for a coon's age." He cocked a finger at her and pulled an imaginary trigger. "You need to work on wifely obedience, you know that?"

Franny bit back a smile. "Yessir."

"Then get that cute little fanny of yours over to the saloon, and while you're there, issue my invitation."

"Yessir."

Dressed all in black, he quickly disappeared again when he moved back into the shadows of the building. Franny stared after him until her eyes burned. It was silly. Absolutely silly. But, in her mind, it was like a premonition. There one minute, gone the next.

Taking herself firmly in hand, she took a deep breath and started up the street toward the Lucky Nugget. As she walked, she imagined what Chase would say if she told him of the thoughts that kept creeping into her mind. That she was being silly. That God didn't rain punishment on people's heads. That she had as much right to happiness as anyone.

Somehow, thinking of what Chase might say wasn't as comforting to her as actually hearing him say it.

As it always was during the day, the saloon was gloomy and dark when Franny stepped inside. Several years back, Swift Lopez and the previous owner of the Lucky Nugget had gotten into a fight and sailed through the plate glass in the front window. Because plate glass was fearfully expensive, the opening had been boarded up. Convinced the window would just get broken again in another fight, Gus had never seen fit to install new glass after he bought the place.

A lone customer sat at a corner table, but the shadows were such that Franny couldn't see him clearly. The darkness suited her. If she couldn't make out the man's features, then he probably couldn't make out hers. She felt safer that way.

Gus was behind the bar polishing glasses. When he spotted Franny, he raised a hand in greeting. "Well, now, if it isn't my favorite gal comin' back to her old haunts!"

Franny laid a hand on the banister as she started up the stairs. "Only for a minute. I just wanted to see May Belle for a second."

"She's gonna be next to leave, I hear," Gus said with a good-natured shake of his head. "Marryin' up with that ornery old fart, Shorty. Can you believe that?"

Franny continued up the stairs. "I think it's wonderful."

"Yeah, well." Gus slung his towel over his shoulder. "I s'pose it's fair. She put in a lot of years here, and everybody deserves a happy retirement. I have to tell you, though, that this old place just won't be the same, what with both of you goin' respectable on me and gettin' married. I reckon I'll have to run me an advertisement in the San Francisco paper to find me some replacements. It ain't just everybody interested in this kind of work, you know."

Franny hesitated in her ascent. For all his bluster, Gus had been kind in his way, and he had always dealt fairly with her. That had been especially true these last few weeks. Since meeting Chase, she had seldom been available to his customers. That had to have hurt his business. Yet he'd never said a word to her.

"Gus, I'd like to thank you. For being so understanding and—"

He waved her words away. "Go on with you. There ain't nobody more tickled than me to see you find a little happiness, honey. From the first time I clapped eyes on you, I knowed you wasn't cut from the right cloth for this kind of life."

The customer in the corner shoved back his chair and lurched to his feet. "No, she sure as hell isn't."

That voice. Franny's stomach dropped, and she turned a stricken gaze to the speaker. Tipping his hat back, he stepped slowly from the deeper shadows in that section of the room. As he moved into the spill of light from the open doorway, she saw that his blue eyes burned like hot coals in his pale face.

"Frankie," she whispered.

He took another step closer. "No. Not cut from the right cloth at all. She came from respectable people."

"Oh, Frankie."

For the space of several heartbeats, he simply stood there and stared at her, his gaze searing. Then tears sprang to his eyes. "I came into town last night," he said softly. "With my friends. We heard tell that for ten bucks, a fellow could have himself the prettiest little whore this side of Frisco. A little blond name of Franny." He gave a harsh laugh. "Isn't that funny? I came here twice hoping to buy a poke with my own sister."

Franny's legs tried to buckle. She grabbed the banister with both hands so she wouldn't fall. "Frankie, I . . .

I can explain." Shaking, shaking horribly, she moved back down the stairs. "Please, Frankie. You owe me the chance to explain."

Those eyes. Filled with undiluted rage and tears. They cut into her. "So you can tell me more lies?" He hooked a thumb toward the upstairs rooms. "Like how you work as companion to a rich old lady named Mrs. May Belle?" He laughed again. And then, slowly and with exaggerated clarity, he said, "Have you any idea how I felt last night when I heard one of the miners in here say that the reason Franny wasn't available to customers was because she'd gone and got married? That it might've been to Chase Wolf, 'cause he was the only fellow in town anyone knew of who'd got hitched. My ears perked up at that because Chase Wolf had come to our house to court my sister."

Franny touched a hand to her throat.

"It was then I realized. Franny, Francine. Blond. Pretty. My sister, the whore." His voice started to shake. "There I was with my friends, praying they didn't realize. Listening to them bemoan the fact that they'd rode all this way, not once but twice, and still hadn't got to fuck my sister!"

Franny flinched and closed her eyes. She heard Gus slap down a glass.

"See here, now, young fella. There's no call to get filthy-mouthed. She asked for a chance to explain. Maybe you'd best listen."

Frankie swung to jab a finger at the saloon owner. "You just shut up!" he cried. "This is between her and me, no one else."

"Then you keep a civil tongue," Gus shot back.

Franny held up a quivering hand. "It's all right, Gus."

Frankie spun back to glare at her. In that moment, Franny knew what it felt like to die inside. Frankie, her little brother. Oh, how she loved him. And now he was looking at her as if she were slime. She didn't think anything could hurt worse than that. Until he began to speak again.

"I don't *ever* want to see you again," he said in a raspy voice. "Do you understand? Not *ever*. I won't have your kind near my mother or sisters. Step foot on our land again, and I'll—" He broke off and shook his head. "Don't try me. That's all. Because whatever I do, it'll be bad. Real bad. I might just pull out the rifle and shoot you."

Franny knew better than that. But the hurt that had prompted him to say such a thing couldn't be ignored. "Frankie, sometimes we don't have choices." She stepped closer and reached to touch his sleeve. "I only did it because I loved all of you."

He jerked his arm away. "Love? No choices?"

"Frankie, whatever else I am, I'm also your sister."

He retreated a step. "You're no sister of mine. And the rest of the family will feel the same when they hear what you've become."

"Frankie, no!"

As he strode from the saloon, Franny hurried after him. Outside on the boardwalk, she caught his arm. He flung her away with such force that she sprawled against the front of the building. "Don't put your vile hands on me."

"You can't tell Mamma!" she cried. "You'll break her heart, and she has burdens enough."

He turned, lunged off the boardwalk, and struck off up the street toward the livery. Franny ran after him. Passersby on the boardwalk turned to stare curiously, but this was one time she couldn't worry about being conspicuous. Clasping her brother's sleeve, she cried, "Frankie! Please. Just give me five minutes to explain. That's all I ask. I only did it for you and the others. The money I made, it all went to support the family!"

He whirled to face her, his face contorted, his eyes filled with hurt and mindless anger. "Oh, yes, the money! Dear God, when I think of the times you handed me money. I took it, never dreaming—" He broke off and grabbed her arm, his grip biting. "You whored to get it. You lay on your back, spread your legs, and *whored* for it. Then you brought it fresh from their filthy hands and put it into mine?"

Franny winced as his fingers dug deep into her flesh. "Frankie, please."

But he wasn't listening. Spying two men on the boardwalk, he jerked her a few steps toward them. "You gents want a whore? For ten dollars, you can have a poke. Line right up! She isn't particular."

Shocked, Franny stared stupidly at the men. They stared back. Directly into her face.

Wheeling back around, Frankie cried, "Did you lie to Chase Wolf as well? Does he know what kind of filth he married?"

Franny bent her head, knowing even as she did that it was too late to hide her face. Even if she had been able to, Frankie had just called her a whore and said Chase's name in nearly the same breath.

Within an hour, everyone in town would know.

Franny, Chase Wolf's new wife, was the whore from the Lucky Nugget. After this, he'd never be able to hold his head up again. And the shame would extend to his family. To his parents, who had been nothing but kind to her. To Indigo and her husband and children, who had befriended her when no one else would.

With her head bent, Franny's gaze was fixed on the ground. At the edge of the boardwalk, a stubborn, straggly dandelion thrust its tattered yellow face toward the sunlight. Dandelions, daisies. They weren't so very different. *"Stay with me,"* Chase had whispered. But that wouldn't be his sentiment now.

A dandelion. Trying to thrive where it didn't belong. Just like her. *"Let Him lift the glass, Franny, and rearrange things. Let him pluck you up from one place where you never belonged and put you in another.*

Weightless. She felt weightless. Like dandelion fluff blowing on the wind. It was so easy to let go and float away. So easy.

Chase had finished fixing the buckboard and was in the house impatiently awaiting Franny's return when a knock came at the door. He wasn't prepared for the sight that greeted him when he opened it. Flanked by Gus and May Belle, Franny stood on the porch, her head bent, her shoulders slumped.

Before he ever glimpsed her face, Chase knew something was horribly wrong. He grasped her by the upper arms. "Franny?" No response. He glanced at Gus, then at May Belle. "For God's sake, what happened?"

"Her brother," Gus replied hoarsely. "He was waiting for her over at the saloon. I didn't know who he was, Chase. I'd've stopped him if I'd known."

"Frankie?" Chase asked.

He drew his wife across the threshold. She moved under his direction, but with the same limpness with which she stood, as if there was no life left in her. Fear clutched Chase, an awful fear. He had never seen anyone behave this way.

"Yes, Frankie," May Belle confirmed. "I had my window open, and I heard him carrying on out in the street. It was pretty bad, Chase. Pretty bad. Franny trying to make him listen, begging him. He called her a whore and offered to sell her to some men on the boardwalk."

"Oh, Jesus."

Imagining the things Frankie might have said to her, Chase was filled with rage. His first thought was to find the little bastard and stomp the fire out of him. But he quickly set aside the urge. Frankie could go straight to hell, for all Chase cared. Franny was all that mattered.

He drew her into the circle of his arm and led her toward the settee. Loretta came bustling from the kitchen. When she saw May Belle, she missed a step. Then her gaze turned to Chase and her new daughter-in-law.

"Oh, lands. Another attack of the nausea. Shall I put on some tea?"

Chase carefully lowered his wife to the cushion and crouched before her so he might see her face. Blank. He searched her eyes for any trace of expression, and there was nothing.

She was gone. Only a shell remained of the girl he loved so much. Chase caught her face between his hands. "Franny?" he said gently.

When his mother saw Franny's eyes, she crossed herself. "Sweet mother of God. Chase, what's wrong with her?"

His voice strung taut, Chase said, "She's just slipped away for a little while, Ma. It'll be okay."

Chase had to believe that. To think otherwise was inconceivable. Clinging to his composure, he pushed to his feet. "May Belle, Gus, thank you for bringing her home. I appreciate it."

"No trouble." Gus dragged his gaze from Franny to look at Chase. "I'm sorry. I started to give the boy what for, but she asked me to stay out of it."

"I understand. She's real protective of her family."

May Belle's lips were quivering uncontrollably. She clamped them together and drew a sharp breath through her nose. "I saw it happening," she said softly, "but I couldn't get down there quick enough to stop it."

"It's not your fault," Chase assured her. "One of them was bound to find out sooner or later."

Chase felt as if he was talking from deep within a barrel. A sense of unreality surrounded him as he saw Gus and May Belle to the door. When they had gone, he went back to Franny, sat beside her, gathered her onto his lap. Like a sleepy child, she pressed her head against his shoulder. Limp, lifeless. Nothing he said seemed to reach her. Every time he looked into her eyes, he wanted to scream. He was vaguely aware of his mother hovering over them, offering water, tea, a cool cloth, anything she could think of that might help.

Time dragged by on leaden feet. With each minute that passed, Chase felt more afraid. She was gone. He couldn't believe it. People didn't just slip away.

Here in a minute, she'd blink and come back.

Here in just a minute . . .

When an hour had passed, Chase began to feel panicky. He tried talking to her, calling to her, but she didn't respond.

"Ma, can you go for Dr. Yost?" he finally asked. "Maybe he'll know something we can do for her."

Getting her medical care. It was all he could think of to do.

"Bed rest," Dr. Yost advised gruffly after examining Franny. "Lots of peace and quiet. Get what food and water you can down her. Probably be best to stick with liquids so she won't strangle."

Drawing the quilt over his wife, Chase sank onto the edge of the bed and looked up at the doctor. "That's all you can do? Prescribe bed rest? Isn't there an elixir or some kind of—" He gestured wordlessly with his hand. "Something. There has to be something you can do besides prescribe bed rest!"

Behind Dr. Yost stood his parents. Chase glanced at his father and saw the sadness in his eyes. He closed his own, struggling to keep his fear at bay. This couldn't be happening.

"Son," Yost said kindly, "I've seen cases like this in the sanitariums, but damned few. I'm not up on all the treatments, so I have to go on common sense. The girl's been through a traumatic experience. It seems to me that peace and quiet should be the best thing for her. If we're lucky, this is just a result of shock, and she'll be right as rain come morning."

"You sound dubious."

The doctor looked uncomfortable. "It isn't that I'm dubious, exactly. I've just never seen shock have this effect on a patient. All the folks I've seen in this condition were—well, they were in what I call a stupor."

"A stupor. And what, exactly, is that?"

"It's a different kettle of fish from shock, by far."

"How so?"

The doctor tugged on his ear. "I'm sure this is probably just shock, Chase. So why get into that? No point in crossing bridges before we get to them. Right?"

A chill washed down Chase's spine. "In other words, you don't want to worry me."

Dr. Yost sighed. "It would be more accurate to say I don't want to worry you needlessly. Let's see how she is come morning. I lay odds she'll be fine."

"And if she isn't?"

"Then we could be dealing with something more serious."

"A stupor," Chase supplied.

Yost tugged on his ear again, which was obviously a habit of his when he was put on the spot. "I didn't say that."

"But you're thinking it."

"Damn it, boy. You're asking me to diagnose something I know nothing about. I haven't been trained to treat crazy folks."

Chase shot up from the bed. "She isn't crazy!"

"Chase Kelly," his mother intervened. "Calm down. Dr. Yost meant no offense, I'm sure."

"How in hell did he mean it then?"

Looking decidedly wary, Yost glanced at Franny.

"I'm not saying she's crazy. I'm just saying I don't know much about stupors." He rested a kindly hand on Chase's shoulder. "I'm almost sure this isn't a stupor, son. She'll be fine in the morning, mark my words."

"And if she's not? How long do these stupor spells generally last?"

Yost shrugged. "Different lengths of time, I reckon, depending on the patient."

"On an average?" Chase pressed. "A few hours, a few days? How long?"

The doctor drew back his hand. "I can only go by the patients I saw in sanitariums, Chase, and they were serious cases."

"And?"

"Well," he said hesitantly, "some of those folks never snapped out of it."

"Never?" Chase's heartbeat escalated. "Are you saying that if she's not better by morning, that she might never get better?"

Yost pursed his lips. "If she's not better by morning, there's a good chance she's a lot sicker than I hope. I just told you, I'm no expert on this sort of thing, and if she doesn't snap out of it, I'd be overstepping my bounds to say what's wrong with her or how long it might last."

Chase had the unholy urge to grab the doctor by his shirt and shake answers out of him. He barely restrained himself. This wasn't the doctor's fault, and losing his temper wouldn't help Franny.

Sinking back onto the bed, he braced his arm on his knee and dropped his head onto his hand. He said nothing more. There was nothing to say.

*   *   *

Chase refused to leave her. His mother brought lunch upstairs, a sandwich for him, broth for Franny. Not wanting anyone to care for his wife but him, Chase held her in the circle of one arm and coaxed the liquid into her mouth. She didn't swallow, and the broth ran back out at the corners of her lax lips. He tried again, and again. Loretta finally assisted him, holding Franny's head and massaging her throat to make her swallow, while Chase tipped bits of liquid into her mouth.

Looking down into Franny's expressionless eyes, Chase finally realized why Dr. Yost had looked so bleak. Most patients in a stupor probably didn't last long. Even if he got a rubber tube to feed Franny, broth wouldn't be enough to sustain her indefinitely. .

"She'll snap out of this," Loretta assured him. "Just you watch. She'll be all right."

When Chase looked into his mother's eyes, he knew that despite her confident air, she was as frightened as he was.

In the late afternoon, May Belle came by to check on Franny. Loretta showed her up the ladder into the loft. At the unfamiliar swish of silk skirts, Chase looked up, identified the caller, then bent his head again, all his concentration focused on the girl he held in his arms. Braced against the wall, he felt as though the logs had made permanent trenches across his back.

May Belle sat down on the edge of the bed. "I hope it's all right, my coming over and all. I figured what with everything else, I couldn't do much more damage."

Chase frowned slightly. "Of course it's all right,

May Belle. You know my father welcomes you here."

She smoothed her skirts. "Yes, well. Your father is a little too kind for his own good sometimes."

Chase was too worried about his wife to take issue with that.

"What did Dr. Yost have to say?" she asked.

Numbly, Chase recounted his exchange with the doctor. Clearly distressed, May Belle took hold of Franny's hand. "She'll get better, Chase. I've no doubt."

Chase wished he felt as positive of that.

"And when she does?" May Belle finally asked. "What're you going to do then, Chase? Have you had time to think about that?"

"I'll get on my knees and thank God."

"No, I meant—" She broke off and swung a hand. "Well, you know, about the marriage, and all. Can you still have it annulled?"

Chase jerked his head up. "Pardon?"

May Belle stared at him for a long moment. "You aren't planning to, are you?"

"Planning to what?"

"Back out."

Chase had the feeling he had missed something somewhere in their exchange. "Back out?"

The older woman's eyes filled with incredulity. "You plan to stay married to her?"

"Why wouldn't I?"

"Well, because. Frankie—the things he said. Him bringing up your name. The gossip will never quit. Those men on the boardwalk, they saw Franny's face, plain as day. Folks suspecting she might be the upstairs girl from the saloon, that was one thing. But them knowing it for sure? Your family has to live in this town. A scandal like that—well, it's no small thing."

Chase's pulse quickened, and in a flash, by listening to May Belle, it hit him. "My God." He curled his hand over Franny's silken head and pressed his lips against the backs of his knuckles. "Oh, God. She thought I wouldn't want her anymore."

Silence fell. May Belle finally broke it by saying, "No matter how much you love her, Chase, you have to think of your family."

He had a hysterical urge to laugh. All afternoon, he'd been thinking that the hurtful things Frankie had said had caused all of this. "Oh, May Belle. Thank you."

"Thank you?"

Chase looked up at her, his eyes flaring with hope. "Yes. I'm so incredibly dense sometimes. She thought I wouldn't love her after Frankie exposed her publicly. Don't you see?" Tears burned under his eyelids. "She didn't think I'd love her anyway."

The aging prostitute searched his face for several seconds. "But you do," she finally said softly, her gaze softening. "Regardless of the consequences for your family. Regardless of everything, you love her anyway."

Chase swallowed. "God, yes. I just wish I could convince her of that. What can I do, May Belle? You understand how she thinks better than anyone. How can I prove to her that she's worth loving? Nothing I've said seems to have gotten through to her."

Her eyes swimming with tears, May Belle said, "Be patient. You have to understand that things have been different for you, Chase. Your ma and pa. You grew up knowing you'd be loved, no matter what. Gals like me and Franny are lucky even to have friends. Our families turn away. The rare man who shows an interest usually turns tail in the end. Feeling worthy of love—well, that's something we learn when we're kids, isn't it? From our families."

"I never thought about it."

"Because you never had to. Your family has always loved you. For us whores—well, it doesn't always happen that way. Fact is, most times it doesn't."

"Which is why Franny went to such lengths to keep her secret from her family," Chase whispered.

"Of course. She feared they'd turn away. And, bless her heart, that's exactly what happened. It'll take time for you to heal that wound. Loving her through thick and thin will do it eventually. But don't think it'll happen overnight. The people who should have loved her, no matter what—well, we know how that went. Her own brother, and he tried to sell her to strangers. To shame her. That kind of hurt can't be erased, not unless Frankie should come crawling back, asking for forgiveness. And that isn't likely."

Chase smiled slightly. "May Belle, promise me you'll never move so far away I can't hunt you up when I need to understand this girl."

"What?"

"I could kiss you. You haven't said a damned thing I didn't already know, but, like you say, I look at things so different that I—" He laughed softly. "Thank you, you gorgeous creature, you! You've just told me what I have to do."

"I have?"

"Franny doesn't believe anyone will love her if they

know. Don't you see?" Chase pushed erect and lifted his wife off his lap. She stirred slightly, but her eyes remained focused on something he couldn't see. "I have to prove to her she's wrong. The best place to start is with her family, just like you said."

May Belle reached out and grasped his arm. "Chase, that could be a mistake. They may not be as forgiving as you and yours are. Trust me, I know."

"Forgiving?" Chase rose on a knee to exit the bed. "May Belle, if anyone has something to forgive, it's Franny." As he strode from the room, he said, "I can't take time to explain it all right now. Just trust me when I say that when I get done with them, her family will be the ones asking for forgiveness, not my wife." When he reached the ladder, Chase yelled downstairs. "Ma, can you get me a blanket?"

He circled back to the bed to gather Franny up into his arms. May Belle followed in his wake as he carried his burden downstairs.

Loretta came into the sitting room from the kitchen. "A blanket?"

"Franny and I are going to take a little trip," he said softly. "I don't want her to get chilled."

"A trip? Chase, she's in no condition to go anywhere."

"Ma, please. The blanket?"

Loretta cast a concerned glance at May Belle, but then she went to the bedroom. She returned a moment later with a quilt folded over one arm. As she handed it to Chase, she said, "What are you going to do?"

His throat aching, Chase repositioned his wife in his arms. Looking over her blond head at his mother, he said, "Franny and I are going to go make a miracle."

Loretta fastened bewildered eyes on him. "A what?"

"A miracle," Chase said as he carried his burden to the door. "The deaf shall be made to hear, and the blind shall be made to see."

20

The Graham house was lit up like a Christmas tree when Chase drew the wagon up near the porch. Both arms aching from trying to drive with one arm while he held Franny with the other, he looped the reins around the guide and then sat there a moment, flexing to get the cramps out. Franny sat quietly beside him, her slight weight leaned against him, her gaze still fixed on something he couldn't see. During all the long hours of the trip, she hadn't spoken or moved on her own accord.

Jumping down from the wagon, Chase caught her behind the knees and around the shoulders to lift her off the seat. As he turned with her toward the house, it occurred to him that the wish he'd made when he first saw her was about to be granted. He was going to fight a mountain lion for her. And, by God, he was going to win.

He strode briskly up the steps. When he reached the door, he didn't bother to knock. He just drew back a foot and booted the damned thing open. Under such force, the door slapped the interior wall. Everyone inside the house whirled to stare. The girls were in the kitchen, washing dishes from the evening meal. Mary Graham sat at the table, snapping peas into a large bowl. Frankie and Matthew were sitting hunched over a checkerboard in the parlor area. Chase couldn't recall ever having seen so many expressions of condemnation in one room. Clearly Frankie had wasted no time in hightailing it home to share his news.

How dare they? Chase looked from face to face, acutely aware of the slight burden he held in his arms, of the suffering she had endured. How could any of her family look upon her with scorn?

Life went on, Chase noticed. They'd obviously managed to eat. And they'd eaten the food Franny had bought for them. Nothing new. She'd been feeding the whole ungrateful lot of them for nine years. Well, they were about to learn just how dearly she had paid to keep their goddamned larder stocked. Chase caught the edge of the door and hooked it closed with his foot. The resulting *thwack* of wood against wood made all of them jump.

"Frankie?" Mary Graham called. "Is something amiss?"

"It's all right, Ma." Frankie pushed up from his chair. "You and that woman aren't welcome in this house," he said stonily. "Get her out of here."

"Francine? Is it you?" Mary called. "Do hush, Frankie. Your sister will always be welcome in my house."

"As the prodigal child?" Chase demanded coldly.

"Because it's your *Christian* duty to forgive and love the sinner amongst you?"

Chase ignored Frankie's threatening stance and strode directly to the table where Mary Graham sat. The smells of roast beef and potatoes blended with the sweet scent of the freshly picked vegetables. Partially resting Franny's weight upon the table, he sent the bowl of snapped peas flying with a sweep of his arm. Alaina squeaked as the porcelain hit the floor and shattered. Peas went in every direction. Not caring, Chase carefully laid out his wife on the table before her mother.

"I've brought you what's left of your daughter," he said raggedly.

Mary Graham's sightless eyes homed in on his voice. "Chase Wolf?"

Frankie came into the kitchen. "I asked you nicely to leave."

Chase shot him a cold glare. "You call that nicely? I'll deal with you in a minute, young man. Meanwhile, kindly keep your mouth shut and your ears open."

When he turned back, he saw that Mary was running her hands over Franny. "Oh, dear God. What's wrong with her? Is she sick?"

Chase braced his hands on the table and leaned forward. "Sick? I wish to God she were. Then maybe a doctor could make her well. Plain and simple, the girl's heart is broken. I've brought her to you because as much as I love her, I can't mend it." Pitching his voice a little lower, he added, "You are the only one who can, and I believe you know why."

"I won't have you upsetting my ma like this," Frankie objected and came striding toward the table.

"Take that piece of trash back where you found her. Get her out of our home."

That cut it. Chase turned and caught the boy across the mouth with the back of his hand. Frankie staggered under the blow, managed to catch himself from falling, and straightened, holding his wrist to his lips.

"Don't *ever* speak to or about your sister in that manner again," Chase said in a dangerously silken voice, "or so help me God, I'll beat the living tar right out of you. Do you understand me, Frankie?"

His eyes glittering with anger and hatred, Frankie muttered, "You can't come in here and throw your weight around. I'll go get the law."

"You do that," Chase said softly. Turning back to Mary, he said, "When you get back, your mother will see to it that your bags are packed and waiting for you on the porch. Won't you, Mrs. Graham? You know which side your bread's buttered on, don't you?"

Mary closed her eyes.

"Closing your eyes won't help," Chase whispered savagely. "You're already blind." He leaned closer. "Only not quite as blind as you've pretended to be. You knew. I saw it in your face the day I met you. You knew! All these years, you knew."

"Stop it," Mary whispered. She ran trembling hands over her daughter's hair. "What's wrong with her? It's not—it's not something catching, is it?"

For the first time in his life, Chase wanted to slap a woman. He knotted his hands into fists where they rested on the table. "And if it were? Just think of it. You could make her feel guilty for another ten years and reap the rewards."

Mary Graham's face drained of color. "What are you accusing me of, Mr. Wolf?"

"I think you'd better leave," Frankie injected.

"I think you'd better shut up," Chase shot back. Keeping his gaze fixed on Mary, he said, "We're going to get to the bottom of this before I go. The easy way or the hard way. Your choice. But one way or another, my wife's going to hear it from your lips. Admit it, Mrs. Graham. You've known all along what Franny was doing to support this family. Haven't you?"

She propped an elbow on the table to press a shaky hand over her face.

"If you love her," Chase prodded, "and I know you must, then, for her sake and for the love of God, admit it!"

With a broken sob, she said, "God forgive me. Yes, I suspected."

With a derisive snort, Chase said, "You suspected?"

"Ma?" Alaina's voice was shrill. "What are you saying?"

Chase straightened. "The unspeakable truth, Alaina," he said more calmly. "Your father was killed. Your mother is blind. She had eight children to feed, one of them sickly and in need of elixirs to keep him alive, and she had no way of earning the money to support you all." Chase cut a glance back at Mary. "To keep starvation from the door, she had to make a decision no mother should ever have to make. Isn't that right, Mrs. Graham?"

"Don't," Mary whispered. "Say what you must to me, but not in front of the children. Grant me at least that."

Chase raked a hand through his hair and glanced from child to child. All but Jason were present. Seeing their stricken expressions, he was nearly swayed from his purpose. But then he drew his gaze back to Franny. No one had protected her from the ugly realities. In contrast, her brothers and sisters had been too sheltered. It was time they shouldered at least some of the burden. Franny couldn't carry it alone anymore. It was as simple and as heartbreaking as that. All of the kids, save Jason, were old enough to hear the truth, and for Franny's sake, Chase was determined that they would.

"I'm sorry," Chase said softly. "But the way I see it, I have to choose between my wife or all of you. That isn't a choice. As much as it may hurt you to face this, you'll never know a measure of the pain that Franny has suffered. And all for what?" He looked to Frankie. "So her brother can spit at her feet and disown her? So he can scorn her for being a whore and offer to sell her to strangers?" He glanced at each of the girls. "So her sisters can curl their lips and feel self-righteous?"

Silence fell over the room. A shocked silence.

"It's time they know the truth, Mrs. Graham. All of it. About the measles epidemic and Franny bringing it home. How, deep down, you blamed her for your blindness and Jason's idiocy. In a sense, she was even responsible for your husband's death, wasn't she? If not for your affliction and Jason's, he wouldn't have had to work such long hours to pay the doctors and buy medicine. He might not have taken that job, roofing the church steeple to earn extra money. Isn't that right?"

"Stop it," she cried raggedly.

"I can't," Chase said hoarsely. And it was the truth. Not because he wanted to draw blood with words, but because he was drawing tears. From Franny. She still lay motionless on the table. Her expression hadn't altered. But there were tears in her eyes. Silent tears.

"You're making me sound like a monster," Mary accused.

"No," Chase retorted. "A mother who loves her children. A mother who sacrificed one to save the other seven. I don't judge you for that. I know Franny wouldn't either. But I do judge you for the way you went about it."

Pausing for emphasis, Chase settled his gaze on Franny's pale face. "She loves all of you so much, she would have done it, regardless. You didn't need to make her burden greater than it already was by heaping guilt on her. But that's exactly what you did. She disobeyed her parents. Nothing big. Just a typical infraction, common among kids that age, and while doing it, she contracted measles. You've held that over her head for nine endless years."

"You know nothing!" Mary cried. "How dare you come in here and start flinging accusations. You know nothing about this family, or about me."

"I know that for nine years, you pretended you didn't know how she earned the money to feed all of you. The truth is, you not only knew, but probably arranged it."

Mary Graham flinched as though he had struck her. Chase saw Franny squeeze her eyes closed. He felt sick. Sick to his soul. But he couldn't stop. She had to hear it. And she had to hear it from her mother.

"Taking in laundry to earn extra money. The madam from the brothel seeking Franny out on the street, your sending her to the establishment to pick up the soiled linen. It sounds innocent enough, but I kept coming

back to the madam seeking Frannie out on the street.
Whores don't dare do things like that. They start trying
to talk to innocent local girls, and they get run out of
town on a rail."

Chase leaned closer. "But that madam approached
Franny, bold as brass, didn't she? And once Franny
started doing the brothel laundry, the madam suggested
other ways she might earn money. A lot more money.
How dare the woman take that risk? If the girl had
gone home and told, the brothel would have been shut
down. Yet she tried to recruit Franny, not once, but
several times, seemingly with no fear of consequences."

"Stop it," Mary whispered.

"No. I think you spoke with that madam, Mrs. Graham. That's why she wasn't afraid to approach Franny,
because her mother had given her blessing. Didn't you?
Because you were desperate. Your baby was dying. Your
other children were hungry. And Franny was your only
way out."

Mary Graham's sobs became more broken. "You
have no right. And no proof. Lies, all of it. Lies."

"I don't think so," Chase retorted evenly. "I admit, it
took me a while to fit all the pieces together. The pity is
that Franny never did. You knew exactly how to play
her, didn't you, Mrs. Graham? How to wield her guilt.
You used it against her like a finely honed knife, justi-
fying your actions the entire time because if not for
her, you wouldn't have been in this mess. Isn't that
how you reasoned? The sacrifice of one child to save
the others. What better choice than the child who inadvertently caused all your woes?"

"No."

"Oh, yes. On the surface, it wasn't obvious. A gentle blind woman who seemed to love all her children, who attended church every Sunday, who in her naïveté didn't suspect where her beautiful eldest daughter got the exorbitant sums of money needed to keep this family going. It all looked good. Sounded plausible. But something about it always seemed off plumb to me. I kept circling it, remembering all Franny had told me. And I have to tell you, long after I first started to suspect, I kept shoving the thoughts aside because I didn't want to believe it."

Showing no mercy, Chase moved in for the kill.

"You know what my first clue was? The day I met you, you heard my footsteps. Scarcely anyone can lay brag to that. I walk like an Indian, toe to heel, and make hardly any noise, even in boots. But you homed in on me exactly, by sound. The blind develop acute hearing. Don't they, Mrs. Graham? To compensate for their affliction."

"So? How does that—"

"Because," he broke in, "you had to have heard Franny when she got up that first night and put on her special dress. You had to have heard her sneak out of the house to leave for that brothel."

"No. No, if I'd heard her, I would have stopped her."

"Exactly," Chase said softly. "Only you didn't. Not because you didn't hear her, but because it was what you wanted her to do, what you'd been praying she would do. Because it was the only way for this family to make it. Why, in God's name, can't you just admit that? I understand it's painful for you, that you wish to

God doing such a vile thing was never necessary and that it breaks your heart to admit, even to yourself, that you did it. But better that than making this girl bear all the shame alone!"

"You're accusing me of pushing my daughter into prostitution!"

Chase ignored that. "I could believe you didn't hear her that first night. But what of all the other nights, Mrs. Graham? Were you conveniently deaf those times as well? And when she returned in the morning? You had to have wondered where Franny had been and how she'd gotten her hands on so much money. But you didn't ask, did you? Not about her absences or about the windfalls. You didn't need to. Because you knew."

"Oh, God . . . Forgive me, Francine. Forgive me."

Chase closed his eyes, relieved yet filled with regret. His voice hoarse with emotion, he said, "She forgives you, Mrs. Graham. The trouble is, she can't forgive herself."

"Ma?"

At the sound of Frankie's voice, Chase opened his eyes to see that the youth's face had gone absolutely colorless.

"Ma?" he repeated. "Say it's not true. That you never."

The plea was heartfelt. It went unanswered. Mary Graham just sobbed and shook her head. The other children seemed rooted, their eyes filled with incredulity and shock. It gave Chase little satisfaction to destroy a family in this way.

Frankie backed slowly toward the door. Watching him, Chase could almost taste the boy's anguish. "Don't, Frankie," he said softly. "You're not a little boy anymore. You can't run off to lick your own wounds when your family needs you."

"My ma pushed my sister into"—the tendons along Frankie's throat distended as though he might strangle on the words—"being a prostitute? To support all of us? My own mother?"

Chase took a ragged breath and turned his gaze back to Franny. She lay now with her arms hugging her waist. Her eyes remained closed, and tears still streamed down her cheeks.

"Your ma did what she had to do," Chase said softly. "What else could she do, Frankie? Go get a job? She's blind. The only other option for widows with children is to remarry, and what man wants to marry a blind woman with eight children? Jason was sick. If he hadn't gotten his elixir, he probably would have died. And on top of that, all you kids were going to starve." Chase looked the boy dead in the eye. "If your ma could have, I'm sure she would have gone in Franny's place. But blind women don't bring top dollar in places like that. Do they, Frankie? Pretty little girls with golden hair do."

Mary sobbed again. "Oh, God . . . Oh, God . . ." She curled her arms over Franny. "My little girl. God forgive me. My little girl."

Frankie leaned his shoulders against the door, his gaze fixed on Franny. "I was so small then, she seemed grown-up to me," he said shakily.

"Well, she wasn't," Chase said sharply. "It was just her misfortune that she was the oldest. Except for order of birth, it could have been Alaina or Ellen. There isn't a person in this house who should look down his or her nose, that's for damned sure. She sacrificed things beyond your imaginations to feed you all."

Frankie's larynx bobbed. "I never thought. She was just a little girl, wasn't she? Only Theresa's age."

Theresa was standing near the sink, her small hands clutched around a towel, her blue eyes the largest thing about her. She was developing breasts, but just barely. Looking at her, Chase felt heartsick. Franny had become a prostitute at her age.

"The way I see it, Frankie, you failed to think about a lot of things," Chase remarked. Inclining his head at the boy's new coat, he said, "I see your sister gave you the money to buy the ready-made suit jacket and vest. That's not to mention the fine tobacco you smoke or the money you planned to spend in Wolf's Landing at the saloon, we won't mention for what. What were you thinking, son? That the money grew on trees at the landing? Did you ever once consider that maybe you should get a job?"

Frankie's face twisted and he ducked his head. Acutely aware of Mary Graham's soft sobs, Chase looked at Alaina.

"And you, young miss. Sixteen years old. When Franny was your age, she was supporting this whole family. What have you done to help? Have you taken in laundry? Mucked out stalls for the neighbors? Have you even done any of the sewing for your younger brothers and sisters?"

"Franny always did it," the girl said lamely.

"Franny has always done everything for you," Chase came back. "That's what I'm trying to make you see." He took a long hard look at each child. "All of you are old enough to appreciate that. Money doesn't just fall into people's hands. You have to sacrifice to get it. Your sister sacrificed her life." He looked at Theresa. "No one bought her rhinestone hair combs when she was your age." He shifted his gaze to Alaina. "She never got to wear dancing slippers. No boys ever even invited her to a dance." He glanced over his shoulder to meet Matthew's gaze. "You want a hunting rifle. Not to feed your family, because Franny has seen to that. You want to use it for sport. Franny never had time to play at your age."

Chase paused to let all he had said sink in, his gaze on Franny's pale, tear-streaked face. He prayed she was hearing every word. In a quiet voice, he told them about her dream places, how she had survived the ugliness in her life, how carefully she had guarded her anonymity to protect her family, how pregnancy had foiled her. He ended by telling them about Toodles, who had known all the bad things about her and loved her anyway.

Alaina moved closer to the table. Frankie pushed away from the door. "What I said to her today—that's why she's like this. Isn't it?" he asked shakily. "It's my fault. All my fault." A sob caught in his chest. "Francine? I didn't mean it. Forgive me for what I said. I didn't mean it."

Mary Graham caught her breath, moaned low in her throat, and whispered, "I'm the one responsible for this, Frankie. I'm the one who should beg her for forgiveness."

Chase laid a hand on Franny's hair and bent to kiss her forehead. "She doesn't want any of you to ask for forgiveness," he said softly. "All she's ever wanted from any of you was one simple thing."

"What?" Alaina cried brokenly.

Chase took a deep breath. "To love her anyway. That's all. Just to love her anyway. From where I'm standing, I don't think it's a hell of a lot for her to ask. Do you?"

Mary Graham made a strangled sound and tightened her arms around her daughter. Alaina hugged them both. Chase watched for a moment, but only for a moment.

Then he walked out. Those were the most difficult ten steps he had ever taken.

Once on the porch, Chase sank against a support post, his body aching with exhaustion, his heart aching even worse. He loved that girl in there so much. To leave her here, even though he knew it had to be this way, was the hardest thing he'd ever done in his life.

The door to the house opened behind him, and a wedge of golden light fell across Chase. An instant later, the hinges creaked closed, and the artificial illumination blinked out. Footsteps crossed the porch. Frankie came abreast of him. After a moment, he sat on the step, draping his arms over his knees, hands dangling.

For a while neither of them spoke. The horses hitched to Chase's buckboard nickered and swished their tails to chase away mosquitos. The high-pitched melody of crickets drifted on the warm night air. Chase looked up at the stars, at the moon, and wished with all his heart that he could take Franny home with him now.

"I guess you think I'm a pretty awful person," Frankie finally said. "That I'm spoiled and selfish and that I don't love my sister like I ought."

Chase winced. "The fact that you realize I might think all those things tells me they aren't true," he finally replied. "Awful, spoiled, and selfish people seldom realize how awful, spoiled, and selfish they really are."

"So you do think it's how I acted."

Chase sighed and joined him on the step, "Frankie, I think you're a little late in growing up, that's all. I'm not sure you can be blamed for that, not entirely. We grow up when we have to, and nobody's required that of you. Franny's made life easy for you. Maybe a little too easy. I think by doing that, she could feel the sacrifices she had made were all worthwhile. She gave you and the other kids all her dreams, made them possible for you. Does that make any sense?"

"I guess." He fell silent for several seconds. "I'm sorry for the way I acted."

Chase turned to regard him. "Yeah? Well, I'm sorrier. I shouldn't have hit you. I reckon I owe you one free punch."

The boy managed a lopsided grin. "You busted my lip."

"I apologize."

"Accepted."

The boy offered his hand. Chase shook with him. Once that was done, Frankie heaved a weary sigh. "Is Francine going to be all right, do you think?"

Chase gazed off into the darkness. Oak trees dotted the property, resembling gigantic mushrooms in the moonlight with their billowing tops and stout trunks. "I don't know," he finally admitted, and saying those words was the greatest agony of his life. "I just don't know."

"What can I do to help her?" the boy asked.

"Love her," Chase said huskily. "Love her no matter what." He took a ragged breath. "That's what brothers are supposed to do."

"I always loved her. Even today when I was saying those cruel things, I loved her. I was just . . . sick inside and hurting. I wanted her to feel as bad."

Chase clenched his teeth. Looking at it objectively, which was no easy task, he could see how Frankie must have felt. "What you did today—you have to undo it somehow, Frankie. You have to put your own hurt aside and concentrate on hers. Do you think you can do that?"

"I already have."

Chase nodded. "I figured you had. Or you wouldn't be out here." He turned to study the boy's profile. "Have you ever looked into still water and seen your reflection?"

"A few times."

"When the wind blows hard, or if the water is disturbed, ripples distort your image," Chase murmured. "You can look until your eyes burn and can't see yourself clearly." He curled a hand over the boy's shoulder. "You are Franny's pool of still water, Frankie. Today, the terrible secrets she has kept from all of you became like the wind or a disturbance in the pool, and she got lost in the blur. No matter how hard she stared, she couldn't see herself anymore, only the ugliness.

"What you must do is make the pool tranquil again so the surface is smooth. Your love for her will be the sunshine that casts her reflection on the water."

"I don't understand."

Chase smiled slightly. "Yes, well, I learned from a very wise man that we ponder what we don't understand. I want you to think about it and find your own way. When you were small, you had a great need, and Franny was there for you. Now the wind has switched directions. She needs you. Desperately. You have to be her looking glass."

Tears welled in the boy's eyes and, shimmering in moonlight, spilled over onto his cheeks. "In other words, I'm her mirror, and you want me to make sure she sees a pretty reflection."

"Exactly. If you think about it, Frankie, we all get our reflections from the people who love us. It's their opinions that shape our opinions of ourselves. Franny isn't sure she's worth loving any more. You must convince her that she is."

"I'll try."

"If you get to know your sister," Chase said softly, "really get to know her, the reflections she sees in your eyes will be beautiful because she is beautiful."

"You love her a lot, don't you?"

"Yes, a lot."

"Is her baby yours?"

"Yes, mine."

"Then why are you going to leave her here? That's what you're going to do. I can tell by the way you're acting."

Chase dragged in a deep breath and exhaled on a

sigh. Spreading his hands, he studied his palms. In simple terms, he explained to Frankie the Comanche belief that yesterday no longer existed and that a person should always walk forward with his gaze fixed on the horizon. "In Franny's case, that belief doesn't apply," he concluded. "She can't leave yesterday behind because too many things happened that were never resolved. She must walk backward in her footsteps and make peace with who she was yesterday before she can deal with who she wants to be today."

"You could stay and help her. I know you want to, and we can make room."

To resist that temptation, Chase pushed to his feet. "I'm not a part of her yesterdays, Frankie. I'm her today. My being here would only make it difficult for her. She needs all of you, not me. She needs you to love her anyway before she can believe I will. Can you understand that? She's suffered a lot of hurt at your mamma's hands. I don't blame your mamma, don't get me wrong. In truth, I pity her because she was ever put in such a situation. But the bottom line is, she inflicted the wounds, and she's the only one who can ever completely heal them. Her and all of you."

The youth hugged his knees. "If I need you and send a message, will you come?"

"Hell bent for leather." Chase stepped to the buckboard, fished under the tarp, and withdrew a bag of gold pieces. "There's enough in here to pay expenses this next month. Before that runs out, I'll make arrangement at the bank for a draft." Chase put the money into Frankie's hands. Looking into the boy's eyes, he said, "You're nearly a man, son. It's time for you to assume the responsibilities of one. I'm counting on you to take care of this family and my wife."

"I will."

Chase climbed into the driver's seat, unlooped the reins, and then gazed somberly into the darkness ahead of him. He didn't want to go. Though he knew he was doing the right thing for Franny, the only thing, he kept remembering the promise he'd made that he would never leave her.

"Frankie, if she comes around and asks after me, will you give her a message?"

"Surely."

"It's important that you tell her exactly," Chase said huskily. "Tell her that when she's ready to come home to me, I'll be waiting for her in our dream place."

21

Waiting . . . To Chase it seemed that August was a million years long. Once a week, he received a letter from Frankie, updating him on Franny's condition. She was doing well, the boy said. Her stupor spells came on less frequently with each passing day. Her appetite was picking up. She smiled often and seemed to be finding peace within herself. Toward the end of the month, Chase made arrangements at the bank to wire money to Grants Pass. Meanwhile he went to work in the mine with his father and Jake to offset the drain on his savings that support of the Graham family constituted. Though he didn't particularly care for mining, it was better than leaving Wolf's Landing and putting even more distance between himself and the girl he loved.

September rolled around eventually, and the days

mounted, taking them inexorably toward autumn. Frankie's letters began to arrive less regularly, and he never mentioned whether or not Franny had plans to return to her husband. Chase told himself it was understandable that the boy should write less. He had taken a job, and with the passage of summer, school was once again in session. But deep down Chase feared he was lying to himself.

Losing Franny. It had been a possibility from the first, and he had chosen to take that risk to give her this time to heal. But to face the reality that she might never come back to him? Chase recalled the emptiness in her eyes and told himself he had done the right thing. But knowing that was little consolation for his loss. With each passing day, he faced the fact that the longer Franny stayed away, the less likely it was that she would return.

Not that he blamed her. In Grants Pass no one knew her terrible secret. Here in Wolf's Landing everyone did. Knowing her as he did, Chase couldn't blame her for not wanting to come back and face the ugliness. He wouldn't blame her if she never did.

At the end of September, Frankie wrote to thank Chase for wiring them money a second time, but then informed him, politely, that the family had made other financial arrangements. Their mother was taking in ironing, something she could do by feel. Alaina was doing odd jobs. Theresa was cleaning for local women. Matthew had a job as a stock boy at the general store. Ellen had a clerical job in an attorney's office. Franny was doing handiwork, which was selling quite well on consignment at local shops. Frankie still had his job at the livery and had recently started earning more money by chopping and stacking firewood for people about town.

Chase took the letter down to the creek to read it and reread it, trying to find meaning between the lines. No mention was made of Franny's coming home. Ever.

That afternoon, Chase accepted that the girl he loved might be forever lost to him. His only solace was that she was no longer lost to herself.

May Belle and Shorty set an October date for their wedding. The Wolfs received an invitation, and Loretta responded by offering to have an informal reception for the couple at their home. Chase would have preferred to ignore the entire shindig, but given the proximity, he couldn't. The simple ceremony was to take place at the community hall. The local preacher had agreed to do the honors. The morning of the wedding, the Wolfs set up makeshift tables in their backyard for the reception that afternoon, then went to the hall to decorate and arrange the guest seating.

At two, Chase walked back to the hall with his family to witness the ceremony. Indigo looked lovely in white doeskin, her tawny hair held atop her head in a gleaming twist with pearlescent hair combs Jake had gotten her for her last birthday. The kids were slicked up in their Sunday best. Hunter wore his dress buckskins, which was about as fancy as he ever got. Loretta floated along beside him in blue alpaca.

"I swear, Chase Kelly, a body would think you were going to a funeral. Did you have to wear black?" his mother asked.

Chase tipped the brim of his hat lower over his eyes. "Uncle Swift always wears black, and you never complain at him."

"Your uncle Swift wore black long before he came to Wolf's Landing. You, on the other hand, were raised to appreciate the appropriate types of clothing for different occasions."

The truth was, Chase felt as if he were going to a funeral. No matter how he tried not to, May Belle made him think of Franny, and thoughts of Franny made him feel as if a knife were being twisted in his guts. He took a deep breath. "I'm sorry, Ma. You want me to go home and change?"

Loretta gave him an exasperated look. "Lands, no. Then you'd be late!"

"Not many folks will be there," Chase qualified.

"Most of the town. Preacher Thompson has worked very hard to get people to attend as a gesture of acceptance. For May Belle's sake, you understand."

Chase figured his ma had been stirring that pot of stew herself and smiled slightly. "Well, maybe no one will notice me."

Once inside the hall, Chase joined his family in a middle row and took his seat. Staring straight ahead at nothing, he was aware of the benches being filled but scarcely spared a glance for the occupants. Distanced from his surroundings as he was, he experienced a jolt when he found himself looking into green eyes.

As though being jerked from sleep, Chase blinked and focused. Green eyes. Beautiful green eyes and a face so sweet he had every curve memorized. Franny. She and her family were entering the row directly in front of the Wolfs. Before taking a seat, she had turned to meet his gaze.

Chase felt as if the bench disappeared from under

him. Franny. She smiled slightly, nodded to his mother, then lowered herself onto the bench. He stared at the back of her blue dress. Most of her clothing was still hanging in his room. He didn't recognize this garment and wondered if she had made it. Her Wheeler-Wilson was still at his parents' house, but judging from Frankie's last letter, Chase guessed Mary Graham must have a sewing machine.

The wedding ceremony began, but Chase heard little of it. A hundred questions circled in his mind. The one thought that came clear to him was that Franny, his wife and the mother of *his* child, had not taken a seat with his family but with her own. Though she had acknowledged his mother with a slight nod, she hadn't him. An uncertain smile, yes. But in his books, that didn't count for shit. This was a public slap in his face. As clearly as though she'd said it aloud, she was announcing a severance of ties between them.

Chase's first inclination was to get the hell out of there, but his pride held him back. If he stormed out, everyone and his brother would know how badly he was hurt, including Franny. God knew he loved the girl, but he didn't want her coming back to him because she felt she had to. Feeling lacerated, Chase managed to sit through the entire ceremony and congratulate the bride and groom at its conclusion.

Though it was the hardest thing he had ever done, once the formalities were over, Chase waited outside the hall for the Grahams. Vowing to himself that he wouldn't reveal his pain by so much as a flicker of cheek muscle, he pasted a smile on when Franny came out the door on Frankie's arm. Chase noticed that her belly preceded her, and his gaze dropped to the sizable protrusion that couldn't be concealed by her dress. His palm ached with yearning to touch her there, to feel for life. His child because he had claimed it. But that was his problem, not hers.

"Franny," he managed to say in a warm, welcoming way. "You're looking good."

Those big green eyes of hers clung to his. Chase glanced away, knowing he'd do something stupid if he didn't. Like snatch her up and spirit her away. There was too much of his father in him, he guessed.

"You're looking good, too," she replied in a tremulous voice. "I'm glad to see you, Chase. So glad." She seemed to grope for words. "I . . . um . . . started to write but I kept tearing up the letters. Some things just can't be said on paper."

In other words, she preferred to break his heart in person. Chase steeled himself and met her gaze head-on. "Frankie wrote regularly."

Two bright spots of color flagged her cheeks. "Yes, well, it was inexcusable that I didn't. I know it's been a very long while." Her voice wobbled and she compressed her lips for a moment. Then, killing him heartbeat by heartbeat with those imploring eyes of hers, she said, "Please tell me you're not angry."

"Of course I'm not. I understand you've been through a difficult time, Franny."

"Then why—" She swallowed and averted her gaze for an instant. Looking back at him, she said, "Then why are you being so cool toward me?"

Cool toward her? He felt anything but. "I'm sorry. I guess seeing you took me by surprise." He forced himself to grin. "Say . . . While all of you are in town, you should have Frankie get your things. I bet you're missing that Wheeler-Wilson something fierce."

She gazed up at him for a long moment. "Yes, something fierce. That, among other things."

"We'll be around the place all day. Ma's throwing a shindig to celebrate."

"I know. She sent us an invitation."

That was news to Chase. He curled his hands into fists, wishing they were around his mother's little neck. "Oh, she did? Well, great. I'll look forward to seeing all of you there." That was the biggest lie he'd ever told. He not only didn't look forward to such torture, but was determined not to put himself through it. He'd spend the day along the creek somewhere and spare himself that dubious pleasure. He extended his hand to her. "Until then?"

She scarcely touched her fingertips to his. "Yes, until then."

Blindly, Chase turned away. He didn't bother to wait for his family, and he didn't head toward home. Instead, he took a page out of Franny's book and slipped away to a special place where the world wouldn't follow him.

"What do you mean, you aren't attending the reception?" Frankie demanded to know. "Why on earth not, Francine? What'll Chase think?"

Stubbornly clinging to the seat of their wagon, Franny gazed straight down Main, refusing to look at her brother. "I'm simply not going, that's all."

"But Ma and the kids already went! What're you gonna do, sit here and draw dust until they come back?"

"Yes."

Frankie groaned and climbed up to sit beside her. "Francine, you aren't making good sense. You've been nervous as a cat waiting for this day. You made a pretty new dress. Now you're planning to go home with us?" He leaned around to see her face. "Excuse me, but there's one minor detail you're forgetting. What'll your husband have to say about that?"

Franny gnawed on the inside of her lip. "Nothing. He suggested you stop by their place to get my things, as a matter of fact."

"He what?"

"You heard me."

Frankie sighed. "Then there's a misunderstanding."

"Indeed, and on my part." Franny blinked to keep her eyes dry. "He doesn't want me anymore, Frankie."

"Oh, for pity's sake." Her brother shoved the heel of his boot against the footrest. "That's the silliest thing I've ever heard. He loves you like crazy."

"He certainly didn't act it."

"Then it's up to you to talk to him and get things straightened out."

"He'll think I'm clinging." She turned stricken eyes on her brother. "Frankie, look at it from his side. Everyone in this town *knows* about me. I can deal with that now. Truly, I can. But a man—well, to have people whispering about his wife? Chase is a good person, and I'll be forever grateful for all he's done for me, but I won't push myself on him. He was polite when he greeted me."

"That's significant?"

"Chase isn't the polite type."

Frankie rubbed his hands over his pant legs. "Francine, he loves you. I know he does. And if you don't go talk to him, you're always going to regret it. But I guess that's your decision to make."

He climbed down from the wagon.

"Where are you going?" she demanded.

"I'm leaving you to your foolishness," Frankie huffed. "If you want to throw away something as wonderful as what you and Chase could have, just because you're scared to go talk to him, then do it. But don't expect me to sit here and show support while you ruin your life."

"Scared? I am not scared. I'm trying to be fair to him."

"Right," Frankie scoffed. "The truth is you're afraid he'll send you away, that he'll confirm your worst fear and tell you he doesn't really love you."

Franny closed her eyes. "I couldn't bear it if he did."

Frankie sighed. "Yeah, you could. That's not to say it'll happen, but if it did, you could bear it. You have a lot of people who love you and will be there if things go wrong."

With that, her brother walked away.

It took all Franny's courage to enter the Wolfs' backyard. Loretta greeted her warmly. Hunter gave her a hug. Indigo seemed elated to see her. Franny glanced nervously around, refusing offers of food and refreshment. She spotted Frankie, who gave her an encouraging wink.

Turning back to Loretta, Franny said, "I don't see

Chase. Have you any idea where he is?"

Her mother-in-law's face fell. "No, dear. He disappeared after the ceremony, and I haven't an inkling where he got off to."

Aching, Franny pasted on a smile. She congratulated May Belle and Shorty on their nuptials. When Indigo brought her a plate heaped with food, she pretended to eat. All the while, her stomach was twisting and she felt as though her legs weighed a hundred pounds each. Feeling horribly conspicuous, she milled through the crowd toward her family. She had nearly reached them when a large, heavy hand curled over her shoulder. She glanced up into Hunter Wolf's dark face.

"Follow your heart," he said softly, "and you may find him."

Saying nothing more, he turned away.

Dream places. Memories. Cool autumn sunlight where once he had danced under summer gold with an angel in his arms.

Chase sat on the creek bank, his arms resting loosely on his upraised knees, his gaze fixed on the rushing water. He willed the current to carry away his pain. On the crisp air floated the scent of woodsmoke, a sign that winter was nearly upon them. He wondered how many other winters would come and go before he began to forget.

Franny . . . The pain inside his chest was so acute it nearly took his breath.

In a rush of wind, autumn leaves were caught from their branches and flung in a dizzying spiral around him, a kaleidoscope of earthen colors, burgundy, orange, brown, and gold. The chill that caressed his cheeks also touched his heart.

Franny, his green-eyed angel. Though he had searched for them, he had seen no shadows in her gaze when they spoke. The time she had spent with her family had healed her, just as he had hoped. But it had left him bleeding.

"Chase?"

For an instant he thought he imagined her voice. Then he turned to see her standing several feet from him, fragile and fair, her green eyes like a promise of spring in a splendor of russet. Startled, he sprang to his feet.

"Franny," he said nonsensically. "I didn't expect to see you here."

She glanced slowly around them, her gaze lingering on those spots where they'd made love the previous summer. A slight smile touched her mouth. "Where else would you expect to see me, Chase, if not here in our special place?"

Not daring to let himself hope, Chase averted his gaze. "If you sought me out to ask about a divorce, that'll have to be your doing. I don't believe in them. But I won't contest it."

She hugged her waist and shivered. "I see."

"I won't sign any papers," he added. "So don't ask. It's against my beliefs, both Comanche and Catholic. I don't want to be difficult, understand."

"Please, Chase, be difficult."

"What?"

She came a step closer. "Be difficult. Yell at me if

you like. Tell me I'm thoughtless and selfish, that you'll never forgive me for staying away for over two months without writing to you to explain. You can even hate me a little. But when you're all finished, be difficult. Don't try to send me away."

"Send you away?"

She raised her chin a notch. Her eyes shimmered with tears as she met his gaze. "I love you," she said simply.

"You love me." Chase bit down hard on his back teeth. "Two months your brother wrote to me, and he never once mentioned your coming home. What the hell was I supposed to think?"

"I'm sorry if I hurt you."

"Is that why you're here? Because you realized you'd hurt me?"

She studied his face for a long moment. "No. I'm here because Frankie said I'd be sorry if I didn't risk it."

"Risk what?"

"Risk your saying you don't love me anymore."

"I've been waiting here for two endless months, and you thought I didn't love you anymore? Jesus Christ! I'll never understand you, you know that?"

"Do you really need to?"

"It'd be a leg up on complete befuddlement."

"I wasn't sure that—" She broke off and compressed her lips. "Do you love me, or not?"

"Don't ask damned fool questions."

"Would you just give me a damned fool answer?"

"Yes."

"Yes? Is that all you can say?"

"I love you," he ground out.

Using the scuffed toe of her shoe, she made a line in the dirt. Her eyes dancing with mischief, she held out her hand to him. "Then step over here, Chase Wolf. Stop being mad at me for things that happened yesterday."

He narrowed an eye at her. "You're pushing your luck, you know."

"It's your belief. A Comanche one. Like a dutiful wife, I've adopted it."

"Conveniently, I'd say."

"Ah, but it's such a beautiful concept. The moment's past, correct? Forever lost to us. You shouldn't waste a second of today worrying about what's already behind us." She wiggled her fingertips. "Come on. Let's make a special place, Chase, a dream place just for us and our baby. I want to make every second of today count. It's all any of us have, you know. Just this moment and hope for the future."

It was an invitation Chase had never expected and, despite the fact that he was still tempted to wring her neck, it was also one he couldn't refuse. "You're saying all the right words," he whispered, "but do you truly feel them? Are all your yesterdays behind you, Franny?"

"Completely. It was your gift to me, Chase. All wrapped up in magic. Today and all my tomorrows. I'm making a fresh start. Won't you share it with me?"

Instead of taking her hand, he launched himself at her, lifted her into his arms, and spun in a dizzying circle with her clasped to his chest. She gave a startled laugh, and the sound warmed him clear through.

Franny, his green-eyed angel. As agonizing as the two months had been, she was worth the wait. He felt as though he were holding heaven in his arms.

"I love you," he whispered fiercely. "I love you so much."

"And I love you."

Though Chase knew it was fanciful, it seemed to him the wintery sun brightened momentarily, and he couldn't help but wonder if the Great Ones weren't smiling. All his life, he'd heard his father's song. The words whispered through his mind now, and he realized the last part of the song, the most beautiful part, had finally come to pass.

In a swirl of autumn leaves, a man, a woman, and an unborn child spun in an endless circle, their union the final fulfillment of a prophecy older than the ages, that the Comanche and his golden-haired maiden would find a special place where they might live in harmony and give birth to a new nation where the songs of the People would be sung forever.

Epilogue

Dressed all in white, the symbol of purity, Franny stood at the back of the church, her trembling hand resting in the bend of Frankie's arm. The organ music began, softly at first, then increasing in volume until the air vibrated. Frankie stepped forward to begin their march down the aisle. She moved beside him, feeling as though she were floating.

In addition to a crowd of well-wishers whose number exceeded her wildest fantasies, Franny saw the beaming faces of those in her family on one side of the church. On the other she saw the faces of people she had come to love only recently. The newlyweds, Shorty and May Belle, Indigo and her tall, handsome husband Jake, their two children.

In the next row stood Swift Lopez, a lean, dark-haired, dangerous-looking man with a mischievous twinkle in his eyes that warmed to a lambent gleam every time he glanced at his lovely wife, Amy. In contrast to her delicate blondness, two dark-haired, black-eyed little boys stood beside her, one holding her skirts, the other her hand.

Tears stung Franny's eyes when she saw her mother-in-law, Loretta. She managed to blink the moisture away. But only for a moment. When her gaze shifted to Hunter Wolf, who loomed beside his wife, Franny couldn't control the tide of emotion that welled within her. Dressed in buckskins, as always, he looked pure Comanche and fiercely proud of the infant grandson he held in his strong arms. Though Franny searched, she could detect nothing in his expression to hint that the baby wasn't of his blood.

Her baby, Chase's son, Chase Wolf, Junior.

Scarcely able to see through her tears, Franny moved past her parents-in-law and fixed her gaze on the tall, dark-haired man who awaited her at the altar with an outstretched hand. Trembling, she closed the distance and took her place beside him. Together they turned to face the priest, Father O'Grady, who smiled warmly and blessed them by making a sign of the cross above their heads.

Sunlight arced through the stained glass of a window. A hush fell over the church. Franny felt warmth flow over her, and through her tears she saw a halo of golden and rose-colored light surrounding her.

She knew it was foolish. Absolutely fanciful. But she couldn't help wondering if that mystical light wasn't a sign from above, God's special benediction. She closed her eyes and let the warmth of it fill her, completely at peace with what she once was and who she had become.

Sometimes, she realized, God did still make miracles, even for the least of his children. Her miracle stood beside her, a stubborn, infuriating, insistent, absolutely wonderful man named Chase Kelly Wolf who had given her the sweetest gift a man could give a woman, love of herself.

Comanche Magic by **Catherine Anderson**

The latest addition to the bestselling Comanche series. When Chase Wolf first met Fanny Graham, he was immediately attracted to her, despite her unsavory reputation. Long ago Fanny had lost her belief in miracles, but when Chase Wolf came into her life he taught her that the greatest miracle of all was true love.

Separating by **Susan Bowden**

The triumphant story of a woman's comeback from a shattering divorce to a fulfilling, newfound love. After twenty-five years of marriage, Riona Jarvin's husband leaves her for a younger woman. Riona is in shock—until she meets a new man and finds that life indeed has something wonderful to offer her.

Hearts of Gold by **Martha Longshore**

A sizzling romantic adventure set in 1860s Sacramento. For years Kora Hunter had worked for the family newspaper, but now everyone around her was insisting that she give it up for marriage to a long-time suitor and family friend. Meanwhile, Mason Fielding had come to Sacramento to escape from the demons in his past. Neither he nor Kora expected a romantic entanglement, considering the odds stacked against them.

In My Dreams by **Susan Sizemore**

Award-winning author Susan Sizemore returns to time travel in this witty, romantic romp. In ninth-century Ireland, during the time of the Viking raids, a beautiful young druid named Brianna inadvertently cast a spell that brought a rebel from 20th-century Los Angeles roaring back through time on his Harley-Davidson. Sammy Bergen was so handsome that at first she mistook him for a god—but he was all too real.

Surrender the Night by **Susan P. Teklits**

Lovely Vanessa Davis had lent her talents to the patriotic cause by seducing British soldiers to learn their battle secrets. She had never allowed herself to actually give up her virtue to any man until she met Gabriel St. Claire, a fellow Rebel spy and passionate lover.

Sunrise by **Chassie West**

Sunrise, North Carolina, is such a small town that everyone knows everyone else's business—or so they think. After a long absence, Leigh Ann Warren, a burned out Washington, D.C., police officer, returns home to Sunrise. Once there, she begins to investigate crimes both old and new. Only after a dangerous search for the truth can Leigh help lay the town's ghosts to rest and start her own life anew with the one man meant for her.

COMING SOON

Tame the Wildest Heart by **Parris Afton Bonds**

In her most passionate romance yet, Parris Afton Bonds tells the tale of two lonely hearts forever changed by an adventure in the Wild West. It was a match made in heaven . . . and hell. Mattie McAlister was looking for her half-Apache son and Gordon Halpern was looking for his missing wife. Neither realized that they would find the trail to New Mexico Territory was the way to each other's hearts.

First and Forever by **Zita Christian**

Katrina Swann was content with her peaceful, steady life in the close-knit immigrant community of Merriweather, Missouri. Then the reckless Justin Barrison swept her off her feet in a night of passion. Before she knew it she was following him to the Dakota Territory. Through trials and tribulations on the prairie, they learned the strength of love in the face of adversity.

Gambler's Gold by **Barbara Keller**

When Charlotte Bell headed out on a wagon train from Massachusetts to California, she had one goal in mind—finding her father, who had disappeared while prospecting for gold. The last thing she was looking for was love, but when fate turned against her, she turned to the dashing Reade Elliot to save her.

Queen by **Sharon Sala**

The Gambler's Daughters Trilogy continues with Diamond Houston's older sister, Queen, and the ready-made family she discovers, complete with laughter and tears. Queen Houston always had to act as a mother to her two younger sisters when they were growing up. After they part ways as young women, each to pursue her own dream, Queen reluctantly ends up in the mother role again—except this time there's a father involved.

A Winter Ballad by **Barbara Samuel**

When Anya of Winterbourne rescued a near-dead knight she found in the forest around her manor, she never thought he was the champion she'd been waiting for. "A truly lovely book. A warm, passionate tale of love and redemption, it lingers in the hearts of readers. . . . Barbara Samuel is one of the best, most original writers in romantic fiction today."—Anne Stuart

Shadow Prince by **Terri Lynn Wilhelm**

A plastic surgeon falls in love with a mysterious patient in this powerful retelling of *The Beauty and the Beast* fable. Ariel Denham, an ambitious plastic surgeon, resentfully puts her career on hold for a year in order to work at an exclusive, isolated clinic high in the Smoky Mountains. There she meets and falls in love with a mysterious man who stays in the shadows, a man she knows only as Jonah.

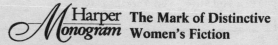

Harper Monogram The Mark of Distinctive Women's Fiction